When Killers Collide

Tom Olsinski

PEGASUS BOOKS

Pegasus Books
3338 San Marino Ave
San Jose, CA 95127
www.pegasusbooks.net

First Edition: January 2016

Published in North America by Pegasus Books. For information, please contact Pegasus Books c/o Janet Cole, 3338 San Marino Ave, San Jose, CA 95127.

This book is a work of fiction. Any resemblance to actual persons, living or dead, events, or locales is entirely coincidental.

Library of Congress Cataloguing-In-Publication Data
Tom Olsinski
When Killers Collide /Tom Olsinski – 1st ed
p. cm.
Library of Congress Control Number: 2015953637
ISBN – 978-1-941859-38-4

1. FICTION / Thrillers / Suspense. 2. FICTION / Mystery & Detective / Hard-Boiled. 3. FICTION / Thrillers / Crime. 4. PSYCHOLOGY / Psychopathology / Compulsive Behavior. 5. TRUE CRIME / Murder / Serial Killers.

10 9 8 7 6 5 4 3 2 1

Comments about *When Killers Collide* and requests for additional copies, book club rates and author speaking appearances may be addressed to Tom Olsinski or Pegasus Books c/o Janet Cole, 3338 San Marino Ave, San Jose, CA, 95127, or you can send your comments and requests via e-mail to contact_us@pegasusbooks.net.

Also available as an eBook from Internet retailers, from Pegasus Books and from the author's platform: www.TomOlsinski.net

Printed in the United States of America

For Stefanie, Craig & Cara,
Justin & Kim

"I became insane with long intervals of horrible sanity."

Edgar A. Poe

"Men are not prisoners of fate, but only prisoners of their own minds."

FDR

PROLOGUE

Under a cloudless sky, the soft wind failed to cleanse the air of the past, while history eroded the present. Abandoned buildings interrupted miles of the soy and cornfield horizon with a grim reminder of failed dreams. Passing visitors never heard ghosts festering in the desolate soil of disappointment. Legions of buried families bequeathed their genes for future generations to inherit and act upon.

Infertile dirt blew across the fading shrubs that thirsted for rain. Gray remnants of a wooden fence joined with the rusting barbed wire that surrounded the parcel of land off the highway. East of the property, cars raced past on Interstate Road 65, between Chicago and Indianapolis. The license plate description of Indiana as the *Heartland of America* often amused truck drivers as they hurried across the flat mundane landscape with minimal observations. On that day, the roadside was a beehive of police activity.

At the small barren plot in Lebanon, Indiana, Scott Avilia mingled with his crew. They had just begun to dig the foundation for a new *Happy Hoosier* gourmet pork tenderloin restaurant the day before. The springtime sunshine reflected off the yellow and green John Deere digger, as past and present collided, and workers unearthed the first human bones.

"Hey, buddy. We hit something bad," announced the helmeted worker to Avilia, who shined in a white shirt and tie.

Scott Avilia felt his high hopes for the corner location plummet. He bought the site on the cheap at an auction after the county assumed ownership of the lot when taxes weren't paid. His construction team was there to excavate for his future business.

The two men noted the grassy mound with darker soil and peered into the hole. A white skull faced them from the dirt—like it was shouting for release. Unable to avert their eyes from the sight, the men retrieved their cell phones, pressing numbers with their nimble thumbs. The worker called his construction boss for direction, and Avilia dialed 911.

The highlight of Detective Robert Mannion's workdays came at lunchtime, which was ruined. He asked for a to-go container and briskly walked to his Lebanon Police car. There weren't many murdered bodies found in rural Indiana, so he appreciated the gravity of the message. Still annoyed at his interrupted meal, he tossed the Styrofoam container onto the car seat, turned on the siren and squealed out of the parking lot.

Mannion arrived on scene and approached the man in the shirt and tie.

"You the guy who called 911 and said there were dead bodies buried here?"

"Yeah, we found one here…" Avilia answered.

Mannion glanced at the skull.

"…and it looks like there may be *more*," he nodded, referring to the other grassy mounds.

"I'm on a deadline. I need to get this cleared up," Avilia insisted.

Mannion ignored the comments and called for assistance. Within the hour, uniformed police personnel with shovels and sniffing German Shepherds overran the property. The cops came in all shapes and sizes, with the youngest doing the digging. Police gathered across the landscape, like the clouds that had suddenly accumulated in the Indiana sky.

Ginger Adams from the police communications department joined Mannion. Her thick auburn hair blew in the breeze.

"When you look at it now, you can see some minor mounds where the spring grass looks a little greener," Detective Mannion mused. "You would never notice it before this skeletal discovery."

Mannion was a Crime Scene Supervisor and one of the two detectives in the Lebanon Police Department. Among the uniformed cops and jean-clad workers, he stood out in his navy Stein Mart polyester suit. His shoulders remained broad from high school football, but his stomach strained his shirt buttons with each passing year.

"I see what you're saying. It doesn't look good," Adams agreed.

Across the pebbles in the faded soil, they walked to find a clear space.

"It must be a killing field," Mannion muttered.

Searchers discovered additional graves in the distance

"Maybe it all happened a long time ago and the killer is dead?" Adams suggested.

Ginger Adams possessed natural enthusiasm that enhanced her technical skill. She would deal with the media and frame the stories instigated from the horrific discovery.

"This is all very exciting. Before my media buddies arrive, you may want to order tarps to cover each located remain… in case it rains."

Mannion called out the order to a uniform.

"I can't imagine who could *do* this," he complained.

"You know, Detective, there is a murder every 36 minutes in the US, and only about thirty percent of all murders are *solved*," she informed him as Mannion walked over to coach a young officer.

Robert Mannion came from an Irish family of saints and sinners. His deceased parents had been teachers. Both his uncles had been police officers while his aunt had a criminal past. Bernie was a decorated hero in the Midwest who had retired in North Carolina. Emmett was killed as a 9-11 first responder at the World Trade Center. Aunt Rosie idled in prison for grand theft auto after assorted run-ins with the law.

Most people that Robert met on the job seemed just as destined for existence at the extremes. The good people became pharmacists, while the bad element, who engaged in all manner of criminal activity, were eventually incarcerated. The bad players were born that way and created outcomes like the one before him. That killing field demonstrated the legacy of a bad person, and it was Mannion's job to find the bastard who was responsible.

"Be real careful," Mannion told the man with a shovel. "Just identify where there's a body, and stick one of these little Neon cones at the location. The forensic guys from the city will bag the results, and share what they discover."

To those rural Indiana cops, "the city" usually referred to nearby Indianapolis.

For the time being, the techs controlled the crime scene. Over time, police presence would increase with inquisitive captains and crime scene specialists. Perhaps even the Chief would show up for a crime of such magnitude. The FBI would investigate, and like green flies on dog crap—the press would swarm over the debacle.

He listened to his supervisor on the cell phone.

"Make sure your guys do everything by the book, Robert. We'll have more scrutiny than ever on this one."

Mannion nodded habitually, despite speaking with someone who couldn't see him. While talking, he glanced at his car, hoping he could go finish his sandwich in the air conditioning—something that would be impossible.

A young cop approached with a cloth parchment in his hand. His tan uniform appeared cleaned and ironed.

"Hey boss. Check *this* out!" he exclaimed, holding out a tattered small black eye patch. "It looks like we have a one-eyed killer... maybe a *pirate?*"

"Listen Cyclops," Mannion scolded, "you know this is a crime scene, right? Where are your gloves? Put that patch back *exactly* where you found it and act like you've been to a crime scene before. Don't remove anything else, okay?"

The man left as Adams approached.

"Finding evidence?" she asked.

"At this stage—who *knows?* There is so much debris here. He's new and learning. But I don't *get* it. This is Indiana! We don't have serial killers here. Bank robbers like Dillinger—we have. Drunk drivers, domestic partner abuse and *Breaking Bad* methamphetamine labs—we have. But a true *serial?* Probably never! You expect that in LA or Boston..."

"Well, we have one now," Adams interrupted. "And don't you remember?—we had that Baumeister guy, over in Westfield a few years back, who killed gay men from Indianapolis? And before that, there was 'Mad Dog'..."

"I got it. I guess there are crazies everywhere."

Mannion watched the officer's movement for any discrepancies to his orders.

"Do we know who owned this land previously?" Adams asked.

"This used to be known as the 'goat house' years ago. It was a little gray and white shuttered house that always seemed empty. Goats wandered from the bordering farm. Best we can tell, the old house they demolished yesterday has been vacant for several years."

"Are you getting enough resources to help on the facts?" Adams injected. "The media will have a hundred questions."

"I've also got the city boys doing some computer searches," Mannion nodded. "But a house like this might have had renters and welfare tenants, and maybe even some squatters. It might be a challenge to find the actual proprietors. Over the years, anyone could have used the lot as a burial ground. Anyone from the highway could stop here. The killer could be someone from Chicago, or anywhere. Time destroys many things, including evidence," "True, but there may be a link why the killer chose *this* location. My bet is the perp was an Indiana resident," she guessed.

"Yeah probably, but there aren't many witnesses to this burial ground. Someone once thought this area could be a new housing development. They even built the Trophy Club Golf Course down the road and there are a few nice brick homes nearby. The plan didn't work and the area became just another forsaken American dream."

He hated rambling, which he usually did in front of a pretty woman. Adams brushed dirt from her suit as a sudden breeze came from the cornfields.

"Looks more like a nightmare now. How many have they found?"

"So far—six skulls and bones, but it looks like there'll be *more*. Apparently, this collection isn't recent,"

He realized the timeframe of these murders coincided with his Uncle Bernie's time with the Indianapolis Police Department, which meant he would have to interrupt Bernie's retirement in North Carolina.

Scott Avilia approached the officers while wiping the sweat from his brow.

"So, what's the deal, officer? When can I resume digging the foundation for my restaurant?"

"It's *Detective* Mannion, and your sandwich shop will have to wait until we sort out the dead bodies. *Sorry* for the inconvenience."

Mannion glared at Avilia, challenging him to respond. The landowner scurried back to his SUV and drove off.

"He's probably rushing off to see his lawyer, like a concerned citizen. The media will be here soon," Adams advised as she surveyed the application of crime scene tape.

Mannion's attention was suddenly diverted to an oncoming vehicle.

"Yeah, and it looks like our esteemed ME has arrived."

Adams walked toward the highway to re-direct a slowed vehicle. A dirty Ford station wagon with plastic wood panels chugged into the lot. Dr. Ikram Patel, the Medical Examiner, held the steering wheel with both hands. His faded brown suit, elbows and knees shining, looked like he had slept in it.

He walked around to peruse the coned areas, mumbling advice to several young cops. He knelt to poke at some of the remains with a yellow pencil. He approached Mannion.

The men shook hands.

"So, what's the word, Doc?" Mannion asked.

"Hello Detective. So far, I count eight remains—all women. They were relatively young, maybe in their twenties. Like her—"

Patel nodded toward Ginger Adams as she walked away.

"We'll need to wait until I examine them on the table. They've been here for maybe a decade, more or less, the poor souls."

"Were any of these remains recently added to this graveyard, Doc?"

As the grizzled man with thin gray hair shook his head, Mannion smelled a hint of booze. "Graveyard, hardly—"the doctor answered with bloodshot eyes that had no doubt seen too many horrors. "It's more like a collection of connected bones from a torture chamber, vestiges thrown into the ground. Maybe those damn goats ate some of the remains. But horrific actions were perpetrated on these young women. Burial was not done with any care. It's more like a dumping site, actually. None of the remains here are recent... and there's something rather unusual I observed," said the doctor.

He looked about in a surreptitious manner, as if sharing a state secret with Mannion.

"No doubt—murder is the ultimate destruction of the victim's dignity and is surely the cruelest of deaths. But Detective, I had a brief look at several of the remains, and there's something very odd."

"Okay, I'll ask..." Mannion sighed. "*What's* so odd—beyond eight *dead* women buried in a goat farm, ten years ago?"

"Well, in those remains ... in the cervical area ... I found the skeletal remains of another creature in each of the dead women—a skeleton inside a skeleton, as it were. Very odd indeed! I can't determine yet if it was inserted pre or post mortem. Another revelation I expect when I examine them on the table. But it seemed very odd to say the least. I thought you should know."

"You say *creature?* So what? There are mice and squirrels all *over* these empty lots, Doc!"

"So true, yet this may have been... inserted. I can't be sure..."

Mannion shook his head and looked across the field of activity. A simple lunch had already evolved into all hell breaking loose.

"Are you saying the killer inserted *vermin* into the privates of these women, *while* they were being murdered? Let's keep that tidbit between you and me for now. We don't need to exacerbate a media feeding frenzy. And you said that none of these women were killed recently..." Mannion asked.

The medical examiner nodded.

"It appears that way. At least none of these poor souls unearthed so far today, Detective. But the man who did this... these killer types don't just stop. You can be sure there are other sites somewhere. They keep killing until they are caught or die. Just like this ground... somewhere you'll find other killing fields."

CHAPTER ONE

In the 1950s, the Albertson Hotel was a residence of famous New York literary elites. Sixty-five years later, it stood as a forgotten relic that failed to update. No one famous lounged in the lobby anymore. Across the worn marble floor of the hotel Harry Powell ambled to the rear of the lobby.

He hung his jacket and tossed the paper bag, containing a sandwich of deviled ham on rye bread, on top of the file cabinet. He pushed his time card into the antiquated punch machine under the clock.

Miguel Rodriguez leaned his pear-shaped body against the concierge table, as he flipped through the New York Post.

"How you doin, Harry, my man?"

"I'm good, Miguel. We need to get mats on the wet floors, with all this chilly rain. Also, here's that book *Bennis on Leadership* we talked about. Hope it helps."

Harry handed the paperback to Miguel.

"Thanks, *Amigo*. This will help me prepare for my new B&B business."

Rodriguez returned his attention to the newspaper.

"Lots of crazy *shit* going on! They found a bunch of dead women in Indiana from some serial killer. He's probably in New York now."

"Any issues here tonight?" Harry asked.

"Eh, *one* thing—but first... you decide on the Rolex yet?" Miguel answered, wriggling the garish watch. "It's looking good."

"What? No thanks. My Bulova still works," Harry said.

"Your loss, *Amigo*. This is a real steal!"

"Now tell me now about the *one thing* tonight that you mentioned," Harry insisted.

"Oh yeah—just that one thing... There's a guy in Room 1755—and he's dead," said Miguel.

Harry shook his head with concern.

"Great. Are you *sure* he's dead? Maybe he's sleeping off a drunk. How long has he been that way?"

"He's dead, but I don't know how long. House cleaning found him earlier," Miguel repeated.

Harry brushed his hands back across his damp hair.

"Earlier? Like *when* exactly? You didn't call the cops?"

"No. The boss told the staff to wait until *you* came on duty…you having been a cop."

"Great. Remind me to thank the boss. I'll call her," Harry said

"I wouldn't do that, *Amigo*. She doesn't like being called during the graveyard shift."

"She needs to understand that this should have been called into the police immediately," Harry interrupted.

"Whatever, my man. That's why I got to leave this fuckin city… dead bodies showing up, and the next terrorist attack is coming any day now, Harry."

"So you've said."

"Serious man—I *hear* things. I warned you. They will attack the subway with Sara gas. They're testing shit right now. That's why I take the bus. I can jump off any time."

"I think it's *Sarin* gas. I walk to work because it's free, not because of terrorism paranoia of what might be lurking on the subway," said Harry.

"Every day bad shit happens. Those terrorists are relentless, Harry. It's only a matter of time before they succeed again. They're moving in everywhere. But where better than this city? I got canned foods and purified water all set, Harry. You do that, like I told you?"

"No, Miguel. I got a cramped place, so there's nowhere to store stuff for Armageddon. Now, tell me about this dead body."

"Stuff is for survival, *Amigo*. You get yourself some Dinty Moore and canned peaches. Nine-eleven wasn't the last shot. You'll see. Just like that Army psychiatrist at Fort Hood—it's gonna be somebody who lives here—domestic terrorists. I gotta get outta here!"

"Yeah, okay. But terrorists could attack a city of any size. Now, what do you know about the dead guy here in the hotel?"

"Name is Jakowsky, or something Russian like that. He was always complaining about the weather. Always wore that old raincoat," Miguel answered.

Harry rose.

"I'll go upstairs and check him out. Then we call the cops"

"I'll cover the lobby," Miguel nodded.

Harry pushed button number seventeen in the elevator. As he proceeded down the stale hallway on the frayed carpet, a familiar pungency alerted him to the odor of death. When he was a Chicago detective, he'd stood over many dead bodies. Yet on that night the coppery scent of blood was not present. When he reached number fifty five on the door, he stopped.

He used his pass key to enter and begin to search the cramped space. He was barely able to open the bathroom door without hitting the bottom of the bed. The bright electric light inside exposed cracked caulk and soiled towels. In earlier work, Harry had discovered suicides in tubs of tepid, brownish water, but not here. He only whiffed remnants of cheap cologne and the stench of an unflushed toilet.

In the distance, omnipresent sirens framed the city outside. Living in New York made people immune to noises. Noise just existed as part of the background, like the crickets in a country location.

A couple of Chinese take-out food cartons sat on a table, like tiny white houses. Chop sticks protruded from one of the containers. An open suitcase sat on a chair, with assorted men's clothing scattered out of the carrier. In the closet, a long raincoat hung from a hook, and a pair of shoes sat on the floor, giving the appearance of a lurking demon.

Harry approached the bed. A blanket quilt covered the lump.

That blanket probably hasn't been washed in over a month.

Unless a person was fully clothed, merely sitting on that bed was a health risk. More and more often in modern times, bed bugs were infiltrating hotel rooms, even the upscale establishments. Yet Harry knew that F. Scott Fitzgerald would never have stayed at the Albertson after the way it had deteriorated.

Harry carefully pulled back the quilt, when to his alarm, a man's head appeared. Matted, gray hair strayed out at angles atop a pale, wrinkled face. Dark eyes stared ahead in death. Out of habit, Harry placed a forefinger on the man's cold neck for a pulse, but he felt nothing. He slid the quilt further down in order to see whether there were any signs of violence or a struggle.

The body was clothed in a tee shirt and boxers. The smell worsened, causing distasteful memories to overwhelm Harry's mind.

Death wasn't proud. Death was what it was—smelly and alone—a finale no one wanted to attend.

This decedent was probably just another old man who died alone in his sleep. Harry observed the tissues and hotel hand cream on the table next to the bed, imagining the guy was whacking off when his heart stopped.

A man alone in a city, filled with hookers of all persuasions who could have shared his last amorous adventure... Instead, he played solitaire!

There was no wedding band on his aged, liver-spotted hands.

Alone we came, and alone we departed. All this guy's family and friends became ghosts on the road.

Harry reached over, closing the dead man's eyes before returning the quilt cover. Though there was no disturbance at the scene, the detectives would investigate whether the death was the result of something more than natural causes. Harry saw his own face in the dead man's— the final scene of his own future.

Harry examined the room before going downstairs to call the cops. Glancing away from the bed, a wallet sat like a frog on the nightstand. He used his pen to flip open the wallet and removed a North Carolina driver's license, which read:

Lawrence Anthony Janakowsky
1111 Military Cutoff Road,
Wilmington, North Carolina 28405

He also found a five dollar bill and a North Carolina Private Investigator's License in the wallet. Scrawled on the back of one of the man's business cards was a phone number beginning with area code 910. In the same handwriting, he read, "*MLF-DD-Cp LeJ?*"

At first, the letters meant nothing to Harry, but then he remembered the Marine training base in North Carolina at Camp Lejeune. Closing the wallet on the table top with his pen, he searched the man's jacket, finding a paper note, folded in the inside pocket. He removed the item, unfolding it, and read the half-page newspaper ad:

CELEBRATION ON THE RIVER

***JULY FOURTH INDEPENDENCE DAY ***

- *See Cape Fear River, filled with Navy, Army and Marine ships!*
- *Hear the Marine Band play your favorite patriotic music!*
- *Watch the colorful fireworks, sponsored by Wilmington Bank!*
- *Eat and shop at street vendors along the riverfront!*
- *USSNC Special Olympics tour and luncheon!*
- *Special children's activities in the Cotton Exchange parking lot!*

The advertisement contained key points highlighted in white Starbursts under the red headline on a blue background. A tagline along the bottom read,

A Big Day of Celebration with Fun to Be Had by All!

Penciled across the top corner someone had scrawled, "*opp?*"

Harry returned the paper to the dead man's jacket pocket.

What is a dead PI from North Carolina doing in NYC, and why was he carrying this newspaper advertisement?

Harry departed the room, closing the door behind him.

Harry spoke to Miguel in a quiet voice after returning to the lobby.

"Well, he's dead now—that's for sure. His name was Lawrence Janakowsky—with a driver's license from North Carolina,"

"Yeah, I know. Want me to call the cops now?"

"Listen, Miguel," Harry asked. "Besides cash, did you take anything—like a wedding ring?"

Like a cat puffing up to appear bigger to an attacker, he stretched himself to his maximum five feet five inch height to glare up at Harry, who was six feet tall and fifty pounds heavier.

"What are you askin me? You sayin I'm a *thief?*"

"Well, you knew his name and where he was from—so you probably looked in his wallet. Plus, there's only a single five in his wallet—for a city visitor? There were no loose bills on the nightstand and no jewelry? I'm just asking…"

"Hey, man—there's a guest directory I could have used. Up yours, Harry! Why you accusin me? "

Miguel approached Harry, scowling at the bigger man.

"Take it easy, Miguel. I'm just asking before the *police* arrive and examine everything."

Harry knew that whenever a stiff ended up in a hotel room, vultures swarmed before the police arrived. He could have ignored what he saw, but he couldn't help the way he was wired: sometimes not legal, but *right*—sometimes not politically correct, but *right!* At his age, Harry especially treasured his integrity, since it was pretty much all he still possessed.

"Maybe the guy has some family who really needed the cash, Miguel, or a *wife* who would appreciate the ring?"

"Hey, maybe *I* got kids who need new shoes, Mr. Perfecto! Some of us got *familia* to care for, *Amigo!*"

Harry winced at the dagger-like comment.

"You don't want the cops asking about this, do you?"

"Fuck em, Harry. You think *they* wouldn't take shit lying around? I just beat them to it. *Verdad!* You *never* took nothin, Harry, when you wore the shield?"

He stared down into Miguel's eyes.

"Never... nothing... ever!"

As Miguel twitched an eyebrow while reaching his hand into his back pocket,

Harry felt his muscles tighten in preparation of a physical response.

"Okay, Mr. Perfecto, you never did anything wrong, huh?"

"I never *stole* anything," Harry insisted. "But I've done plenty wrong. It's your choice, Miguel."

"And you do what *you* gotta do about what someone may or may not have taken from the room, *Amigo?*"

Miguel's eyes flittered about the lobby, as if looking for rescue.

"I'll call the precinct and tell them we have a stiff," Harry stated. "No apparent crime. Then I'll call the boss and let her know about her decision to leave the corpse here all this time."

The ensuing hours were filled with official police activity until sunrise. The police indicated they would have to await the official ME lab results, but that the death looked like a coronary event.

Harry called his hotel boss and told her the importance of calling the cops immediately when they found the dead body. The replied directive came from the screeching voice on the phone.

"Give the passkeys to Mike right now, and you are to vacate the premises immediately!"

Harry dropped the phone into its cradle with final closure. He was stunned at the harsh suddenness of the order, but to his surprise, he was also relieved. He signaled to Miguel.

"Here you go, Miguel—my keys and ID. I'm no longer an employee here."

"She *fired* you, *Amigo*? I told you not to call her at *night*. I'm sorry to see you go, but you will escape the next terrorist attack. No one is safe. When my B&B opens in New Hampshire, you will visit, okay?"

Miguel looked at the keys as if they were toxic waste.

"Does this have anything to do with that dead guy?"

"Not that I know of… why do you ask?"

"One of the older cops—the one dressed in a suit," Miguel whispered, leaning in. "Well, he told me to tell you it maybe *wasn't* a heart attack."

Nodding, he backed up and resumed flipping pages in the *Post*.

"Well now, isn't *that* interesting," Harry said to himself.

Remembering the dead guys' note, Harry Googled and found an "MLF" that could have been a minor terrorist group, with a New York post office box location. "DD" came up blank. And "Camp Lejeune" was the Marine camp in Jacksonville, North Carolina.

Harry's phone buzzed as he prepared to depart. It was an old cop friend who now worked in North Carolina.

"Harry! It's me—Bernie. I broke my leg. I need your help right away with the agency. Lots of cases and I need help!"

Harry exited the hotel lobby, to pack up and head south, to help a friend and get some answers.

CHAPTER TWO

The husky, middle-aged man steered the Crown Vic along Military Cutoff Road. Bernie Mannion survived harsh Chicago, endured Indianapolis, but now he loved Wilmington. His retirement from the Indianapolis Police Department (IPD) led to him becoming a licensed Private Investigator in North Carolina. A man had to make a living!

Bernie sought a simple life, which required plenty of good food, enough booze and a little poontang. Cialis worked wonders sustaining his attention. Like the song said—*whatever gets you through the night*. He had the pension money to pay for it. And then his PI license afforded him a legitimate reason to carry a gun, which he had done for half his life. He felt naked without a piece.

As he drove past the crepe myrtles and palms, Bernie mused that *a man becomes the place where he lives*. He found Wilmington a city escaping a singular identity. Was it a historical locale, since it was a railroad center in the early 1800's? *Yes, but routes changed and the trains disappeared.*

And then the Yellow Fever epidemic came. At one time, the city led the world in shipping turpentine from the surrounding western forests, so was it an industrial city? *Yes, but demand changed.* It was a city linked to history the British once occupied during the Revolution, and the Civil War closed with the capture of Fort Fisher. Military links continued with the current tourist landmark, the USS North Carolina, a retired battleship that went to Pearl Harbor before fighting battles around the world. But it was more than that.

Presently, was Wilmington a college town? *Yes, certainly.* Wilmington College (WC) educated over twenty thousand students per year on a sprawling, verdant campus. Was it a river town? *Yes.* The Cape Fear River flowed through restored areas, where pirates once wandered the alleys along cobblestone streets.

Restaurants, bars and ghosts currently shared the northern shore side of the river. The former rice paddy wetlands grew *au natural* on the southern side. Was it a beach resort town? *Yes.* While Wrightsville Beach aligned east of the city, Kure and Carolina beaches were also nearby. Atlantic Ocean waves crashed along the eastern city side, while the river framed the southwest. So, was it a tourist town? *Yes.* The city swelled in the summer, as hotels flashed "No Vacancy" signs.

Was it an active military town? *Certainly* the largest ammunitions storage depot in Southport, Military Ocean Terminal Sunny Point (MOTSU), near the entrance to the Cape Fear River, was kept nondescript for visitors. But there were active encampments and military training areas—all within an hours' drive. Wilmington had all these personalities, but what Bernie loved most was the glistening ocean and all its white boats.

At the behest of a Safety Patrol Officer, Bernie slowed the white Crown Vic he called *Moby Dick.* In stalled traffic, he idled near St. Matthew Church on Eastwood Road after a Sunday Mass. The flashing patrol car lights brought back memories of his police days and the event that drove him to Wilmington—alone. Some incidents of the past were never forgotten, but they showed up unexpectedly, like clouds on a previously sunny day. He recalled the very reason he was in Wilmington.

In Indianapolis, he and his wife, Ethel, had agreed to sell their Broad Ripple house and were packing for imminent retirement in places like Arizona or Florida. All they were seeking was peace and quiet. He could still hear her screams so many years later.

That fateful day was also a Sunday, when he obliged her by driving her to church services. Bernie joined her for Sunday services, but he held no religious beliefs. As usual, he drank too much on that Saturday night, after he had pulled a double-shift to increase his police retirement benefits.

Their garage seemed to have shrunk over the years. It barely accommodated the two old cars they owned. The kids had left the nest, but their junk remained behind. Ethel refused to discard what her children abandoned, and the clutter became permanent.

Ethel always waited outside the garage doors to enter the Lincoln Town Car. She wore a floral dress with the pearl necklace her children had given her to wear to church.

"It's easier to get into the car from out here," Ethel often told him.

Bernie noticed that part of her difficulty in entering the car inside the garage went beyond the clutter, but that her weight had increased considerably. Hell, he was fatter too, but being a cop kept him somewhat active. When the kids flew the nest, Ethel stopped any known activity besides watching TV and eating.

On that fateful day, Ethel waited outside the garage door for the car. Maybe it was the hangover, but on that Sunday, Bernie had accelerated a little faster than usual. It was a straight exit—a mundane act he had performed a hundred times previously, without incident. Later, he wondered if Ethel had dropped something and bent over to pick it up or if she was distracted by a phone ringing? He would never know, and that haunted him more than any cold case.

As the car accelerated out of the garage, Bernie felt a thud and wondered what happened. *Perhaps his golf clubs had fallen again and he ran over them?* Perplexed, he waited for Ethel to open the passenger door so he could ask her. She had sat next to him for almost thirty years. He looked to his right and the seat remained unoccupied. He strained his neck to look back and saw no one.

The first tingle of anxiety greeted him seconds before he heard the sound. At first, he thought it was a kitten crying. Then his police adrenaline mode kicked in. Bernie slammed the Lincoln gears into park and leaped from the car. He ran to the back of the car and looked around the empty driveway in the still Sunday morning. There was only that kitten whimper.

Searching in the direction of the fading cry, he looked under the car, and there was Ethel! She lay trapped beneath the oil-stained chassis—her floral Sunday dress splattered with blood, her face turned away from him, perhaps to avoid a final accusatory admonition.

Later nightmares altered situational truth, and he fancied her looking at him and pleading for his help. If he could have lifted the car, he would have.

How could she have gotten under the wheels? He had only moved the car a few yards into the driveway. Should I have driven it back into the garage? But that would have run over her again. Should I have tried to pull her out?

But her heavy torso was locked in place. He needed help. As he always did when driving, he sought Ethel's direction, and yet she couldn't answer him that final time. All he heard was her fading moan. He punched 911 into his phone.

Within minutes, vehicles screamed closer and emergency personnel surrounded him. Feet scrambled around his driveway. Sirens blared. A tow truck lifted the Lincoln. Ambulance lights flashed. He heard words of condolences and comfort. An unfamiliar voice asked, "How could this happen?" Neighbors patted Bernie on the shoulder, asking if he needed anything.

The next twenty-four hours were a blur, filled with completing forms and enduring the restrained observations of those around him. Nurses looked at him like he was an old fool. Who *else* runs over his own wife in the driveway? He didn't need others to accuse him. Self-recrimination oozed through every pore.

Ethel died from internal hemorrhaging. People who didn't know her expressed their sorrow. Bernie heard the word *tragedy* used quite often. No one ever verbalized it, but he knew what they all thought: *You are an idiot, Bernie Mannion! Were you drunk? Did you do it on purpose?* They never said such heinous things, but he knew their thoughts. He loved Ethel like no other. He wanted her next to him forever.

Soon afterward, Bernie took full retirement and forgot about Sedona and Sarasota, which Ethel preferred, choosing a fresh start near the ocean—in a place where no one knew him. He couldn't depart the accusatory stares in Indianapolis fast enough. He chose North Carolina for his relocation—with his new best buddy, Johnnie Walker.

As months passed, the vivid memory of that fateful Indianapolis Sunday receded to a memory file. The horrific images from that Sunday returned to him, as if it were yesterday. That moment killed his beloved Ethel and destroyed his hope. Gone was his life companion, on the precipice of their anticipated best years together.

That single action alienated him from others he'd once called friends and family. Only his old friend, Harry Powell, kept in touch. His children sent Christmas cards and text messages on his birthday. Ethel was dead and that was the tragedy. Her painful death was his fault, and yet he cried for himself.

Better I should have died that Sunday morning!

Minutes of inattention ended one life and destroyed another. The last best hope in life was that, at some point during living it—all that a person did wrong would suddenly be corrected through some final act of helping others. He hoped for such a future in Wilmington.

A gesticulating traffic cop blasted his whistle, directing Bernie to proceed with church traffic. Bernie happily accelerated Moby Dick to escape his morbid memories.

Moby Dick approached the strip mall, and the storefront emblazoned with the slogan: *Private Detection and Solutions.* Bernie took whatever cases came his way to stay busy, and Mannion Investigations stayed busy enough in the small storefront office on Oleander Drive. His schedule crowded with divorces, missing persons, and scud work to help assorted lawyers. The police pensions paid his living expenses, but he needed to fill his time to block Ethel's ghost from visiting.

He better understood the stories he heard of defrocked clergymen who, once they abandoned celibacy, became seekers of what they had never enjoyed. In Wilmington, Bernie sought what he hadn't experienced as a monogamous married man. He had worked all his adult life to provide for a family, but he decided to acquire what he had always wanted for himself.

When his phone beeped, he noticed the ID showed area code *317*, so he knew it was a voice from his Indiana past.

"Hey, Uncle Bernie—this is Robert. How're you? Got a minute?"

Bernie recalled that his nephew had never called after Ethel's death and assumed he was not calling to check on his health.

"Sure, Bobby, what's up in the Heartland of America?"

"We have an odd case here, from a long time ago. It's up in Lebanon—not exactly your Indianapolis arena, but I thought I'd run it by you. You were *the man* in those days—investigating homicides in the city. Anyway, we found bodies near a deserted house on Interstate 65. Some wacko killed twelve women and buried them in the lot. The Medical Examiner thinks they've been dead eight to ten years.

In his profession, Bernie's nephew, Bobby, was known as Detective Robert Mannion.

Bernie parked Moby Dick in the strip mall lot.

"Is the ME still Patel, who drinks too early? He used to be down in Indianapolis."

"Yeah, some things don't change," Robert chortled. "He told me he rinses with mouthwash before seeing corpses, if *that* makes any sense."

"Yeah and I weigh over two hundred pounds because of a hormonal imbalance," Bernie laughed. "Who were the victims?"

"They were young women, in their twenties and thirties—mostly hookers and druggies."

"People less likely to be reported missing," Bernie mumbled.

"Did you have any case of women and burials like this?"

"Certainly not a dozen dead, but let me think," Bernie answered, pausing. "I drove Interstate 65 enough times over the years. I even wasted a nice Saturday walk once, playing golf, when Trophy Club first opened. Are you talking about the lot with that dilapidated gray and white house with a green roof?"

"Yeah, that's the property. You've got a great memory."

"It always seemed abandoned," Bernie admitted, wagging his head. "We never had any suspected serial killer or cold case mystery. We had a couple of whack jobs, but they were caught. In my day, most one-eight-sevens ended up being one spouse killing the other. So what makes this one special, other than a serial killer in the heartland?"

Silent hesitation pervaded both phones. Bernie thought he had lost the cell connection, but his bars showed full power.

"Robert, are you still there?"

"Yeah, I'm still here, Uncle Bernie. Are you getting enough private eye cases down there in North Carolina?"

"I'm as busy as I want to be. I may hire some more help."

Bernie shifted the walking cast on his recently broken foot.

"That's good. They say North Carolina is a nice place to live. Get a boat yet?"

"I'm working on it. What is it, Robert? You're dancing around. Is there something *special* about this case?"

"We have no people of interest yet. We're trying to track down whoever lived in the house, but it was a rental and it had squatters, so official records may be murky. It's just something *about* them—the bodies. The ME's looked at all the bodies now, and they all have the same... It's *weird* shit!—that's why I called you... to see if you ever had even one case like this."

Bernie looked at the dashboard digital time and realized he had an appointment in five minutes.

"Lay it on me, Nephew. I'm sure I've heard worse." "Like I said—the dead were all women in their twenties, many with blondish hair. Each had... the weird shit—they had a *creature* in their private area."

"They had a *creature*?" Bernie repeated, his face contorted.

"Yeah, doc wasn't sure. They're bringing in some animal expert from Purdue University Veterinary to check it out. They're thinking a gerbil or hamster, or something like that…"

"I remember that housing area never quite developed and wild animals definitely roamed about. Old wood structures have plenty of rats and mice, so maybe some post-mortem situation," Bernie suggested.

"Yeah, that could all be true, but the doc thinks differently. Doc says that before these women were murdered, they were tortured and these creatures were… put inside them, while the creatures and the women were still *alive*."

Bernie used his handkerchief to wipe off the beads of sweat that rolled down his face.

"You're telling me this guy put mice inside their pussies— like a fucked up Tom and Jerry Show?"

"Tom and Jerry? Who's that?"

"Never mind, just an old cartoon. Bobby, you gotta tell me more," Bernie urged.

CHAPTER THREE

Night brought coolness outside the public bathroom in the rest area along Interstate 70. Lloyd Curtin breathed free air for the first time in many years. Inside prison, he was the recipient of pain, while outside, he could return to being the deliverer. He dragged the lifeless woman along the overgrown crabgrass, past the picnic tables. When he neared the brush, the tree frogs ceased chirping. After lying her corpse on the fragrant earth, deep inside the shrub covered periphery, he completed his vile actions.

Lights flashed from the passing trucks on the highway. After he finished, Lloyd returned to the highway, passing unnoticed by several truckers, asleep in their cabs. Lloyd considered himself to be a pirate of sorts, and he continued east toward the Atlantic Ocean, driving at night, when the sun didn't burn his eyes. He sought family and peace, which had abandoned him in Indiana.

It had been weeks since his long drive from Tennessee to North Carolina. As he approached a church in Wilmington, he noticed a brass cross aspiring to heaven from the vaulted roof of the brick church. A thousand believers attended the three Sunday masses, two in English. Broad parishioner demographics covered a range from seniors, beseeching heaven, to children attending the connected primary school.

On that sunny bright day, the single white male in his thirties drove along Eastwood Road and glanced at the bike path on the side of the road near the church. Heavy shrubbery created a natural look to some. But for Lloyd Curtin, it presented an opportunity to snatch a jogger alone near sunset. The urges he fulfilled at the rest areas along U.S. Route 70 on his trip to Wilmington had continued. Aspirations to upgrade from hookers in Indiana brought him to the church.

Lloyd pulled into the parking lot past the St. Matthew Church welcome sign. He came to hunt every Sunday over the last month. Over his omnipresent tee shirt, he wore a stolen long-sleeve plaid Tommy Hilfiger. It was better to hide the tattoos on both his arms in order to blend in and to avoid recognition.

In oceanfront Wilmington, where his relatives had links to a pirate past, Lloyd locked his van to protect the booty. He kept his action kit inside his "pirate ship," hidden under a mattress next to a tiny cage and bottles of water. A worn paperback copy of *The Collector*, by John Fowles, sat cover down on the passenger seat. Lloyd walked among the faithful into St. Matthews and sat in the rear of the church. As military jets roared across the sky and rattled the church roof, no one noticed the sociopath among them. People didn't care about Lloyd as long as he didn't bother them.

Lloyd turned up his collar and hung his head, as if in silent prayer. Six years and twenty-three days of incarceration weighed on his appearance. His pale skin contrasted with the tanned residents around him. He needed to be careful about the acne on his neck, which reddened with too much sun. Exposure would be painful.

Wax candles flickered on the altar. Baskets of lilies rested on the marble floor. Lloyd wished closer proximity to the altar so that he would be able to smell the faint fragrance of the floral bouquet. Whenever a woman entered his pew, he inhaled for the chance at perfumed excitement. Each fragrance elicited recall of previous pleasurable events.

He attempted to sit alone in different sections of the church. He even attended Spanish language Mass, although he did not understand the language. That lingual lapse didn't perturb him, since he wasn't attending Mass to worship. Searching for prey, he focused on his targets, which were pretty women in their twenties.

Avoiding his predatory stare, perfect little families sat around him and misdirected his memories. Lloyd envied those families, smiling at each other. Despite being raised in family filled Midwest trailer parks, where Lloyd escaped tornadoes every year, he could not avoid turmoil from uncaring adults. His chain smoking mother kept the double-wide fairly neat.

When his drunken sperm donor visited between jail terms, it was usually to take cash and punch the woman he called his "bitch-wife." Occasionally, the man belt-whipped his bastard son. When the man, who Lloyd refused to call "Dad" wasn't present, his mother made all the family decisions.

When his mother didn't pay bail, she entertained nocturnal guests, who left crumpled cash on the kitchen table. On those nights, Lloyd listened to his mother groan along with a grunting man who had joined her in bed. He couldn't understand what sleeping together meant—when they obviously weren't doing much sleeping.

Soon he understood too much. Lloyd recalled a beer-bellied guy in a wife-beater shirt, who gave him a crumpled five dollar bill and told him to "go get yourself a six pack and relax." Lloyd was twelve years old. The urges that sometimes overwhelmed him were just beginning.

His mother made him feel weak. Sex and pain always went together. Lloyd aspired to be the man of the house, so his being unsupervised opened the door for him to *act* like a man. Trailer park residents kept the local law busy, meaning Lloyd became accustomed to nightly kaleidoscopic visits from police cars.

He secured a hunter's knife and hid it under his cot. Before sleep, he fantasized about blade insertion when he jerked off. Men were expected to do things to women that had nothing to do with love. In prison, he had time to read about regressive necrophilia in the library. The knife wasn't his penis, which worked fine. It was a *tool* for another purpose—power. The urges *had* to be followed. There was no *choice*, except death. Lloyd knew what he was, and he accepted it as his life.

Weeks earlier, on his first visit to St. Matthews, he was fortuitous enough to find a copy of the church registry. Inside were photos of parishioners, with matching names. The directory became a starting point to learn more on-line about potential targets. Some women were more open than others and allowed access to their social media pages—along with full information, like their locations.

Lloyd smirked in satisfaction, fascinated at the ease required to learn about people. Despite an IQ below one hundred and a *passed-without-earning-it* diploma from special education classes, he was becoming computer capable. *What do teachers know?* He felt smarter than most formally-educated people. They had money and time to go to fancy schools. Colleges sold them their degrees that society misunderstood as education. Real education came from the streets. Even his mother admitted that Lloyd became smarter than she'd expected—before she tweaked herself to death on methamphetamines—the hillbilly heroin.

The church service began as diminutive Father Rodrigo, in colorful vestments, approached the altar, accompanied by three female altar servers. Lloyd looked at each girl, but they were easily under sixteen and too young for his plans. *You are not a perverted pedophile, interested in kids,* he congratulated himself.

Looking up at the massive olive-wood statue of Jesus Christ that hung above the altar, he noted that the nails were displayed correctly, which was through the wrists—unlike some crucifixion scenes that showed nails through his hands, where his body weight would have ripped through the flesh, causing him to fall to the ground.

Dead on the cross, the face of Christ meant nothing to him. Lloyd was attracted to Christ's torture, which led to His agonizing death. Lloyd preferred the horrific flesh-shredding scenes in Gibson's *The Passion* movie.

Catholic Churches were easy to access and Lloyd could maintain anonymity. He savored penetration into these collective good souls by his pirate persona. Since he didn't even drop a dollar into the collection basket, Lloyd laughed that he could listen to music, eat bread and drink wine—all free of charge.

After Mass, he could go to the parish hall for free donuts. None of the older ushers who stood about in their ill-fitting suits ever questioned his attendance. They reminded him of bank guards. His jeans were clean enough, and he usually brushed back his straggly hair.

The only discomfort Lloyd felt came when the priest directed the attendees to share the sign of peace. Lloyd received the friendly handshakes and words of peace from those around him, but he resisted eye contact, since he feared others could peer into his soul and expose his inner urges.

While the Mass began, Lloyd examined the women attending church. He watched the television procedural shows and knew the psychobabble about the abusive hooker mother who birthed the psychotic killer. That oversimplified image—compared to a life like his own—nearly made him laugh. Television profilers always described the criminal as a white male in his thirties. *Such brilliant deduction, Sherlock! Who else? Pimply teens and old farts?* Lloyd knew real life was much scarier than fiction could possibly imagine. He read true crime books. The obligatory red and black covered paperbacks taught him a lot.

Like everyone, he was born to act a certain way. That was the way it was: a man played the cards in hand dealt in life. Alcoholism was an illness from alcohol craving. The fat guy overate because of his desires before becoming obese. Why was Lloyd any different? He was born with urges, just like the others, and he responded.

Bad shit came his way, as it did for most people. *So what?* It was like being gay. He didn't choose to be the way he was, so he just played it out. On most days, he liked who he was and lived his life. He was blameless. Yet as he came to the Cape Fear coast, he let his image of being a pirate blossom, because he was *Born to be Bad*—just like George Thorogood sang.

Lloyd had a simple goal with his targets, and that was to *own* them. Also, he had a simple goal with cops, and that was to defeat them. He could win by controlling the women before death and defying capture so that he could continue his passion. He was never going back to jail. After all, with pirate blood in his genes, he was smarter than all of them. Taking the women made him feel all-powerful.

He looked around the church and recalled his mother telling him about an uncle—unlike the ones who stayed overnight, who she referred to as "visiting uncles." She described an Englishman, an Uncle Kevin, on her father's side, as someone paid by the Queen to be a "gentleman adventurer" for a government fee, to steal for the Crown. Some people called them pirates.

Generations earlier, Uncle Kevin had ended up in Wilmington, near the Cape Fear River, where denizens of the pirate trade gathered. During long hours in a tiny cell in Tennessee, Lloyd's obsession with this family legacy lured him to North Carolina. In addition to pirate ghosts, Lloyd knew that his brother, Jeff, was flourishing financially, presenting him with a freeloading opportunity.

A middle-aged woman with glasses at the tip of her nose stood to read a letter from St. Paul. Lloyd decided she resembled all of his grade school teachers.

How useless they were, as they punched a clock to get a government pension.

They ignored a unique child's actions that included using a magnifying glass to light ants on fire and plucking legs off grasshoppers. Maybe if they had reacted earlier, Lloyd would have lived a different life. He wasn't responsible for who he was. He was dropped by a whore, abandoned by a sperm donor and ignored by teachers. His genes made him who he was, and the people in his life hadn't helped improve anything.

The congregation stood in unison to hear Father Rodrigo read the day's Gospel, but all Lloyd heard was *blah blah blah*—like the cows in a Larson comic. While the congregation prayed, Lloyd's head filled with expanding clouds, gathering in a storm. His head churned as the ominous clouds darkened.

Under his shirt, a creeping sea monster tattoo began, just above each wrist, and wound about his forearm, culminating in a burst of crimson at his shoulder. The sharp-toothed monster devoured prey on each of Lloyd's shoulders. A damsel in distress with exposed creamy white breasts succumbed in the salivating serpent's mouth. Across his back, another graphic battle occurred, where a leering bearded pirate with a black eye patch and a knife in his mouth leaped aboard a frigate to ravish a voluptuous harlot. In the universe of Lloyd Curtin, women were victims and pirates were winners.

While the congregation listened to Father Rodrigo struggle through a sermon of broken English, Lloyd used the time constructively. He examined the parishioners. Over the past few weeks, he had identified women who fit his criteria. Targeting churches started as a game, but it quickly became a realistic part of his plan. He had worn out enough honky-tonk barmaids and truck-stop sluts. Church women would never talk to him, but he would still possess them and be all powerful.

In no particular order, Lloyd targeted regular church attendees. *Target one* sat serenely, like a petite ice queen. She held her shoulders back to accentuate moderate breasts. Sometimes, she distributed the communion wafers, and Lloyd liked to receive the host from her directly into his mouth. A full gulp of the wine followed. Lloyd laughed that Catholics allowed pirates to partake of their sacred sacraments.

Dark roots betrayed *target two*, who bleached her hair blonde atop a thin figure and pursed lips. She wore horizontal black-framed eyeglasses. Gliding across the church like a model, she presented herself so prim and proper. Extending her well-toned arms, she led the singing of the psalms.

Target three had more meat on her bones and could be called *zaftig*. Probably once a drop-dead gorgeous swimsuit model, she presently displayed curvy expansion that brought strains to her designer clothes.

Lloyd's fourth candidate shook her long brunette hair as she walked across the front of the church to share a reading. She displayed a perfect high-arched ass, more common in younger women.

The fifth had the face of an angel, enhanced with colorful makeup. Her shiny russet hair hung as a frame for her cherubic face. With dark almond eyes and a Roman nose, she appeared as if she was painted by a European artist of centuries past.

Father Rodrigo spoke in an animated manner to draw the congregation's attention, but Lloyd's thoughts were elsewhere. He would penetrate each woman beyond their body and into their souls. Ultimately, he would control them completely. No longer would they look down their flaring nostrils at him—like he had leprosy.

Not handsome enough for them? My lingo isn't slick with praise? Can't make them laugh?

Perhaps not, but he could use his power to possess them by ending their lives—the ultimate ownership.

The sixth target could have been a waitress at a Raleigh truck stop. Her heavy breasts strained against even loose tops. Despite the adopted foreign child that clung to her, she retained the appearance of a coffee-slinging slut, with raven black hair.

The seventh was a woman who looked like a late-stage teenager, with a shapely body and pristine face. Always in tight jeans and sports tops, he imagined her hanging out in Hollywood, waiting to be discovered. Flowing blonde hair framed translucent skin around enormous eyes.

Father Rodrigo ended his sermon with a sign of the cross, and then all stood to pray for others. Christians were an odd crew who loved their enemies and turned the other cheek—enough reason for Lloyd to disdain them.

Target eight possessed a Mediterranean face, with high cheek bones and a large, inviting ass. She displayed dangling earrings and artistic makeup. Lloyd questioned what she was doing with her short, bald husband. He imagined her sweating and screaming with Lloyd.

As the Mass progressed, the congregation knelt, and when Father Rodrigo raised the oversized host above the altar, Lloyd visualized his targets kneeling before him.

A possible *target nine* walked back from receiving the host with a bouncy stride. Contrasted to styles today, she wore short and tight, white shorts and a bold, horizontal striped blouse. Thick, strawberry blonde hair surrounded a face like those on the Miss Clairol hair color boxes.

His *tenth target* stood out with lustrous red hair and full lips. High heels enhanced her height, and she appeared proud of her tallness. Often seen alone, she came unadorned by make-up. Lloyd imagined her afire when he controlled her.

A college girl became his number eleven. She sported a classy Celtic face that had clear, white skin, framed by onyx hair. Lloyd envisioned her as a gymnast with flexible form.

The twelfth candidate stood erect as the lead singer in the chorus. Her curly brown hair cascaded across broad shoulders of a strong physique. She sang with confidence and never wore a bra. When singing, her sensuous movements shouted to Lloyd to take her. The candidate quantity appeared appropriate.

Which one would he take before she cheated on her mate and stole away with his child? Which of these whores would someday make their child watch her nightly degradation? Forget the guy on the cross above them all—Lloyd would become their true savior.

Those were his twelve—twelve women, twelve apostles, twelve months, and he liked the number twelve. He would own them, one-by-one. The urges were accelerating since his arrival.

Online social networking helped him gather pertinent tidbits about each woman. Some were business achievers. Others participated in local clubs and teams. A few played tennis and some golf. Others jogged daily at the same time and place. At his keyboard, he knew where they went each day, and who they knew.

Good thing for libraries and free access!

As Lloyd passed on the wicker collection basket without a contribution, he sensed an urge to act. He would select one of his targets to spend more time with him.

Maybe I'll send them all untraceable emails and determine if there is any interest? Maybe I'll call them to determine who will agree to donate stuff from their garages to help handicapped Haitian orphans?

Each target had exposed enough so that Lloyd could customize the bait on his hook. He believed that at least one out of the twelve would voluntarily meet him. Ten percent wasn't too much to expect. One lucky woman would be the first Wilmington wench to please the pirate king!

His plan grew closer to reality each day, with only one decision remaining: *Who will I make my first choice?*

As Mass concluded, Father Rodrigo blessed everyone, telling the congregation to "Go in Peace." As everyone stood and moved toward the exits, Lloyd inhaled perfumes, perusing the crowd. *How did I miss her?*

She sat in a pew in the far corner of the church. As she walked, her blond ponytail bounced seductively. Lloyd leaned forward to see her long, white legs, sprouting from khaki shorts. Her muscular calves looked like those of a tennis player or runner. Her erect demeanor made it seem she was trained to stand at attention.

He returned to his van, which had an outfitted interior like a pirate ship. He thought of his van, with a black interior and white exterior, as the reverse-Oreo. As he moved, the sun reflected off the diamond earring dangling from his ear. He had pilfered the jewelry during his latest relocation job.

Sliding between parishioners, he maneuvered behind "ponytail" and watched her ass cheeks move up and down in harmony. He approached closer, but couldn't smell any lingering perfume. She accelerated her pace to a small car before some kids jumped in front of Lloyd, blocking his pursuit.

So Lloyd watched blonde "ponytail" sashay to a Toyota. As she departed the parking lot, he noticed an Army bumper sticker on the rear fender. To Lloyd, she became *Army Girl*. Stepping off the curb on the exit road, he peered at the departing Corolla and noticed license plates that were from Maine. He considered adding her to his twelve, or using her to replace the next target.

Lloyd sat alone in his pirate ship. After the satiation of his desires, he planned where to dispose of the body. Unlike barmaids and hookers, for the target list created at church, availability guided his selection. For as long as he could remember, the urges had come—beginning with the plucking of fly wings. Eventually, he progressed to mice and rabbits. Joy came from the actions rather than the outcome. His joy increased with a woman in a new hunting ground.

After evaluating the parade of targets from Mass, the urge became unstoppable. No rest would come without appeasing his desires. He was right to feel better, after all. To relive the pleasure, he removed and retained the usual trophy.

In the moonlight, Lloyd stopped the van. Dragging the corpse of church target number two into the wetlands, he returned to the van unseen. Inside the black garbage bag and weighted with a cinder block, she would never be found. Lloyd drove off with a smile on his face. The pirate had arrived in peaceful Wilmington.

CHAPTER FOUR

Kiki Sanchez turned off the engine of her lime-green convertible Volkswagen. She enjoyed coming to the Mannion Private Detection and Solutions Agency, mostly because she liked working for old Bernie. He never hit on her, like so many creepy old farts, who ogled her tits like hungry babies. Bernie basically let her make her own work hours, which allowed her to pursue music gigs around town.

Guys could play guitars, but they were always looking for a female singer who moved provocatively and knew the words to their cover songs. That week, she would sing with the *Flying Fools* at the *Mayfaire Summer Music Festival*. She had several different colored cheap wigs, so no one recognized the same singer in different groups.

Kiki opened the bottom drawer of the filing cabinet to put away her Sak purse and sneakers, and slip on the low heels for work performance. Leaning over, she exposed the butterfly tramp stamp on her lower back, above the red thong band. She also had a turtle tattooed on her ankle. In the back supply room, she started the coffee maker that Bernie found too confusing to operate. The bells atop the front door alerted her to Bernie's arrival.

The burly man in an ill-fitted suit limped in with a cane.

"Good morning, Kiki. How was your weekend? Wild and crazy, as usual?" "You should only *know*, boss."

She flipped her purple and black hair in a humorous imitation of a flirt.

"How are you getting around, Captain Ahab? What can I do?"

Kiki spoke with compassion for the man who easily weighed twice as much as she did. His tan summer suit and faux Panama hat contrasted with her colorful combination of red-and-yellow top, with pleated plaid skirt.

"Just get me some coffee, please... and then come and sit down. I've got a couple of things to talk to you about."

Kiki smiled at him as she completed the task.

"What's up, boss?"

She drank purified water from a huge pink bottle through a bent straw.

"Well, you know we have been busier—with more clients—and with my busted leg and all… I'm bringing in an old friend to help with the business."

"You mean Harry Powell—Vietnam veteran who was a decorated Chicago cop. Plus, you two knew each other in Indiana where you were a cop. He retired to Maine, where he was a hero. Something called a Convictions Integrity Unit in Chicago stripped him of his pension—says he shot the guys who assassinated his wife, even though they were both shot during a felony. A bank in Maine foreclosed on his cottage, and then he ended up working hotel security at some fleabag NYC hotel. "

"Yeah, how did you…"

"Elementary, my dear boss—I run this little shop of horrors."

She sipped from her water bottle.

"He'll be here tomorrow? Do you want me to greet him? No, that's okay. You'll take Moby Dick to meet him and share dinner, since he's driving down from the Big Apple. Oh yeah, he'll be living at *The Hampton Inn* for now, then who knows?"

"I didn't know he was a hero in Maine."

"Yeah, the headline read 'War Hero Saves Couple." Small town called Higgins Beach, but a big deal to the deli owners who were being robbed. Your Mr. Harry happened to walk in and got wounded in a shoot-out that saved their lives."

"What happened to the perp?" Bernie asked.

"Shot dead."

"So you learned all this history? What do you *think* of him?"

"The newspaper had a recent photo of him. Tough but nice. He looks like an aging 'Mad Men' character…"

KiKi smiled at Bernie.

"It's a cable TV show?"

"Okay. Well, if *I* can add something. About a year ago, Harry's daughter and grandson were killed in a car accident on the way to see him—wiped out his family. Maybe he's recovering, if possible. He's a stand-up guy. You can trust anything he says."

"There's a *but* coming here, isn't there?" KiKi smiled.

"But he doesn't… he *won't* perform all the tasks required in a profitable private investigation organization. He has his *own* set of rules, you might say."

"*Organization*, oh you mean like the two… or now *three* of us? You mean Harry won't snoop around and take dick and beaver shots of cheating spouses?"

"Probably not. Harry's a by-the-book guy. He'll probably handle the more… *sophisticated* cases we get."

"Like the *second* item on your agenda?"

"Well, we also have a new client. She'd worked with another PI, but he passed away so she contacted me. A woman…"

KiKi leaned forward, crossing her legs.

"Are you telling me her husband is cheating on her and I get to take some *dick* pictures?"

"No. This case is quite different. And I've got to tell you, Kiki… it might be somewhat dangerous. There are some questionable people involved—maybe bordering on violence, and I wanted to warn you to see if you were still okay."

"Hey boss, don't be so paternalistic. This is the road I've *taken*. I told you I won't carry a gun, because I'd never shoot anyone, but I can help in other ways. I meet tough guys at the clubs all the time. I can handle myself. Thanks for worrying, but no need. I carry mace and a blade. What's this damsel in distress's name?"

Bernie appeared stunned.

"*Mace and a blade?*"

"No BFD. And the new *client* you were bragging about?"

"Oh, you don't already *know* her profile?"

"Hey boss, I only check out what might impact me," she answered.

"Technically we're employed by Mr. JD Henzlein. David Dodd is his client, and he's up in Camp Lejeune. But I expect she'll be involved in this complex case. Her name is Mrs. Morderca. Carolyn."

"Okay, I got it. What else?"

Bernie answered, his face serious.

"These folks may be involved in some… terrorism."

~~~~ ~~

Harry Powell scratched his facial stubble as he drove the Taurus southward. His urgency came from the phone call he received from Bernie Mannion earlier:

"I broke my fuckin leg. I'm gonna lose the damn business if I don't get help soon. I don't wanna hire some dick. I need you here, Harry."

Harry winced from pain in his knee as he accelerated the four-cylinder engine.

So he was the better alternative to some dick, which was comforting.

Recent phone calls were always bad news. He willed the bad news into the past, filed on a shelf, to be forgotten. Wilmington was a final chance for a comeback in his shattered life. He had stumbled into the declining stages of mediocrity.

He squinted, as the road signs were harder to see, and his sense of direction faltered. New music seemed foreign, with noise and lyrics he couldn't follow. The daily news was filled with places around the world whose names he barely recognized. As he approached North Carolina, the car drifted across the lane markers. He drove slower as the road grew darker. Exit sign lights reflected on his right hand atop the steering wheel.

The wrinkles were becoming deeper. Why was he aging so fast? Wasn't it a few years ago that he couldn't understand the old farts who hung around too long at the job? They didn't accept the time to move on. Slowly, he questioned if he was becoming one of those guys.

Miguel's words about domestic terrorist fears in the city floated around in his head—but that dead PI was from Wilmington. And that serial killer story from Indiana...*when Bernie and I were both working there almost a decade earlier. I'll help Bernie in his PI business, and hopefully, I'll find answers to many questions. Is this trip to help a friend, help myself, or to find Carolyn?* He missed the calls to crime scenes to catch criminals.

Bernie needed help, but Harry needed to do something impactful with his time. It was a chance to move forward, and a chance to help people. He was alone, driving monotonous miles through New Jersey, on past the blinks that were Delaware and Maryland, across a stretch of Virginia, and finally onto the dark roads of North Carolina.

Green signs with white letters flashed around him, like windows to a future. Time sped by him like the directional signs.

I know I can't go back, and thinking about the past wasted the present, and yet his life existed in the past. The present sucked for assorted reasons, but he didn't deserve any better. What did they call it? Karma? For the people he killed, for the lives he abandoned, this was his outcome—driving down a dark, empty road to a small town in North Carolina. Harry Powell—this is your life. Live it!

He followed signs for Wrightsville Beach and headed south into northern Wilmington, looking ahead to the final chapter in his life.

The radio directed his thoughts. He raised the volume when Bob Seger sang about his drive against the wind. *Where had all his time gone?*

"Time heals every wound," a nurse promised him in the recovery room after he was shot in Maine during the deli confrontation.

He knew the falsehood of such an observation. Time simply progressed rapidly, devouring days allocated in a life. *Actions and people made time worthwhile.*

A helicopter whirled overhead in the dark. Several empty Red Bull cans banged on the floor. Glen Campbell sang about a rhinestone cowboy, and all the compromising. He nodded. As the car accelerated, he squinted to read the green directional signs, heading to a job as a private detective in Wilmington, North Carolina.

~~ ~~ ~~

Johnny Cash sang about hurt and pain as Harry pulled the car into a jammed parking lot. Valet parking wasn't a common occurrence in his life. Bernie was finishing a Johnny Walker Black when Harry walked inside. The busy wait staff scurried around a room that was filled with jovial after-work drinkers and diners.

"We're always meeting in seafood restaurants. How's the broken foot?" Harry asked, extending his hand.

"It hurts like hell. That's why I drink."

Bernie signaled for a refill and displayed his cane.

"Wait a minute," Harry interrupted." *You* said you broke your leg and you were laid up. All I see is a walking boot and a single cane. That's a miraculous recovery! What is it… you *fractured* one of those little bones?"

Despite feeling somewhat scammed, he sat and smiled.

"Hey, it *is* broken, and I *do* need your help, Harry. Your limp looks better, but you look like *shit*. Lose your razor?"

"It's good to see you, too Bernie. Have you been on a diet?"

"Ha! Yeah, a diet of eating whatever the hell I *want*! No police annual physical bullshit. Wasn't it Will Rogers who said he never met a food he didn't like?"

"It was *something* like that. It was a long drive in a hurry, but I'm ready to go. What cases do I need to work on?"

"Hey—slow down. This is the South, not New York. You always get right to the point. Want a drink?"

Bernie ordered another JWB and Harry requested Belvedere, on the rocks.

"I arrived like ten minutes ago," Harry began "So I'm staying at the Hampton Inn down the road… for now."

"*Belvedere?* You're stepping up, Harry. How did you like Kiki at the office?"

"Your office was closed. It's a long drive from New York City."

"It could be *our* office, Harry! I'm thinking Mannion and Powell. MP—like your old job, eh? Private investigation work today is much more sophisticated. For me, it's all about cash flow. It's a way to supplement my paltry, inflation-shrunken, tax-depleted pensions from Indiana and Illinois. And when Social Security comes, it won't even pay my bar tab. I need current income, so I don't run out of money over the thirty years I plan to live."

"You're an optimist," Harry laughed. "Two pensions aren't *enough?* Did you buy a boat or something?"

"Actually… I did, but she's only twenty feet. Those docking costs in the slips are high, but I'm not living in Arizona. It's heaven out there on the water. You gotta come out with me, Harry. Just a man and the sea… and some alcoholic enhancements… and maybe someone in a bikini…"

"I don't wear bikinis," Harry smiled.

A young waitress placed the drinks in front of the men.

"*Thanks*, darling," Bernie offered as he watched her walk away.

"Hey, by the way—you ever hook up with that cutie, Carolyn, from Maine?"

"Carolyn left Maine, Bernie. She had a family emergency down south. I haven't heard from her in quite some time."

"To old friends and new adventures," Bernie announced, raising a toast.

Harry raised his own glass.

"Life is like boxing, Harry. You get hit, but you gotta keep moving and throw some punches. A wise man once said, *you judge the character of a man, not by how often he gets knocked down, but by how many times he gets up.* Cheers!"

After a few minutes of catching up, Bernie pulled several manila folders from his leather briefcase.

"Let's see… missing kid from Figure 8 Island, security support at Wilmington College (WC), an uncle charged with being too friendly with neighbor kids, Marine court martial, a guy who thinks his wife is cheating with another woman—the usual stuff."

Bernie dropped the pile of folders on the table.

"Very organized, Bernie, I'm impressed. Got any cases involving the MLF?"

"The MF? Motherf…"

"The M-L-F—the Military Liberation Front, a little terrorist group I read about."

"Nah," Bernie sighed. "To be honest, *KiKi* does all this. She's great. You're going to love her. She's just like a daughter to me."

"What do I do? Do I just *pick* a case?"

Harry leaned forward as the alcohol hit his empty stomach. He could see the dead guy he found at the Albertson Hotel in New York.

"You know a private eye named Janakowsky, here in Wilmington?"

"There are a 100,000 people living here, Harry. Let's see… Jankowski? *Doesn't* ring a bell."

Harry recalled the newspaper advertisement found in the dead man's jacket in the hotel room.

"I understand you're having a big Independence Day event in Wilmington on the Cape Fear River?"

"Yeah, what a surprise, Harry. It happens every year, usually around early July, like the Fourth?"

"Nothing being investigated about that event?" Harry asked.

"Not that *I* know about. Who *cares*?"

Bernie smiled and motioned to the pretty young waitress.

"You a native North Carolinian, sweetheart?"

"No, I'm from Michigan. I came here for school. I major in marine biology at WC. Can I recommend an appetizer?"

Her smile exposed a perfect row of white teeth. Bernie strained to read the name badge on her chest.

"Well, Bethany, for me, you can acquire another JWB, and the flounder. Harry?"

"I'll have the shrimp scampi," Harry finally submitted.

"You know why I eat *flounder*? It has both eyes on the same side of its body, so it can detect things better... like *me*."

Bernie laughed.

"The court martial Marine interests me the most," Harry concluded as he focused on the folders.

"Nice *ass*!" Bernie nodded.

"The Marine?"

"No! That cute little Bethany. Don't you notice women anymore?"

"Women? Sure, but not teenagers. What about the Marine?"

"The Marine is up in Jacksonville at Camp Lejeune. It's a touchy, complicated case, but there's a client here in Wilmington that may be more urgent... and more money for us." Harry recalled the script on the advertisement he found on Janakowsky, which read *MLF-DD-CpLeJ.*

"Does the Camp Lejeune case involve somebody with the initials DD?"

"What's all this *about*, Harry? Are you bringing a case with you from New York? I got enough here."

Harry leaned in, speaking quietly.

"On my last day in security at the Albertson Hotel, we found a dead guy, alone in his room. He was a PI from Wilmington, named Lawrence Janakowsky. Written on a July 4th ad in his pocket was *MLF, DD* and *Camp Lejeune.* Coincidence?"

"Listen, Harry—I'm sure all things will be revealed in time, but right now we got more lucrative cases I need you focused on, okay?"

"Don't tell me that involves the cheating spouse?"

"No," Bernie protested "This one's new. No folder yet. There's a wealthy professor living in Landfall, which you drove past. Her name is Annabelle Radinsky-Wade. She claims her adult daughter went missing. No sign of any crime. The daughter's a beautiful redhead. Police figured either she hooked up with some beach bum or swam out too far in a riptide. After 48 hours, the cops gave it a look, but it went cold fast. The professor thinks I... *we* can do better.".

"A rich professor? Isn't that an oxymoron?"

"Not anymore, Harry. You need to get with the times. In our day, municipal employees were at the bottom of the pay scale, but not anymore. The president at Ohio State made almost two million last year. Plus, our professor inherited big bucks, and she's younger than us, Harry. And I hear she's hot!"

When their food arrived, Bethany served each of the men. "Is there anything else I can get you?"

Bernie started to make a comment, but he deferred to Harry.

"No, this all looks fine. Thanks for now," Harry answered.

After she left, he turned to his friend.

"I thought you were going to make some sexist remark about what she could *get* you...."

"You underestimate me, Harry. There's more than meets the eye to Mr. Bernie Mannion."

"You haven't *met* the professor mother of the missing daughter?" Harry asked.

"Not yet. I just got the referral from JD. Plus, this widow is hot. Did I already *tell* you that?"

"I thought you preferred younger women, Bernie?"

"Well, Harry, I'm like a whale... I catch what swims my way."

"One more question before I finish eating and head back to the hotel. You see the story about the bodies from a serial killer they found in Indiana?"

Bernie finished his drink and nodded.

"Creepy shit, my friend. Thank God there isn't anyone like that here in Wilmington! "

CHAPTER FIVE

Lloyd looked up at the massive man who spoke at him.

"You can crash here for a few days, man. I'm on a ride to Los Angeles, and I'll be back in a week. Remember, don't smoke no shit in here or fuck in my bed. Then you need to find your own crib, man. I don't need a roommate."

With that farewell, Big Bob was gone, leaving Lloyd alone in the apartment. The nauseating oil stench from the garage below would have to be tolerable until he found his own place. It beat bumming off the pier and sleeping near the beach. There were public restrooms and there was beach access near some of the restaurants. The food in the dumpsters wasn't all bad, as long as he retrieved bread and vegetables and avoided spoiled seafood.

After being released from prison in Tennessee, Lloyd stopped along the way in Kentucky and West Virginia. He secured a moving gig and would stay until he located relatives. Almost all the money the truck driver paid him went to buy the van parked out front. He found it on Craig's List, and he paid cash so there would be no identification.

They concluded the deal on a Sunday afternoon in the empty parking lot of a closed *Chick-Fil-A*. Lloyd wore a baseball hat and shades. He found old license plates in a dumpster, and he put those on the van.

Like most national carriers, Weston hired truck drivers, who then hired manual labor. Most weren't too particular. The driver paid loaders like Lloyd cash for a day's work—no benefits and no paperwork. It was straight work for pay. May through August was the prime times to get hired, when loaders earned almost a hundred dollars a day.

Drivers picked guys like Lloyd, who were young enough to carry heavy furniture. Although wiry, Lloyd lifted weights to enlarge his biceps. Drivers liked his tats, but concerned about customers, they told him to wear a long sleeve shirt to cover up on moving days.

He found it funny that drivers picked him, based on appearance, when he would steal anything he could get his hands on. Like a house cat that crashed against windows at birds it could never reach, Lloyd always sought treasures that others owned. He settled for what he could get.

Lying on the mattress, he inhaled from a joint.

Screw Big Bob!

He had the van and he had sold a pair of pilfered gold cuff links at the gold exchange store. The wealthy insurance executive would never miss them. It was easy to rob a customer in the moving business. *Just hide the booty in an empty mover's box to be taken out to the truck for breakdown. Then shove the loot into a corner to grab later.* Rich people all had coverage, so no one lost anything. Lloyd survived through his version of unapproved wealth distribution.

He inhaled as his thoughts drifted back to his youth. He saw himself standing near the trailer where his mom lived in Indiana. Removing the wings of the flies he caught, he enjoyed watching them crawl about aimlessly, desperate to take flight before he squashed them.

He liked grabbing cats when he could, but they were tougher to catch, so they were a rare treat. After stunning one tabby with a rock, he hung it by the paws from a clothesline. Once the cat awakened, Lloyd smiled when it screeched and then gleefully watched the cat wobble away in pain when he cut it loose.

At least I cut the early ones loose.

Allowed to keep one pet, he had a brown and white hamster that he named Skippy. He kept it in a perforated Ked's sneakers box. One rainy day, as Lloyd removed Skippy from the box, an urge struck him. The squirming creature's heartbeats throbbed into his fingers. Without thinking, he pressed his thumb and forefinger around its neck. When the tiny bones crunched, like walnuts in a nutcracker, he felt a thrill.

It gave him pleasure in taking a life. The tiny animal died quickly, and he dumped it on the gravel outside the trailer so his mother would think it had escaped and was killed by a cat. To keep him occupied, his mother would supply him with another creature. The urges he felt that day would never abandon him.

There was familiarity about dead Skippy's face that reminded Lloyd of what a teacher described about Lloyd as having "dead eyes." The fat hag made him attend psychological counseling that ended up going nowhere. In those sessions, they gave him new Crayolas and told him to draw pictures, so he gave them what they wanted, green trees and brown houses, with smiling stick figures holding hands.

Never once did he use the gloomy black Crayola. No red blood covered any of the images he drew. Such total bullshit, but those state experts got paid by the hour and acted like they didn't give a shit, which they didn't. Schools claimed to protect kids, but they didn't care. Lloyd was always just promoted to the next grade level as someone else's problem.

In a photo on the bureau, Big Bob stood next to a little old woman. She was maybe five feet tall, and she looked like a hand puppet next to Big Bob, who was easily three hundred pounds and six foot six. With fawning maternal love, the cherubic, gray-haired woman looked up at Bob.

Lloyd had no such photo of the woman who gave birth to him. If they had a similar picture, his mother would have been glaring at him with crossed eyes, filled with regret about how she let herself get knocked up. Her round pig-like nose and pencil thin lips completed the worn face, framed by straw-like, bleached hair. Lloyd closed his eyes to visualize his mother beneath a grunting visitor. Combined with the stench of cigarettes and booze, he recalled the deflated sounds of release and exhaustion.

Lloyd peered into the dusty mirror atop the bureau, squeezing a white pustule on his acne-scarred face, resenting his mother for the bulbous nose he had inherited. *A man can't escape his history.*

The urge to hunt returned. The urges abated when he was in jail, but they had returned with a vengeance. His only choice was who and where. Lloyd inhaled the last of the weed and smiled with anticipation of the fun to be had.

The afternoon sped by as he worked on the interior of his van. He had to clean it from his first adventure with a church lady. On the floor, he placed a plastic covered single mattress that he found discarded on garbage pick-up day. He stole tools from a truck driver and used them to install shelves for holding liquids, duct tape and plastic ties. His hit kit neared completion. Two bright orange street cones sat in a corner.

Beneath all his stuff, he hid an Ultron stun gun that he considered an upgrade from the chloroform of his pre-jail hunting. It was easier to acquire a stun gun than draw attention to himself in buying a drug like chloroform. He threw in a cheap paint brush and tray in case he was ever pulled over and a cop asked what he did.

What could I say? Handyman, painter, pirate… and killer?

The van was his pirate ship that sailed atop the macadam waves of highways, to pillage wealth and rape fair maidens—all to fulfill his childhood inbred urges. It's what pirates did. Sometimes, Lloyd felt like wearing the shoplifted black eye patch, especially after being in the Cape Fear home of his pirate ancestors.

In a white van similar to a hundred others, Lloyd drove along the streets of Wilmington. For his immediate target, Lloyd had a sketchy plan. A few joggers were vaguely familiar. He might have seen one at church. He might have seen her dance in a strip club, but he wasn't sure. He did know one of her activities. She jogged near the beach, where he could grab her.

Many single women lived near the beach. He preferred sunset, because the shadows covered him from being observed. He retained a legitimate confidence about being able to operate undetected, based on a decade of free reign. No one got wise to him in Indiana.

Above the sandy beach the vast sky flowed with mauve and crimson. He parked the van near the Johnnie Mercer Pier in Wrightsville Beach. He watched women the way a hawk watched rodent prey. He planned to use the Ultron taser to stun her asleep. When she awoke, he would convince her he had a sexual problem. He just wanted to come on her, and then he would release her, unharmed. After hearing the promise of release, targets initially gave into his desires. They wanted to believe his promises. He gave them hope. As time passed, they would beg to be released, even offering him money, and some gave lame excuses, like pregnancy, disease, a heart condition or some other lie. A few women claimed they were on the rag, thinking that would bother him. They didn't laugh at his stuttering then or look in disgust at his acne. Terror in their eyes was the best response he could hope for.

Women are whores who should be eliminated before they harm innocent offspring!

Some were pampered poets with unrequited love. Others were pseudo athletes who sought to seduce rich professionals. But whatever guise they assumed, he knew they were whores who would use sex to seduce some handsome sap into becoming husbands in order to obtain wealthy lifestyles or cash on nightstand tables. It did not matter what the currency was, since they were all sluts, who sold what they had for what they wanted—except for with Lloyd, who owned them and *took* what he wanted.

As "Lloyd, the pirate" moved stealthily along the streets, his urge grew more intense. He checked the rearview mirror and saw no cops. There was just a stream of carefree beach-goers, near the cusp of the vacation season. Everything became secondary to his urge. Demand accelerated for a target, the urge growing and consuming his body. His long-fingered hands tingled with excitement. He crouched behind the steering wheel, like a panther in search of satiation. He did not consider every woman who passed the van. Only young solo women without dogs were targets.

After fifteen minutes without a target, he drove the van to another location to avoid suspicion. He tugged down on the black baseball hat with the gold "P," in honor of his pirate ancestors. As sun set, he turned toward the small bridge over the inter-coastal waterway on Wrightsville Beach. Driving ten miles an hour, he ogled the joggers along the tree-lined street. The more he saw, the more his building to explosion increased.

They ran on the walkway under the row of live oak trees. Some were in pairs, but most were solo. Some were men, but most were women. Young women jogged in their sporty, tight tops and brief shorts, with muscular legs, shapely asses and bouncing breasts.

Since there were houses, and people lived along the Inter Coastal Waterway, his actions had to be sneakier than at the isolated truck stops. He couldn't simply perform, dump and depart like he did with lot lizards on the road who just finished blowing a truck driver for ten bucks. They never suspected Lloyd was anything more than another Alexander Hamilton. But under the darkening sky at Wrightsville Beach, he needed to set up his ruse to fool his prey.

He parked the van in a break in the sidewalk, where municipal utility workers performed repairs. He set up the orange cones, indicating ongoing work. With the setting sun, the tree-lined sidewalk became less visible from the waterfront residences. A few cars drove past, departing the beach area. A bankrupt gas station bordered the waterway and filled the gap in waterfront residences.

These runners may be tourists or locals. I don't know or really care. The young women ran off calories to maintain those luscious figures. They are here for the taking. I want one now!

The urge exceeded any hesitancy about visibility. The blood that had filled his head with cautions flowed south—to that part of his manhood that responded without any thought. Risk enhanced his excitement. These were classy ladies, in a rich area, and not some hick-town hookers. He had to act smart. He depended on the willingness of humans to help each other.

His bony fingers drummed the steering wheel. Joggers passed him, hardly noticing him, like he was an invisible man. The red-headed runner looked familiar.

Was she from church? Was she a dancer?

He couldn't recall. The new weed was stronger and fogged his recall. Yet he gravitated toward the red hair on that tall woman. He fancied to call her "Big Red" in his mind. She wore a chartreuse pullover and tight black shorts, down to her knees. Her long strides progressed after she passed Lloyd. From the side door of the van, he exited and strategically maneuvered the two orange cones onto the walkway, and he positioned them so that, upon her return, Big Red would need to jog toward the trees and away from the street, not disturbing the working man.

Lloyd watched Big Red run east, off Wrightsville Beach, toward the bridge into Wilmington and waited patiently for her return. Approaching night limited visibility. A few others ran past him—no men, no couples, no dogs. Lloyd kept the side door opened and the Ultron in his left hand.

Squinting, he watched Big Red return toward the oceanfront condos, becoming the solo runner. She was taller than most of the women. As she neared, he could see perspiration covering her face, and her large breasts bounced a welcome to Lloyd. He bent over the cones and pretended to be working. No one was behind her. Darkness crept across the tree-covered sidewalk. She seemed to slow her pace as she detoured.

Heart throbbing, Lloyd threw his forearm across the woman's chest. The blow stopped her cold and she fell to the pavement. Before her breath returned to scream, he grabbed her sweaty arm and shoved the Ultron onto her exposed neck. Spasms shook her body, and she went limp. Lloyd grabbed her long limbs and tossed Big Red into the van. He inhaled her floral scent. After slamming the side door shut, he opened the back door and returned the orange cones into the van.

Jumping into the driver's seat, he accelerated away from the enclave. Maintaining twenty miles an hour over the draw bridge, he drove toward the city. At a traffic light, he turned right, into a foreclosed office complex and settled the van into a deserted back corner. Not a sound could be heard after he cut the engine.

He climbed into the back of the van. After duct-taping Big Red's mouth, she slightly awakened and wriggled in discomfort. Noting that she had awakened, he admonished himself to become more adept with the Taser to sustain longer sleep.

Her skin shined with perspiration as he ran his hands across her soft body. Beyond the sweat, she smelled like gardenias... and fear. Her petite nose flared, and suddenly her green eyes opened and enlarged. Quickly, he turned her onto her stomach. Overcoming the slippery skin, he fastened plastic strips around her wrists behind her back. He licked sweat from her forearm and inhaled her beauty.

I own her now!

As he forced off his jeans, Big Red stirred a little more. He slid her long body onto the old, stained mattress, lying atop her, with his lips pushed onto her left ear.

"I own you," he whispered.

He peeled down her tight, black running shorts and licked her sweaty hip. She squirmed under him and tried to scream. He calmed her with words he had used before.

"I won't hurt you, if you do what I say. I just want to *come*, and then I will release you. If you fight me, you'll make me have to kill you."

Lloyd liked to deceive women. It was the pirate way. Once the women yielded, he unleashed his passions to satiate his urges.

He smelled grilled steak in the distance from a local restaurant. Some men salivated at the aroma of a steak, and yet Lloyd felt a similar hunger. Big Red's green eyes darted in panic. She felt the response to his hunger, as he tore off his shirt and began to ravage his preferred meal.

Lloyd knew he had unlimited time for pleasure. Having also smelled the cooking odors, a hungry brown gerbil in a cage jumped about. It hadn't eaten in days.

CHAPTER SIX

Gray military helicopters thumped above the green ocean, while white waves crashed the beach in Wilmington, North Carolina. The trio flew along the oceanfront border, causing sun-tanning visitors to scan the sky for the American logo. As summer commenced, tourists began to swarm the local beaches, like wasps at a picnic. Many wondered why the military machines had infringed on their peaceful environment.

Visitors often asked residents if the helicopters indicated a terrorist alert, but residents accustomed to the military activities calmly accepted the omnipresent training exercises. Wilmington residents pacified guests with their perceived truth that the helicopters bolstered national defense through training. Often it was the Coast Guard patrols. And sometimes, they would add a tongue-in-cheek, "You can't be too careful protecting where terrorism may attack next!"

Surfers in black wet-suits struggled to ride the gushing waves toward shore. Assorted sun bathers scattered across the shell-covered beach. The number of summer tourists would peak on Independence Day. A young man with six-pack abs worked his muscular legs in synchronized movement as he jogged with pods in his ears. He never heard the helicopters—only the hip-hop music he preferred.

A shapely female with dark hair lay on her stomach in a black bikini. A three-year-old boy in a neon swimsuit chased sea gulls in a futile attempt at capture. His sister frolicked nearby with inflated plastic aids on her arms. Their mother sat watching them while reading a worn paperback.

The young blonde woman in a one piece turquoise and black swimsuit jogged along the beach. Running like she was being pursued and aware of the helicopters, she didn't look up. Instead, she focused on her strenuous running routine body burn. Her ponytail bounced behind her tight figure with bent arms swinging and legs churning, like a machine in motion. The strain helped clear her mind of the piled up issues in her head. *Memories of her wartime experiences were well worth evaporating. From current conflicts, she needed a respite.*

Carolyn Morderca slowed her run to decompress. The fresh, salty breeze cleaned her lungs with a redeeming spirit, like a vent removing smoke-filled air. Her muscular arms dangled at her side. The sounds of waves splashing returned to dominate the beach after the helicopters passed over. A couple of pale, flabby men standing nearby in shallow water ogled her physique. Ignoring their not too subtle appreciation of her figure, she strode into the ocean.

She smiled, enjoying invigoration from the cooling water. Her one-piece swimsuit wasn't in fashion, but her battlefield scars didn't need scrutiny. The undulating water caressed her. After a few minutes, Carolyn marched from the ocean and removed the barrette to loosen her pony tail. Shaking her blonde hair free as she reached the public access walkway, she departed the beach.

Past the palms and crepe myrtles, Carolyn jogged up the stairs to her air-conditioned apartment. She reviewed the numbers on her pedometer in satisfaction. After she got showered and dressed, she dropped to the floor in a push-up position. Instead of exercise, she reached under the bed to retrieve the security box. She checked the contents inside and double-checked the Glock handgun that remained oiled and loaded. She couldn't be too careful, as she would soon be meeting with her brother, David Dodd, and his new friends.

David's girlfriend, Jasmyne, and her brother, Karim, were part of a small campus group that aspired to confront the local military complex. David had gone along with them during a campus protest, which started all the trouble. To Carolyn, he portrayed his involvement as a dupe. The Marines didn't see it that way. David kept blaming others, despite his stupid actions. Yet Carolyn grew up with David, and she was convinced she still knew him.

Knowing a person in their earliest years is really when you understand a person best. Does the essence of anyone really change that much after they evolve into adulthood? Some individuals change, but most don't. Doesn't the sneaky child become the stock-fraudulent adult? Isn't the psycho serial killer the same boy who tortured animals? Change happened, but not easily, and not often to the core of a person.

Carolyn doubted David had changed all that much from their times together. Despite her doubts concerning his integrity, she loved him unconditionally. But still, she packed the gun.

Carolyn poured a sweetened iced tea and stood on her patio. Visible in the distance was the collapsing end of a wooden pier. The decaying wood that endured the erosion of constant battering by the Atlantic reminded her of a life, battered but not broken. White waves crawled along the black water, like snakes.

Are these waves the same that once touched my toes in Maine?

The ocean offered security and peacefulness, like a link to aboriginal beginnings of man that were inescapable.

She looked down at the families below her patio as they walked to the beach together. Family history never truly escaped subsequent generations. She and David had grown up in rural North Carolina, where tourists never visited, as locals referred to the area as "the backwoods." When her father died, she was almost a teenager.

Her mother used her and David like trained seals to fulfill her base desires. Carolyn's dad would have been thrilled to see her as a decorated war hero, but her mother carped about Carolyn receiving recognition for murdering innocents in a peaceful land, which America had illegally invaded. Carolyn never shared the truth about her combat experiences with her mother.

Better both parents are now gone, avoiding the controversy of David's court martial.

The sun reflected off a million tiny seashells on the distant beach, as if they were buried treasure washed ashore. Her dad brought shells like these just for her when he came home from his trips. Her friends envied her having the shells as if they were diamonds. The remnants of her past presently resided in an old Candies shoebox.

Her rule-bound father and liberal-hippie mother never really connected. David and she believed that their parents had sex twice—to procreate them. Carolyn believed family could determine *who* individuals were, but it was life experiences that made a person *what* they were.

Her glass on the patio floor rattled from the vibration as another helicopter flew past. A fan of history, she knew that Wilmington remained a city, surrounded by a military presence, dating back to the British occupation during the Revolutionary War. Nearby historic Fort Fisher was the final fort captured in the Civil War, and a fatal blow to the Confederacy. Presently, Yankee tourists walked over the structural remains of the fort on their way to the North Carolina Aquarium—the present trampling the past.

She could always recognize her Corolla, with the Army recruitment bumper sticker she hated. Next to her car in the lot, tourists unpacked their vans. She lived alone and liked to watch TV shows about the pop idol roller coaster lives, enthralled at how they celebrated fame in one sequence and then quickly became destitute. She particularly savored the final minutes of the show. In that segment, the celebrity either made a spectacular comeback or died. Carolyn considered her life like one of these episodes.

What will become of my life? Maybe David and I could escape our past and share an idyllic future in paradise? We can control our future.

But she needed to extricate David from his legal quagmire in the Marines for such a future to exist. Like the TV shows, she tried to envision a sunny ending, but she always saw the final scene fade to black. With chilled Riesling in hand, she rested her sand-covered feet on the balcony railing, feeling adrift, like someone too young to retire and too old to cry.

Atop the television sat a single black seashell. Harry Powell gave it to her when they first met in Maine, where she had gone to recuperate after her military discharge. They became close— too close for her. Then David called her in a panic, and she abandoned Maine and Harry for North Carolina.

She looked up at the moon. As a child, she recalled watching reruns of *The Honeymooners*, when the face of the man in the moon evolved into star, Jackie Gleason. On that night, the lunar view reminded her of another man and the recuperative nights she savored talking with him in Maine. She imagined that the lunar shadows created a facial impression of that square-jawed man. Despite all her best intentions, she could not forget Harry Powell.

She peered into the night where, in the distance, the vast black ocean stretched between houses in her view. Moonlight reflected off the sliding-glass doors. How far north across the water could she see?

Events had quickly occurred during her final days in Maine. It was like a sporting event she replayed, trying to slow down choices and improve the outcome. Harry Powell could have become someone she loved. Yet she ran down to Wilmington with only a precursory explanation, and a nebulous one at that.

Hesitant to share her fear of intimacy with Harry, she exaggerated David's urgency. Much of what she told Harry was untrue, which was her plan. She committed to total honesty only to herself. Genuineness encouraged entrance by others, and she swore no one outside her family would ever access her again—not even the ruggedly handsome Harry Powell.

Carolyn refilled her wine and assumed a lotus position on the couch. She sipped the sweet wine and tried to block the images of her Army days in Iraq, but she failed. Sporadic gusts from the ocean swept her hair and opened windows in her reflective soul.

She recalled a scene that contained assorted faces with unshaven, slobbering leers. It was a muggy night, after a mission that had gone bad. Her unit watched what appeared to be a family, travelling together by wagon, so the team relaxed their guard. The family turned out to be combatants, who began firing at her team. The ambush and subsequent explosions destroyed her convoy.

She lay in the dirt, staring into the lifeless eyes of her friend, Sergeant LeRoi Mitchell. The other three members of her team also appeared fatally wounded. Injured but alert, she was cornered by the enemy and alone. The convoy's women and children picked at the bodies of her team, like vultures on carcasses. They took anything not attached, and then scattered into the distance. The smelly men dragged her beyond the walls of a destroyed hut.

Although stunned into initial submission, adrenaline from fear and loathing filled her veins. She fought ferociously for escape from the claws of the savage enemy. They spoke what sounded like gibberish to her, but clarified their intent when they chanted the words.

"Fuck her. Fuck the Yahnkey."

Carolyn tasted the gravelly dirt, as they pushed her deeper into the barren desert soil. One man sat on her shoulders and held her head down, while saliva dripped from his yellow tobacco-stained teeth. The drool made her want to vomit. Another pinned her arms by squatting on them, so close that she could smell his fetid breath. He assumed the role of perverse cheerleader, repeatedly screaming to his peers to "Fuck her!"

Pain seared through her right shoulder from the explosion. Held down, she couldn't see the barbarian at her feet, but she felt him tear off her pants and force her legs apart. She kicked, scratched and screamed with all her strength against the pressure, but the trio overwhelmed her. An animal-like grumble came after the beast at her feet raised his tunic and leaned into her.

As his manhood pierced her, she twisted her hips off the ground to push him off, but she failed. She pressed her elbows into the gravel to force herself up, but the man on top of her was too heavy. He slapped her across the cheek, demanding submission. Thrusting and grunts pierced her as the trio continued the violation.

The men switched roles and took their turns fulfilling the vulgar chant. They chose different orifices to penetrate. When she clenched her jaw to prevent one entry, they twisted her already damaged arm, forcing her to open her mouth. At some point, they tore away her bra and gnawed at her breasts like rabid wolves. She thought the attack would never end. Her mind finally imagined a peaceful oasis to escape the horrid situation.

After what seemed like hours of continuous attack, she had no remaining defenses. Blood dripped onto her parched lips and she hoped water would follow. Her face now buried in the sand and her right eye swelled closed. With her left eye, she strained to see over her crushed cheek bone. Repeatedly, she tried to scream, but her parched tongue was stuck to the roof of her mouth.

One of the men offered her a stick that had a cloth at the end, with water on it. She tried to lift her head and open her mouth for some satiation, but all she saw was a blur of men standing above her. Then she heard the men's gruff laughter as they shoved the cloth into her mouth, which became saturated by the same source of liquid, as all three men urinated on her swelled face. They shared cruel laughter.

"We fucked Yahnkey... fucked you good!"

She tried to look up at them in one last effort at defiance as they emptied themselves on her before covering up. Through one eye slit, Carolyn watched them scamper like hyenas into the dark streets. Overcome by darkness, she collapsed into silence.

Days later, Carolyn awakened in a US Army hospital, looking at the wrinkled face of a woman who might have been a nun. A doctor who came to visit described her injuries. He kept trying to comfort her by saying she would heal—like he knew what he was talking about. After she began to recover, the Army sent her home with an honorable discharge for injuries sustained in combat. While her wounds qualified her for the Purple Heart, she would never tell anyone what *really* happened in Iraq, and she invented more traditional reasons to explain her disability exit from the army.

She worried that a legal file existed somewhere with pictures of her torn torso abandoned in the desert, like a corpse. Officials retained proof of the incident that would be filed under combat injury, but the reality of her wounds was far worse. Her broken bones and ripped flesh would heal, but she knew the degradation and internal penetration could never heal or be forgotten... never! *Revenge filled her thoughts.*

The wine in the Riesling bottle disappeared. She did not drink red wine, as it reminded her of that bloody night in Iraq. The hint of crashing waves could never drown out the memory of that brutal intrusion into her very being. On many days, she raced into the waves, trying to be cleansed by the incoming salt water, but to no avail.

Never could she allow another stranger to get too close. No stranger could penetrate her shield. She nodded in a silent reappraisal of why she had to leave Harry in Maine. *He'd come too close, and that could not be tolerated.*

Carolyn glided into the bedroom and lay on the unmade bed. On her side, she pressed her knees together in a fetal position. David remained her only blood relative and, while he was troubled, she had to help him, no matter what. When she showed up in Jacksonville to visit him, she immediately knew he needed more help than she could offer. That was why she hired the inexpensive private investigator, Janakowsky.

Soon it was time to meet David. She dressed casually, dabbing *Obsession* behind her ears. Descending the stairs, she got in her car and drove north on Highway 17 to Surf City in order to meet David, her handbag weighing heavily with the loaded Glock.

CHAPTER SEVEN

Two massive men in tee shirts walked along the hot streets of Jacksonville, looking like caricatures of military warriors. The garish yellow sign exploded in black print: *Saigon Sal's Military Surplus Store.* Any visitor to the military town of Jacksonville, North Carolina noticed the *Saigon Sal's* sign among the plethora of stores. Depending on the viewer, Sal's contained memorabilia, or merchandise, that could fill miles of shelves. Young visitors knew little about the history of Saigon in the Vietnam War, but they shopped at Saigon Sal's anyway. Ho Chi Minh City today was just another place. History faded like bones in the sun.

Everyday Saigon filled the headlines long before either of the two men were born. The young people who came to Jacksonville didn't drive the Blue Star Memorial Highway for the scenery. Rather, they came to fulfill their commitment to the US Marines Corps at Camp Lejeune or the Air Force Base at Camp Geiger. Handmade signs hung on the Camp fences to welcome home friends and family members who had heroically protected their country. The facilities dominated the exit off Highway 17.

The Marine duo felt engulfed in the massive military presence within the mostly rural area.

"The fucking military is *everywhere* around here. We can't escape them," David Dodd complained.

"That's for damn sure. What can you name from Washington DC heading south to Charleston? I see visitors passing the clandestine CIA headquarters in Langley VA, where the Office of Terrorism Analysis (OTA) thrived," Rock Morton added.

Not to be outdone, Dodd continued.

"...and their training sites in Williamsburg. Plus, the Navy ships docked in the harbor at Norfolk VA!"

"Besides here, the Marines are also based in Quantico, Virginia," Rock said.

"Oh yeah? How about Fayetteville NC? There's *Pope Air Force Base* and *Fort Bragg,* which contains the secret operations records in the Delta Force archives?"

Caught up in the discussion, Morton beamed

"Well, don't forget Topsail Beach, where rockets were once tested as *Operation Bumblebee* and the second largest port for the confederacy in Wilmington with Fort Fisher!"

"In your *face*!" Dave countered. "I got you, fucker. How about across the Cape Fear River, where the MOTSU Arms Storage Facility hides in Southport? It holds the largest munitions supply in the military."

"Nobody even *knows* about that. I got Parris Island off the coast of Georgia, where the Marines do intensive training. And The Federal Law Enforcement Training Center was also in Georgia. Gotcha, ass wipe!" Rock taunted.

"Oh yeah? What about the Citadel, the Military College of South Carolina, in Charleston? Booya! Done and done."

The men jostled as they continued their walk.

Since the terrorist attack on the World Trade Center, Americans accepted a defensive strategy at home. The military presence enveloped some residents in a comfortable cocoon of protection and pride. Yet others felt it pervasive and aspired to minimize its existence. These Marines represented this dichotomy of opinion. While several of their friends wanted to see the presence destroyed, Dave and Rock tolerated the need, but they wanted to escape its presence.

"'We gotta get outta this place, if it's the last thing we ever do,'" they sang.

Inside the camp walls, red brick buildings with gray roofs portrayed the encampment as similar images found at college dorms or a prison. These conflicted images weren't far from the dual reality.

Sprouted around the camp were various retailers. Sycophantic businesses decried the state of government expenditures on the working military personnel. Large storage facilities like *Rent & Save* accommodated the arriving Marine recruit's excess stuff. Tire stores proliferated on street corners, with a preference for outdoor displays. Low end hotels for visiting family and friends offered cheap nightly rates.

The sleazier joints like the *Iron Rod Motel* advertised hourly rates. Barber shops were also common, despite most Marines displaying the same buzz cut. More Iroquois styles appeared among the men, where the American Native style became avant-garde. Dave and Rock sprouted that look.

Park and Pawn shops provided a good source of needed capital. Personnel who defended the Republic often traded items to these facilities for cash to pay for recreation or liquor. Expectedly, the area also sprouted an array of tattoo parlors, continuing the tradition of a century of Marines, who emboldened their skin with displayed viewpoints and reinforced the inked stereotype of a warrior.

Both men had been customers at every one of these businesses during their brief time in the Marines. On his right arm, David Dodd displayed a tattoo, which pictured the Shores of Tripoli invasion, sponsored by a bewigged Thomas Jefferson as an American flag unfurled in the background. Dodd's six foot six, muscled frame protruded from his tight fitting Saigon Sal tee shirt, which had arrows aimed at his exposed biceps and read *These Guns are Loaded*.

Despite the appearance of a comic book hero, with bright blue eyes and short cut blonde hair, David also had a tiny tattoo scrawled on his upper thigh: MLF. This abbreviation stood for Military Liberation Front, the group he joined when he met Jasmyne on campus at Wilmington College.

And the man walking with Dodd—everyone called him "Rock." Rock had a Marine emblem tattoo on his left forearm and a peace symbol, bordered with barbed wire, on his right bicep.

Nothing appeared new on their stroll, and they tired of looking around town. They sought respite and entered the cool shade of a familiar bar.

"What the fuck do we do now?" Rock McDaniel asked.

They sat across from each other at the pine table in the *Outside Inn Bar*, sharing beers.

"We drive down to Wilmington tomorrow and connect with Jasmyne and Karim to meet with my man, JD. He'll have more information of what we do next," Dave advised.

"JD Henzlein is just a scumbag lawyer wheeler-dealer, Dave. It's all about money to him. He has no message other than to make money," Rock insisted.

Dave pushed the lime wedge down into his Corona and wiped his mouth on his forearm.

"Hey, cash is okay. It's all green, man. How many people do anything for more than that? Jasmyne is unique in wanting to change the world. She truly believes that we can influence military decisions."

"What about that group she belongs to, the MLF? What are they about?" Rock asked.

"It's pretty loose," Dave answered. "Not like an organization, just people with ideals. They think we've gone too far with our military might. They protested against the water contamination here at LeJeune. They fight against the proliferation of military sites on the Atlantic Coast."

"Yeah," Rock agreed. "That stupid campus protest in Wilmington that got us into this shithole mess."

"Hey, we can invade countries all we want," Dave complained, "but we never change their fucked-up cultures. They flourish under dictatorships and violence like they have for centuries. Who the hell are we? Some dudes seek change, at the cost of their own life and freedom. Others bitch and moan and just chase the almighty dollar."

"What about us, Davey? We kind of do both."

"We're pragmatic revolutionaries," Dave insisted.

"Yeah, but you got the MLF tat…"

"Me and Jasmyne got shitfaced that night, what can I say?" Dave grinned.

Rock leaned forward. His physical appearance mirrored Dave's and, except for Rock's black hair, they could have been mistaken for twins. They were perfectly-conditioned, human military machines, trained to kill enemies throughout the world. Some guys in the Camp called them "Salt and Peppa."

"You want another beer?" Rock asked.

"It's kind of early in the day for a six-pack, man. It's only 10 a.m.," Dave answered.

"So put a fucking cornflake in the brew and you got your breakfast!"

"I'll skip having another right now," Dave smiled. "I got to meet somebody in Surf City later, and I don't need a buzz on."

"Are you meeting some rich bitch cougar?"

"I'm meeting the last of my family, Mrs. Carolyn Heather Dodd Morderca. My big sister escaped the Yankees up north to return to her southern roots to help me."

"She's going to get you out of this court-martial shit?" Rick asked. "Is she a lawyer? Will she help me?"

Dave finished drinking from the clear bottle, resting his massive hand on Rock's bouncing leg.

"No, she's not a lawyer, but she talks like one. She helps me and that helps you. Carolyn has military credibility, since she received the Purple Heart for combat injuries. She believes she's here to help me evade the false accusations of sexual bias."

"Her presence here ain't going to interfere with our fuckin fourth demonstration, right?" Rock asked.

"No, nothing will interfere with the July *event* to wake up all the apathetic assholes. We're progressing well with JD's plan. Some of the needed weapons are already stored in the *Rent & Save* storage locker."

The men tossed crumpled dollar bills onto the counter and departed the dark bar. Squinting in the bright daylight, they walked to the Iron Rod Motel. Rock rented a room for the special hourly rate, and Dave joined him. For the hour, they cast aside the macho facade they maintained inside the camp gates with their dog tags. In the room, they savored furtive unification before returning to the confines of Camp Lejeune. They wanted to enjoy this shared fulfillment before violent events consumed all their time.

~ ~ ~~ ~

The attractive couple with identical blonde hair sat at the corner table. They attempted dialogue over the boisterous crowd in the *Oceanside Bar & Grill* in Surf City, a small beach town in the center of Topsail Beach. While known as a military post during WW2 and presently for the loggerhead turtle hospital, the locale served as an equidistant meeting point between Wilmington and Jacksonville.

The beach town formula played itself out in the bar, as off-duty military and summer break college students combined with unlimited cheap alcohol in an environment of fun and rowdiness. One-dollar longnecks brought them into the bar, where Jäger shots soon followed. Carefree youth shared laughing, hook-ups and fist fights. Odors of beer, urine and vomit filled the arena for social interaction—never to be fully replaced by electronic social networking. Abundant sunshine, Atlantic waves and fine sand provided recuperation for this nighttime crowd.

At a table covered with empty Corona bottles, the beautiful pony-tail blonde woman conversed with animated hand gestures to the super hero-shaped man. The woman would have enticed other men's attention, if she were alone. Even by Marine standards, the man's physical presence intimidated most people. To patrons this couple might be perceived as a romantic couple—not the siblings they were.

"Your friends aren't going to make it, David?"

"It's just you and me, Sis."

"You're in deep shit, dear brother."

"Don't overreact, Sis. It's the reason there are lawyers. JD has contacted a Marine shark and... with *your* help... y'all get me off," he replied, swigging a longneck.

"You trust that guy, JD Henzlein, way too much. Your situation may be more acute to the Marine brass than their contaminated water lawsuit. Those wells were closed for decades, and the litigation may take as long. But they *will* want your situation resolved quickly as an example to others. Your new friends threaten the establishment. You understand that, don't you, David?" she asked, her eyes locking onto his.

"So what? Shit happens, and dues must be paid. Jasmyne says we need to make noise, since other people don't. As for Henzlein—maybe you don't like JD because he ogled your tits and grabbed your knee?"

"Trust me—he never touched me with either hand. If he had, he would have lost it. His undressing vision was sufficiently vile. I know the type. He oozes slime!"

"Calm down, Sis," David whispered.

"You should stay away from him and, quite frankly, the others, as well." Carolyn warned.

"Hey, JD is full of ideas and opportunities, Jasmyne will change the world and Rock is my friend. Karim is a little crazy, but that's life. They're good people—not like that biased bastard, Colonel Bogart,"

"Then why the urgent call to drag me down here? If you're so well represented, then why the panic?" She leaned closer. "Why the hell am I here?"

"My fucking life is on the line, Sis. The Marines want to screw me. They toss me out with a record, and I can't get hired. I'm broke. I need all the help I can get. But you have the military imprimatur—with a Purple Heart and all. The military respects its own heroes. JD may look like a gigolo, going to seed, but he works the system. To be honest, you're the visible hero in support of her persecuted sibling.

Plus, your physical allure may distract the judge, who I hear likes the ladies."

"Please, David, don't be so superficial. You and I know that appearances can be deceiving—just a façade."

Dave Dodd stopped drinking.

"Since you were old enough to walk, people perceived you as the pretty innocent. I was just the big dope. You're right. Appearances were a façade. But you're a real hero."

"I was no hero, David. Plus, I was in the Army—not the Marines. I was just one of the boots on the ground. I fought. I got hurt. I came home. No big deal. And you admit partaking in the protest against the Marines, you and your little campus radicals. So really, are you so innocent?"

"No one is *totally* innocent, Sis. But Rock and I joined a little campus protest is all, and that's being blown way out of proportion. There were plenty of *professors* marching, and nobody's threatening them. Colonel Bogart is just out to get me because of my alternative lifestyle. You got the disability pension, and I won't get squat!"

"So he overreacts to a *protest*? Aren't there campus protests every week?" Carolyn asked.

"We were wasted and wore our uniforms, and we didn't figure on the surveillance cameras. Cameras are everywhere, with someone watching everything, like on that TV show, *Person of Interest.*"

"Are there any further messages your *cell* intends to send?" Carolyn asked, staring. She twirled her half empty beer bottle.

Dave leaned his broad shoulders back and raised his translucent eyebrow, displaying how impressed he was by Carolyn's apparent knowledge. He felt like he was playing in a Texas Hold em Tournament, and the flop was about to be displayed.

"Listen, Sis, I'm not part of any terrorist *cell.* It was just a college protest Carolyn, you're my only family."

His hand covered both her hands.

"You are who I love. I have no other allegiance."

"What about Rock and Jasmyne?" she asked.

"Dalliances in transition," David insisted, starting on another Corona.

"So I'm here to convince the Marines of your innocence, is that it? And offer you an honorable exit, instead of the brig?"

"Well, that and one other little thing. This chick I told you about—Jasmyne—she's been a positive influence in helping me see the bigger picture, but she might be knocked up and won't consider aborting the piglet. I thought you could talk her into doing the practical thing. I don't even know if it's my kid, and I sure as shit ain't going to marry her."

"Seriously? What can *I* do? I hardly know her," Carolyn protested.

"Talk to her—woman-to-woman like."

He handed Carolyn a card with phone numbers.

"You can convince her I'm not the daddy-type."

Carolyn considered her brother. David excelled in sports, but he'd skipped too many practices. Low grades indicated a short attention span, and combined with minimal effort, was a formula for failure in school. She thought that the Marines would straighten David out, and while she didn't trust him, she felt guilty for bringing the Glock, which weighed heavily in her purse and on her mind.

He leaned back and grinned as Carolyn yawned.

"It's time to go home," she said. "I'll see what I can do about Jasmyne, David."

She stood and hugged her brother goodbye before leaving the noisy bar. Dave remained behind, as the night was just beginning.

CHAPTER EIGHT

Professor Annabelle Radinsky-Wade lived in Landfall and felt she belonged there. Good genes and Pilates classes helped her maintain the figure of a woman half her age. While she always had good tits, the marvelous young surgeon from Duke reduced the sag and added inches. Colorfully-enhanced and eyelash extenders made her eyes stunning. Botox smoothed her forehead and erased the crow's feet around her eyes. Only her neck belied her actual age, but scarves hid the obvious disparity between a wrinkled turkey neck and her unlined facial contours. Her wardrobe filled two master closets and the fifth bedroom in her house.

Acres of million plus dollar McMansions were surrounded by a ten-foot white wall. Guards at security gates checked all entrants to keep the riff-raff outside. From the leather seat in her red Mercedes Brabus SLR Roadster, she nodded at the waving guard as she drove into Landfall. Her six thousand square-foot home, with five bedrooms and seven baths, sat on the corner, surrounded by ten-foot tall Magnolias. She didn't care if the space was too much for her and Rhett, her Siamese. She glided past the country club and golf course, where her husband, Lars, had passed.

Young millionaire Lars Wade had met a barista graduate student, whom he called Belle. They were married for a decade when he died from a heart attack. Lars had just missed a birdie putt and crumpled to the green. His cigar-smoking golf buddies thought it would have been a good way to die, if he had only made the ten-foot putt.

As a result, Annabelle had the time and money to pursue ideals learned as an undergraduate in sociology. Her inherited wealth was derived from an invention that Lars created decades earlier. He was a young, tinkering pharmacist when he came upon the idea of a small plastic ring for toothpaste tubes, which allowed a color to come out with the white toothpaste.

In those days, anything but white was revolutionary. After selling the patent for this striping device for millions, his lifestyle changed from labor to leisure. Thereafter, he dabbled in antiques and played golf.

"Only in America," he would often say to their social contacts.

Annabelle played the country club wife, while festering to be more. So after Lars died, Annabelle did three things—she finished her doctorate degree, with a thesis entitled, *How Individuals Changed the World*; she bought a red Mercedes convertible; and she dyed her hair blonde. Friends said she never looked better.

The transformation from grieving widow to college professor came easily. All she had to do was convince the National Rural Water Association (NRWA) to donate a grant to the University, and a course was created with her as the instructor. The hundred thousand she donated to the NRWA didn't hurt. Her course began with efforts to expose the water contamination at Camp Lejeune and expanded to broader military actions.

I can make a difference. I hate what the military is doing, whether local intrusion or global invasions. How would we feel if Russian troops showed up in Wilmington to dictate our actions? Who helped her when she needed it?

She spent three hours a week teaching class, and maybe an hour in administration. Her assistants did everything else, like grading papers. It was a sweet gig that allowed her time for other activities.

Even before her husband's death, her sexual attentions had wandered. Lars' passion for Annabelle waned after the first few years of marriage. Golf seemed to offer him more pleasure, as indicated by his comment during his weekly poker games.

"The best hole I can get into is on a green."

Because Landfall wives never appreciated the looks Annabelle solicited from their husbands, Lars' passing increased their apprehension, dissolving most of her social links. She chose to enhance her pleasure in life, which meant more sexual experiences while supporting world changing activities—escapades *outside* Landfall. Off-campus trysts became routine. She frequented bars downtown, along the Cape Fear River.

The smells of the river included the aroma of the past. Ghosts remained in riverside mansions and alleys. Along the shadowy cobblestone streets, filled with ancient pirate ambiance, she would visit bars and meet strong young studs. They were often from Camp Lejeune, and they frequented the *Pirate Cove Bar*. The young warriors sought a chance to blow off steam, away from the evaluative eyes of their superiors at the training facility in Jacksonville.

On that night, she needed an escape from worrying about Natasha. The police didn't seem to be concerned about her missing, but JD had set Annabelle up with a couple of private investigators. For the moment, distraction was the agenda.

The *Opium* preceded her sashay into the *Pirate Cove Bar.* Her arrival time afforded the studs enough opportunity to lubricate their bravery. Women who ventured inside joints like this usually had a similar purpose. Some of them were professionals, but many were hair-stylists, looking for a military pension to take them away from the hourly work week.

By that hour, the lower hanging male fruit had been plucked. The remaining men understood she meant to hook-up as soon as she entered the raucous bar. Night and alcohol enhanced her beauty. *Fat Tire* neon signs glared in the window. Baseball games decorated the corner televisions. Most eyes were on the blonde, who penetrated the tacky bar with a flourish.

Annabelle perused the room for her type—the tall ones that worked out and had some color. With her former dancer's legs well-exposed, she sat at the bar and ordered a Metropolitan. She dangled a black high heel for all to lust after. Pete, her favorite bartender, was off duty and the new guy didn't know her… yet. She scanned the room with a disguised condescension of these Neanderthals that served a singular purpose. In her experience, it was rare that the first dude to hit on her would emerge as the Annabelle prize winner for the night.

But maybe that night would be different.

"Hello, Miss. May I buy you a drink?"

Pretty unoriginal start, but he had an electric smile atop a muscular six feet. His dark hands had long fingers, which she knew translated to other enlarged endowments.

"Sure, Marine. I'll have another Metropolitan. Thanks. I'm Annabelle."

She offered her bejeweled hand.

"How did you know I was in the Marines? I'm Corporal Lance, at your service."

"Are you really… *at my service?*" she asked.

"I could be."

When he smiled, she read his lustful gaze as more confidence than anxiety. As her eyes worked over him, she drank from the second cocktail. Her legs swung to face him as his eyes followed her movements. She read his mind, crawling up her thighs. Her chartreuse fingernail touched the opal pendant hanging near her cleavage, as if reminding him of some expensive attributes he shouldn't ignore.

"Where are you from, Captain?"

"Kansas, Ma'am… and I'm a Corporal,"

"It's Annabelle, Corporal Lance. Kansas? Are you a farm boy? Are you used to working hard with your hands?"

"Well, no, Miss Annabelle. I'm originally from Kansas City… so more of a city boy. Are you from here in North Carolina?"

She laughed, projecting her most welcoming smile—one that combined deception with welcome.

"Oh, no… no one is *from* here, where I live. I just settled here years ago."

"Your *husband* work here?"

The question came with a look of hesitancy. She liked them somewhat unsure at that point, but confident enough to close the deal.

"Now, what would I be doing in a joint like this if I had a *husband* hanging around? I'm just a lonely widow lady, living alone in a big empty house, trying to keep myself… satisfied," she whispered.

His hungry stare scanned her while his tongue crossed his lips— actions that made her feel wet below. When she looked up, he was staring at her chest and she swore he blushed through his dark skin. Annabelle decided right then.

He's the one for tonight.

"Do you like cats?"

"Cats, yeah sure. They're okay, I guess."

"How would you like to see *my* pussy… cat?" she asked.

A few minutes later, they left the *Pirate Cove* together, hand-in-hand.

The next morning, after cleansing herself of the insatiable Corporal Lance, Annabelle drove to the WC campus. She liked the way her figure elicited stares, but she reinforced separating business and pleasure.

A cat doesn't pee in its own bed.

Summer course load was lighter, so she had few official classes on that day. But such availability afforded her the chance to counsel a group of quasi-graduate students. The small group had formed a campus approved club called *Beyond America* that focused on an alternate view of American history, using the Zinn textbook as guide.

Originally, they simply discussed what was wrong with America. For the past year, however, they focused on the US military and had initiated a campus protest against water pollution in Camp Lejeune. Members created a message of protest, based on their hatred for military intrusions in their homelands. Annabelle started as a peripheral advisor and developed into the group's mentor. Her link to the Military Liberation Front added guidance and linkage to the class. This small cell of blossoming activists helped fulfill her goal of changing the world. An unforgettable event would explode the image of America's military might on Independence Day—right there in peaceful, little Wilmington.

CHAPTER NINE

Harry leaned back in his beach chair and burrowed the bottle of vodka-enhanced diet Snapple Iced Tea into the shaded sand. The ocean sparkled like diamonds before him like memories of his idyllic days in Maine. After leaving the cement jungle in New York, he reconnected with the beaches to rejuvenate himself. His goals were simple, like helping friends and enjoying the beach. Harry always smiled at the beach, as did most people.

The town of Wrightsville Beach included several miles of sand and improved revenue by installing parking meters from March through October. Harry learned to keep a roll of quarters in his Taurus. Eight coins bought him an hour of beach bliss, which was all the time he had available. In Wilmington, Bass boat shoes fit work or beach. Socks were for tourists.

Fishermen hung lines off the Johnnie Mercer cement pier, which contrasted with other local wooden piers, some of which were approaching collapse from decay. Yet to Harry, the aging piers had more appeal. The cement pier stood like a structured, well-planned life that afforded an individual immunity from the oceanic ravages. Haphazard lives experienced more and even collapsed from the beatings that existence delivered, like the eroding salt water against wood, but such existence felt more alive and engaged. Harry wanted to believe that.

He never ceased to be amazed by the variety of seashells. On the beach, he always looked for unique shells and shoved them into his pocket. A white and gray seagull strutted across the tan sand to beg for food, like a cat Harry once knew. Waves crashed high toward the shore and the movement massaged his tired soul.

Beach attendees ranged in age, from grandparents to toddlers. Frisky teen couples wrestled in the sand, oblivious to the stares of passersby. Occasionally, a woman would walk past Harry and smile at him as sand flies nipped at his feet.

When had those veins appeared?

Sandpipers, as they sought nourishment, scurried about in a silent ballet, avoiding water. A week earlier, Harry watched a tow-headed boy run past him in quixotic pursuit of the birds. Just when the boy came close, the bird would fly away in an immortal symphony of man's pursuit of fleeting happiness. The boy looked at Harry and waved at him while his mother, who held the hands of her daughter, caught up with her son.

The boy reminded Harry of his deceased grandson. Learned from his days in the Midwest, Harry reflexively smiled and said hello. The young mother returned Harry's greeting. She reminded Harry of the actress who married Tom Cruise and sort of disappeared. Her short-cut, black hair contrasted with the blonde children, while her petite nose and thin lips allowed her large brown eyes to dominate a face anyone would call pretty.

From his chair, Harry watched the children collect shells from the moist sand. They grasped these tiny treasures from the beach like they were gold. The two adults watched the children frolic.

He glanced over at the young woman.

"Can I *ask* you something?"

She looked down at Harry and flashed the look of a woman who had endured too many weak pick-up lines.

"Okay…"

A salmon and yellow bikini clung to her youthful figure, exposing muscular abs. Her thin hand shaded her eyes, despite the available sunglasses resting on her head.

"Are these children… *yours?*"

"Please don't tell me I look too young?" she sighed.

Harry laughed at her rebuff and stood up, while hiding his wince from a stiff knee.

"I just wanted to ask you: Do you realize how *wealthy* you are… having these children?"

He wondered whether she was surprised at his question or if she had caught a whiff of his alcohol breath.

"Why… yes… yes I do!"

She gripped the thick sunglass frame and covered her eyes.

"That's all I wanted to say. I hope you spend this time with them as often as you can…"

He paused in awkwardness.

"Sorry. I didn't mean to preach. It's nice to meet you."

Harry looked away from her and sat, his decrepit chair almost tipping over. His mouth now dry, he wanted to burrow in the sand for his Snapple.

"Thanks… I will. And by the way—the children *are* mine."

She paused and, with hands on her hips, looked down at Harry.

"I'm Holly."

She extended her hand. "It's too bad their father can't enjoy watching them grow up."

Surprised, he stood.

"Hi. I'm Harry Powell."

They shook hands.

"I hope he isn't like me—busy with work?" he said.

Her eyes looked down and almost closed.

"I shouldn't have said anything. No, it's not that he's too busy. He's no longer with us," she answered.

They watched the children run in jubilant beach freedom.

"Sorry, I didn't mean to get so personal," Harry stammered.

"Well, Greg was stationed in Camp Lejeune, and then one day he was shipped out. He was killed in Afghanistan. It was the first week he was there."

She peered out at the ocean and adjusted the sunglasses on her face. Harry felt like a jerk for bringing up a gloomy topic on such a sunny day. Once again, his knack for making stupid comments to pretty women displayed itself.

"I never should…"

"You were in *another* war, weren't you?" she asked.

"Yes, I was—a lifetime ago, in Vietnam. How did you know?"

"Something in your eyes told me. There's a darkness that says you're familiar with death and destruction. Sort of sadness…"

She touched his muscular forearm.

"Sorry, I didn't mean to suddenly get so personal. That's not like me at all," Holly gushed.

They shared a laugh—like people experiencing unforeseen linkage.

The little boy waddled toward his mother, his tiny hands overflowing with shells.

"Hello, little man. Put them in here."

Harry held out an empty plastic baggie, used for peanuts, which he had eaten.

"Wow, thanks!"

Triumphant, the boy ran to show off to his sister the container full of his shells. After a while, the boy began tossing wet sand at his sister, who screamed louder than was necessary. They resumed splashing in the shallow water.

All of a sudden, Harry lurched into the water toward the girl. Tearing off his Cubs cap, he scooped into the water and whisked the contents away from the children. The boy screeched, fleeing to his confused mother, while Harry pulled the girl up in his arms and carried her to her mother.

"It was just a jellyfish. No worry, but they do sting."

"You okay, little lady?" he asked the wide-eyed tyke.

After the incident, the children, under their mother's supervision, collected their beach bags. A breeze splayed dark hair across her picturesque face, like cracks in a glass window. Her alabaster complexion contained inquisitive furrows.

"It was nice to meet you, Harry Powell. And thanks for saving my daughter."

"No problem. I enjoyed meeting all of you, Holly."

Harry returned to this same section of Wrightsville Beach several times since that meeting, always hoping to see Holly and her children again. And one day, he felt like a kid, watching the prettiest girl at school, walking toward him. Holly carried a large brown paper sack and a beach blanket. The children carried toys. The little family spread out the blanket and sat on it.

"You're the *baggie* man!" the boy shouted at Harry.

For a reason he didn't understand, Harry dumped his vodka Snapple into the sand and ambled across the sand toward the family.

The children devoured their fruit and then ran along the shore, forgetting their mother.

"Hello, Harry. Want an apple slice?" Holly asked.

"No, I'm good. I had a cheese sandwich."

"Harry? Do you have… family here?"

He slowly shook his head.

"No, I don't… have any children or wife. That's a long, sad story. Do you have any *other* family?"

"Well, I have a father-in-law—General Sabbatino. He can't get down here from Camp Lejeune for our Memorial Day lunch, as planned… So, would you like to share some baked organic chicken with the three of us? We can meet near the pier. A person shouldn't be alone. It's not exactly the Fourth of July, but it is a holiday weekend and all."

The children descended on the blanket.

"We're hungry, Mom…"

They attacked the Livey's Health Food Store bag like seagulls at an unguarded picnic. Holly distributed bunches of grapes.

Harry looked at her with eyes glistening, like the shells in the sand.

"I would be honored. I'm fortunate to have met you," he stammered.

Holly grabbed his hand and pulled him toward the tumultuous waves. She splashed water over Harry's tee shirt as the children joined the couple's laughter. The sky was never bluer nor the sun brighter. He couldn't recall the last time he smiled so genuinely. He peered up at the solar source of the diamonds, sparkling atop the ocean and appreciated the experience. He treasured the little family and hoped he would share their peace.

~~~~~~

As usual, Harry awoke minutes before his alarm clock went off. The neon digits blared the time in his face, while he tried to focus on his current location. Harry shaved and completed his attire with a client meeting: blue blazer, button-down, khaki slacks and boat shoes. His reddened nose and pink cheeks reminded him of the wonderful day at the beach with Holly and her children.

He strode toward the lobby in search of his private eye partner. Glancing across the crowded breakfast area, he saw Bernie, commandeering a table covered with several emptied cereal bowls, filled Styrofoam plates, drained juice glasses and an empty yogurt cup.

"You know this is only for *guests*, don't you?"

Bernie, who sat reading the *USA Today* sports section, wore a shirt with a palm tree pattern that hung over his tan slacks, with a matching suit jacket that rested over a chair.

"Baseball is in full force, Harry. We need to go down to spring training next year and see some games. I hear there are lots of Baseball Annie's around the ballparks, looking for action. Sit down, Harry. Have some breakfast. *My* treat!"

"It's complementary, but thanks. Forget your tie?"

Harry stood to get coffee.

"Can I get you something more, Bernie?"

"No, I'm good. Chicks love to help guys with canes," Bernie smiled, as he devoured a forkful of scrambled eggs.

As if on cue, a fortyish blonde, with dark roots, came over to Bernie.

"Here's a little fresher coffee. Now you let me know if you need anything else, sugar."

She sashayed back to the kitchen entrance, with Bernie watching.

Coffee and yogurt in hand Harry sat.

"Hey Harry—don't forget you're in Wilmington now—very casual. The regular attire here is sandals, shorts and a tee shirt. So I'm way ahead of the game... you can't see my toes. Besides, I can better hide my heat this way, *and* not sweat my balls off. We ain't lawyers. "

Bernie bit into a buttered muffin and eyed the buffet for more fodder. Harry glanced down at his watch. They had an appointment in twenty minutes with a client. He brought out the folder that Bernie gave him to review.

"Is your gun necessary, Bernie? I meant to ask why you told me to bring mine."

"Just a precaution, is all. Mr. Smith and Mr. Wesson make me feel younger—like it's my performance-enhancing steroids."

Harry returned his attention to the folder.

"Mrs. Annabelle Radinsky-Wade is the client. Her daughter, Natasha, has disappeared? The police *aren't* looking into it?"

"No, they *are* looking into it... but not getting anywhere. There's no sign of any crime, no ransom note. Almost a week, and it's a cold case to them. Annabelle's a friend of JD Henzlein, my business associate. Mrs. Hyphenated name just wants to talk to us. We can get some billing-days' work out of it. Plus, I hear she's hot. So, let's go get Moby Dick and make some money!"

Within minutes, Bernie's Crown Vic pulled through the entrance gate into Landfall. With a bizarre English accent, the car's GPS voice directed Bernie to turn the car several times for their destination.

"Nice GPS voice, Bernie," Harry remarked.

"Yeah, it adds class to being told what to do. KiKi hooked it up for me with the accent and all."

Bernie carefully maneuvered into a driveway framed by brick borders. Solar panels covered the roof. The four car garage doors were closed and a fire-engine-red Mercedes sport model sat in the driveway. The plates read *WC#1Prof.*

A woman opened the front door of the house. The men noticed her body before her face appeared in the doorway.

"Hello gentlemen, I am Professor Radinsky-Wade."

The woman, who wore extreme makeup, was dressed in a red scarf, white blouse and a tight black skirt, inches above her knees. Bernie and Harry followed her direction into the designer living room. Harry nudged his partner to stop staring at the woman's ass. From a doorway, a brown Siamese cat peeked at the visitors, but it kept its distance.

"I'm Bernie Mannion, Professor… and this is my associate, Harry Powell. We are both former police detectives. Now, we help citizens as licensed Private Investigators. JD said you might be in need of our services?"

Bernie handed her one of his business cards, which she ignored.

"Please have a seat. Can I offer you something to drink… sweet tea or coffee?"

"Thanks, some sweet tea would be great," Bernie nodded.

"No thanks for me, Mrs. Radinsky-Wade," Harry interjected. "This is about your missing daughter, I believe? When did you last see her?"

"Yes. Call me Annabelle, Harry. My daughter is Natasha Radinsky. She used… uses my maiden name. She's a student at WC. She's been missing for several days now, but I was told I cannot demand a missing person's report, since she is over eighteen years of age. I am her mother and I cannot seek a missing child? Isn't that ludicrous? The police don't seem to have any answers, and I don't have much faith in them locating her. I thought it best to initiate a private investigation."

When the professor left the room to get Bernie some tea, Harry pulled out his old notepad and clicked a plastic Albertson Hotel pen. Bernie had a PDF in his hands. The Professor returned and handed Bernie a tall glass of iced tea.

"When exactly was the last time you talked to your daughter? Does she live here with you?" Harry asked.

"No, she's twenty years old and has her own apartment near the college campus," Annabelle answered. "I saw her for dinner at the Indochine Restaurant last Sunday. We had Pad Thai."

Harry read the room and saw wealth everywhere, but with a certain coldness that reminded him more of a museum than an inviting home of familial warmth.

"Here's a recent photo and some other information I put together. I thought you would want to know."

She handed the photo and a blue sheet to Harry. Bernie sipped his tea and shot a questioning look at Harry. The men looked at the color photograph of a gorgeous young woman. Red hair framed, high cheekbones and perfectly-enhancing make-up—likely from a professional photo shoot.

Harry wondered how much the pose represented the person, since she looked provocatively at the camera. Natasha looked very little like her mother. The stat sheet pre-empted most of their questions.

"What do you think has happened to your daughter, Annabelle?" Bernie asked.

"Well, to be frank, I fear she may have run off with some scurrilous scum. She's very popular. At first, I thought nothing of it. She's an independent woman, capable of taking care of herself. But she hasn't replied to any of my texts."

Harry recalled the case in Indiana where Indiana University co-ed Jill Behrman had gone missing for months and was eventually found murdered by a creep who had been stalking her.

"Was she seeing anyone?"

"No one regular that I'm aware of. She has many friends. You can see why from her picture. She loved running along the beach. Natasha was getting her MFA and worked part time as a hostess at The Oceanic Restaurant during school breaks."

Annabelle posed like someone about to be photographed.

"Was she involved with any radical groups on campus… like the MLF?" Harry asked.

"Radical? No. She doesn't have a political bone in her body."

"So she worked and went to school full-time?" Bernie asked.

"Yes, detectives—financially, she didn't need to work, but I raised her not to rely on inherited wealth. I *earned* my doctorate and became a full professor. I was also fortunate that I inherited money from my late husband, which I don't depend on. I have been quite successful on my own."

She waved her ring loaded hands at the walls.

"All this material crap was left by my late husband, Lars."

While Harry scanned the gilt-edged frames of oil paintings along the walls, Bernie eyed Annabelle's legs.

"It seems like everything we need to know is on this sheet you prepared," Bernie concluded. "I know JD—Mr. Henzlein talked to you about our fees, so if it's okay with you, we can begin focusing on this situation immediately. Despite my busy schedule, I'll make your case a priority."

Annabelle nodded and stood.

"We'll do all we can to find your daughter," Harry promised.

Annabelle grabbed Harry's arm as the two men were leaving the home.

"I'm pleased you'll be working on this case, Harry. Perhaps we can meet to discuss your plan… over drinks at La Scala?"

Harry courteously smiled in agreement.

Bernie angled his cane into Moby Dick and slammed the door. The air conditioner blew loudly as Harry slipped on his seat belt.

"Well, shit! She sure seemed to like you, Harry."

"Yeah, it was probably the blue blazer. By the way, what's the La Scala?" Harry asked.

"Where her hyphenated highness wants to consult with you? It's a fancy Italian restaurant-bar, with more plate than food and subpar lighting, making it hard to read a pricey menu—but good for a rendezvous… or so I've heard."

"Okay…" Harry shrugged. "I'll follow up on this blue sheet of acquaintances she gave us. I'll also check at the morgue."

"Yeah, you pursue the daughter's disappearance. She's probably shacking up with a summer gigolo. Keep a list of every minute you spend, as its billable time. Even when you sit on the beach and watch the waves and you're thinking about this case, we should bill her for your time. I got other cases to follow."

As they drove off, Professor Annabelle Radinsky-Wade peered through the white plantation shutters. A tentative smile strained against her tight skin. Investigators like Janakowsky and Mannion were much the same—tired ex-cops, billing time. But that other man, Harry, seemed different.

His earnest focus appeared passionate and intense, but his square jaw and chiseled features also intrigued her. The look from his laser-blue eyes almost made her cum. Her thumb and forefinger caressed her right nipple through the silk blouse. This Harry Powell seemed young enough to sustain her pleasure, and old enough to know how. After finding her wayward daughter, he could be some fun—*providing he focuses on me, and not the MLF.*

CHAPTER TEN

Harry's call to the local cops confirmed no activity in searching for Natasha Radinsky. Nothing indicated any crime. Many college students took the end of a semester to wander off, in search of their muse, like Calliope.

He listened to the rant about police budget cuts, which allowed enough staff to focus on cases where an actual crime had occurred. After he expressed his empathy about the budget state of law enforcement, he accepted his solidarity in seeking answers in the woman's disappearance. The morgue hadn't received any young women in several months. Hospitals were no help either.

Harry initiated a search into the disappearance. Driving near the campus of WC, he parked at the Soft Shore Apartments on Racine Avenue. Apparently, he drove the cheapest car in the lot. There were plenty of parking spots, since the regular sessions ended in early May and didn't resume until mid-August. The azaleas had already lost their brilliant blooms and bordered the lot as green background.

Among what Harry called garden apartments, he located Natasha's apartment and used the key her mother supplied. On the blue sheet, her mother mentioned she had leased the apartment year-round—unlike many of the students who rented for the school semester.

The locked door displayed no signs of attempted forced entry. Inside the sun-drenched apartment, he smelled faded perfume, burned food and sweaty clothes. Generic beige walls held few decorations. Partially-filled coffee cups were scattered atop the kitchen countertop. In the living room, a leather couch, covered with silk pillows, faced a flat screen television on a table with scattered DVDs and Netflix envelopes.

Encompassing pink décor assaulted his vision in the bedroom. Window blinds, lamp shades and a bed comforter blasted shades of pink. He deftly dodged landmines of scattered designer clothes on the floor. The closet contained shoes, tossed everywhere. Foot attire ranged from worn running shoes to shiny high heels.

From behind him, a voice came from the living room.

"Tash? That you, girl?"

Harry turned and peered into the living room, where a smiling young woman with an athletic frame greeted him. She wore black shorts and a turquoise tee shirt, emblazoned *Wilmington College* across her chest.

"Hi, I'm Harry Powell. I'm a Private Investigator working for Miss Radinsky's mother... and *you* are?"

"Sunrisa Mitchell. I live down the hallway. When I saw the door open, I thought maybe you were Tash. Obviously not."

Sunrisa examined Harry like she was buying a used car.

"When did you last see her?" he asked.

"Maybe like four days ago. We did a run. Everyone scatters in summer, so I figured she went off somewhere."

"Any idea where she went? Maybe taking summer classes?"

Sunrisa laughed.

"Mr. Harry, she wasn't taking *winter* classes, so I doubt it."

"Not taking classes, huh? Isn't her mother a big shot professor here?" he asked.

"Not that I know about. Plus, it wouldn't matter who her momma is, since the law doesn't allow parents to know grades and attendance stats about their kids in college. Privacy laws, you understand."

She smiled and angled her head toward Harry. On white sneakers, she bounced like she was ready to run.

"I see. Is anyone else here who might know where she went?"

"Not sure anybody else is around. Tash was always into something. She worked over at the T and A Restaurant—great name, right? They might know more. She dated a bunch of people, but no one serious. We linked because we both run."

She bent taut legs at the knees and stretched.

"You run, Harry?" she asked with a grin.

"Not unless somebody's chasing me."

"And I'll bet a lot of ladies have chased you, Harry."

"Well, I'll check with her employer. Thanks, Sunrisa,"

Harry sought water for his parched throat.

Sunrisa spun around.

"Anytime. See ya, Harry, P.I."

She jogged out the door.

Harry perversely missed having Bernie present for a comment as he continued inspecting the apartment. He saw a photo of the mother-professor with a silver-haired man—probably Natasha's father. Another silver frame held a glamour head-shot of the stunning Natasha—like the one her mother had given him.

He observed car keys atop a small cloth purse on the kitchen ledge.

So she didn't drive anywhere herself.

Inside the purse, he found an overstuffed wallet and scattered, crumpled single dollar bills, but he found no driver's license.

Runners carry minimal ID.

He searched for but couldn't find an apartment key.

Maybe she went for a local run?

Other than her absence, nothing appeared amiss, but Harry sensed dread.

People didn't disappear. Usually they just didn't want to be found or were dead.

After a fruitless visit to the Campus Administrative Offices, where nothing could be shared, he drove to the T and A. The gray building with orange signs turned out to be what was once called a "Tittie Bar." He recalled the professor telling him that her daughter worked at some upscale seafood restaurant on the beach. *Not quite.*

The manager hadn't arrived and the staff mentioned that Tash worked here but she hadn't answering her cell for a few days. There were no concerns by the staff that she didn't respond, as she was on-call for when they needed extra staff.

The burly bartender, Spike, hid behind an unruly Van Dyke and had the letters *F-T-P* tattooed on his fingers. Harry knew that someone advertising *Fuck the Police* wouldn't help him much.

"Maybe Tash is sharing cabin space with one of the vacationing professor-types on a little off-the-coast adventure," Spike offered.

"Professors *date* students?" Harry asked.

"Student? I don't think Tash was a student. She just lived near campus. 'Dating?' What are you… from the 60's? She hooked up now and again, but she had no regular if that's what you mean. People come and go, man. Tash liked to party… liked to dance, you know what I mean? She's a fun girl. You interested in anyone else, or just Tash?"

Harry frowned and turned away from the pimp proposal to return outside to the cleansing sun. The day grew hotter and he left the car door open to cool off. Natasha didn't much resemble the person her mother described—only the photo seemed accurate. But then, *many people were often not what they seemed, especially to parents.*

Harry accepted that, after his own poor performance, he was the last person to judge the closeness of a parental relationship.

If Natasha wasn't a student and wasn't doing much waitressing, what was she doing lately? Hooking up with a professor?

Her mother paid the rent, so there didn't seem to be any financial need. Except for some pot, he observed no drugs. But women who went missing always brought out the pessimist in Harry and increased his sense of urgency.

~~ ~~ ~~

Carolyn slid into an open space near the beach entry. She disliked the US Army decal, but she bought the car at a bargain from a guy leaving the army. Carrying the Red Sox blanket she bought one September day at Fenway with Harry and Bernie, she trudged through the grassy public access to the beach.

She enjoyed visiting Topsail Beach in the daytime, and she relished the feel of the centric beach town called Surf City. Topsail was a long public beach, twenty-some miles north of Wilmington. The horizon that greeted her must have appeared like heaven to believers. A bright, cloudless North Carolina blue sky framed the white waves atop the vast green ocean. In cheap flip-flops, she stumbled across the walkway onto the fine sand. There, the sand was all soft—unlike the shell-scattered sand on Wrightsville Beach, and there were no parking meters to worry about.

Her brother, David, and his girlfriend/significant other/slut of the day, Jasmyne, were already ensconced on the beach, with assorted sun protection paraphernalia. Their physical disparity made them an odd couple.

While David stood a muscular six feet six inches, the girl next to him looked like a small person out of a Peter Jackson movie. Jasmyne was five feet tall at best, with sprouting dark tufts of hair from her armpits. Carolyn found Jasmyne to be one of those people who thought they were interesting and talked too much to demonstrate their erroneous perception.

Carolyn had only met the woman once before and retained an instant dislike. *But aren't first impressions usually accurate? Maybe no woman is good enough for my brother?* Hardly that, but he deserved better than that loathsome troll, with black-rimmed eyeglasses and mangy hair.

Jasmyne often repeated what she heard on NPR and quoted MSNBC talking heads that no one ever watched. She apparently linked with David when he took a campus course, sponsored by the Marines, in conjunction with WC. Carolyn had few political views, but extremists annoyed her because they always assumed that only they were correct. Yet she desired to maintain civility.

"Hello David... Jasmyne."

"Hi Sis. Great day, isn't it? I thought we could talk better here than in some smelly gluten-filled diner. You okay I brought Jasmyne? You two haven't had a chance to talk much, unfortunately."

"Hey Carolyn..." Jasmyne smiled. "Are *you* as pissed as I am about the delays to the Marine lawsuit on the water poisoning that those assholes covered up? I have an article in here somewhere."

She searched in the turquoise bag, labeled *WC*, pushing aside an email and notes from Professor Radinsky-Wade about the MLF.

"Not really," Carolyn answered as she tossed her red white and blue Sox blanket on the hot sand and sat down. She wanted to avoid an argument—like the last time they met, when Jasmyne defended 9-11 as something America deserved as retribution for all its evil acts around the world.

"I came here to receive an update from David on his court progress."

"Chill, Sis. Have a Blue Moon."

He opened the cooler and pulled out a cold beer.

"Remember? You were going to *talk* to Jasmyne. Now is your chance."

"No open liquor in North Carolina, dear brother. Besides, you and I have other more serious matters to discuss."

"Oh relax! The fascist beer police aren't out today," spat Jasmyne. "*I'm* looking forward to this summer, when imperialist America, after flaunting intrusion around the world, celebrates the Fourth of July on the Cape Fear River."

When she looked toward David, she smiled in a duplicitous manner that caught Carolyn's attention.

"Really, I didn't think you were so patriotic," Carolyn mused.

Her brother covered for his girlfriend.

"Jasmyne just loves all the colorful diverse fireworks and all..."

"I want to tell the government to shove their policies up their ass," Jasmyne hissed. "A wise woman once said, 'Swords will be extended until intruders leave our land.'"

"Sometimes we try to help others," Carolyn blurted.

David shot a disapproving glance at Jasmyne.

"This isn't..."

"This isn't the time—I know," she sighed. "I just think this particular Fourth will be a memorable one, don't you, Davey Do?"

She leaned forward and pouted her lips, beckoning at David, who awkwardly gave her a kiss. He changed the topic.

"As to the court martial, Sis..."

"So where do you stand now?" Carolyn asked.

"Well, that fucking Colonel Bogart wants to bust my balls. I don't fit his image of a Marine, so he makes a BFD out of nothing!"

"Are you referring to the protest on campus, against the military?"

"Yeah, me and the guys were there, and we thought it would be a hoot to march along. Who knew there would be a camera? Colonel Bogart is making it like some kind of terrorist treason."

"WTF? Buck Bogart is a fascist asshole," Jasmyne interjected.

"And once again, that's the *only* activity they have against you?" Carolyn persisted.

"Yeah, it's like I told you, Sis."

"Davey doesn't *lie!*" Jasmyne shouted at Carolyn.

"I never said he did. I just want to be sure what they have..."

Carolyn glared at the unkempt imp with her scrunched up venomous face. The woman had no idea what her brother was capable of doing.

"They don't have *shit!*" Jasmyne yelled. "This is just so typical of the oxymoronic government intelligence. They're big brother—trying to show how macho tough they are against innocent people, who were just exercising free speech. We'll see how they handle the real event soon enough."

"What *real event?* Who's *they?*" Carolyn asked.

"Rock is my BFF and Karim Nissim is Jasmyne's brother," Dave explained. "Jasmyne thinks global and knows there will be worse events. If Colonel Bogart wasn't driving this personal attack, we would get warning letters and all would be forgotten."

Carolyn began to feel uneasy sitting with the couple.

"David, what happens if you *are* dishonorably discharged? What would you do?"

"We'd be financially fucked," Jasmyne replied—for David. "With no health insurance coverage for the baby!"

She grinned.

"Baby?"

Carolyn felt a powerful headache coming on and recalled David mentioning the pregnancy, but she had hoped he was premature.

"Yeah, your brother knocked me up. It's confirmed, so in about seven months, you'll be Auntie Carolyn."

Jasmyne sneered at Carolyn—like the child was a demonic deliverance that could be used as some sort of tool. Carolyn glared at her brother, who shrugged his shoulders and sucked from his longneck bottle of Blue Moon. Jasmyne returned to her magazine.

Only crashing waves and squawking gulls intruded the silence. The ocean crawled closer to the trio that sat contemplating their next action. Carolyn tingled in rage and deployed all her willpower to restrain it. The Army taught her to kill, and in that moment, she wanted to snap Jasmyne's neck.

~~ ~~ ~~

Harry embraced full detective investigator mode. A website called *Endgame* opened various electronic doors for finding a missing person. Tash hadn't used any credit cards in five days, and there were no food or gasoline purchases. *Maybe she was searching for who she would become?*

In recent times, collegiate years were used more for self-reflection than the short term goals common to Harry's past—like when Harry ended idyllic days on the Bloomington campus of Indiana University to fight in a faraway jungle, where he believed he would help oppressed people fight for freedom—all for nothing. Over the years Harry became a self-taught person.

Following the guide from Annabelle, Harry checked with the manager of the Oceanic Restaurant on the beach.

"No Natasha Radinsky has been working here."

Harry took a seat at an outside table on the wooden pier of the Restaurant, and figuring it was lunchtime, he stayed. While awaiting his baked oysters, he scanned the beach view. When eating alone,

Harry liked to stay busy, so he resurrected a black notepad that had served him well in previous investigations and jotted down some options.

Natasha lived alone// Missed her normal routines for 3-5 days// Not attending any classes at WC. Not showing up at her real waitress gig at T&A. No job at Oceanic//Not running with a friend. Friends lost touch with her. No signs of impending danger or violence. No ransom demanded of the wealthy mother// Car keys remain in her apartment//No body found.

Ran off somewhere voluntarily... Spontaneous vacation... Accident - amnesia? Found injured? Check hospitals again.

Hooked up & may reappear hung-over to resume life... cell- unreachable? Check GPS with carrier?

Abducted, murdered? 70% of murder/abductions = by people the victim knows... another 20% = robbery or extortion, not seen here... result = 10% which is a random stranger with no theft or personal link, = serial killer? Why no body found in a week?

Why people murder? Love or hate, money, revenge – Random psycho?

Who murders? Close friend/family/lover gone astray. Business arguments. No suspects known. Maybe a hook-up gone bad? A stranger/psycho/stalker attracted by Natasha's appearance?

Harry mulled over *murderers* in his notes. Some people expelled from the womb were just bad people. Call it genes or their bloodlines, whatever. They were born bad and would end up bad. Along the way, they would harm others until they were stopped. Harry had little compassion for them, but he focused on saving the potential victims.

Others had something happen to them in life—like a kick in the balls. But they didn't stay down or turn the other cheek. They decided to initiate revenge through a conscious choice, which might have been understandable, but was equally reprehensible.

No one Harry came across in his initial investigation seemed to fit any of these motives. Relationships were few, money was plentiful and apparently drugs were not involved. No one identified any conflict in her life.

The scariest killer of all was the sociopath, with no linkage to the victims and a deep psychological need to kill. *Is my background dealing with the dregs of society making my current view more cynical than necessary?*

Nothing indicated a crime, violent or otherwise. But in the worst case scenario, fatalities usually occurred within forty-eight hours.

Maybe she went off on a yacht with a professor, like the bartender offered? He had seen car keys in the apartment, but her Prius wasn't in the apartment lot. The only items Harry perceived as missing were her apartment keys, driver's license and smart phone. Annabelle said Tash had the Android version. Harry had the phone store use the GPS capability, which indicated a non-working unit. Its last location was Wrightsville Beach, where Sunrisa said they jogged.

The waitress slid a plate of baked oysters in front of Harry.

"Something to drink, sir?"

"No, thanks. I'll stick with water. I'm working."

He felt odd saying he was working while eating on the sunny pier. As a black and white striped sailboat drifted by on the sparkling ocean, he wished his case was as clear. He appreciated that his life had a purpose—to find a missing woman. Detection came from making inquiries and connecting the answers. Harry preferred the direction of his tasks to be straightforward—black and white. But this case was beginning to seem more complex.

Needing to speak with Annabelle, he returned to College Road and the brick entrance of WC. Everything he needed to know wasn't on Annabelle's fact sheet. When Harry informed the security guard that he wanted to see Professor Radinsky-Wade, the middle aged guard responded "Annabelle?" with a raised eyebrow that Harry thought included a smirk. He parked in the visitor's lot.

He walked past corkboard walls, filled with opportunities for unpaid internships, seducing students to work for free and an enhanced resume. The brass sign on the door announced Professor Radinsky-Wade. No one was there, causing him to presume they took late lunches. The unlocked office door allowed Harry the opportunity to look around, and her cluttered office made Harry feel claustrophobic.

One wall, with displayed award plaques, caught his attention. Several were from important sounding groups, unknown to Harry. Many pictures displayed Annabelle, standing next to silver-haired men. In every group photo, Annabelle wore a red dress and stood out from the gray-suited men, like they were her backup singers.

Scattered papers filled a credenza. Harry scanned the desk for family photos and found only one of Natasha with her mother. It featured Natasha on a balcony in a black cap and gown, probably from high school, while her mother wore a shoulder baring dress that, predictably, was red.

He leaned against a battered bookcase that contained sociology tomes and a thin Saul Alinsky book. A thick text by someone named Zinn read, *A People's History of America*. Another section of the wall displayed the educational tickets of entry to WC.

He read the walls and discovered that the Professor had graduated from Queens College in New York and received advanced degrees from Western Carolina University. There were also some honorary awards from WC. Harry picked up a heavy silver pen from the desktop, which contained letters that read, *Henzlein Realty*.

Harry looked for hints related to Natasha and found none. The only local item that caught his eye was a folded newspaper advertisement. It was the same one he found in Janakowsky's pocket—the celebration on the Cape Fear River on Independence Day. While the people in Wilmington probably loved fireworks, the professor didn't impress him as a fireworks fan.

Leaving the office and walking toward the exit door, he heard a vaguely familiar voice in the distance. Near the exit sign, he peered into a glass door. In a nearly-full tiered classroom, fifty students sat slouched in their chairs wearing flip flops, tube tops and shorts and looked like they were attending a beach party. Professor Annabelle Radinsky-Wade strutted on the lower level stage, lecturing. Harry entered the back of the room and sat in the last row.

"That's why just watching current events pass you by while squandering time is unacceptable," the Professor admonished. "The military establishment is just the tip of the proverbial iceberg, infiltrating our state with their fascist plans and their penis-enhancing weaponry. We are a patriarchal nation of male aggressive attackers. Whoever does not agree with our America first view, we attack and destroy…"

She paused for effect as she sipped from a plastic water bottle.

"And to do what, protect our way of life? We add more military sites daily, while fighting against free day care. Zabernism pervades our lives. We destroy the ozone layer and produce landfills, with poisons and tons of plastic bottles… like *this* one!"

She tossed the uncapped bottle against the note board, leaving a dripping stain of water.

"This imperialist country tries to enforce its capitalist agenda on every other country. How? By sending storm troopers to kill anyone who disagrees with them! Your parents won't have to suffer from world hatred. You will!"

As the professor scanned the audience, Harry slouched in the back row, trying to avoid her gaze.

"So, as your peers dissipate their precious time twerking—you should *do something*! Blade chopping helicopters that slice up endangered brown pelicans should instead be looking for industrial polluters, like the greedy cement-making corporations that are destroying our very planet. Instead of invading other countries with storm troopers, we should use our wealth to cover our millions of healthcare uninsured. Remember that governments will pay attention if you *take action*. Don't be a spectator in your own life! Don't make money. Make a *difference*!"

Harry watched her work the room and felt his face redden.

Does her collegiate audience understand the hyperbole she's using to incite their disruptive views? They all looked so young.

Glancing around the room, he doubted the youngsters appreciated what the military did for them every day. They could not be living off their parents and sitting in college if they weren't protected from all the anti-American scum in the world. *Had they forgotten the thousands of civilians slaughtered on 9-11?* On campus and in that room, Harry felt like a stranger in a strange land.

The professor continued.

"Save fucking for the night and make a positive difference during the bright sunny day!"

The professor stood center stage with open arms, engulfing the applause that her comments elicited. Harry admired her impeccable timing and recalled Johnny Carson saying how important timing was for an exit. During the tumult of adulation, Harry quickly stood and exited with a Groucho-like walk. He pushed the back door open and escaped the building, feeling like he was being rescued by fresh air.

As he stopped his car at the light to exit the college campus, he assimilated ominous links between the vitriolic professor and a society in conflict.

Was any of it relative to the missing Natasha Radinsky?

Annabelle said her daughter was apolitical, but had she been wrong about her daughter's politics— like she had been wrong about her jobs and school attendance?

Was she hiding some terrible truth? Where was Natasha?

Harry was going to find out.

CHAPTER ELEVEN

Colonel Albert "Buck" Bogart lifted his leather Titleist golf bag into the trunk of the Chevrolet, with identification tags clinking as they fell. Buck admired showing off his golf experience—Sawgrass, Pebble Beach and Pinehurst. Conferences offered him a chance to travel on the government dime and, while it did not pay fees, due to rules for government employees, the host group conveniently supplied golf passes. The day's meeting in Wilmington afforded him an afternoon to play eighteen at Landfall.

After golf, Buck returned to his hotel room. That night was *road time*, which meant calorie-free meals, unlimited booze and maybe a little mistress on the side. When the hotel room phone flashed with a message, he hit the button and listened to an unfamiliar female voice.

"Colonel Bogart? I may be able to help you defend contamination claims at Camp Lejeune. I was hoping I could get a few minutes of your time to discuss the matter. Perhaps we could meet for drinks at the Chop House Restaurant next to your hotel. Is seven o'clock okay? My name is Heather Kenan. Thanks."

Bogart jotted down the number before flipping on ESPN and lowering the volume. From the voice on the message, he envisioned a hot, young woman with flowing blonde hair and a deep tan, like a television sports reporter.

As a member of the committee investigating disaster claims, why shouldn't I meet with a potential constructive source? "Hello, this is Heather."

"Hello darling, this is the Colonel. I understand you can *help* me?" Bogart began.

"Why hello! Yes! Colonel Bogart—I have information that may refute claims regarding the Camp's contaminated water."

"I see. What are you wearing, Heather?"

"Excuse me?"

"Right *now*, what are you wearing?"

"Well, I just took a shower, so basically a towel..."

"Now darling, don't wear much more tonight. I'll see you at the restaurant bar. By the way, how will I recognize you?"

"I have red hair and will be wearing a green dress," she answered in a sultry voice.

"Red hair, huh? You must be a feisty one. *Are* you?"

"I'm just a patriot trying to help the Marines, Colonel."

"Okay Heather, I'll meet you for drinks in a half hour."

To Bogart, her words sounded naïve, but her voice sounded experienced. He hung up the phone and used his cell to call the wife in Jacksonville. Sports highlights played on the TV, as he lay on the bed with legs stretched out.

"Oh the usual, honey. I'm tired after the meeting all day. I'll just walk up to the corner deli and get a salad."

"*You* mean it was hot on the golf course and *you're* off to get a steak," countered his wife of twenty-six years.

Bogart smiled into the phone, considering the woman who knew him all too well. He glanced at the steel Rolex, purchased in Singapore, calculating that he had fifteen minutes to kill before he went to meet Heather, so he continued to talk to his wife as part of the "home maintenance" he lectured to his recruits.

Sixteen minutes later, he walked down the driveway to the restaurant bar and greeted the stunning woman with red hair. He gulped down two Bombay Sapphire Gimlets on the rocks while she sipped a Prosecco. He noticed how her thick hair accentuated her white skin, with no tan, and no ring either. They shared small talk as he waited for the environmental pitch.

"I'm guessing you have no information on the law suit, do you?"

She laughed like a coquettish teenager.

"You're very perceptive, Colonel!"

"So what's your angle, sweetheart?"

"I work for Landfall Properties, and I watched you play at the golf tournament today. On an impulse, I guessed you were staying alone overnight. I wanted to get up-close and personal with a powerful handsome man like you. Besides, my fiancé is serving overseas, and I hate going home for another night with his dopey dog, Elvis."

"Is your fiancé in the Marines?" Bogart asked.

"No, he's in the Army in Germany… just hanging around, as bored as I am."

"Yet, you wear no ring?"

"Nor do *you*, Colonel," she laughed.

As her alabaster hand caressed his tanned bulging forearm, he sensed a flash of warning.

Was it danger or seduction?

"I don't know, Heather. I've got a busy day tomorrow."

"Let me show you the moonlit beach as part of my customer service," she urged. "Consider tonight a respite from your responsibilities... where you can get whatever you want."

She smiled and finished her wine. Buck Bogart felt a tinge below the table.

"When in doubt—act" had always been his motto.

Why not have a little fun and give her a thrill?

He paid the bill in cash and they left together. Heather drove the Colonel over the drawbridge to nearby Wrightsville Beach, where they shared another drink at the Blockade Runner Resort. They sat secluded at a corner table, separating only once, when he had to use the head. Upon his return, he appreciated the refreshed drink that he called a "Loaded Arnold Palmer."

After the drinks, they walked out the rear lobby toward the beach. With his arm wrapped around her in the silky dress, he let her lead him to the promised moonlight tryst. At that hour, the breezes kept most guests off the beach. Past the tall grasses, they moved in unison.

The drinks loosened his sausage sized fingers to grope for her breasts. They wobbled a few steps before falling together onto the beach sand.

"You promised me *whatever* I wanted," he mumbled, as he squeezed her shoulder.

Happily he discovered she wore no bra.

"So I *did*, Colonel, and I will fulfill the promise of the *what,* but the *where* is my choice, and I prefer the section of beach with softer sand, without the shells."

The black ocean crashed, unseen, as clouds drifted across the full moon. The environment had changed over a few hours, from a sunny carefree day, into a shadowy night that could be romantic or ominous. Bogart leered at the stunning woman who stared back with bright blue eyes. Her tight, shapely body felt smooth in his rough hands. She removed her dress easily over her head as he dropped his slacks. His excitement grew and he lowered his gruff face onto her bare breasts.

Heather stared up at the star-filled night sky, the undulating swish from the waves beating behind her.

"All I want is justice," she said to him before he shoved his tongue into her open mouth. "Don't you?" she asked when he came up for air.

He maneuvered her body so that his erection pushed against her rump. Bogart kissed her shoulders and squeezed her breasts, ready to say anything to avoid interruption.

"Of course, darling—give justice to all. Do I *know* you? Listen, sweetheart, just open up those sweet legs. You're going to howl at the moon and tell me you liked it. Then we can discuss... justice."

Popeye-like forearms pushed her into a squatting position like a dog.

"Anything I wanted you said... anything... and I want a hole in one—right now."

Bogart tried to force his erection into her, but she reached back and grabbed his tool, leaving him sweating profusely and moaning. It wasn't that hot and he wasn't that drunk, so he was confused. As her hand slipped a condom on his manhood, his heartbeat hastened so much that he knew he would explode from her touch.

He tried to pull her closer, but she slithered away from his presently involuntary thrusts. His heart accelerated and his erection escaped his control. She turned to face him and squeezed him until he finished ejaculating. Then she slapped his face and glared into his contorted face.

Next, she kneed him in the crotch, stripped him of the condom and pushed him backward onto the sand, leaving him grasping at his shrunken manhood and hyperventilating. From a fetal position, he cringed in pain as his enlarged eyes stared up at her.

Slipping the green dress back on, she looked down at him like he was dog shit. He groaned in discomfort, finally understanding his physical reaction wasn't normal. With the moon over her shoulder, she hovered above him with a hate-filled face, glaring down at him. Her soft beauty was replaced by a harsh glare that burned like lasers into the prone man. Her hate-filled face was the last thing he would ever see.

"You liked your loaded tea sweet, didn't you? Well, it contained a bonus— and that's *killing* you right now. You were never going to touch me, asshole! Never, you stupid moron! I know all about you! You aren't going to hurt any more innocent people. Die... you bastard! Die!"

"What the fuck?" were the last words of Colonel Buck Bogart. His naked torso lay prone next to the tall, wild grass. His grizzled right cheek sweated into the glassy granules of sand. A raven squawked from beyond as the ocean waves crashed onto shore and filled the night.

Heather returned to her apartment and tossed the red wig on a chair before entering the cleansing hot shower.

On the next day, local news reports described the deceased, abandoned body of a man, having likely suffered a heart attack, found on the beach. The same news source promised more information about another fatality involving a young woman who had fallen down a flight of stairs and died of a broken neck. One accident and one natural death were soon filed and forgotten.

A file buried in a locked military cabinet contained the documented connections between Colonel Bogart and the campus radical, Jasmyne Nissim. Sperm samples confirmed that the young woman had been sexually assaulted before the fall down the stairs. Lab tests identified the sperm found on Nissim was that of Colonel Bogart. His preliminary toxicology tests showed his death from an apparent heart attack. Since her attacker was dead, the case was closed, with no need for salacious scandal mongering. Working with local police, military leaders kept their house clean of scandal. All documents were labeled *Confidential*. There were no more stories, no more headlines, and no more court martial.

Dave called Carolyn as she drove toward Camp Lejeune.

"Hi Sis—I don't know how to tell you this. You aren't going to believe what's happened. My friend, Jasmyne... she's dead. I was out of town with Rock. They found her at the bottom of stairs, where she apparently fell."

"I'm sorry, David. I know you liked her... and the baby?"

"Huh? Oh yeah—they never said anything, so I guess the baby's dead as well. They asked me where I was, and Rock confirmed that we were out of town. It's all so incredible."

"That's unfortunate, David."

"And the other unbelievable coincidence—Colonel Bogart—the guy leading the prosecution against us... he just had a fatal heart attack. Can you believe it? In fact, he was found dead with his pants down at Wrightsville Beach. There are all sorts of rumors…"

Carolyn pressed the accelerator and saw the signs approaching the Camp.

"How're you doing, David?"

"I'm okay, I guess. I know you didn't like Jasmyne, but she meant well. Her brother, Karim, is going fucking nuts and believes that she was *pushed* down the stairs. He even heard a rumor that Bogart's semen was found on Jasmyne. He thinks there's a military conspiracy."

"It will all be forgotten soon," Carolyn assured him.

She turned on the windshield wipers as she drove through a sudden rain storm.

"I'm happy about Bogart," Dave sighed, "but I'm numb about Jasmyne. But I guess I caught a major break. The Corps is keeping things quiet. I know I sound like a jerk, but I feel like… celebrating!"

She exited the highway at the Camp Lejeune sign.

"And so you shall, David. I'm almost there to be with you."

CHAPTER TWELVE

JD Henzlein had entered the funeral parlor. The old maid—the aunt who no one liked—lay on display in a coffin. The downtown Patrick Funeral Parlor seemed too large for the number of mourners. Deceased Aunt Priscilla rested as the final representative of her generation.

The downtown cobblestone streets of Wilmington used to be the home of wholesalers and whorehouses, but they were presently lined with restaurants and boutiques. Sailing ships used to dock on the river pier, where now tour boat operators, dressed in pirate costumes, hawked cruises of the nearby wetlands.

The stately funeral home of white clapboard with green shutters sat blocks north of the downtown waterfront. The historic section sprouted when wealthy sea captains built the largest homes atop the hill to assure safety from flood waters and intrusive derelicts. The old mansions had evolved into lawyer's offices, investment firms and funeral homes.

Jefferson Davis (JD) Henzlein approached the coffin, gazing down on a relative he hadn't seen in years. Aunt Priscilla looked like an overweight old man wearing excessive face makeup. The scent of scattered floral bouquets reminded him that he hadn't sent any flowers. Grabbing a blank card from an ignored table, he jotted his name and switched it out for the card on a large floor display.

After sporadic introductions, twenty relatives, unknown to each other mingled about. Observing his distant family relations, JD realized he may have been the only one who had no tattoos and all his teeth. Clearly absent were condolence hugs at the loss of a person few knew and fewer liked. The women gathered in one corner and shared rumors. The kids ran about, oblivious to death and the men went outside to share smokes and scores of sports events.

JD looked with disdain at his remaining bloodlines that ran through this crowd. It was hard to believe that long distant relatives had owned nearby peanut plantations and approached being wealthy. Having a similar background, he went to Duke Law School and built a successful real estate business, while these Neanderthals regressed to trailer park public assistance life. He believed a man could always grow past his birth influence, if he wanted it and tried hard enough. You can leave the genes behind and create your own identity, like he had.

The diminutive clergyman gathered the family to sit in a circle for an impromptu 'sharing'—he asked each relative to share what they recalled about Aunt Priscilla.

"She spoke her mind... you always knew where you stood...."

Such reiterated comments caused heads to nod in solemn agreement. JD determined that Aunt P had a big mouth and nobody liked her.

After the reverend departed the stultifying confines, a cousin approached. Leaning toward JD, he whispered.

"Jefferson, ain't it? Hey—do you want a shot of Old Grandad?"

The cousin showed the flask in his jacket. "I just wanted to tell you something the reverend needn't hear."

"No thanks, and it's JD. And what is it he shouldn't hear? "

"Aunt Priscilla *has* something in her casket... something that the church doesn't approve of."

"What is it? Drugs?"

"No... Squeeky—in her will, she demanded that she be buried with her favorite pet, a cat named Squeeky."

"The cat's in the coffin?"

"Well, sort of. Its ashes are in a container, near her feet."

The cousin looked around the room in evident fear that the dialogue would be overheard. JD wasn't clear on the etiquette in response to such a disclosure. *Congratulations? Why am I being told? Because I'm the oldest cousin or a lawyer, or because I'm the only man whose jacket matches his pants?*

Instead, he relied on his often-used hollow reply.

"I'm sure she appreciates your courtesy,"

JD checked his Rolex and searched for the exit sign. Soon, he would escape to his air-conditioned Escalade. He had to check on a commercial development in Porters Neck, acreage in Jacksonville and duplexes in Topsail Beach. And forget about the Hampstead housing failure. He didn't need whatever his old Auntie might have left, but he felt a vestigial obligation to attend the services.

Friends and family shared a cold cuts buffet the next morning in a dilapidated church. When the Kool-Aid ran out, the mourners escaped. At the burial site, JD stared down at the fraying green carpet that reminded him of a miniature golf course. The service ended and proceeded to Aunt P's house. Someone mentioned sharing whatever remained in her modest home.

Like pirates seeking treasure, JD watched as cousins looked through the remnants of a life. The scene reinforced that a person's legacy was not found in their possessions. The immortality that a person created remained in the hearts and minds of the people they influenced during their life.

As the daylight faded, the cousin with Old Grandad in his jacket gasped. "Oh, shit!"

At first, JD thought it was a normal response to these macabre maneuvers. His cousin stood in the kitchen with a colorful jar in his hands. He looked at the others who had gathered to see what caused his outburst. He read from the labeled jar in his hand.

"*Squeeky*," he said, displaying the contents.

In their haste to bury the old woman, a mistake was made so that ashes from a source other than Squeeky had been interred with the coffin.

Relatives shifted in awkward silence. No one moved. JD thought about dumping Squeeky's actual ashes into the freshly-disrupted earth at the cemetery on his way home. Yet before he could share a proposal, another cousin grabbed the container with Squeeky's ashes and carried it outside. He returned in two minutes to the kitchen, fondling the empty cat urn.

"Well, Squeeky is buried with the *flowers* now," he said.

JD stared in silence.

Even in death, a person can't direct wishes fulfilled!

Escaped to his Escalade, he paused, looking back. All the stuff that accumulated in garages became worthless fodder for some uncaring relatives to toss away, like so much garbage. As the air conditioner blew, he had put the vehicle in drive when a face suddenly appeared in the driver's side window. He looked at the man, who had unkempt hair scattered atop an unshaven face—and who was very late for the funeral.

"Hey Jeff—it's me—Lloyd... *Val's* kid," Lloyd Curtin offered.

JD lowered the window. While he wore his summer-weight, black Armani suit with a white shirt and Garcia tie, Lloyd wore a black Members Only jacket, stained jeans and a tee shirt. JD was clean-shaven, with trimmed hair and subtle cologne—compared to a guy with a soul patch, disheveled hair and the distinct body odor of one who had sweated without showering. The latter stood with hands in pockets, leaning into the Escalades' window. His ball cap—turned backward—made his ears look like butterflies, attached to his head. JD wished he had departed earlier.

"Nice ride, bro," Lloyd smiled.

JD reached out his manicured hand and grasped the proffered unwashed hand of Lloyd Curtin. JD winced at the nibbled nails that dotted the grubby fingers.

"We are *not* brothers, Lloyd—we're half-brothers at best. Nevertheless, how are you, my friend? You missed the wake and funeral… and even the burial by the way! You still tweakin?"

"Nah, I got clean in the joint, man. I just use weed and drink beer now. I'm clean. I would've been earlier, but I got tied up on a business deal."

Lloyd looked over his shoulder, as if he were being pursued.

"Well, I see you're out of jail. Did you escape?"

"I did my time, Jeffy boy. Coulda used a good lawyer, but I never got that education given to my *richer* cousins."

"I go by *JD* now, Lloyd. I'm sure you could have… I do mostly real estate law. How long you been here in North Carolina?"

"I been here a coupla weeks. I'm working for Weston movers now—executive position—coordinating relocations of corporate executives and all."

JD smiled.

This fool must be an executive of loading trucks and stealing what he can!

He prepared to drive off.

"I got no wife and no kids… you? I'm looking on e-Harmony for the perfect woman to date," Lloyd offered with a Jack-O-Lantern smile that seemed creepy.

"Look, Lloyd—I need to be somewhere."

"Well, I was saddened enough to read the *ol-bitch-erary* in the paper about old Auntie's demise, but I was gonna look you up anyway, brother."

"Yeah, well we missed the chance to reminisce about the good old days that never happened. If you're in the will, the executor will notify any recipients next week. Your cousins are *inside*, looking for any abandoned loot."

"Hey, shit—I'm not looking for anything, bro. Did they already go through her garage stuff?"

Lloyd's dark eyes peered into the car's leather interior, like he might be targeting a laptop, causing JD to check that his locks were engaged. He automatically reached for his business card, but he paused. He didn't want this odiferous half-wit showing up at his office.

"Where are you *staying*?" JD asked. "I'll give you a call."

Lloyd rubbed his stubbly chin and his thin mouth twitched.

"Okay, call me, man. It's just that I'm staying at someone's crib temporarily… while I save my executive commissions to buy my own place on the water."

JD paused in silence, and he had already shifted back to drive when he had an epiphany.

Maybe Lloyd can help me with a special downtown business project on July Fourth—something that an ex-con might consider doing?

"Okay. Tell you what—meet me for breakfast at Louie's Saturday morning, and we'll talk."

"Thanks, man. We *pirates* got to stick together."

Lloyd looked back at the trailer.

"Excuse me? What pirates?"

"You know—old *granddad*… and I don't mean the whiskey."

"What the hell are you talking about, Lloyd?"

"Our granddaddy's the same, even if our hound dog daddy knocked up different bitches. You know granddad, the pirate, came ashore near the Cape Fear River. He was a real sumbitch scallywag and got into all kind of trouble on land. I think they eventually *hung* his ass," Lloyd grinned.

"Whatever. I need to be somewhere. See you Saturday."

JD looked in the rearview mirror as Lloyd's head grew smaller in the darkness, like a remnant from his past, crawling up from the primordial ooze of generations, leaching nourishment in the present. He accelerated to escape his familial past.

Lloyd backed away and stumbled to his van.

Maybe I can still find some stuff here tonight after everyone leaves.

He parked on the dirt road and waited for his cousins to depart. The cover of darkness allowed him to enter the gravel driveway unseen. The vultures had taken all the goodies from the place. Only a broken bureau and a three legged table greeted Lloyd's invasion. He opened the closet to find a bunch of bent wire hangers, and nothing else. The stench of cat pee and old age convinced him not to crash there.

In an open bureau drawer, he found a single earring, wedged in the corner. He hoped it was a diamond, but he would accept zirconium. It shined nonetheless. Through the warped door, he entered the carport.

The cracked floor smelled of burned oil and leaked fluids. He looked under a tarp at two bald tires propped against a wall. A dirty throw rug lay atop something else. Lloyd pulled it off, discovering a storage chest under the grime. The rusted crisscrossed metal exterior remained, with rusted lock in place.

Instantly, he fantasized about his lineage to pirates' plunder. Popping the lock, he opened the top to his treasure chest! Beyond the dust, he smelled decay. With little lighting, he made out several VHS movies, like *Arsenic and Old Lace,* and magazines, like *Women's Health.* Every magazine cover promised a diet to lose weight.

Further down in the chest, he found some woman-on-woman magazines that aroused him. There was probably lesbian porn on the unlabeled tapes—if he could just locate an old VHS player. There were papers under the porn, so maybe he would get luckier with some light.

He lifted the old chest and placed it into his van, careful to make sure the chest did not touch what remained in the wheel well—a plastic bag containing a lifeless body.

It was time for Lloyd to dispose of the stiff. Better he should drive and find a location.

I'll hit a Denny's and have a Grand Slam breakfast. I need to kill some time so no one sees me dump the body.

After exiting the driveway, he waited until he got to the road before turning on his headlights, headed toward the ocean. He held a full treasure chest and a ravaged wench in his pirate ship.

CHAPTER THIRTEEN

As the sun settled behind the beachfront properties, Harry Powell stood alone at a bridge that penetrated the residential section of Wrightsville Beach. He had driven along the path that Natasha was known to run. It struck him that quite a few of the joggers were women who exercised on this oak-lined street where the sidewalk stretched from the inter-coastal waterway to the local museum parking lot. To Harry, it seemed like an ideal lurking place for a killer to watch runners parade before him. A killer could crouch like an arcade shooter, aiming at moving targets across his sight line.

To gain the perspective of locals, Harry parked in a utility repair ramp near the waterway and interrupted runners before nightfall. He showed a photo of Natasha to all the joggers who stopped for him. The blue blazer made him look official, almost like a cop.

He found people in Wilmington to be friendly. They stopped if they thought they could help. The resort-like area contained a disproportionate number of shapely female runners. Harry figured he wasn't the only one new to Wilmington who noticed as much. To the wrong person, such awareness created a perverse opportunity.

A gap between runners allowed Harry to consider the nagging question about the car keys found at Natasha's apartment. From her campus residence, the distance here was more a drive than a run. Then it hit him.

I never checked the brand of the car keys in the apartment to see if they matched Natasha's missing car. What if they weren't her keys? Odd but possible, I'll need to follow-up.

A young man with six-pack abs slowed his run. He wore shorts and expensive running shoes, along with an I-pad on his biceps. He removed the ear buds in response to Harry's gesture.

"Hi. Thanks for stopping. I'm trying to locate *this* missing woman. Have you seen her?"

The man kept churning his muscular legs while taking the photo in his hand. Harry felt hopeful, since a dozen runners had instantly replied they didn't recognize Natasha.

"*Yeah*, man. She looks *familiar*. I think she worked at the bar down the street, the T&A maybe?"

"That's right. Have you seen her recently? She jogged along this road and…"

"Maybe I saw her a week or two ago at the bar. I see lots of runners along here, but not her. To be honest, she seems more like the *night time in a bar chick*, you know?"

He handed the photo back to Harry and resumed running.

Harry noted the ear buds that many of the joggers wore disallowed them to hear screams for help. After several more negative responses, he accepted closure from the darkness that crept around him. Sitting in his car, ready to depart, he was startled by someone knocking on the driver's side window. Then he noticed the flashing lights of the cherry top.

A uniformed cop directed him to lower the window.

"Please put both your hands on the steering wheel where I can see them and give me your driver's license, sir."

"I can't do both actions at the same time, officer. May I reach into my pocket with one hand?"

He handed the officer a copy of Bernie's PI license and his Maine driver's license.

"What *gives*? Are you Bernard Mannion or Harry Powell?"

"I'm *new* here, officer. I'm Harry Powell, working for Mannion and Associates Detection and… we're private investigators."

He had started to search for a business card when the officer shouted at him.

"Put your hands where I can see them, sir! What are you doing out here?"

"I'm working a case looking for a missing woman. I learned she sometimes ran along this road. Professor Radinsky-Wade hired our firm to help find her daughter, Natasha."

Harry grabbed the photo on the front seat and showed it to the policeman.

The officer returned to his patrol car. After the usual delay, the officer dismissed Harry.

The name on the cop's badge caught his attention.

"Thanks, Officer Jordan. Are you guys working on finding this woman?"

"I'm not allowed to discuss police business with you, sir. Please move along."

After confronting that private eye, Officer Malcolm Jordan had a night of one DWI and a public intoxication warning. He slowed his police cruiser to take a break. *At four in the morning, a human being should not be awake.* They stuck him with this lousy graveyard shift. Visitors never linked Wilmington with the birthplace of the famed basketball star he called "the other M. Jordan." But Malcolm Jordan was a municipal employee, fulfilling his sworn duty. He could catch some shut-eye and still get paid. During most of his shift, anything that moved was either a creature or trouble. They had little trouble here.

As he sat in his patrol car nested near where he rousted the PI, his eyelids became heavy. Missing women weren't uncommon in a tourist area. It wasn't Aruba, though. Missing people eventually showed up, with made-up excuses. Women were like that—there was always a story—like the one Latonia gave him all the time.

Nothing appeared straight-forward and simple—divas displaying drama. The silent street scene before him was set against a black sky. With chin hitting his chest, his head snapped up. An unmarked van drove past. Through a sleepy haze, the digital clock numbers read *four zero five.* His head nodded back down. The van had both taillights working and drove at a proper speed. *Probably just some fisherman getting an early start.* He fell back asleep.

Inside the van, Lloyd peered anxiously in his rearview mirror. *Was that a damn police car behind the bushes on the side of the road?* He watched his speedometer and slowed as he veered over the drawbridge. He kept driving west, carefully watching his speed. Sweat beads appeared on his forehead. He could always say he was returning from a funeral and wake.

It took only ten seconds for him to stop the van on the overpass. He tossed the duct-tape, cinder block-weighted garbage bag into the dark water. No one could have seen him. His plates were unidentifiable. The unlabeled white van resembled a hundred others. *What the hell was a cop doing there?*

He felt livid at first—like when he was busted for meth in Tennessee. *I should have done a drive-by first to see that no one was on the other side of the overpass. But who would figure a cop sitting there at four in the fucking morning?* He needed to be calm. There was no movement. *The cop was probably asleep.*

He continued along the barren Martin Luther King Highway toward the airport. Looking back, he confirmed that no one was following him. He had some clean up to do, and knew a safe place. If he cleaned everything thoroughly, no evidence would be found.

Slowly, he approached the lighted self-serve storage area near the airport. He would add the clasp of red hair he folded into a baggie to his trophy collection. As he opened the metal door to the storage unit, he smiled. *Once again, the successful pirate has returned alone and unnoticed.*

~~~~~~

The morning greeted JD with a bright sun in a cloudless sky—a sunglasses morning for sure. Henzlein tried to shake the cobwebs from his head while driving on Market Street to his office. His Escalade maneuvered past some relic, hogging the left lane in a Camry, but his gaze diverted from the septuagenarian to a sexy teen.

Her ass caught his eye at first, a high-arched bottom in cut-off jeans pranced on the side of the road, waving a sign that advertised a car wash for her high school. He liked what he saw—long, blonde streaked hair, blowing in the breeze. Feeling devilish, he pulled up next to the hottie and lowered his tinted window.

"Hi, mister! Get a car wash? The money goes to our senior trip…"

He lowered his Oakleys to the tip of his nose, looking her up and down. *Tall and lithe—like a beach volley ball champion.*

"What do I get for my contribution?" he asked in his most mellow realtor sales pitch voice.

Like a young actress, she reviewed JD with large brown eyes and a wisdom beyond her years. She appeared innocent, but sexy—all in one stunning package.

"That depends on the… *size* of your contribution."

She smiled at him. Three other girls focused elsewhere and topless boys washed the cars. He took out his billfold and peeled off a U.S. Grant fifty-dollar bill, holding it out for her.

"I wish I had one with Robert E. Lee, but such are the spoils of war."

"Awesome! Thanks, Mr. *Real Law,*" she beamed, causing JD to recall his customized plates.

"What's your name, honey?"

"Amber."

"Like the missing girl?"

He released the currency to her.

"A girl is *missing?*"

She folded the fifty in half and slipped it into her top instead of the plastic container in her hands.

My kind of girl! He looked at her decal covered fingernails.

"Say Amber—you're a senior. Are you eighteen years of age? Would you be interested in a summer internship?"

She smiled with her chin down and eyes looking up at JD. He was accustomed to that look from some women who caught his pitch and promised interplay. The girl oozed the sloe-eyed seductive look that could elicit a rise out of any man.

"I just turned eighteen last week. What does an intern have to do?"

She leaned on one leg, with the other one crossed in a way that reminded JD of a Russian tennis star.

"We can negotiate the specifics, but I guarantee you'll have fun and earn some money. *Call* me."

He handed her his business card and moved forward. As he watched the applied suds enclose the Escalade, he figured he *deserved* some relaxation. He begrudgingly wrote two alimony checks each month, and for that he received no satisfaction—only grief.

Reviewing his iPhone *Notes* list, he had an ATO fraternity get-together in the following month. He had to schedule another planning meeting with the three stooges about the July Fourth demonstration. Then there was another contribution session with Annabelle, who liked to experiment, and who had recently mentioned a three-way. *Maybe Annabelle would like Amber?*

The clean water currents cleared his windshield as the Escalade glided past the cleaning area. In a quick sideways glance, he caught Amber still shaking her ass when he accelerated across the suicide lane into ongoing traffic. He anticipated a wonderful summer of diversionary frolic, along with the financial gain of clearing half a million dollars on Independence Day. *Sweet!* However, he did not know that he had just invited the source of his demise into his life.

~~~~~~

Bernie Mannion slowed Moby Dick into a parking space near his office. He was uneasy with the new business cards. The script read, *Mannion & Associates Detection and Solutions.* It looked *better* than a Mannion & Powell partnership. The former sounded like a bigger organization with many associates. *And who knows if Harry will stick around?*

A mess greeted him inside the office door—folders on the floor and desk drawers tossed about. His desktop computer was trashed. KiKi kneeled on the floor, gathering scattered documents. With a reddened face, she gazed up with tear-filled eyes.

"What the *fuck*, Bernie? Who *did* this?"

Her hands flapped like a penguin's flippers.

He had never seen her cry, but she was close to it. He approached and dropped his beefy hands on her thin shoulders.

"Are you all right? Come and sit down. Let's just look and see what's missing, okay?"

She nodded and stood, while pressing down her plaid mini skirt. Rings covered most fingers on her hands.

"I came in early, and this is what I found. I had the laptop home this weekend, but they still tore apart the docking station and my hard copy files. There's nothing worth stealing here, Bernie. Why mess everything up?"

"I'm not sure why anyone would *do* this," Bernie answered, shaking his head.

He looked about, like the detective he had once been. Carefully, he tried to figure the focus of the break-in.

"Okay KiKi, I'll take care of this mess. Why don't you go down and get us some bagels and coffee?"

He placed his hand on her shoulder and handed her a twenty.

"Gotcha, boss. But what is this all about? Who *did* this?"

"I have no idea."

He knew too much about recent warnings and didn't want KiKi involved.

"On *my* bagel, get me cream cheese and lox and…"

"…and capers, no onions—I know! Okay, boss."

Bernie watched KiKi as she left the office. She was small-town born and had never experienced the violence that filled the worlds Bernie knew. Her short skirt and tight top were fun for her. She remained blissfully unaware that some pervert could misread her attire as an invitation. He worried about how he could warn her about the reality of the world without diminishing that sparkle in her eyes? It would be like a father telling his children that he wasn't as good as they thought.

He leaned his cane against the metal desk. When the computer files weren't located, this trashing represented a crude message from people Bernie was up against. The wall calendar reminded him that he didn't have much time to resolve the danger. Events would be completed on July Fourth and then, maybe he would be able to sleep again. *Maybe.*

CHAPTER FOURTEEN

The bustle of breakfast diners filled the booths at the *Sweet and Savory Restaurant*. Scrawled specials, written in chalk, covered a blackboard. Harry sat across from Holly.

"Thanks for taking the kids to summer camp. It's nice having adult company," Holly offered as she finished her steamy green tea.

"I should be thanking *you*, Holly... for letting me share time with your family. Reminds me of missed opportunities."

"You're too hard on yourself, Harry. Live each day the best you can and take advantage of the situation now. What are you trying to change about yourself?"

"I just want to be like the Bee Gees and keep *stayin' alive...*"

"I don't know who the BGs are, but... how will your life be different a year from now?"

"Maybe I won't... be *alone*."

"*Aht lo leh vahd*," she whispered.

"Okay, I don't know the lingo or the meaning."

"It's Hebrew. *You are not alone.*"

"Thanks," Harry said, surprised. "*You* know Hebrew?"

"No, I saw it on an episode of NCIS."

"Ah, yes. One of my favorite shows, as well."

"It's not my thing, but let me tell you a joke, Harry. See—there's this guy who shares lunch with his peers at work and complains every day about the sandwich he brings. 'I hate cheese sandwiches,' he says to everyone. The next day, they meet for lunch and again the man complains: 'I hate these cheese sandwiches.' Finally on the third day, he complains once more about his cheese sandwich lunch, until one of the other guys asks, 'Why don't you tell your wife you don't like cheese sandwiches?' The complainer replies, 'My wife? I'm not married.' And then the other guy asks, 'Then who *makes* the cheese sandwiches you bring every day that you hate?' To which the complainer replies, 'I make them myself.'"

Harry laughed and accepted that maybe he brought too many cheese sandwiches into his life.

"Think about it, Harry. I need to be at this woman's house for visiting nurse assistance. See you tonight."

She grabbed her purse and, before racing from the restaurant to her car, she kissed Harry on the cheek. He watched her exit while appreciating how easy dialogue came with her. As he finished his coffee, he considered his episodic sex life through the years. But now he desired a broader partner.

Unlike Bernie, he was not interested in having some chippie to massage his ego. He wanted a peer, who could share his interests and time together—maybe even laughter and there would be a second chance with children. Plus he liked the sound of "Holly and Harry."

When he opened the door into the offices of Mannion and Associates, cheap bells rang above the door. Disarray across the office greeted him, while he thought he smelled urine.

"Nice mess, huh? You should see the back room," Bernie called as he entered the front area, limping on the wooden cane.

"New cane?"

"Yeah, a step up from the aluminum mini quad. It's maraca wood. It's kind of classy, huh? The original detective Poe had one of these bad boys."

"Nice—especially if you *need* it. What were the intruders looking for, Bernie? Any idea who did this?"

"I have no idea. Maybe some bored kids?"

Harry noted the lack of eye contact from his old friend.

Door bells tinkled to interrupt the pause between the two men. KiKi bounced open the door with her butt and carried a tray of coffees and bagels. Her maroon-streaked hair shined in the morning light.

"Good morning," Harry called as he reached out to help her with the tray.

He sat the food on a desk. KiKi knew which unmarked bagel and coffee were meant for whom. With delicate hands and black fingernails, she handed Bernie his coffee and bagel, removed her breakfast and flopped into her chair, leaving a single coffee.

"Is this coffee for me?" Harry asked.

"Sure… NBD."

"Thanks, KiKi."

There was much he wanted to say to her, but he always felt like he was intruding on her and Bernie. After devouring his bagel in silence, Bernie stood.

"Well, I have *clients* to see. KiKi—will you clean up the rest of this mess? There's nothing missing. Probably some kids. Harry, how goes the missing girl case? Let's walk and talk."

Bernie held open the front door and Harry followed him outside. Harry spoke first.

"Is KiKi okay?""

"Yeah, she's just upset about some stuff and playing protector for me. Anyway, *about* the partnership…"

"I know—I've already been demoted to associate," Harry chided.

Bernie limped toward Moby Dick, grumbling.

"Does *everyone* know more about what's going on here than I do? Well, the cash flow for the agency is bad right now and…"

"It's okay, Bernie. I came here to help you out. I don't even have a license. It's about the work for me. When you no longer need the help, I'll be gone."

Bernie turned.

"Whoa, slow down! I *need* you—it's just that I got a lot of things going on, in addition to the missing girl."

"We need to talk more, but I have to meet a priest about the *missing girl*, whose name is *Natasha Radinsky*, by the way," Harry reminded him.

"I know… Annabelle's kid. What's the priest connection?"

"I'm just following up on a lead," Harry explained as he leaned across the top of his Taurus. "One more thing—you're buying a new *boat*, and yet tell me you have *cash flow* problems? You've got paying clients, and the rent on this office must be paltry. So, what's going *on*, Bernie?"

Bernie tossed the cane on the passenger seat and spoke from behind the Crown Vic's steering wheel.

"Don't worry, Harry. This too shall be revealed."

"Sometimes, a man reaches for what is beyond his grasp and falls hard. Not good—especially at *our* age, Bernie. It becomes harder to get up. Whatever you're messing with is probably something you should let go or get help. Let me know when I can help."

"Thanks, Harry. I'll let you know."

Harry drove in the direction of St. Matthew Church. After he parked, he walked past a modern school, bordered by a black iron fence, while reflecting on his unfenced school days.

Like the bank robber, Willie Sutton, replied when asked why he robbed banks: "Because that's where the *money* is," Harry entered the church because it was where he could find the priest listed in the church bulletin he found in Natasha's apartment. A church document didn't seem to fit with the profile forming of Natasha, and so it intrigued Harry.

Odors of incense and flowers greeted him as he walked across the thin commercial carpet. Each year, he lost another connection to his past, and that made him feel like an intruder in the holy place. *Maybe my church absence contributes to the emptiness in my lonely nights?*

A small man in khaki slacks and a casual white shirt approached him.

"Are you, Mr. Powell? Hello, I'm Father Rodrigo. You called and said this was urgent? Please have a seat."

Harry missed the identifiable attire of black cassocks and Roman collars. He liked white jackets on chefs and habits on nuns.

"Please call me Harry. Thank you for seeing me, Father. I'm a private investigator, helping the family of Natasha Radinsky. She's missing and we're trying to locate her."

Harry showed the photo of the young woman to Father Rodrigo.

"Does she look familiar?"

The priest took his time examining the photograph.

"I don't think so, but we have *many* visitors."

"Ms. Radinsky's mother is Professor Annabelle Radinsky-Wade over at WC. Do you *know* her?"

The priest smiled with a subtle acknowledgement.

"I know *of* her, from the newspapers. But she is not a parishioner here."

Harry applied learning from his earliest years of detective work to go beyond reading faces and peruse locales. From a pile of books on the table, he reached for one.

"Those are meant for parishioners," the priest commented. "It's the Church Membership Directory. The missing girl—do you think she's been injured?"

Harry turned each page, searching for a familiar face. At the back of the book were listed names and addresses, along with phone numbers and some e-mail addresses.

"For now, she's just missing. I don't see Natasha in this directory, but with this personal information at the back, couldn't anyone learn information about a parishioner just by grabbing one of these books? If they wanted to stalk someone, this could be an aid?"

"My son, we don't think that way here. The parishioners *are* the church. We encourage everyone to interact and know each other as followers of Christ. We are all His children."

"Perhaps I've been around bad people too much, Father. But anyone could enter the church and find information on a pretty girl and make her a target."

"I suppose evil can enter anywhere, my son. Why is it you think Ms. Radinsky is a parishioner?"

Harry unfolded paper and handed it to the priest.

"I found this newsletter in her apartment."

"Ah, this is our weekly church bulletin, from... two weeks ago. We hand these out after every Mass on the weekend. And certainly, she could be attending services and *not* be a member of the church— we don't require admission fees or inspect attendees, Mr. Powell."

"Perhaps *another* priest?" Harry asked.

"I'm afraid in these... how do you say... economic times, I'm the only priest here at St. Matthews. If this young woman is in some trouble, I would like to help you anyway I can."

A sudden impulse hit Harry.

"Do you have surveillance cameras here?"

"No, no cameras."

Harry handed the priest a business card as he turned to depart.

"Call me if you think of anything. Thanks for your time."

"I will, my son. Unless you need it to help you, I will also take that directory back now. I'll watch and, if I see your missing woman, I'll give her your card. Perhaps you will return to Mass here some day? *Via con Dios.*"

Harry returned the directory. He didn't know what to say, so he departed but blurted a stupid "*adios.*" *Perhaps Natasha came here seeking solace in a harsh world? Maybe a devil stalked her in this angelic place.* Harry knew the odds of survival after someone went missing more than 48 hours. *How had the priest known I'm a lapsed believer?* He walked outside and considered he might return to attend Mass once again. Driving past the brilliant pink flowers of the crepe myrtles that surrounded the church parking lot, he realized he needed professional help.

He nodded at two uniformed cops, taking a cigarette break, outside the backdoor entrance of the Wilmington Police Department. It used to feel like home when Harry entered a police facility. Too many years had passed.

Waiting on a bench, Harry recalled a similar feeling when outside his commander's tent in Vietnam, decades earlier. His attendance had been ordered to explain a firefight with the Vietcong. Mostly, Harry recalled the big guy from Arkansas. George stood tall in the foxhole and didn't react fast enough to enemy fire. Harry tackled him like a linebacker and they both hit the wet earth.

He could still smell the fetid earth on his cheeks. Confusion reigned as others thought they were fighting until shots from the smarmy jungle penetrated their group. George and Harry regained their positions and returned defensive fire. Soon, there came a silence from the Cong. The battle finished, the platoon walked away.

Minutes later, a young girl approached their victorious unit. She offered a white and yellow flower to big George, who leaned over to take the gift with his good old boy smile. Being cynical, Harry sensed something wasn't right, but his seconds delay from thought to action proved fatal. The cute little girl was still smiling when she exploded. With her limbs flew shrapnel that penetrated several American soldiers. A bomb had been strapped to her back. George fell like a fallen tree trunk. The explosion blew his chest open. Harry tried resuscitation until the medic pulled him off.

He had saved George's life only to see it lost within minutes, and it grated at Harry. He wanted to leap into the jungle and attack the sneaky bastards who sacrificed a little girl instead of fighting face-to-face. But the self-proclaimed North Vietnamese soldiers had run off to hide for another attack. Big George lay dead because Harry hadn't acted fast enough.

A throat clearing cough interrupted Harry's reflection. He followed directions and sat in front of a desk.

"So, what can I do for you, Mr. Powell?"

The man facing Harry could have been his brother. Like aging football linebackers, they had identical quasi-military haircuts and showed no paunch below their broad, muscular shoulders. Their piercing eyes met as the square jaws faced each other across the battleship gray metal desk. The nameplate identified *Paul Spano, Chief of Police, Wilmington.*

"I wanted to introduce myself, Chief Spano. I'm new here in Wilmington, working as a PI of sorts. My name is Harry Powell, and I figured you might want to know what I'm doing."

Chief Spano read the business card.

"What does *of sorts* mean?"

"Well, I came to town to help my old friend, Bernie Mannion. Do you know him? He owns a licensed private investigation firm. Mostly, he works for lawyers and performs investigative tasks. Bernie broke his leg and he asked me to help."

"Yeah, I know the ilk—taking beaver shots to help screw a guy with alimony. What are you *looking into* right now, Mr. Powell?"

Harry noted an unlit cigar rested in a Hot Wings shot glass.

"Please, call me Harry. Professor Annabelle Radinsky-Wade hired us to look for her missing daughter, Natasha. Do you have any news?"

Chief Spano pounded at his keyboard and read the screen. Harry figured he was either checking out himself, or Natasha, or both.

"I don't hang with many professors, Mr. Powell. Have you learned anything about the adult Ms. Radinsky that would indicate any criminal activity?"

"No, Chief. I haven't—at least not yet."

"Wilmington is a relatively small town, Mr. Powell. There aren't many incidents I'm not aware of here. The girl was recently reported missing. Nothing seems amiss. College kids go off all the time here as summer arrives."

"But she...."

"Your attention is duly noted. Call me when she shows up. I see you have a license pending, and your background checks. I also see you were on the job in Chicago, so you know I can't share police data with a civilian. Just keep me informed about anything on Annabelle's daughter."

The chief stood up, indicating the meeting was over. The men shook hands with equal pressure. As Harry turned away, the Chief called out a final comment.

"By the way, welcome to Wilmington, Harry. Keep your eyes open." Spano scratched his forearm where the tattoo of the Marine icon spread. As Harry departed the station house, marshmallow-shaped clouds drifted across the sky. He always "kept his eyes open," but he wondered why the chief of peaceful Wilmington would offer him such advice. The words were reminiscent of Bernie, advising him to bring his gun. Glancing at the sky, he worried that maybe a hurricane was coming.

CHAPTER FIFTEEN

Bernie leaned on his maraca cane and ambled past the community events board in Louie's Diner. He ignored a sign for the Independence Day Gala Celebration on the Cape Fear River pier downtown. Placing his cane on the ledge of his favorite booth, he slid onto the vinyl seats. The waitress filled his coffee cup.

"Ready to order, hon?" she asked with a voice that sucked on too many cigarettes over too many years.

"Waiting for a lady to join me, Darlene. Coffee for now. It's *business*," he answered defensively while perusing the dining room, sparsely occupied by an aging clientele. His gaze shifted when she entered the room.

If there had been a crowd, their heads would have turned to look at her. Blonde hair framed a thin face, atop an athletic figure. Swathed in red halter top and white shorts, she sported long shapely legs, giving her the appearance of a real life Barbie doll. Like a runway model, she strode toward Bernie and sat across from him, smelling of floral perfume.

"Good morning, Carolyn. It's private here," Bernie announced, defending the place he chose to meet. "Is your brother, Dave, joining us?"

Bernie wasn't certain why he needed to meet with Carolyn, now that Harry was in town. It seemed like a good idea when he scheduled the breakfast.

"No, Bernie. I told you that David was unavailable, which was why you wanted to see *me*. Isn't *this* what you planned?"

The waitress reappeared with a small pad and retrieved the pencil above her ear.

"Are you ready to order, hon?"

Carolyn raised her eyebrows.

"Coffee with low fat milk and an English muffin, dry. Do you have fresh fruit?"

"We have packets of strawberry jam."

She dismissed Carolyn, speaking to Bernie.

How about something to eat for *you*, hon?"

"Give me Number Five with bacon, eggs fried medium and rye toast buttered."

The waitress departed.

"*Friendly* service," Carolyn remarked. "So, what's new on the case for David? I assumed that is why you wanted to meet?"

"Listen Carolyn, a PI usually works for lawyers, with expectations of privacy. In your case, I sort of have two clients, maybe three. JD Henzlein is the lawyer and David is *his* client... so *you* are, well... I guess I could say a friend, and..."

The waitress returned with a full breakfast plate for Bernie. She dropped a soggy muffin smeared with butter in front of Carolyn.

"I asked for this dry and I don't have coffee," Carolyn complained.

"Gotcha," the waitress winked while removing the muffin. She soon returned with an overdone toasted muffin and a coffee and creamers for Carolyn.

"Anything else you need, hon?" she asked Bernie, who declined.

Bernie devoured a crisp piece of bacon from his fingertips, as he shoveled eggs and hash browns into his wide mouth. Carolyn nibbled the burned muffin.

"The waitress a *friend* of yours?"

"Naw, just that I eat here a lot," Bernie answered between mouthfuls.

"Why did you want to talk to me alone, Bernie?"

He adjusted his position in the cramped booth and filled his mouth with food. Carolyn stared at him. Her large blue eyes were inquiring, yet they were cold, like those painted on a doll.

Bernie washed the food down with a long sip of coffee, wiped his lips with the napkin and leaned toward her.

"Carolyn, I do need to talk to you about our roles and the mess your brother is in. But there's something... more personal."

Carolyn checked her smart phone.

"Does this have anything to do with that stupid radical group that David's troll girlfriend was involved with? She's dead and David isn't involved with them anymore."

"Harry Powell is here in Wilmington," Bernie blurted. "He's working for me—helping me out since I broke my leg and all."

He grabbed for his empty coffee cup as Carolyn brushed an errant blonde strand from her forehead. She looked again at her phone, as if the device, like some presidential teleprompter, would provide her with directions on how to react.

"I see," she said without expression. "Does he know about *our* situation—extricating David from the Marine court martial?"

"It's been *tough* on Harry. You know that his daughter and grandson were killed in a car crash?"

Carolyn shook her head in denial as he continued.

"His estranged daughter was coming to visit with his grandson when their car was demolished by a head-on collision with an eighteen wheeler just outside Portland. They were both killed instantly. It was the only family Harry had left."

"I didn't know. How *is* he?"

"Well, it's been a bad time for Harry. He lost the beach cottage due to some legal bullshit. And if that wasn't enough, he apparently had his police pension from Chicago rescinded, due to a civil suit about a shooting years ago."

Carolyn looked up at Bernie, her expression making her appear like a picture on a billboard, with frozen facial features.

"Why are you telling me all this bad news about Harry Powell? What does this have to do with my brother's court martial, Bernie?"

"I didn't plan on doing so, but you asked how he was."

"I meant, like alive, working and stuff," she countered. "Not his perfect storm tragic life story. It's not like it was *my* fault, or is *that* what you think? Because I left him in Maine, all this happened?"

Bernie proffered his large hands in an open gesture of compliant innocence as the waitress finally appeared with a muddy glass pot.

"More coffee?"

"Sure."

This time, both cups were filled.

"Listen, Carolyn, I don't know anything about what went on between you and Harry in Maine. Harry didn't handle all this *tragic life* well. Who would? He ended up sort of wasted in New York. And I really needed some stronger legs here. He's working on another case, but before I get him involved, I need to know if you have any issue if he were... helping with your brother's situation?"

"I thought the court martial was almost resolved," she said, her voice suppressed. "Why bring someone *new* into the case?"

She remained motionless, except for her thumb that flipped screens on her phone.

"You are mistaken to worry about such triviality, Bernie. I haven't thought about Harry Powell in a while. As to his working on the case, who cares? As long as he doesn't muck up David's release. Quite frankly, you could have just phoned me if that was all you wanted to tell me."

"You want that check together or separate?" the waitress interrupted.

"I've got it," Bernie insisted.

He anticipated a warmer, more compassionate response about Harry.

"Well, I'll see you later this week, with JD and Dave," he mumbled.

Carolyn whisked away without a goodbye, walking out the diner door with a purposeful stride that he took as annoyed. *She was warm in cold Maine and frigid in hot North Carolina. Go figure!*

"She your daughter?" the waitress asked with a sarcastic smile.

He slowed at the exit, watching Carolyn walk past Moby Dick before reaching her car. In the strong sun, her blonde hair appeared almost white, making Bernie consider that Carolyn could be *Harry's white whale.*

~~~~~~

Annabelle appreciated the cherry wood in the library. Her husband insisted upon it when they built in Landfall. 'Gives the place a look of class,' he used to tell her. She had to admit he was correct. The room differed from the white-trimmed southern styling throughout the house.

On the writing desk lay business papers, mostly from the college. The pile included one document from the MLF. At either end sat two framed photos. One displayed her late husband, Lars, at a business session, and the other a portrait of his daughter, Natasha. The girl came to live with them at sixteen, after her birth mother died. She'd clearly cut all ties—except financial—and gone out on her own.

Annabelle sat on the silk-covered loveseat, awaiting JD's visit. He was not really a friend, not a random pick-up, and not technically her business advisor or realtor. He wasn't a cohort from academia in shared political ideals to change the world. Although he wasn't any one of these, he played all these roles in her life.

JD liked to party more than those tenured at the college, and he possessed skills beyond young studs. He looked like what a fourth Kennedy son might have been, with the broad shoulders of a young Ted, the hungry eyes of a vital Bobby and the relentless dick of John.

JD *Kennedy* would have been something, with all that money to support his conniving deals. His morality would have made old man Joe proud of his feats—between the sheets and in business. But instead of such royal beginnings, JD Henzlein descended from local white trash. A man never fully transcended his past, but JD escaped the poverty mire through education and work. He made something of himself, with a Duke Law Degree, a cunning mind and eight hard inches.

The checks for JD had already been written. Annabelle projected the July Fourth Display as an orgasmic conclusion to the foreplay of her local work with the Military Liberation Front. She envisioned newspaper headlines that would impact a complacent society. Her satisfied smile gave way to erotic thoughts of JD. Closing her eyes, she grooved into the silky cushions in anticipation of an afternoon delight.

JD maneuvered the shiny black Escalade through the Landfall security gates. The professor always left her front door open for his afternoon visits. Most of the house smelled like floral scents, but the study permeated with leather, old books and memories to give the room an odor—like history. Previous generations, trapped inside pages of old books, sat on the shelves, watching him perform. JD entered the room and saw Annabelle waiting for him on the loveseat. She wore a cream-colored dress, with lace on the short sleeves. JD liked her flushed appearance for his attendance.

"Hello Annabelle," he said as he rested his leather briefcase on a Queen Anne chair that matched the blue and gold-striped design on the loveseat. She sat there like a queen and patted the empty spot next to her with regal direction.

"Oh, JD, my feet are so sore," she said, lifting her bare right leg.

JD removed his suit jacket and folded it onto the desk chair. In this room, he played a role. He smiled at the hungry eyes that invited him, as if he were the jester come to perform for her highness—just another compromise he made on the road to his horizon of wealth.

JD never abandoned playing this role of hired servant to the rich. Handsomely paid for his time, he leaned toward Annabelle. With her delicate foot in his hands, he bent to kiss her pedicured toes. He licked the arch toward the heel and then caressed her ankle, working his way toward her thigh with soft kisses. The pungency at the top of her thighs both repulsed and excited him.

She looked down at him with the condescension of the rich on the groveling poor—like he represented the lower class desire to satisfy the upscale Landfall lady. With an appreciative gaze, she smiled at him. Slowly, he slid her dress up, knowing she wouldn't be wearing underwear. His knees hit the floor, while his head nestled between her thighs and the Brazilian cut. Ringed fingers weaved through his thick hair. He imagined her hands held the hairy head of a silverback gorilla as she moaned in pleasure. He probed and nibbled expertly until she came the first time. Then she directed him to enter her to create a *second chorus of Afternoon Delight.*

An hour later, Annabelle and JD were fully clothed and seated on her private patio.

"We do need to talk *some* business," he said as he sipped the Johnnie Walker Blue.

"You mean you want a *check*," Annabelle offered with a smile. "It's okay darling, I get it…very well, in fact."

She crossed her legs and straightened her dress while sipping a Long Island iced tea, her newly-applied lipstick staining the Waterford glass.

Wisteria climbed the trellis, and fragrant fresh air satiated the humidity. She had moved the papers from the office desk to the glass table outside. JD silently perused the paperwork.

"Any word from those PIs on Natasha?" she asked.

"Some leads, but nothing definite—no signs of any violence or anything. She's just off partying. Maybe she met some stud on the beach and they went off together?"

"Well, she *has* disappeared for days before, but I do still worry. You *know* she was my stepdaughter, right? I mean, I love her and all, but she was Lars' daughter more than mine. I'm sure she'll show up with her hand out, as usual," Annabelle concluded, licking the edges

of her glass. "That new man at the Mannion Agency seems quite...
interesting."

"Powell? To me he seems like a Yankee little rigid about rules."

"With that laser look, he seems like a volcano, ready to erupt.
Better *watch* him. I don't see *him* on his knees," she said.

JD looked at her over his thin reading glasses, ignoring the
teasing remark. For a decade, he learned to tolerate class warfare that
economics brought. Soon, he would be on the other side of the
financial fence so that others would kneel before him.

While mortgage scams were profitable, the Independence Day
investment deal would catapult him over the fence and into the land
of the truly wealthy. The MLF activities provided the cover needed.

"The group requires a ten thousand dollar investment before
July Fourth. Are you still committed?" he asked.

"Yes, I am darling. Are troops being sent to far off lands to
create little Americas? These goons are even intruding on life here in
the Carolinas. Next, they'll be marching on campus in khaki jungle
gear, telling me what to teach. The capitalists need to be dissolved,
and that floating retired relic of war goes down with it. As to my
commitment, may I remind you that *I* was an angel for peace before
you were a Blue Devil at law school?"

He smiled as Annabelle wrote the check to his LLC, which could
be applied to various initiatives after he deducted his twenty-five
percent commission. Like many people who didn't earn their money,
they didn't watch it so carefully. Plus, he shared an attorney-client
confidentiality privilege. Finishing the business process exchanges, he
excused himself before she wanted more.

He drove past the Landfall guard, the air conditioner blasting
into his hot face. Within minutes, he stopped at a McDonalds and
went inside. Past the food counter, he rushed into the restroom. He
turned on the hot water and waited for it to burn his fingers. From
the wall dispenser, he pumped creamy soap until it filled his cupped
hands. Lowering his face, he forced the scalding water and soap into
his mouth and face. With the bitter, soapy water, he repeatedly rinsed
his mouth. Annoyed there were no paper towels, he pushed his face
under the hot air dryer, vigorously rubbing his chin and cheeks in a
futile attempt to remove the stench of that bitch!

He gazed into the mirror. *Soon this afternoon of groveling will be just
another short chapter, added to overcome my past.* He had financed his climb

up another rung on the ladder—past those lazy losers in his family. He exited the men's room. *I swear to God I will never kneel again. My personal Independence Day is arriving soon!*

CHAPTER SIXTEEN

Lloyd kicked open the back door of the unfinished model home. *Pirates don't wait for handouts like JD might offer—they pillage and plunder!* This was how Lloyd ended up here. Unlike the locked storage area, here the rent was free.

He carried the rusty treasure chest from Auntie's garage inside and dropped it on the plywood subfloor. From the cooler, he grabbed and chugged a bottle of Bud Lime. He tore off the rusted lock, his heart pounding. A pirate treasure chest—his financial future secured.

He knew there was a reason to drive all the way there. His genes had a positive outcome, after all. The top layer of yellowed newspaper pages were tossed onto the floor. *Where is the gold?* He grouped the VHS tapes with the women magazines. With the chest completely emptied, he sat on the floor and examined his booty—rubber-banded S&H Green Stamps booklets, cigarette coupons, with pictures of Sir Walter Raleigh clipped together in piles, brittle yellow pages of newspaper articles with titles like *Hurricane Comes Closer* and an antique map.

He savored the treasure, like it had all been left to him in her will. At first, he believed the map to be an old pirate buried treasure map, but it turned out to be a useless advertisement from a car dealer, promoting various Cape Fear dealership locations. *Damn it!*

His snobby brother, Jeff, tried to con him into paying some rent on an old Monkey Junction condo, but this uncompleted house suited Lloyd much better. *No one will see me here. No one ever visits these abandoned sites.*

Since Jeff's Real Estate Company halted building on the dream of a new community, or plantation as they called them, he felt entitled to camp there. Tall weeds on adjacent barren lots helped his privacy. No one driving past on Highway 17 would have noticed another van, coming and going. *No one noticed anything in that old house near the goat farm in Indiana, so why would anyone pay attention here? People worried about their own shit and ignored what went on with strangers. I'll hide in plain sight.*

He drove toward Wilmington, stopping at a gas station to fill up and read the local newspaper. There was nothing in the Wilmington Star-Gazette about any Big Red, dumped in the waterway. Now with a personal burial ground, he could accelerate his attention on the church ladies.

He parked in the lot behind St. Matthews Church and joined the congregation as they entered. He sat in a back pew, where he casually checked out the parishioners. The early arrivals prayed. The short priest greeted the congregation in his Hispanic accent. Lloyd called him *Father Taco*. Lloyd guessed Americans didn't want some jobs, like being priests, so some foreigner had to take on the role.

Maybe half of his original twelve targets appeared at the Mass. During the communion service, almost all the church goers went up to receive the host and wine, the body and blood. Lloyd watched the communion parade proceed like a beauty pageant, meant just for him. *Summertime in the south was the best at seeing the real figures.*

Just before the ushers at the end of the line chugged the last of the wine, Lloyd noticed a familiar blonde with a pony tail. When she proceeded to receive communion, her muscular arms and legs moved in a military manner. He had dubbed her Army Girl. Lloyd had never approached a woman he feared could physically defend herself. Her thin stomach indicated "single with no kids," which brought less urgency to report her missing.

Mass ended, and the parishioners exited the back of the church. Lloyd walked slowly and maneuvered himself to walk behind Army Girl. She shook Father Taco's hand and received his blessing. Lloyd brushed past the priest and maneuvered through the congregants until he caught up to Army Girl. He inhaled, but she gave off no scent.

She approached the parking lot. The tight khaki shorts were worn to excite him. He watched each cheek rise and fall as she walked faster on long muscular legs. She wanted Lloyd to take her and show her what it was like to be pillaged by a real pirate. Lloyd approached Army Girl, but he heard a click from the keys she aimed to open the locks on a gray car.

He noted the *Army Proud* decal on the rear bumper. She quickly slammed the door and Lloyd heard the locks click closed as he walked past without pausing. He memorized her Maine license plates and would enter them into his cell phone.

Climbing into his van, he brushed aside the hanging Pine Tree air freshener. Starting the engine, he tried to position his van behind Army Girl's car, planning to follow her to her residence. Catholics courteously let everyone into the exit line, which mired him in enough traffic to let Army Girl escape. She turned east toward Wrightsville Beach.

He would attend the same Mass next week and park near the "Army Proud" Corolla from Maine. Then he could easily follow her and learn precisely where she lived. Too bad she wasn't in the church directory, resting on the front seat next to him. *The Internet's such an easier way to infiltrate the lives of targets today.*

He floored the accelerator on his pirate van, driving west, out St. Matthew's parking lot. Maybe he was making a mistake with a military woman who attended church, but his urges inexplicably demanded upgrades for enhanced excitement. Army Girl would collide with a real killer—a pirate named Lloyd. Other targets might be easier, since he had addresses, family connections and personal social network information, but Army Girl excited him more.

In the Hooter's parking lot, Lloyd parked and turned off the ignition. He was proud of his van. The pirate decal added more identity to the inside wall of the van. While nondescript white and unidentifiable outside, the pirate van interior flourished as his black lair, like a reverse Oreo. With Army Girl gone, he flipped the church directory pages and reviewed his yellow post-it notes next to the photos of his favorites. He picked several options that he saw at church earlier. Inside Hooter's, Lloyd enjoyed a burger while he checked out social media to learn more specifics on the day's targets.

The restaurant air conditioning worked against the expanding heat between Lloyd's legs. The young waitress leaned over the table to take his order and show off her breasts. She presented herself as accessible, but almost too easy. *Not enough of the hunt here, too much like the past, with easy targets and almost willing participants.* Lloyd wanted more of a challenge—the thrill of the hunt. The urges were beginning to overwhelm him and only action could offer calm.

From his window seat, he scanned past the closed on Sunday *Chick-fil-A* restaurant across the street, to find the sign he sought for his next stop—*Pet Land.* They were open on Sundays and sold creatures other than cats and dogs. Each of his purchases came from a different store, and they were always in cash. If stores had surveillance cameras, his sunglasses and pulled down cap would hide his face. *Another little Lloyd could easily be obtained.*

The waitress placed his food in front of him and sashayed away, her exposed tits and inviting ass triggers for the afternoon's delight. Lloyd grinned and bit into the rare hamburger. While he savored the juicy blood that dripped down his chin, he licked his lips and an erection began. *It's time.*

That evening, in the woods behind the unfinished house on Highway 17, Lloyd buried the pillaged body of church target number four.

~~~~~~

As morning came, Harry Powell sat in McDonalds, devouring an old favorite—a steak and cheese bagel, with black coffee. Once a quarter, Harry satiated his desire for the delicious high calorie fast food. On that Monday, he ate with the justification that he needed strength to find a missing woman. Each hour that passed, he felt more like he was hunting a killer.

His foreboding dominated considerations about Natasha. He had never met the young woman, but he had come to think he knew her. Her mother's reactions seemed a little cold and distant, atop her voiced concerns. *Who prepares a fact sheet rather than discuss her daughter?* Harry knew he should not criticize any parent for relationships with children after his own pitiful parental performance. *What did my mother often say to my father? "You should be the last one to talk."*

What young person today leaves their wallet and car keys if they plan an absence for any length of time? Harry sipped the hot coffee. He knew that if Natasha had been taken against her will, she wouldn't survive the first forty eight hours, which had passed. Nothing indicated she ran off with anyone or had been taken. There were no kidnap demands, despite a wealthy, prominent parent. There were no apparent jealous former lovers and no motive except a pretty woman crossing the path of a perverted predator. There were no apparent links to subversive campus groups. No one saw anything. No one heard anything. No body found.

It was common in today's transient society—singles disappearing for a few days—summer beach romances and what did they call it? Hooking-up? Such couplings were not planned. They were a normal part of the dating game. And a mother not in panic, but more annoyed.

He sensed that people wanted to avoid being seen making judgments on others, so they avoided any advice. Parents avoided comments about the lifestyle of children for fear of losing their friendship. Annabelle told him it wasn't the first time she had lost touch with Natasha, but Harry recalled the recent TV trials of a pretty young mother who everyone believed murdered her daughter. That mother hadn't called the cops for weeks, despite knowing that her little girl was missing, and yet she was acquitted. Harry considered the professor, but nothing indicated a motive for murder. *She may have challenged the cops even before Natasha was actually missing.*

While finishing his breakfast sandwich, Harry realized the onions would leave a bad breath odor, but he savored the taste. Sometimes a person endured long-term discomfort for short-term pleasure. A young mother walked past him, followed by her small daughter who carried a Happy Meal.

Seeing them take a booth, he recalled a birthday party picture of his grandson, Christopher, at a McDonalds. Framed and on a table, he examined it as he awaited their visit to his Maine cottage. Portland Police said the Mini Cooper never saw the truck swerve into their lane.

The sixteen-wheeler crushed the Cooper and its passengers beyond recognition. Chances to hold his grandson on his lap and read him stories instantly vanished. Harry had never made the time to tell Christopher how much grandpa loved him. The same held true with his daughter, when being a cop took precedence over being a father.

He arrested criminals and put them in jail to protect strangers. While he earned money to pay for it, he never knew the white-picket-fence tranquility of a normal family life. Every year, time moved faster. He accepted that his dream of a family would never be fulfilled.

After the fatal car accident, Harry had told the lawyers to cease battling to retain the Maine beach cottage. Diminished of any fight, he even surrendered against the civilian review board in Chicago that rescinded his pension—all because they claimed he had planned to kill the thugs who assassinated his wife. They were criminals, caught committing a felony, and he had shot them all dead. The past had beaten Harry and he knew it.

Wiping the counter clean, Harry pressed the wrapper and napkin into his empty coffee cup. He tossed the trash into the receptacle and walked to his car. Behind him, he heard the child laughing with her mother as they shared breakfast. *Good times I'll never experience!*

KiKi Sanchez greeted Harry at the office and resumed aligning files. Harry noticed the chartreuse stripes in her hair.

"Good morning KiKi. Hey, the office looks great. You did a lot of work. Thanks."

"You're welcome, Harry. Want an Altoid?"

She pushed a small tin at him.

Harry sucked on the mint and found his chair. *I should have skipped the onions.*

"Thanks. Has Bernie arrived yet?"

"Bernie is never here this early. He says this early hour is for the support staff—meaning me. Do you have any news on the professor's daughter?"

"Natasha? Nothing much new on that, but as a young woman of today, let me ask you—do you ever go *anywhere* without your cell phone?"

"Are you *kidding* me? Never! How could anyone reach me? Or how could I reach anyone... unless..."

"What?"

"Unless I really wanted to chill and be left alone. Then I might turn it off. Or if I was with a special someone, or if some asshole was bothering me, I might go to airplane mode. If I wanted to be sure I had some peace, I would shut it off, but I would never ever leave it home."

"If you had it with you and it was on, would there be any reason not to answer repeated attempts to reach you?"

"Only if caller ID told me it was someone I didn't want to talk to... or if the battery died. Or I guess I could be in a low availability zone, with no cell service."

"Those still *exist* today?"

"Yeah, a few. Worst case could mean I can't answer it... that bad things happened..."

KiKi was a caring person—not a taker, but a giver. She even cared about a girl she had never met.

"And if you went jogging, would you take car keys?" he asked.

"Not if I were jogging nearby. But if I wanted to run at the beach, I would have to drive, since there aren't any busses to the ocean—last I heard. Things have changed, Harry. We can go anywhere and have total links to anyone. We have these…."

She wagged her shiny iPhone toward him.

"Plus I have all my keys here—house keys, car keys, library card, Harris Teeter discount plastic—lots of stuff."

She dangled a turtle decorated ring. Harry considered her answers. The only keys at Natasha's apartment were car keys, with no house keys attached. *Does it matter?* There was something he was missing, but he couldn't place it. He checked his notepad list. He had covered Natasha's friends, employers, mother, neighbors, college and random joggers—even a priest. He talked to the local cops. *Who else might know something? Maybe another visit to her apartment is needed.*

"You *do* know you can put all your little scribbled notes into that device you think of as a phone, right Harry?" KiKi asked, as Harry checked his notes.

"Yeah, thanks KiKi. Old habits die hard," he laughed.

"Your phone is vibrating," Kiki told him.

She picked up the office land line, becoming distracted. His reaction time to the vibration was so slow that the phone notified him of a missed message. He clicked on the voice message icon and heard terse words from Chief Spano.

"We have a 187. We found the dead body of a young woman."

CHAPTER SEVENTEEN

Hands choking the steering wheel, Harry raced over the drawbridge into Wrightsville Beach. As he approached flashing lights, the police commotion reinforced his sense of gloom. Police diverted traffic, causing Harry to pull into the History Museum parking lot. He hurried along the sidewalk under trees, which shaded him from the morning sun.

He passed the alcove where he had showed Natasha's picture to joggers. This street was part of her runner's route. Harry wanted the world to be a nicer place, but it wasn't. The flashing lights visualized the terse verbal message of a crime. The quantity of personnel present indicated a very serious crime. *I hope this isn't Natasha Radinsky!*

He approached the first uniform and displayed the borrowed PI license—like he was Bernie Mannion, adding, "Chief Spano has requested my presence." They let him pass and returned to their preoccupation with traffic control and annoyed tourists.

"Hey, Harry—over here," the Chief called.

Harry walked across the street to the edge of the small bridge that entered the residential area. A clear blue sky surrounded the rippling waterway with bordering palm trees. *Not the place for a corpse.*

Chief Spano stood next to a large woman in uniform. She directed a few official-looking types, probably detectives and medical examiners.

Harry had been a part of such scenes and didn't miss the part of the job when someone reported a corpse. No matter who they found, the person had family who would mourn. *Most people weren't good or bad just somewhere in between.*

"Hey Chief—thanks for the call."

"Harry Powell, this is my counterpart in Wrightsville Beach, Police Chief Belvich. This is her jurisdiction, but we're working on this together. Thanks Kristine," Spano said.

Harry shook the hand of the sturdy chief who had steely eyes and authority that went beyond a badge.

"Is the body you found that of Natasha Radinsky?" he asked.

Spano grimaced and turned slightly toward the black bag on the pavement.

"It's possible. What do you think?"

Spano removed the unlit cigar stub from his lips before he unzipped the body bag.

Harry's knees cracked when he bent over for a closer look. The bloated white face had matted reddish hair. He tried to mentally compare it to the color photo of Natasha, but suddenly, the face morphed into his late wife's face—from the moment when he went to the Chicago morgue for identification. *This distorted face is familiar.*

"Harry, you okay? The weighted corpse loosened when the body bloated and an arm extended above the water surface. The exposed hand caught the eye of a local guy arriving to fish off the bridge," Spano commented.

Harry stood, continuing to stare down at the face. His knees wobbled and his stomach churned. *I've been showing her picture around so much and looking into her life, I feel like I know her.*

"Sure *looks* like Natasha." He paused to swallow. "Cause of death?"

A sense of defeat engulfed him. Hollowness permeated his being. *My inability to locate her quickly enough may have allowed her premature death.*

"Her mother will need to come downtown for an official identification, I'm afraid. Doc tells me maybe strangulation, but also there are dozens of slashes all over her. You don't want to see her body. It looks like she was held and tortured before being murdered," Spano said. "It never gets easier to see this."

Harry absorbed the pain, becoming overwhelmed with defeat. He wanted Natasha to wake up.

"I called you because a uniform tells us he talked with a private investigator the other night near here. He said the guy claimed this was a likely place for a killing. Was that you, Harry?"

"Yeah, that was me with Officer Jordan. I said it was not likely, but possible. One of Natasha's jogging trails was along here, and it seemed to me a convenient snatch area. But I'm not sure a killer would return her corpse to where he grabbed her. Seems like a double risk to be recognized. Maybe the killer has a weird sense of closure?"

"We'll learn more after the docs conduct an autopsy. We need to help clear this all up and minimize tourist disruption. The mayor doesn't want publicity to scare away visitors. Did your investigation red flag anyone as having the potential to do this?" Spano asked.

"Nobody I spoke with popped out as a person of interest. The usual suspects don't seem to exist. No husband or estranged boyfriends. No jealous roommate. No apparent work conflicts. She didn't appear involved in any surreptitious behaviors. Nothing indicated drugs. Clearly, she wasn't the student her mother thought, but nothing indicated a motive for murder. Maybe it's some travelling wacko, who was just looking to torture and kill a pretty young woman?"

"Hey, this is Wilmington," Spano countered, "but that's my number one fear. An unrequited lover doesn't scare outsiders, but a whack job on the loose gets everyone anxious... especially politicians!"

"Despite residents in smaller cities, who always say that a vicious killer can't exist in their town, they do all the time. Evil resides everywhere."

"Is there anything else, Harry?"

"Something is bothering me, something about her car. How did she get over to this beach area from her apartment, when her car keys are still in her apartment? Too far to jog all the way here, isn't it?"

"Didn't she *work* nearby? Maybe she hitched a ride?

"Well, her mother thought Natasha waitressed at the Oceanic, but that wasn't quite true. She did some part time work at tables at the T&A Bar. She even danced a little at the some clubs. I didn't see her car in either of their lots."

"Good question, Harry. We need to check it out."

When he looked west toward the city proper of Wilmington, Harry shaded his eyes from the bright sun. *Why in a city of so much hope and joy did this tragic death occur?*

"This location is flooded with attractive female joggers," Harry offered. "Sometimes they're in pairs. But too many are solo and too many are running near dark. Too easy for a killer!"

"Yeah, I guess you might see it that way—coming out of Chicago and New York. We southerners see it as an idyllic locale to exercise year-round. Pretty streets in natural wetland environment, between inter coastal and ocean."

"I suppose you're right," Harry agreed. "What we've *been* makes us who we are and how we see things. I guess I tend to look for what a criminal might see. I can't help it. I guess I see evil around every corner."

"Hell of a way to live, Harry."

The medical team lifted the body bag into the ME van for the trip to Brunswick County morgue.

"You ever figure out what she did for a living?" Spano asked.

"Well, different people told me she was a graduate student, waitress, actress, clothing designer, dancer, pro surfer—you name it. She was like many young people—just trying to find her identity."

"That doesn't help us much, Harry."

"Maybe it's like Edison observed after all his failed experiments—this info eliminates who *didn't* kill her. Real life isn't as simple as a novel, with one dimensional characters defined by the role they perform. You know, where all the cops are overweight and divorced? Most people have complex, diverse lives that evolve over time, if you take the time to know them."

"You know, speaking of fiction, I never saw a real life private eye investigating a murder case," Spano mused.

"I get it, Chief. I appreciate your allowing me some inclusion. I know my role here. But Mrs. Radinsky-Wade remains a client. I can bet, with her view of police proficiency, that she'll expect Bernie and me to continue seeking the motive and the killer."

Chief Spano brushed back his hair and looked straight at Harry.

"I understand, Harry. And since her mother is a distinguished professor at WC, with many political friends, I can bet she'll work the system. But you and I are blue bloods who have the same goal that overrides all that bullshit!"

"Make sure the perpetrator pays for the crime and does the time… and doesn't kill anyone else," Harry insisted. "Natasha was an only child. And for a parent who appears not to be that close to her daughter, losing a child is still the worst tragedy anyone can experience."

"Keep me in the loop on whatever you guys find," Spano nodded.

"Thanks, Chief."

Harry returned to his car, imagining what the professor would experience in parental recriminations for what she could have done differently with her daughter. Parents maintained a belief in their omnipotence, despite the growth of their children into self-sufficient, decision-making adults. In life, chapters in a book often ended without any meaningful epilogue.

As he drove back to the storefront office, numbness pervaded his body—as though all acts were meaningless. *Man planned and God laughed* came to his mind. The doorbells announced his office entry, like he was in an old time delicatessen.

"We need to lose those tinkle bells, Bernie," he said as he walked in and saw Bernie at his desk.

Harry didn't notice the cell phone buried against Bernie's ear as he pulled a chair over.

"JD, I'll call you later," Bernie said before squeezing the phone shut in his large hand. "Well, Harry?"

Harry felt awkward and didn't know where to begin.

"*KiKi* isn't here?"

"She'll be back in an hour. What's on your mind, Harry?"

"You *know* they found Natasha Radinsky?"

"Yeah, so I heard. Seems like you're a new asshole buddy of Chief Spano—and his closet of grey suits and white shirts. And it ain't even his jurisdiction. But I still got my connections."

Harry felt a cold resentment in Bernie's harsh tone.

"Did you talk to Mrs. Radinsky-Wade?"

"I was just about to go over to see Annabelle. The Chief just told her personally what they suspected. Obviously, she has to go down to identify the body, but there's little doubt. She called JD and wanted to know where *we* were with finding the killer? To be honest, Annabelle wanted to know if you were just wandering around until her daughter's dead body was found by some fisherman."

Harry dropped his chin on his chest. He felt like a knife had plunged into his heart—frustrated he couldn't find a clue to the disappearance and possibly prevent the fatal outcome.

"I talked to quite a few people Bernie, but that failed to help. After forty-eight hours, you know the odds. So what now, Bernie?"

"Well, we're still on the clock. Asking questions ain't finding answers. She wants answers," Bernie stated.

"I understand. I want to find the killer, no matter what. But it's a *police* investigation now. I couldn't unearth any apparent motive in my days here, so maybe this is random with no connections. Any other dead young women turn up lately around Wilmington?"

"Maybe you should ask your friend, the chief. Wilmington is a low crime place. This ain't murder-city Chicago. Annabelle pays on time, so we continue our work and see what we can find out. I'll talk to Annabelle, so you needn't bother her. I'll calm her, and say I'm working it also, but I got no time, Harry. Other cases—events are getting more complicated... not ready to involve you yet, but JD says..."

"You really trust this guy?" Harry interrupted.

"JD's a *lawyer*, you know. He knows stuff I can only imagine. His links go way back in North Carolina history. Plus, he's lived here most all his life, so yeah, I trust him."

"Seems like a pettifogger to me."

"You do too many crossword puzzles, Harry. JD is like a money-seeking octopus, with tentacles everywhere. Some old timers tell me that relatives of JD's talked Sherman into burning Atlanta instead of Wilmington."

The ringing front bells interrupted their discussion. KiKi Sanchez entered the office with an owner's aplomb. "Oh, hi guys, board meeting?"

She sat, the colorful hair streaks including some bright red that matched the knee-length silk pants she wore. Earrings the size of oranges hung from each ear, and had palm-tree, red inlays.

"KiKi, I need to talk with you," Bernie began as he rose on the maracas cane and ambled to her desk. "Harry was just leaving on a case..."

Harry walked out. While his car interior cooled off, he considered who to talk to. This whole scene wasn't working out, but now he needed to find a killer. First, he would need to learn the autopsy results. His cell phone rang. The familiar voice seemed subdued.

"I'm happy you still use the same cell number," she said.

"This is the only phone I have."

"We need to talk, Harry. I may be in some trouble..."

"Where *are* you, Carolyn?"

CHAPTER EIGHTEEN

Even during the summer, the WC campus entertained students, but empty classrooms were available. The professor joined four male students. Three of them were disaffected rootless losers, seeking identity, and were thus expendable. The fourth was a protégé for his deceased sister by proxy. The group leader loved the irony that all these students attended WC on federal subsidies. In this action, they would attack a part of the very government that paid for their education.

"Karim, please update us on our progress," professor demanded.

"We are prepared for Independence Day. The weaponry has been gathered and the Marine operatives informed. The military presence will receive a strong message that we, the people, will no longer tolerate their intrusion into foreign affairs."

"How much do these two Marines know so far?" she asked.

"Just to the degree they need to know. They believe this is another protest. *I* control the serious weaponry for the main target," he answered.

"I wish you would share with us the entire plan," one of the students, originally from Eastern Europe, complained. Recently, the two fled Boston, after the marathon fiasco. They transferred from a Massachusetts state school to the UNC system. Sometimes, they even attended college classes.

"And if you're captured or found to be a plant? You are new, and know all you need to know for now. On this mission, you're the support. Once you bloody your hands, your knowledge level will be expanded. Someone talked too much, and now my sister, Jasmyne, is dead—murdered by the military industrial complex."

"Karim, we all mourn the loss of Jasmyne. She is irreplaceable," the professor consoled. "And now my step daughter... has been found murdered—and the government knows nothing about who did it or why,"

"I'm sorry for your loss," Karim offered. The others nodded.

"Despite our personal losses, this mission must continue. Let me remind you that the MLF is not an organization with a typical office headquarters or monthly newsletters. Small groups like us, all over the US, work independently to affect change. America shipped thousands of soldiers from the Wilmington Cape Fear port to kill in Iraq, and now we'll show them that they need to stop interfering in other country's politics. We won't deter them with one act, but the accumulation of our actions will make a difference. We will not only destroy symbols, but…"

"Perhaps we should *limit* our discussion," Karim warned, rubbing his leg nervously.

"Of course Karim—you have grown much. I was closer to Jasmyne than my own daughter. But now details are best kept low key. I'm sure Gregor and Pyotr understand we want you… protected."

The two acolytes nodded.

"They watch places like New York and San Francisco closely, but the scrutiny on Wilmington is far less. So it is here that we'll act. After the July Fourth events here, we will take you to a safe location."

"Just be absolutely *certain* you're in the Cape Fear Community College parking lot along the River, so we can escape the downtown chaos," Karim admonished the other men, who nodded like bobble head dolls before being excused.

The leader looked at Karim's eyes.

"Those two will be found when the authorities search for suspects," Karim indicated. "They won't be talking by then. It's all set."

"We also need to scare off the nosy American civilians. I know physical force is not your thing, but we need to have someone get the job done. No one can interfere with our actions," she asserted.

With that final directive, the professor walked down the hall to the office labeled *Professor Radinsky-Wade*.

~~~~~~

Harry recalled his many attempts to locate Carolyn after she ran from Maine—like a hurricane had struck. Yet on a sunny day in Wilmington, NC, she called him.

"Can we meet for lunch today? The Seafood Place, I can be there by two," she said.

Harry considered his conflicting emotions, regret and the reunion. He initially reacted by shaking his head. *Right now, I should focus on finding Natasha Radinsky's killer, not revisiting an old friendship.*

"I'll see you then," he said.

On the pier extension of the oceanfront restaurant, Harry sat at a table decorated with a glass carafe that was filled with seashells. He sipped from the ice water with lemon. Seagulls floated in the cloudless sky, watching to see if diners parted with any errant food. The restaurant had roped off the collapsing section of the old wooden pier to prevent entrance.

Wouldn't it be nice if a person could do that with their life, just rope off the decaying parts and move forward? Wood aged at different rates, much like people, and most days Harry felt aligned with the collapsing area. When he had a purpose, he felt useful—like the stable sections of the pier. He adjusted the small bouquet of violet poesies he'd bought for Carolyn.

"Would you like something else to drink, sir?"

The waitress was pretty and friendly—*the exact demographic that would cause Bernie to offer a comment.*

"No thanks, I'm okay. I'm working."

The ocean reminded him of the good times in Maine, enhanced when Carolyn moved in nearby. After her military discharge, she and Harry linked through the tragedy of common pasts. They shared a love of shells and the ocean. That summer, they enjoyed time together on the shoreline splendor of Maine.

On the sand below, a few middle-aged men tossed nets into the approaching waves, casting for small fish to gather bait for larger prizes. The seemingly futile activity reminded Harry of what it was like seeking a killer.

The detective talking to contacts was like seeking bait that might lead to a larger catch, and eventually the killer. On the beach, the men repeatedly tossed and pulled the nets. Hopefully, their persistence would pay off—better than Harry's efforts to locate Natasha Radinsky. Her cause of death by choking indicated the killer may be a sociopath who wanted to feel her die. Darkness crept into Harry's mind as he tried to focus on the sunny day. *Is this single murder the beginning of a spree?*

He read there was a murder in the US every thirty-six minutes. Anyone of the diners around him could be a killer. According to statistics, a family member or friend would be the most likely target. It was strange how people looked askance at shadowy strangers when they should more rationally fear the person they shared meals with.

Carolyn walked toward him with a purposeful stride. Her squared shoulders leaned back as her long legs strode toward him. She looked thinner than Harry recalled, while the man with her appeared to be her inflated male-version. Carolyn looked like she had materialized from the cover of a J. Crew catalog. The massive man marched in synch with her—he could have been a Marvel Comics action hero.

"Hello Harry!"

Carolyn beamed at him. She reached up and, placing both hands on his shoulders, she kissed his cheek. While he returned the greeting, she appeared different up-close. In Maine, she had been make-up free, but she added lipstick and mascara. He failed to hide his surprise that she wasn't alone.

"Carolyn—hello!"

"Harry Powell, this is my brother, David Dodd."

The muscular young man gripped Harry's hand—like he was trying to impress him with his strength.

"Hello, sir. Good to meet you."

The couple sat at Harry's table. In the bright sun, Carolyn's eyes matched the Carolina blue sky. Harry noted some crow's feet—like she hadn't been sleeping well. Physical presentations from the past don't always fulfill a positive recollection, but Carolyn's physical beauty exceeded his recall. He surreptitiously slid his poesies next to the table pole so they seemed part of the restaurant decor.

The waitress took their drink orders—a Blue Moon for David and a Pinot Grigio for Carolyn. Harry stuck with water.

"So, Harry. It's great to see you. You look good."

Carolyn examined him, politely ignoring his weight loss and haggard appearance.

"I was so sorry to hear about your daughter and grandson. Bernie told me. I didn't know until recently."

Harry mumbled "thanks" and drank his water. At such times, he missed chilled vodka. *She had been here two minutes and already told me two lies.* He looked like shit and she already knew about the tragedy, since she had sent a Hallmark condolence.

It suddenly hit him—*this David Dodd was the DD at Camp Lejeune? The same on the card I found with the dead PI in New York!*

"Before I forget, I have a question—do either of you know a guy named Janakowsky, a private investigator?" he asked.

David responded first.

"I never *heard* of him."

Carolyn paused to think for a minute. Her hesitancy could have been time to reflect or to deceive.

"I don't know anyone by that name," she said.

A third lie.

"I understand you fought in Nam, Harry?" David interjected.

The man had already devoured half the beer.

"Yeah, I was there."

Flashes of steamy jungles and screaming soldiers filled his vision.

"So were you a fuckin hophead like everyone else over there?"

Though Dave exaggerated a wise-ass smirk, Harry wasn't sure it was an attempt to be funny or that Dave was just a jerk.

"I fought in the Marines, a lifetime ago. I fulfilled my duty. What trouble are you in, Carolyn?"

"I guess *I'm* the one in trouble, Harry," Dave replied. "Court martial from the Marines. Some bogus crap…"

He finished his Blue Moon and glanced toward the waitress, waving his empty bottle with biceps that strained his tee shirt. The waitress brought another Blue Moon and they ordered: Carolyn a salad, Harry a fried oyster po boy and Dave a veggie burger.

"David got involved with some protestors," Carolyn began, "and the Marines now want him court-martialed. It was mostly coming from one man, Colonel Bogart. He had a biased vendetta against David."

"It was a fuckin legal campus demonstration against the government's cover-up of water contamination at Camp Lejeune and intrusive politics. There was a movie made and everything, so it wasn't like we were radicals or any of that shit," David added.

Harry noted Carolyn's concerned response to her brother's protests.

"But you're a Marine, so you're protesting against yourself… just because of Jasmyne."

"Sis, Jasmyne opened my eyes to the issues!"

"She was with the *Military Liberation Front*. Have you even heard of them, Harry?" Carolyn asked.

"MLF? Vaguely. Tell me more."

"It's just a small, local college group that protests military intrusion, —no BFD," Dave answered. "It means Big Fucking Deal."

"I see. I understand that Bernie's working on a court martial case up in Jacksonville at Camp Lejeune... so I gather that's you?" Harry asked.

Dave nodded, chewing his food. As they ate, Dave seemed more intrigued by the surfers riding the waves on the beach below.

"Harry—Bernie is helping our attorney. The court martial was trumped up, even before that stupid little campus protest. Bernie gathered information that challenges prosecutorial assumptions of guilt. I wanted to see you and have you meet David... and have you understand our situation. I know you're now Bernie's partner, but..."

"I'm just temporarily here—at Bernie's request—to help him with the agency after his leg injury. Not a partner, just a hired hand."

"Independence Day will be quite the demonstration here, Harry. You don't want to *miss* it," Dave interrupted, smiling a Cheshire grin.

Harry felt uneasy at Dave's expression.

"What happens *after* Bernie heals? Are you staying here, or do you return to Maine?" Carolyn asked, caressing the carafe with shells.

"No. Maine is no longer for me. That's all gone."

She leaned in, eyes glistening. "What about your *girls*—the cats, Olivia and Elaine? Are they here with you?"

"Not quite. Around Christmas, Elaine stopped grubbing table scraps and no longer ate her cat food. She got thinner and thinner, so I took her to the vet in Portland. They diagnosed a kidney disorder. Despite repeated injections, doctors saw no improvement. I told the veterinarians to do whatever was necessary to help her. For several weeks, the poor creature moped about the tiny cottage, until a diagnosis of incurable cancer came and, to stop the suffering, I let the veterinarian put her to sleep."

"So you still have Olivia?"

"Within a week of Elaine's death, Olivia slipped out to the beach and dug herself a hole in the sand before the waves came in. When I returned from shopping, I saw an unfamiliar shape on the smooth beach and ran across the wet sand. Olivia lay there, curled in death."

"You mentioned a *biased vendetta?*" Harry asked.

Carolyn shot a furtive glance at her brother that made Harry feel like the intruding third person on a date between an intimate couple.

"You know, David, Harry helped me a great deal in Maine after I returned... from combat. Always there to help, aren't you, Harry? This bias threat becomes complex..."

Dave interrupted his sister.

"Look, I'm bi, Harry. That means bisexual. I don't lisp and I don't like Broadway musicals, okay? But the Marines don't want me or my *type* in the Corps. Colonel Dinosaur was just the point-person out to purge us anyway he could. The campus protest was just an excuse to get rid of us. That fuckin dickhead!"

The vulgarity and volume of Dave's comment caused other diners to steal glances at the trio.

Carolyn placed her pale hand on Dave's forearm.

"Who is the *us* you mention?" Harry asked.

"In the Marines with me is my BFF, Rock."

"You said *they're* out to get you. You've done nothing to warrant such an extreme response as a court martial?" Harry posited.

"Why assume *we* did something wrong, Harry?" Dave responded.

"I didn't, but you said..."

"Take it easy, David. Harry's here to help us," Carolyn advised.

"Bullshit, Carolyn. He's *one* of them—old school straight bias makes him deaf, typical of his generation of dinosaurs who are unaware of how the world has changed!"

"Harry," Carolyn intervened. "Truthfully, this situation has become a broader issue. His friend, Jasmyne, was part of a radical campus group I mentioned."

"They're social reformers! I'm not a member of some secret society," Dave asserted, "but I *do* support efforts to stay out of other people's business and influence the world. And the Corps doesn't know or give a shit about this little group. They're after me and Rock."

Carolyn smiled at her brother, caressing his blond-haired forearm to calm him.

"Okay, but they are radical people and they protest military actions. David isn't involved with any subversive violent acts, Harry."

The vein in her pale skinned forehead expanded with agitation as the waitress appeared to ask if everything was okay. Three voices replied "yes" in a way to discourage her further attendance.

"I still don't see where I fit in," Harry remarked.

"Well, Bernie's been helpful. That homophobic colonel went after David. Beyond foreign intrusion and the pollution at Camp Lejeune, the geographic area around Wilmington is filled with various military sites that may be involved. Bernie was fact-gathering when something changed the case."

"Okay, I'll bite. What happened?"

Dave leaned forward.

"Two people recently died. Colonel Bogart was found dead from a heart attack, and my girlfriend, Jasmyne, fell down some stairs and broke her neck. She may have been sexually assaulted and pushed down the stairs in anger. Rumor has it that Bogart's semen was found on her. The Marines are keeping it all hushed up."

"Was Jasmyne part of the protest?" Harry asked.

"She was present. But she was a thinker—smart, with strong ideas and plans. So yeah...fuck yeah!"

"I'm confused. You say this Bogart was a homophobe, and that was what motivated him to go after you? *And* you imply that he may have raped and murdered a woman, your friend, Jasmyne, before conveniently dropping dead from a heart attack?"

"We think the official version of heart attack and accidental death is a cover for what *really* happened," Carolyn answered. "We think he killed her and was attacking someone else when he dropped dead. You *know* you can't trust the military or the media. Nevertheless, the official plan still threatens David from getting an honorable discharge."

"Our civilian lawyer, JD Henzlein, is sharp as a razor, Harry, but *you* wouldn't like him because he has his own set of open-minded rules, and old Bernie is..."

"Bernie's been helpful," Carolyn interrupted, "but now we're beyond his level of fact-gathering. We want to put pressure on the Marines to allow David to leave on his own terms, with a clean record. You were a Marine with medals, Harry. With Colonel Bogart gone and the campus instigator dead, perhaps they'll offer David some hush money."

"That doesn't sound like anything *I* could help you with, Carolyn. I'm long removed from the Marines, and those medals come with baggage. My recent legal entanglements with the Chicago PD may not help your case. Besides, I'm working on a murder case."

David pushed back his chair.

"I *told* you this was a waste of time, Sis. I *told* you this old guy would be useless. *Fuck* this melodrama! I need to take a walk!"

He rose from the table, tossed his napkin on his empty plate and exited the restaurant.

"I guess that means *he* isn't picking up the tab?" Harry guessed.

"No surprise there," Carolyn laughed.

They glanced toward the vacated chair.

"You know, Carolyn, at the end of the day Dave may need to accept that we are born alone and we die alone. No one will save us from that reality. I don't think I can help you on this."

"That sounds like the old pessimistic Harry I first met on that battered shell driveway in Maine... when you ogled my breasts," she said, grinning.

"Actually it was your... *derriere.*"

"I didn't know you spoke French?" Carolyn examined the carafe of sea shells and reached out to hold his hands.

"Lots of good memories on the beach, Harry Powell!"

They watched David Dodd walk in the distance, like a sullen Neptune. A bikini-clad woman walked past him unnoticed while he watched surfers, gliding to shore.

Harry recalled New York nights, when he tossed on a sweaty mattress, contemplating questions he would ask Carolyn if he ever saw her again. But as with most of his actions—once the opportunity arrived for him to perform, he just blurted out what came first from his heart.

"Why did you leave Maine?"

The carafe of shells tipped sideways, spilling onto the table. Carolyn averted her gaze toward the beach.

"I *told* you. Family matters. *David* needed me. I'm his only blood relative. They were rushing to judgment."

She looked away from Harry toward the beach and her brothers' disappearing form.

"What about *us*?" Harry asked.

Carolyn handled a few of the loose shells from the carafe.

"Remember the *shells* like these you gave me?" "I recall the shell you left on your final note," he said.

"I couldn't take the next step. We were getting too close, and I couldn't be close with anyone but family."

"We were *friends*—I thought friends for the long run."

Harry felt discomfort in the dialogue and wanted it to end. The distant look in Carolyn's eyes conveyed more than any words. Her ambivalent response brought his disappointment toward anger. He handed his credit card to the waitress.

"It was wonderful to see you again, Harry. I know you understand my actions—family always coming first. Genes and all, you know. I thought I could do this alone, but I may have been optimistic. As a former Marine, couldn't you help me out with David? It's tough enough to get a job *outside* the government today, but that dishonorable discharge stigma will destroy him. Bernie has been helpful, but Harry—you're the best."

"I'll always be a Marine, Carolyn. *Semper Fi.* Maybe this Colonel Bogart had a bug up his ass, but I don't believe the system today would go after your brother just for his sexual preferences. And you already have the help of Bernie and this Henzlein, but I'll look into some things for you."

Carolyn stood and they walked away from the table, but Harry grabbed his posies and followed her. When he caught up with her, she turned.

"Still checking out my *ass*, Harry? Or is it my *derriere*?"

Carolyn smiled back at him and they departed the restaurant. He held the posies at his side, depositing the violet flowers in a refuse container as he passed.

~~~~ ~~

Bernie drove Moby Dick into Annabelle's driveway and parked behind JD's Escalade that always seemed like he'd just washed it. While the white barriers of Landfall kept intruders outside the community, it also retained a certain type of person inside. As Bernie maneuvered up the front brick walkway of the ostentatious house with his cane, he considered that Professor Annabelle probably *belonged* here, but that he and Harry didn't.

"Hello, Bernie," JD said as he opened the front door. "Need any help there, my friend?"

"I'm good, JD. *How's* she doing?"

As if on cue, Annabelle came from the kitchen bar with two iced drinks. She handed one of the Waterford glasses to JD.

"Well, *she* is doing as well as can be expected, Bernie. Thanks for asking. Welcome to the wake. What can I get you to drink?"

"Bourbon is good. Neat."

Bernie placed his Panama hat on the glass table.

"Maker's Mark okay?" she asked over her shoulder.

"Fine," Bernie nodded as he followed JD's direction.

The men sat on the living room sofa, like waiting suitors from another century. The Siamese peeked in at the men and quickly departed. Annabelle returned and handed Bernie a glass of amber liquid, filled to the brim. She sat in the embroidered chair and crossed her legs in her conservative navy blue dress. As if directed to coordinate their actions, all three drank in unison.

"I wanted to tell you how very sorry I am—*we* are—about your daughter... about Natasha," Bernie mumbled.

Annabelle inspected the shade of her Bombay Sapphire gimlet. The men froze in silent respect for her mournful pose.

"Not that it matters, but she wasn't my *birth* daughter. She was my *husband's*, from an earlier dalliance. Nonetheless, I loved her as if she was my own, and I want her killer... castrated!"

"The police are working on the case, Annabelle," Bernie assured her.

"*Now* the sons-of-bitches are paying attention—too late! And how much priority are they giving to some unknown student? They couldn't be bothered when she was *missing*! Really, she never had a chance to make a difference in the world."

"Maybe we should remind the cops that she's *your* daughter—" JD chimed in, "an elite member of the community. That would accelerate their actions."

"No. I don't need to be the target of lurid headlines and twitter attacks all over campus. The little shits talking about me and my tragedy? No, it wouldn't help solve anything—just cause a feeding frenzy among the on-line hyenas."

"The police will come to talk with you," Bernie advised.

"They already did. You both know Chief Spano—with his little American flag lapel pin. He came by earlier and told me personally what they found. I appreciated his courtesy."

"In the future, they can talk to *me*," JD insisted, "since I'll be representing Annabelle, as her attorney."

"Representing her for what?" Bernie asked. "I'm sure the police also want to minimize headlines. I have contacts inside the force that will keep me up-to-date."

"I'll talk to my upper echelon connections in the Mayor's office, so we can avoid any lurid publicity," JD pronounced with flair.

"First, my protégé at the University, Jasmyne—falls down some stairs and dies. And now, Natasha is murdered. Oh my! And Bernie—what in *hell* is your boy, Harry Powell, actually *doing* to find who did this to Natasha?"

"Well, now that the police are involved," Bernie mentioned, "are you certain you want us to continue the investigation?"

"Of *course* I do! I don't expect much from a bunch of municipal employee flatfoots to get anywhere. They work best on easy cases— like arresting protestors at a cement plant and slapping them with records for life. Solve a murder? Maybe if they *beat* a confession from some sap! Chief Spano is just a good old boy. He shared very little with me. He's clueless about who did it, and he deferred disclosure on an ongoing investigation. What can you tell me about her death, Bernie? Was she assaulted sexually?"

"Do you *really* want to get into the gory details right now, Annabelle?" JD complained.

He placed his half-filled crystal glass on the table top. Annabelle grabbed a coaster and slid it under his sweaty glass. She looked at both men, like they were undergraduates.

"I want to know *everything!*"

"Can I get you another gimlet?" JD asked rising to the occasion.

"Thank you, darling. Well—*tell* me, Bernie."

"It appears she was abducted—maybe from where she was jogging. She may have been held for a few days. There were signs confirming sexual abuse. The COD—cause of death, was from strangulation and there were knife wounds. She was…"

"That's enough Bernie!" JD insisted upon returning to the room like a southern gentleman, with a drink for Annabelle.

"No, let him continue."

"The killer dumped her body into the water, where a fisherman found her."

Annabelle sat, unmoving. Her finger ran across a swelling tear in her right eye, careful not to disturb the mascara. She re-crossed her legs and worked on the refreshed gimlet. Her restraint set the tone for the men's anticipatory silence.

To both men, Annabelle finally spoke.

"So Harry Powell will pursue the killer, and the Mayor and police will treat this familial linkage with extreme discretion, correct?"

When Annabelle rose from her chair, she shook the ice in her empty glass and conveyed a request for their departure. Bernie gulped his final taste of Mark and rose to depart.

"I'll follow up with all my sources," JD promised as he stood, offering her a supporting hand. Bernie was reaching for his Panama when his cell phone played the Dragnet theme, indicating a text message.

"How quaint," Annabelle, proffered. "Anything relative to Natasha's death?"

"No," Bernie answered. "Another case. Annabelle, I want you to know that I'm also personally spending more of my time on your case. Again, I offer my condolences. If there's anything I can do, please call me."

"I will contact you, Bernie," JD whispered, as Bernie opened the door.

"Aren't you *also* leaving?" Bernie asked JD.

"No, my friend. The professor and I have some *other* matters to resolve. I'll call you later."

Bernie enjoyed the air conditioner cooling as he sat behind the steering wheel. The humidity reminded him of the muggy Midwest summer days he hated. As he heard Annabelle's front door slam shut, he felt an interstitial chill, linking past to the present. Flipping open his cell, he read the earlier text message from his police contact:

Radinsky MO: gerbil insertion

~~ ~~ ~~

Harry inserted quarters into the summer parking meter at Wrightsville Beach. Over his shoulder, he hoisted the worn folding chair and walked to the location where he had earlier met Holly and her children. With a client's child found dead, he sought a one-hour respite.

Most people created habits of repetitive behavior. Such choices made for easier decision-making—where to put keys, what to wear, and when to eat became manageable relaxation. Such behavior was repeated to create a routine that calmed a chaotic life.

He set up the chair at the rise, where sand dipped down to the ocean waves. The Cubs hat protected his face from the penetrating sun. As the hour neared noon, he watched a small SUV park, and he watched the driver organize children and their stuff for the beach. Each child carried a blanket and bag.

Harry watched her lithe body tread over the sand. Her hips swayed in motion, while she flipped black hair away from the cherubic face. Like a hawk, she watched her children run toward the encroaching ocean, appearing oblivious of the solitary man seated in a bent beach chair.

Harry stood as the family neared him. The children were the first to recognize him and diverted their oceanic direction to greet Harry with innocent "Hi's."

Holly stood before Harry, squinting in the bright sun.

"Hello, Holly. I was hoping to see you here."

Harry wished he had a chair to offer her. She carried an oversized beach blanket with the logo of the Toys R Us Giraffe on it.

"Well, Mr. Harry Powell, how are you?"

"Holly, I wanted to call you, but..." he stammered.

The kids raced to the shallow water that crept along the beach. The girl picked shells, and the boy chased a sandpiper. Seagulls floated above them, seeking morsels of nourishment.

"Don't go in without me!" Holly shouted to the children.

Harry gestured to the sand around him.

"Join me?"

Standing there with all the blankets, sunscreen and beach toys in her arms, she made no attempt to unburden her stuff.

"Where is this *going*, Harry? I thought maybe we made a connection, with Memorial Day together and then breakfast, but then I haven't *heard* from you. Do you want a *beach buddy* or something?"

Harry found her directness likeable.

"Please sit, and we can talk—an hour in your day. I brought some cookies for the kids. They're called the Kitchen Sink from Fresh Market. I know they're not the most nutritious, but they're delicious. They contain some oatmeal and chocolate. Is it okay to give them?"

"Sugar overload to bribe my kids, Harry? Yeah, it's okay."

She tossed the blanket on the sand next to him.

"Your *shovels* and pails!" she shouted at the children.

Harry sat in his chair and reached out to help her organize the beach stuff. His tongue felt glued to the roof of his mouth.

"I'm sorry, Holly. I should have called. I became busy with some serious events. The woman I was trying to locate was found... Regardless, I didn't call."

He stumbled for the words.

"Did you *want* to call me, or did the urchins scare you off? You wouldn't be the first man to avoid a woman with small children."

Looking at her, he was again astonished by her beauty. Her arms and legs were taut, like an athlete's— shaped like a woman his mother would describe as 'never having had kids.'

"I got busy... but I guess I was also a little scared."

"You?—the war hero cop scared of... them, or me?"

She moved the plastic toys around to appear occupied.

"It certainly *wasn't* the children. It was more that you are so... well to be blunt—you're so beautiful and young. I just struggled to believe you could be interested in me, so I convinced myself to avoid rejection and chickened out. And as to being a *war hero cop*, I don't recall telling you my career history?"

"You can learn a lot about someone on Google, Harry. You're *way* too modest, really. You received A Medal of Honor? And I wouldn't have rejected your call. In fact, I was disappointed when I *didn't* hear from you."

Harry warmed at the radiance of her smile.

"Sorry. I shouldn't allow work to override my relationships. I've been trying to improve prioritization, and old habits *can* be broken. I'm now working on several cases, one in Camp Lejeune."

"*Really?* My late husband was there briefly," she said.

"Have you ever heard of a Colonel Bogart?" he asked.

"Not that I recall, but I didn't know many people up there, Harry. However, my father-in-law's a big-shot up there—General Sabbatino. Was there a *murder* there?"

"No. That murder case is right here in Wilmington."

"The young woman they found?—dumped in the waterway?"

"Yeah, that's the one."

"And you didn't come to the beach to think about all that stuff…did you?" Holly asked as she watched her children frolic.

"I take an hour here every chance I get. The ocean helps me think. But today, I *also* came here, hoping to see you all again."

For the next half hour, they talked and laughed. Their eyes only left each other to watch the children, who screeched when Harry presented each of them with the "kitchen sink" cookies.

"They have raisins, so they're healthy," he said.

"I don't even want to *know* how many grams of sugar they have," she said.

The refulgent waves splashed atop the clear green ocean and the water crept closer toward their feet. Holly handed Harry a business card from the Visiting Nurse Organization and wrote her private number on it.

"No excuses now, Harry."

"Thanks," said Harry. "Here's my official card as well—because if you don't hear from me, I must be hospitalized or incarcerated."

"You're *and associates?*" she smiled.

Standing, Holly dusted off sand and looked at Harry, who watched her children and not her ass.

He looks like the old Marlboro man cowboy advertisements when I was a kid.

She smiled, caressing his stubbly bearded face with her long fingers.

"I *like* you, Harry. Call me."

"I will, Holly."

Harry remained in his car after the family drove off, images from black and white romantic movies filling his head. He gripped the hot steering wheel and started the ignition.

"This could be the beginning of a wonderful friendship!"

CHAPTER NINETEEN

Lloyd, the hunting pirate, slouched in the vinyl chair at the Hanover County Regional Library. He finished the article in *Men's Health* about multiple orgasms. Reading magazines for free was enjoyable. Using the computers without being traced was also practical and economical. They erased the server every night.

In addition, he could observe staff and customers. A few library regulars might become another list of potential targets, but most missed the attractiveness of church-goers.

He had procured his library card using a driver's license under the name Timothy Hanover, which he obtained from an identity thief at a bar in Charlotte. Wearing no underwear enhanced abrasion from the jeans. He peered at potential targets as they sauntered past him.

Almost all the customers were alone. He preferred going there an hour before closing. On that night the urge began. His urges were becoming more frequent. When his body electrified he was helpless to restrain the urges. He sought fulfillment... *soon.* No time to check on the church ladies. No time to drive north to the abandoned house.

Past the self-check-outs, he noticed the petite blonde girl. She wore skinny dark jeans that wrapped her ass and showed some light between her thighs. She glided like an angel through the young fiction aisle. Hers was a face of pristine beauty. Young, and eighteen at most, her presence begged him to take her, but he hesitated. *Maybe she is too young for me?*

He walked to the other side of the shelves to look into the angels' face, but she had exited the library. One of the semi-regulars arrived. Atop a protruding forehead, she also had black thick hair, obviously dyed. Wearing round-framed green eyeglasses, she plopped at a table. Her legs shined like sausage casings inside violet stockings. She piled up books to review.

Lloyd returned *Men's Health* and grabbed a *People* from the racks. He walked past Ivanka and looked down to admire her shiny exposed legs. Her ass in the tight purple skirt squeezed through the open back of the chair. In the gray library, her red blouse made her stand out. She strutted like a peacock, with several books cradled in arms that covered ample breasts. He knew Ivanka drove a yellow Fusion, with a sunflower on the antenna and a stupid smiley face in the back window.

He watched from the reading section as Ivanka flipped through pages of an oversized book. He peered over magazine pictures of Jessica Simpson and smiled at the hint of an erection in his jeans. But suddenly Ivanka looked up from the books and stared directly at him. *She's caught me watching her!*

He looked down to avoid eye contact, so he didn't know whether she smiled in appreciation or cringed in fear. After counting to ten, he looked up again. She had gathered several books together and approached the check out. Ivanka wasn't blonde or pretty, but Lloyd was ready. *What is it my momma told me? Beggars can't be choosers.*

Lloyd dropped the *People* onto a table as he walked through the electronic monitors and out the exit to the parking lot. He checked all the cars and found the yellow Fusion parked in one of the *quick visit* thirty minute spaces. The location caused Lloyd to smile, since the Fusion faced trees blocking the view from the Landfall office complex.

Behind him were the cars of the few remaining library customers. He started the van's engine and moved directly behind the yellow car, as if he were waiting for a parking space. He opened the van's sliding side panel. His erection thickened when he moved to grab the Ultron taser to make sure it was juiced.

His tool kit sat prepared with duct tape, plastic gloves, elastic ties, eye patch, serrated knife and Cheese Whiz. The only sound in the van came from clicking nails against the cage by his pet store purchase in Leland—the one he called "Little Lloyd." The urge was peaking. *No choice but to grab her now!*

Ivanka trudged across the parking lot with several large books cradled in her arms. She juggled the volumes to reach for her car keys and popped open the car trunk. She never turned to see Lloyd leap from the nondescript van. He was on her in seconds and pressed the taser to her neck, stunning her into unconsciousness.

Books fell into the car trunk as Lloyd tossed Ivanka into the van, slamming the sliding door shut. After closing the Fusion trunk with his elbow, he hurried into the van, driving off without anyone noticing. Ivanka lay unconscious in the back. He drove past AAA and turned left off Oleander Street onto Wrightsville Avenue, which contained restaurants, doctors' offices and one bankrupt shopping mall. Lloyd drove across the empty mall parking lot and stopped at the far end, near shrubs that hid his pirate ship from the street.

He turned off the motor but let the accessory power keep the air conditioner going. From his kit, he wrapped the black eye patch over his left eye. After locking the van doors, he climbed into the back. Ivanka remained unconscious as Lloyd sniffed her feint lemon fragrance. She began to stir.

He was more experienced using chloroform, so he wasn't sure just how long to apply the new taser, but he was learning. He wanted his victims unconscious, but not too far gone to miss the fun. While climbing over the prone body, he marveled at her soft roundness and she smelled lemony. He removed his boots and jeans.

Sometimes he calmed victims before proceeding. It all depended on the stage of his urges. On that night, he was too far gone for games.

Ivanka moaned when he pushed onto her stomach. He zapped her again with the taser to limit any struggle before she was well restrained. After yanking off her garish shoes, he cut away her purple skirt and red top. The big red lace bra remained in place for the moment. He fastened plastic ties around her flabby wrists and caressed the silky violet stocking covered legs.

Excited, he rubbed himself against her pliant thighs and delicately peeled the stockings off, enjoying their feel and savoring the final withdrawal at her feet. Bending forward, he held her bare left foot in his hands while he licked her toes, causing her to utter a small groan. He tied each foot to the van's side wall with an elastic tie. The ties were strong but had flex to allow movement, like he preferred.

He hadn't held the taser long enough, as Ivanka was awakening. Tearing off a piece of the gray duct tape, he plastered it across her mouth to keep her sounds muted. He didn't want her totally silenced, or part of his fun would be diminished. A sweet citrus scent came from her, like lemons, and maybe that explained why she had a yellow car. He looked out the van windows to see cars driving past on the distant roads, headed home. No one came into the abandoned mall.

He pulled plastic gloves over his hands, pausing to admire his full erection and readiness to have her. When she squealed, he noticed her head lifted up, with bulging eyes. No doubt she was awake. He savored the fear on her face and watched the sweat beads gather on her forehead. *I have all the power now!*

He held the twelve inch hunter's serrated knife to her face and whispered.

"If you scream, I'll cut off your tits and eat them. Are we clear?"

Lloyd adjusted the eye patch over his left eye as she nodded. He peeled off the tape, ready to reapply if she shouted.

"Please! I'll do anything you *want*. Just don't *hurt* me!"

He smiled and felt his erection grow harder, and touching her lip with the knife, he grinned.

"I'm going to do what I want. I *own* you now, Miss Ivanka Fields."

"You *know* me?" she stammered, but she said nothing about recognizing him from the library.

"You are a Virgo, try to eat like a Vegan, but you sneak burgers at Five Guys and go to the library every Wednesday after work. You work in a boring office with a bunch of nerd accountants, who find you an exotic friend in their dull world. Your favorite color is yellow and you wear citrus cologne. You should be more careful sharing. You might attract the wrong type of… friend."

"I'm having my period," she whimpered.

"Really, is that true? Oh goodie! I *love* cherry juice!"

He noticed that she was shaven "down there." He liked that, but would need another trophy source. The urges surpassed his restraint. Jolts passed through his arms and legs, but they focused in his manhood. He had no more control. After he slipped on a Trojan, he entered her.

Dryness demanded that he push hard and she started to scream, so he pushed the tape back over her mouth. The harder he grunted, the higher she squealed. Resistance made it all more enjoyable for him. After finishing, he watched tears drip from her big eyes. Her white belly jiggled on the van's zebra throw rug.

Gripping the handle, he used the knife tip to slowly cut parts of her bra. The material was flimsy for such full breasts. Ivanka began to spasm in fearful sobs. All he could make out was "please," which gave him satisfaction. Straining against the restraints proved useless.

Leaning down, he bit her nipples until they bled. He licked the blood off her big, soft breasts. She jiggled like Jello, so he named her "Jello Yellow." He looked up into her whimpering face. He accepted time for recuperation to have her again, but maybe that would be easier once she stopped breathing. He used the knife to poke holes in her skin and felt aroused each time the blade penetrated her. Blood oozed out. He liked that, too.

He glanced around the interior of his van as it became darker outside. Pirate memorabilia stared at him, like an audience that admired his work and goaded him to rape and plunder. He felt like he complied with what his ancestry demanded. *Maybe I'm a reincarnated pirate, and all this is just fulfillment of who I've always been?* As a child, the urges confused him, but his true destiny became realized in the shadow of Cape Fear pirates.

After another half hour of enjoying her squirming and whining, he reminded her of his power.

"I *own* you!" he whispered into her ear.

After another hour, Jello Yellow seemed to be fading away. He removed a small wire cage from the side van wall, displaying the cage before her mascara-stained face with bloodshot eyes.

"This is little Lloyd. He's very hungry and he wants to *eat* you!"

Her eyes bulged out of their sockets. Lloyd could feel hot urine as she released on his knee which caused him to slap her face for such an unsanitary display.

"How dare you *piss* on me!"

Both his hands tightened the duct tape across her quivering lips.

"Jello Yellow—this is Sir Little Lloyd, the Fourth. He's going to be your new friend."

Ivanka Fields strained against the ties as Lloyd spread her legs wider, which only increased the bleeding.

"I own you, wench, and I'll do whatever I want!"

Atop Ivanka, his eye patch was in place and knife held in his teeth. He twisted off the top of the Cheese Whiz, speaking to the small brown gerbil in the cage.

"Hungry enough, little Lloyd?" he asked in a child-like voice.

He used the knife to calmly spread the orange cheese into Ivanka's hairless opening. A couple of days without food made the little beast very hungry. Mice served the purpose on the Indiana farm, but this was a more refined location.

"Here you go, Ivanka. *Feed* the famished creature, he wants to live. He wants to revenge his ancestor's death at the hands of a heartless bitch like you!"

He lowered the cage between her legs and let the gerbil loose. It nibbled at the cheese trail and crawled inside Ivanka. She screamed and tore against the ties so hard that she tore her flesh. Lloyd moved swiftly, untying her left ankle from the van wall and hooking it to her right ankle so that the gerbil could not exit the way it entered. He had designed a one way street of famish fulfillment.

Ivanka's enlarged eyes darted about in panic, while Lloyd sat there, lubricating himself with blood from his knife. Lying face-to-face with Ivanka, he watched her stare at him with hopeless fear. Her continual high pitched screeching elated Lloyd as his hand caressed her black hair. He pulled off the wig and the short blonde hair aroused him some more.

"I'm a pirate, and you are my booty! Can you feel Lloyd, the Fourth? He's inside you now with his cheese appetizer. Next, he'll be eating you, *devouring* your insides. What you denied to people like me who looked at you, he will take. And what happens when little Lloyd is all full? Sadly, he'll suffocate and die, and then it will be my turn again.

"Do you *like* that? You begged for attention with your smells and colors. You displayed your shiny legs to taunt me. I know you wanted to be taken and now you are. I totally control you, don't I? Can you feel it? Just nodding is okay."

As he held her closer to him, Ivanka tried to nod, but she rolled her eyes upward and passed out instead. Lloyd held her, resting the blade against the furrows of her neck. He squeezed her tight, like she was a life preserver. Finally, he closed his eyes and rested.

The van remained in the dark corner of the abandoned mall parking lot for another hour before he drove off, unnoticed. Everything wasn't perfect though. Lloyd had decisions to make. Water destroyed forensic evidence, and there was so much water in Wilmington. He missed filling a body farm, like the one he cultivated in Indiana. With choices, he had so many decisions to make, and so little time.

~~~~~~

David Dodd left the cramped restaurant to enjoy the incessant waves disrupting the calm shore—like the plans for July Fourth, when *actions* would wake America from a malaise. He rejoined his

sister near the restaurant exit. Carolyn reached up and caressed the
hair behind his ear.

"Looks like you'll need a haircut soon."

"Are you giving Harry Boy trim?" Dave asked, studying his
sister's reaction.

"Harry and I are old friends. No need for jealousy. You didn't
need to piss him off… or do you just *like* doing that?"

"To some people, I do."

He reached out for her hand.

"You certainly didn't help him identify with your position. He
now works with Bernie, so it was only a matter of time before he was
asked to look into your situation. Better he thinks he's on our side
than coming aboard late as an interrogator. We need to keep Harry
close."

"I'd like to keep *you* closer," Dave growled, drawing Carolyn
toward him.

He rested his hand on her shoulder and placed his lips against
hers as his tongue entered her open mouth. Their shared heat
exceeded the southern temperatures. A senior couple walked past
them and considered the young couple kissing, and smiled at their
youthful passion. Carolyn held David's hand, as they walked to the
car and a meeting with their lawyer/consultant in his office.

JD Henzlein positioned his chair to sit taller than all his guests,
so that he could look down at them. Upon their arrival at the real
estate office, he jumped up from his chair.

"Hello, my friends. Come in! Come in. Can I get you some sweet
tea?"

"You got a beer?" Dave asked.

"Sorry, we don't have beer," JD laughed. "This is a place of
business, but we can meet for some brews later."

"Iced tea would be fine for us," Carolyn nodded.

JD directed an associate to bring the beverages. He fantasized
about Carolyn, bent over the edge of his desk under him. Dave sat,
while his nimble thumbs pecked away at his smart phone engulfed in
playing Candy Crush.

"JD, now that Colonel Bogart is out of the picture, when do we
have David returned to good standing?" Carolyn asked.

"I'm working on that, Carolyn. As you know, Dave, there are several balls being juggled at once here. This morning, they made another offer—Non-Honorable Discharge, which is a step up from Dishonorable—and all charges are dropped, with the record expunged. You would enter civilian life with a clean slate. What do you say, Dave?"

"That's not *good* enough, JD." Carolyn answered. "He wants a clean Marine slate, an Honorable Discharge. No deal. What about compensation for slandering his good name? I know the military likes to hide any inconvenient truths. Can't we use the leverage of media fear to extract *more* from them?"

"Carolyn, you *know* David hired me before you came south. It's his call," JD insisted.

Dave looked at his sister and shrugged his shoulders.

"I just want to move on," he mumbled in a non-committal manner.

"Look, JD—and no offense, David—but *he* doesn't have any discernible *skills* to serve him in the crowded unemployment lines. A *job* is what he needs, which will be extra tough with this non-honorable bullshit. They could offer him a *financial* settlement!"

Carolyn sounded like an attorney, pleading her case.

"Maybe they could, but they aren't going to offer any compensation to *my* client, when at one point they were going to throw him in the brig," JD answered, shaking his head. "This isn't *like* a civilian situation. *You* were in the Army, Carolyn. You should know how they work. They don't *appreciate* Marines protesting on campus."

"But the campus protest leader, Jasmyne Nissim, is dead," Carolyn insisted, "and their Colonel may have raped and killed her. You have no business with those protesters now, do you, David?"

"This is all bullshit!" he answered. "They're *homophobes* and we all know it! *That's* what this is all about. Fuck em!"

Glancing down at the table, Dave continued.

"And those *people* you disdain include Jasmyne's brother, Karim, who is a peaceful protestor and student on the WC campus. He puts out a blog in his mother's basement when he's not attending classes. Bogart *invented* motives just to screw us!"

JD looked over at the handsome young man who he totally misread when they first met.

"All this because of your... *sexual* preferences, Dave? Unlikely," JD said, wagging his head.

"What about headlines featuring a Marine Colonel, persecuting gays and raping a student protestor? How would the Marines like that?" Carolyn asked.

"Rape is pure conjecture, my friend. We... or *you* can speculate all you want, but I don't see how this will benefit Dave. The official report says Colonel Bogart died of a heart attack and the woman tragically fell down some stairs. They weren't even together when their bodies were found, and the evidence is now sealed. In addition to your Marine lawyer—as your civilian attorney, Dave, I must recommend you take the deal. If we wait too long, say after July *Fourth*, another colonel may decide to vigorously pursue these charges."

"What's July fourth got to do with anything?" Carolyn asked, glaring at the men.

"*I* understand, JD," Dave sighed. "Give us a day to discuss this and we'll get back to you."

JD and Carolyn both looked at Dave with surprise at his initiative for resolution.

"I need to use the head," Dave announced as they exited into the office foyer.

As he stood at the urinal and relieved himself, JD appeared next to him, but he didn't unzip.

"Tell your boys we're ready to go on July fourth. Don't let your sister get in the way. And what *should* be obvious to you is that after that show, the Marines won't offer you shit. They may even—"

Dave zipped up and turned to JD.

"Take the deal and don't tell Carolyn shit. Rock and I will be gone after July fourth, and I want the legal paperwork solid so they can't retract anything, okay?"

"Okay, my friend. Besides, there are *debts* to be paid off."

Dodd played Texas Hold em with overconfidence. But he needed to pay off Internet debts to some overseas crime syndicate. He had agreed to help Karim create a demonstration with money supplied by some rich donor client of JD's, who hated the military presence. He and Rock obtained materials for Karim.

Following the holiday display, they would leave Wilmington forever. Cash would pay off Dave's debts and leave enough seed money to open a surfing shop in Costa Rica with his soul mate, Rock.

"I get it, JD. Timing is everything in life. We take the deal in writing now and use the interim access to attain more... tools," Dave concluded as he washed his hands.

"And Carolyn doesn't *know* anything, right?"

Dave grabbed JD by the shoulders with wet hands.

"Look, my sister has nothing to do with this shit. It's *our* deal. You get the fuckin cash—we get the weapons. We do our thing on the fourth, and then I'm done, right?"

JD looked up at the flushed face of the massive man to whom violence wasn't theory.

"You'll be home free, my friend."

Dave dried his hands, while JD handed him a blank white business envelope, filled with cash to facilitate the acquisition of G4 explosives.

"Still seems *extreme* firepower for a message!" Dave commented.

"*My* area of concern—not yours," JD advised.

Dave looked inside the envelope, but he didn't bother counting the money.

"Good. There are guys always willing to sell shit for the right price. And those private dicks are staying out of all this, right?"

"Don't *worry* about those guys—they aren't Holmes and Watson. They don't know anything about our July fourth events. But your sister is too close. She *worries* me."

Dave brushed his hair back and looked in the mirror at JD.

"I can control Carolyn. I help you, and then I'm debt free—*my* own Independence Day."

The two men exited the men's room to meet Carolyn, who waited. Unsmiling, she grabbed Dave's arm and led him outside.

"What was going *on* in the men's room, David?"

"*Nothing*, Sis—just some bullshit. I wasn't giving him *head*, if that's what you thought."

He smiled, but Carolyn didn't. After jumping in the Toyota, he resumed his electronic game, while Carolyn slid behind the steering wheel, feeling deceived, dirty and angry. She slammed the door and squealed out of the parking lot.

Back in his office, JD leaned back in his chair, inhaling the aroma of fresh coffee. He saw trouble brewing with Dave and Carolyn. He preferred simple people with obvious motivations. Sometimes Dave was gay, and at other times he was straight— sometimes he was an activist, but he was also a money-grubbing gambler.

And his gorgeous sister, Carolyn, seemed desirable and toxic on different days. JD would be glad when he didn't have to deal with either of them again. He enjoyed being surrounded by young women, who sashayed about him in the office—even those he hadn't screwed yet offered the enticement of silky movement and aromatic allure. He was like the Shah in his *Kasbah*. He never hired a man. *What was the point?*

Women were usually sharper and far better to look at. And even the airheads deployed in showing properties offered occasional blow jobs to remain employed. With the deals coming, JD would be set.

Jennifer peaked into his open doorway.

"Mr. Mannion has arrived."

"Bernie—my friend, welcome. Have a seat. Can Jennifer get us some of her hot… coffee?"

"Thanks, I could use the caffeine, but iced might be better," Bernie answered as he watched Jennifer walk away.

"She has a nice ass, huh, Bernie? You can take a shot, although *you* got that Goth wacko in your office."

"KiKi? She's not a wacko, JD. She's a nice young lady. I couldn't run the office without her." JD leaned back, raising both his hands in defense.

"Sorry, no offense intended, my friend. Now let's talk business. The investment deals you said you would be interested in along the Cape Fear Riverfront downtown. Your presence indicates you're still interested?"

Bernie leaned forward.

"I'm always interested in good investments, JD. A cop's pension doesn't cover everything a man desires, and I'm checking out a new boat."

JD leaned forward, smiling like a shark.

"Well, let's just say that, based on my *connections*, there are some lucrative deals available. The chance to buy in now and make a killing in six months is available for someone with *cash*."

Jennifer returned with their coffee and departed. Then JD reached for papers on his desk.

"Is this illegal, JD? I can't get caught up in any scandal that could jeopardize my police pensions!"

JD frowned.

"*Illegal?* No, not *illegal*, my friend. I'm a lawyer. And our elected officials wouldn't be involved in anything illegal. It's an opportunity to take advantage of future events that will make a killing. Not like that bullshit point-zero one percent the banks are paying. We'll *double* our investment in six months. No risk at all. Upfront cash is required. I personally put half a million into it. If you can…"

"Whoa JD—I'm a retired cop. I don't have half a million. Plus, I need to see some facts about the deal."

JD shuffled through the papers on his desk.

"Surely, you could borrow a hundred thousand from your pension, no? Maybe take a short-term advance from the cash value of your government life insurance. Just realize certain other investors are part of the decision team that will also profit from events, which are directly in their control. I'll give you a list of the properties our consortium, The Wade Hampton Realty Trust LLC, will buy, and then we share in the resale profits in six months. Tax free, by the way. It's simple—we buy low and sell high. Maybe we even receive a government bailout, if something catastrophic happens."

"Like what? Fire, flood, a hurricane?" Bernie asked.

"Shit *happens*. It's coming up on the hurricane season. You know, some sharp people got *rich* in Louisiana from the government payouts after Katrina, as well as that BP oil spill. Like some weasel politico said—*Never let a crisis go to waste.*"

JD slapped a couple of pages with fine print onto his small private copier. He handed the copies to Bernie.

He had no need to share all the details. After the July Fourth fireworks and explosions, the buildings would be declared structurally unsound and smoke damaged. Several investors were leaders who would declare the buildings destroyed. Property owners would receive huge checks from insurance companies and the Federal Agency.

"This is confidential stuff, Bernie. Tell no one, so we make more money. What amount can I count you in for? A hundred?"

Bernie looked at the names on the list handed to him, which included elected officials, who could control decisions. He gave JD a positive nod.

"So *this* is how the rich guys get richer? If you're in for half a million, then I could borrow to double my investment. Boats aren't cheap. I'm in, JD. Make it two hundred."

Bernie reached across the desk to shake hands with the smiling lawyer. He considered mentioning the office break-in but deferred for now.

"Excellent. You're in, my friend. After all, what's life but pussy and profits?"

JD laughed as Bernie stood and put on his Panama hat.

Bernie drove back to his cheap storefront office, which he hated. He hated the humid weather that made him sweat through every shirt he owned. He hated slow moving traffic. Most of all, he hated never having enough money to buy whatever he wanted. *That'll end in a few months with this JD deal.* But he loved the smiling face of KiKi Sanchez, who greeted him as soon as the door opened. Without any forethought, he handed the papers from JD to KiKi for proper filing—a fatal error.

CHAPTER TWENTY

Harry stood alone on McRae Street before a building that resembled a hospital. The glass-front entry witnessed few uniforms, going in or out. Plainclothes entrants swiped pass cards for access. Viewing the Wilmington Police Department from an outsider's perspective reminded Harry of his peripheral role. He was outside, looking in—no longer a part of the blue team that caught criminals.

Several officers were smoking as they talked to Bernie outside the smoke-free environment. Harry approached the trio of protruding stomachs.

"Hey, Harry. Guys—this is my associate, Harry Powell. He was on the job with me in Chicago a hundred years ago."

He slapped Harry on the back.

The men offered perfunctory nods without any name introductions. The men had little need for names, as they already knew Bernie and didn't give a shit about Harry. Besides, the word was out that Powell had linked with Chief Spano, their boss.

"The guys were sharing a little tidbit on the Radinsky murder, Harry. It seems our killer shoved a hungry gerbil up her pussy."

Bernie spoke in the vernacular of his former peer group that demonstrated a commonality with them. All but Harry laughed.

"But when I have to go, the last days of that gerbil ain't bad. I shared my MO info from Indiana. Almost ten years ago, the goat farm murders occurred. This killer could be some weird copycat. Or maybe our killer is Rip Van Winkle and just woke up. Now he's travelling across the country."

Cigarette butts hit the pavement.

"Well, guys, here's my cousin's police phone number in Lebanon, Indiana. His name is *Robert* Mannion. He can tell you all about the victims they found."

He handed his business card to each of the local cops and walked back to Moby Dick, with Harry beside him.

Harry paused.

"I thought *I* was lead on the Natasha Radinsky murder, Bernie?"

"Yeah, well Annabelle wanted some assurances from me. Plus, with the MO found here, I had the info from my cousin. It can't hurt to improve links with the rank-and-file locals. Besides, with all the databases, like VICAP and HSK for serial killers, interstate crime quickly involves the FBI. So we can assure Annabelle that we assisted and earn billable time. Nothing to do with you."

"We don't need duplication of efforts," Harry insisted.

"Why? So you could go to Chief Spano and be a hero? It was *my* intel from Indiana that made the link."

"I was looking into this case at your direction, Bernie. I came here to help you, not to compete for billable hours!"

Harry felt annoyed, but he wasn't certain why.

Bernie acts like a college freshman away from parental controls for the first time. Chasing women too young and boats too big with money he didn't have.

And worse, he assuaged his ego by sharing info with the cops and not his partner. For the time being, Harry had to *help* identify a killer. The men parted ways.

Bernie climbed into Moby Dick, slammed the door and drove off. The hula girl on his front dashboard wiggled. His car phone signaled a *317* number, from Indiana.

"Hello, Robert. Long time no hear from. How are things?"

"Hi, Uncle Bernie. I thought I would call with an update on that farm I told you about. Final body count is twelve women—all under 30. Cause of death is strangulation with multiple knife wounds. "

"Any suspects yet?"

"Not a one. Checking out the property ownership and rentals became a dead end. It's looking like a very cold case at this point. No DNA was found, so he obviously used a condom," Robert remarked.

"Let's hope *more* than one," Bernie joked.

"What? Oh yeah, condoms! Is there anything new with you?"

"Same old shit."

They were about to disconnect when Bernie considered that family ties mattered.

"Hey kid—you want to be a *hero*? Go to your big boss—alone, and tell him you discovered that a dead body with the same MO just turned up in Wilmington, North Carolina. You'll be the star of the Lebanon Police—and maybe get some *national* attention."

"Are you kidding me, Unc?"

"No, I'm serious—dead serious."

Harry read the *Wilmington Star-Gazette* headlines about a young woman murdered in Wilmington. There was no mention of the bizarre MO, or any links to Lebanon Indiana. They didn't even mention that Natasha was the daughter of a prominent local professor.

Clearly, the goal to avoid tourist panic, influenced a low-key approach and inference to a hook-up gone badly. The blurb included that the deceased woman was an exotic dancer, probably to allay public concern that the deceased was *like* them. No doubt the newspaper reporting was influenced by local officials and public concern. Eventually, that cooperation wouldn't sustain, and the truth would spill out like a gusher.

Upon entering the PI office, door bells and a chilly climate greeted Harry, but they had nothing to do with air conditioning. Bernie huddled over his desk on the phone. KiKi stared at the computer, with a pen in her mouth, barely nodding. Harry flopped at his desk. He had felt more value rousting drunks in the Albertson Hotel lobby.

Harry reviewed pink forms that KiKi used for missed phone calls.

"Can I get you a coffee?" he asked KiKi.

Showing great surprise, she looked up at him under the day's pink-striped hairstyle that matched her pink stretch top.

"Sure, thanks. I take…"

"Light crème with two pumps of sugar-free hazelnut, right?"

"Yeah. Thanks, Harry."

She smiled, nodding. The paperwork kept her focused. As directed, she shared nothing about the work with Harry.

Harry gestured to Bernie about coffee and received an okay, along with something to eat. Harry figured an *everything bagel* with a spread, as usual. Sharing food encouraged shared thoughts. He imagined cave people sharing ideas over roasted dinosaur.

He returned with the coffees and a bagel for Bernie.

With Bernie seriously occupied on the phone, he addressed KiKi.

"You ever meet Natasha Radinsky?"

"The professor's daughter? No. But it's *horrible* what happened."

"You've met Professor Annabelle Radinsky-Wade, I presume?"

"Once. Apparently, she didn't like coming to our humble office. When she came in, her nose was up and she ignored the hired help—meaning me. She's a bigwig at the university, and I am just a lowly community college student."

KiKi looked over the coffee cup as she drank the hot beverage, peering at Harry.

"You're looking for her daughter's murderer, right?"

"Yeah, I am. But I'm not getting too far."

"You know her death affects all of us? In Zen, we are *all* connected."

"I've heard that philosophy. I suppose it has some truth. But how the situation of a Sherpa in the Himalayas affects me escapes my simple brain…"

"*I* think we're all connected. So even if I didn't *know* Natasha Radinsky—what happens to her happens to me, like a tossed pebble ripples the still waters of a lake."

Harry listened and nodded. The older he got, the more he realized how little he knew.

"KiKi, did you happen to know about a private eye named Janakowsky?"

"You mean that guy with the crinkly hands who always gave me that creepy look? Like *he* could still get it up!"

"Yeah well, he ended up alone and dead in New York City. Any idea what he was working on?"

KiKi showed no reaction to the fatal news.

"No idea. He came here maybe once or twice and met in the back with Bernie. That last time I saw him here, he appeared enthusiastic about something. I think he used to be a PI around here for years—mostly the skuzzy divorce stuff, I think. I recall cheap suits and not enough deodorant. They never had me do any filing or anything."

"Wasn't he *one* with you?" Harry asked, smiling. KiKi laughed.

"*Touché!*"

"Are your parents still around, KiKi?"

"No. they both drowned near Bald Head Island. They rented a boat for a day and ran into a sudden storm. They left their little daughter—who would be me—with a neighbor."

"I'm sorry to hear about their demise."

"Hey, I had great grandparents who raised me. How about you?"

"My mom died in her nineties. She got sick and lingered in a weakened state, until she told the doctors to let her go. My dad had a heart attack and died suddenly. No death is better or proud."

"Anyone's death *does* diminish all of us."

"What happened to Natasha Radinsky should never happen to *anyone*," Harry said. "Please be careful."

"Warning me? I have no enemies, Harry, or is it because I'm a defenseless woman?"

"Well, the Radinsky killer chose a woman here, and there may have been more. There are evil people who perform unspeakable acts—sometimes without any link to the victims."

"There are also plenty of *family* members," she added, "who do horrible things—even to children."

Harry observed her decline in cheeriness.

"That's true. Most murders are done by friends and family. Over seventy percent of murder victims know their killers."

"You ever have children, Harry?" she asked.

He paused, wishing he were elsewhere.

"Yeah, I even had a grandson. But they're all gone now. Take care of yourself, KiKi."

She nodded as he tossed the empty cup in the refuse.

"Thanks, Harry," she said in a whisper, "for listening, for caring."

She returned to her computer screen and ended the conversation.

"Go find a killer, Harry."

As Harry headed for the front door, KiKi shouted.

"*You* be careful, Harry Powell." She waved a goodbye.

He began reviewing as he drove off. He found no links to a killer for Natasha other than to an MO from a serial killer of the past or some crazy copycat. The FBI would deploy VICAP to scan for a pattern of similar MOs. Harry believed that a killer in Indiana was about to unveil a similar trail of death in Wilmington. Killers go to jail for reasons other than murder, and Harry assumed the FBI would examine recent prison releases.

Harry used the hands-free car unit and spoke with his police source in Indiana, Ginger Adams.

"...the exact location off Interstate 65 where the twelve bodies were found. They'd been dead almost a decade. All corpses had the skeletal remains of a rodent inside them, inserted pre-mortem."

"*All* of them? *Gross!*" Harry cringed.

"Investigators haven't located any suspicious former property owners. Several renters came and went, but none were considered suspects. The land was in foreclosure, and the house was abandoned for years. If it weren't for an entrepreneur, digging to build a new restaurant, the bodies may have remained hidden for another decade. The FBI now believes the perpetrator moved elsewhere or died. At this point, they seem to have no person of interest."

"Tell me more about the victims," Harry insisted.

"All the dead women were in their late twenties to early thirties. None were pregnant, but a couple had previous abortions. Several were identified as waitresses, and a couple was probably hookers. None were married when they disappeared, and one victim had a boyfriend in jail for drug distribution. All had blonde hair, or hair that was dyed blonde. Two of the women were-light skinned blacks, two were Hispanic and all the rest were white. All had been sexually abused, and there was some evidence of a ritual torture, with knife slashing. COD was strangulation. The guy just pressed down on their throats until they suffocated."

Ginger paused.

"The ME believed the killer had post-mortem sex with several of the women."

"This guy's really *sick!*" Harry said.

"The FBI owns the case now and is rechecking the Highway 70 corridor. It isn't uncommon to find lot lizard hookers murdered. The victims were mostly white trash or minorities that didn't carry the priority appeal—as if some rich white woman had been murdered in her Carmel estate.

"Like your rich white woman in North Carolina, right? Watch the heat turn up. Maybe *America's Most Wanted* will pick up on it. Meanwhile, when the Indianapolis 500 race crowd came to town, the news media became bored with old scary stories that had no resolution. As you probably know, Harry, eighty percent of attacks on women are sexually-related."

"Thanks, Ginger. Keep me updated with any new news. They're keeping the MO quiet here for now to avoid panic."

"Sure thing. Come see me anytime you're back in Indy. Good luck."

Pursuing a killer, Harry felt energized. As usual, he would share what he learned with Chief Spano, and hopefully the FBI manhunt would be like a contained one-hour Criminal Minds episode that ended in the perpetrator being captured. But Harry knew it took talent, time and lots of luck to find a random killer.

Usually, the break came when the killer made a mistake along the way. Criminals were aware of the forensics today and protected themselves. There hadn't been any real identifiers, except the creature insertion MO signature. Harry wanted to prevent more murders that were otherwise inevitable. He owed something to Natasha.

Maybe KiKi was right about everyone being connected. He became upset, envisioning the burial grounds in Indiana and the fact that the victims had few mourners. This sick killer had to be captured soon.

His phone indicated a call from Chief Paul Spano.

"We found another body of a murdered young woman, Harry. 187."

Harry's hands clenched.

"Who is it?"

"She was in the little pond near the library this time. Geese were gnawing at her arm. Her name is Ivanka Fields. You ever hear that name when you talked to people about the Radinsky woman?"

"I *never* heard that name. Is the library the branch just outside the *gates* of Landfall? Is there any surveillance video?"

"That's the location. Their security cameras are limited and grainy, but they got her entering the library and then leaving alone. There was a skinny guy with a ball cap and shades who seemed to follow her, but we can't tell much. Looks like a hundred other guys. Now with two murders here, the Feebs (FBI) will be all over this. One of their nerds told me about the picquerism—fancy talk for the cutting slashes. I just thought you should know that your Radinsky wasn't his last victim."

"What *about* the woman? In her twenties, blonde?"

"Relative to the other women, Harry, there's one strange thing—she was kind of full-figured and had dyed *black* hair, but she was actually a natural blonde. You told me the victims in Indiana were mostly blonde, but how would our killer know that about Fields?"

"Maybe the perp is getting impatient, decelerating, or maybe he's not as consistent as the profilers theorize?"

"We don't know much about the victim yet. And keep *this* real quiet from our Wilmington friends, Harry—but it appears the insertion MO was repeated—a gerbil. The FBI is now rechecking all pet store purchases, but there's not much security. We're trying to keep this from the local media, but when the word gets out, I can only imagine the crude headlines. We'll have sensationalist creeps from everywhere!"

"This won't be quiet for long now," Harry remarked.

"By the way, the governor chimed in on the investigation. First, they wanted it kept quiet, and now they want answers *yesterday*. The Feebs have fully taken over, but this is still *my* town and these last two victims are *my* people. My team has got to find this guy fast. He's in Wilmington, and I see no reason he'll leave soon. All hands are on deck, Harry. The Feebs don't like outsiders since they think only they can solve cases. You ever work with them?"

"The FBI are mostly young guys who joined the Feds after college and worked twenty years, climbing the ladder. They're usually pretty sharp, but they're also politically savvy careerists with limited field experience."

"Not many have been cops," Spano added. "I can tell you a detective in a big city after *one* year has solved more cases than a *twenty*-year FBI agent! But they do have big budgets and high tech tools and resources to do a full blitz."

"Teamwork is the key to success, Chief. We use all the tools by all the investigators to grab this guy and prevent more victims."

"No more murders in Wilmington. All hands on deck," Spano repeated before hanging up.

CHAPTER TWENTY-ONE

The air conditioner increased intensity as Harry continued driving. He focused on a serial killer from Indiana, who presently stalked Wilmington women. The Indiana killings of twelve souls spread out over three years indicated a resident. *An apparent respite had passed, but could anyone be certain?* The Feds would check any incarceration record that coincided with bodies found with this weird MO.

If it's the same guy, a Federal database might show who lived in Indiana during those killing years and now resides in Wilmington? If the killer was a tax-paying employee or on any public aid, there should be a paper trail. Maybe even the same credit card used in the two states. Harry thought a moment and realized that he and Bernie oddly fit that description. Harry didn't believe much in a copycat, since Indiana hadn't released the MO information that only the original killer would know.

Harry called the manager at the T&A bar, and she told him that Natasha had done some extracurricular pole "dancing" at the Pussy Galore Club.

He found the strip joint blended among welding auto repair stores. The seedy exterior became darker and smellier inside. During the day, stale beer permeated the air in the lifeless club. Daylight exposed poorly painted walls, with cracks and mold. The night would hide blemishes as the focus moved to human flesh on stage.

"You're a little early for the show," a raspy female voice called out.

"Oh, hello—sorry. I'm not here for the show. My name is Harry Powell, and I've been hired by the family of Natasha Radinsky to try and find who killed her."

"Son of a bitch! I thought cops did that. Are you a cop, Harry?"

"I'm just trying to help a client. I'm a private investigator."

"You look like a cop, Harry," she said from behind the bar.

"I used to be one years ago."

The woman leaned across the bar, displaying ample freckled cleavage. Against pale skin, red lipstick dominated a worn face under shiny pink hair.

"I'm Bunny. I manage this joint. Can I get you a drink?"

She extended her hand and held eye contact with him before releasing his hand.

"No thanks. Did Ms. Radinsky work here?"

"Tash worked her once in a while. She filled in for the regulars. She had a sweet body, but her gyrations were kind of pedestrian. I bet you like an agile woman. Am I right, Harry?"

Harry watched Bunny's thin hand rest on his forearm. A green lizard tattoo crawled up her forearm.

"When was the last time you saw her?"

"Like a week or two ago. We don't exactly keep precise records here."

Bunny's smile exposed a gold front tooth.

"Was any one paying special attention to her?"

"The regulars know not to bother the girls on stage. They just leer and drink. If a stranger acted funny toward the girls, the regulars would probably kick his ass."

"Did Natasha say anything about taking a trip?" Harry asked, considering what Spike had proposed.

"No. Nothing. Not that I talked to her much. Was *she* the body they found near Wrightsville Beach?"

"Unfortunately, that was her. Let me leave you my card in case you remember anything else. You can give me a call."

Bunny twirled the business card in her fingers and looked up at Harry.

"Hey Mr. Private Solutions—anytime you want to stop by, I have an office in the back for... private meetings."

"Thanks, I'll remember that."

Harry smiled and rose from the bar stool to depart, glancing at Bunny, who suddenly remembered something.

"One *other* thing, Harry—there was a guy here a few weeks back that I hadn't seen before or since. He was pounding beer specials and kept telling everyone he was a pirate. The guys ignored him, and he finally left. I can't recall if Tash was dancing that night."

"You remember what he *looked* like?" Harry asked as he thought about the library surveillance.

"Vaguely—he looked just like lots of guys who come in here... with a stained tee shirt, old jeans and hair that never saw a brush. Nothing stood out about him... except I recall he wore a Weston

Van Lines tee shirt, as if that meant anything. We got guys who wear Panthers shirts and they couldn't tackle *me*."

Harry thanked Bunny and departed.

Wasn't the library victim followed by a thin guy in a tee shirt? A moving van company job would fit the killer profile of someone who moved around a lot with cash income without records. Several phone calls to Chicago later, Harry was clear Weston had no local employees, except truck drivers.

He returned to Natasha's apartment. The car keys remained on the kitchenette table. Upon closer inspection, it hit him: *these car keys have a small Mercedes logo on them, like the professor's car. Natasha's Prius keys are missing, indicating she took her car.*

Harry made some calls and learned that the abandoned Prius was located in the municipal parking lot next to the Wrightsville Beach History Museum—near the running area where Natasha's body was found. Further checks confirmed that the Prius presently sat in the city garage, after having been towed for an extended parking violation. The dates from ticketing to towing confirmed her abduction time.

Harry called Spano. Forensics found nothing suspicious inside the Prius. After sharing his suspicion of a moving truck driver link and the car situation indicated she was grabbed while jogging, he added another observation.

"Chief, in the video at the library of the skinny guy following the victim Ivanka—did the photo show any logos on the tee shirt?"

"We got more side shot, so nothing visible. Just a tee shirt and a black baseball cap pulled down over his eyes."

Harry recalled his conversation with Bunny. "Was there a *P* on the cap?" Harry asked.

"No, we don't know. We didn't get a heads on shot, only the side angle. Why?"

"Just curious if it was a Weston tee shirt, like a guy watching Natasha dance at the Pussy Galore Club. This guy claimed to be a pirate. If the guy at the library had a black ball cap with a *P* on it— like the Pittsburgh Pirate baseball team, there might be some link. It may be the same guy, a transient mover type."

"I'll check this out and share it with the Feebs," Spano assured.

A light mist speckled the windshield as Harry drove to revisit the Wrightsville Beach area. This time, it was *on* the hour, so he had to wait for the drawbridge to lower after a sail boat passed. He realized the killer was either local and knew the bridge schedule, or was just plain lucky that the bridge was down on his escape route after dumping the body.

In Indiana, this guy kept the bodies buried in the ground. Now he dumps them in the water—twice. While submersion obliterated forensic evidence, what are the serial killer's trophies now, and where does he keep them? Spano told him that no trophy removal was obvious, *but who knows? Where does he torture his victims? Perhaps this guy uses a van, like that nondescript white one seen at the library, like a roaming domicile... for a roving pirate?*

He still waited at the powered bridge when his attention shifted to his vibrating cell phone.

Carolyn sounded like an intimate ghost from his past.

"Hi Harry. How about tonight—the dinner we *talked* about? Just you and me—like old times?"

"That's fine. Watch yourself, Carolyn. There's a psycho killer loose around Wilmington, and you could be a target."

"Sometimes you sound like my father, Harry."

"Maybe uncle or older brother," Harry laughed.

"Thanks for your concerns, Detective Powell. See you at dinner."

Harry questioned his earlier warnings to KiKi and then to Carolyn. *Does it matter? This killer will take who he wants when he desires. The only way to stop a serial killer is to kill him.* Killing him would save countless future victims, but Harry could never overcome lost family opportunities—even if his efforts saved a hundred strangers. Yet, his present focus would escape yesterday and expect enough tomorrows to justify his existence as a man who caught the bad guys.

The bridge lowered, allowing his return to the city.

~~~~~~

KiKi was working alone, making copies of the supposedly "secret" documents that Bernie gave her, when David Dodd strode into Mannion Detections. His incredible hulk filled the doorway to the extent that his head almost hit the doorbells. Looking like he'd just come from the beach, he was dressed in a sleeveless tee and colorful flag swim trunks, hanging past his knees. He pushed wraparounds atop his sun bleached, Iroquois cropped hair.

"Hey Babe—is Big Bernie here?"

He smiled at KiKi and acted like he possessed charisma, despite the projected disingenuous arrogance that she found annoying. She remained seated, since she had met Dodd several times before, and he always treated her like some obligatory hurdle to get what he wanted.

While his physical representation may have excited some women, she found him more like those steroid-induced body-builders who went too far in their grossly-narcissistic portrayal.

"Mr. Mannion is out on a case, Mr. Dodd, isn't it? Can I take a message?"

She removed the pen from above her ear to write on a pink pad, aiming her hateful laser gaze at the man, hoping he would take the hint.

"Oh, I guess nothing crucial. We're just working on some fireworks. Just let him know I came by. I wanted to talk to him about some questions he had. Yeah, tell him to call me back on my cell. I'm going out to catch some waves."

"You want him to call you about some fireworks, and?"

She wrote the note and made little effort to appear like she cared. She used the acronym "AH" for Dodd—the *Ass Hole*.

"Yeah, tell him it relates to his Big Bang Theory." He smirked. "Thanks Babe. See you around."

He returned the sunglasses to his face and flashed the toothy smile. KiKi laughed at how AH's attempt at a cool exit failed when the door bells tinkled. She couldn't figure out the way the dude acted. He was gay, so it couldn't be a *legitimate* flirt.

Maybe he's a switch-hitter who chases every orifice? What's with his message about fireworks anyway? What's going on here? Bernie is working the court martial case of AH and was involved with Slick Willy in downtown building purchases, but what is this with fireworks? Did this have anything to do with the break-in? The hints piqued her curiosity.

Her bejeweled fingers glided across the computer keyboard, searching for more information. She believed everything could be found on search engines. After all, everyone knew she ran the investigative office. However in this case, for the additional information uncovered, she would have been better off *not* knowing.

~~~~~~

Carolyn Dodd Morderca had free time before dinner with Harry, and St. Matthews Church was on same road as the restaurant. A sign indicated afternoon confessions. She wandered the lobby and found a room labeled *Sacrament of Reconciliation*, where a Father Rodrigo sat. Carolyn entered the room and immediately regretted her decision.

Long unfamiliar with Catholic rituals, she awkwardly kneeled before the man in a black cassock. *Where are the screens to hide my identity?* She sought forgiveness from the God he represented.

"Forgive me father for my sins," she uttered.

In a whisper, she shared her war time actions, mostly silent neck-snaps of enemy lookouts. The priest looked down in receptive contemplation as she generalized her sexual lust without reference to partners. After a pause, she decided against confessing any civilian activity, for fear that the priest might be legally bound to report it. *I never intended to commit sins, and if there's no intent is there any sin? Protection of family exceeded all other laws, doesn't it? Perhaps the absolution might help.* Father Rodrigo blessed her and told her to say ten Hail Mary's for penance. "I will pray for you, my child," he said as she stood.

After departing the confessional, Carolyn kneeled in a pew to pray in contrition. She didn't recall the exact words to the *Hail Mary*, so she winged it. *God will understand.* Others prayed around her. Several older ladies in floral dresses said the rosary, and a woman with a bathing suit visible under her outfit sat with her identically dressed daughter.

A thin man in a tee shirt and jeans sat by himself. Carolyn felt the man's eyes trained on her. *This isn't unusual on the beach, but in a church?* Maybe the warning from Harry biased her attention to the potential of a stalker. She was relieved when the man stood and departed church.

Carolyn prayed to Mary, the mother of a God she didn't know. She could never forgive those who attacked her. Turning her other cheek wasn't an option. Anyone who threatened her family threatened her. Staring at the massive Jesus statue in the church, she wanted to believe that He would forgive her for everything. Catholics believed that forgiveness and redemption were always possible.

Prior to her departure, Carolyn stood and genuflected. As she approached the Toyota, she clicked the doors open sooner than usual. *Am I paranoid to feel predator eyes?* The parking lot was almost empty, except for a few SUV's and a banged-up brown Ford in the priest parking spot. She closed the door locks and turned on the ignition. Inexplicably, she looked in the rearview mirror for any movement, but she saw none. She drove to her dinner with Harry.

From the barely visible spot in the corner of the church parking lot, Lloyd Curtin sat in his pirate ship, fingering his bleeding ear lobe. He had replaced a hanging decoration and inserted the earring found after Auntie's funeral, but the pain still throbbed. When Army Girl exited the church, his attention shifted. He started up his van. *How lucky is this meeting with Army Girl? I just stopped at the church to take a leak. Maybe our interaction is predestined.*

He followed her gray car. Urges began to grow beyond his control. To stay close to Army Girl, he pressed down on the accelerator. Images filled his head as he accepted that he had no choice but to fulfill these unstoppable urges. *There's no sense being a pirate, if you don't pillage and rape.*

CHAPTER TWENTY-TWO

Army Girl drove past beach crowds and parked near her condo. After retrieving mail, she walked casually, unaware of being observed. Lloyd Curtin sat in a van across the parking lot. He watched Army Girl ascend the stairs, lusting for her tight ass atop shapely legs. Arousal made him adjust how he sat.

He peered out the window. The sliding glass doors opened on the second floor, and Army Girl looked around. Now he knew exactly where she lived! The crowds returning from the beach began to party around him. *No one can observe the grab!* Another day would soon arrive when he would take Army Girl as booty in his pirate ship and do what he wanted. *Soon, very soon!* He drove away in frustration.

After showering, Carolyn dressed for dinner—lacy black bra and panties under a short black dress that she slipped over her head. She dabbed Vera Wang perfume behind her ears. The wine bottle was half empty. She exited for the restaurant, selected for its romantic ambience.

Harry waited for her near the waterway as the setting sun created a sky of pinks on the distant horizon behind the white sails of docked boats. In Maine, he and Carolyn were approaching a special relationship, when she suddenly ran off. There were no Virginia Wolf histrionics. From his experience, life wasn't like a stage play with wordy confrontations.

Relationships mostly just faded away in silence, and yet her departure felt sudden and inexplicable. *Family situations don't mean total cessation of current relationships, do they?* Despite trying to forget, her departure continued to pain him. He abhorred old fools and disparaged becoming one.

When she appeared before him, she was as dazzling as any view of nature. Together they walked into the dining room of the Blue Fin Restaurant.

"You look wonderful. Nice place!" Harry remarked, as he looked about the dining room.

"Thanks. I hoped you'd like it. And *you* left the Cubs hat behind!" Carolyn said as she sat in a chair, offered by the host.

Harry wore the blue blazer with khaki slacks, a button down shirt, boat shoes and no socks—as dressy as he got. Carolyn sipped Pinot Grigio, while Harry reverted to his sweating Amstel from the bottle. Across the patio, a piano man played Billy Joel tunes.

"What's on your mind, Carolyn?"

"It's just a reunion of sorts, Harry."

She raised her wine glass to offer a toast.

"To the future—with old friends."

Carolyn clinked her wineglass against Harry's beer bottle.

Maybe it was just the absence of a pony tail, but Carolyn seemed different to Harry. Cascading blonde hair framed her pretty face—though not quite the same fresh face he'd met in Maine. She appeared to have morphed into a serious woman, with a distant, haunting look. They talked about life in the South. She asked about New York. He asked about North Carolina. Several rounds of drinks diminished the restraint.

"You know I came here to help David, but why did you *really* come to Wilmington, Harry?"

"Bernie asked for help, claiming his left leg was broken."

"*Claimed?*"

"Turned out he fractured a small bone in his foot that required a light walking cast for a week. Maybe he was lonely?" Harry laughed.

"I see. Why do you think he really asked you to come down here?"

Harry drank the cold beer on the hot night, appreciating life's simple pleasures. The beautiful intelligent woman also helped. *Tonight should be about the future and positive outcomes.*

"I'm not sure. Maybe he thought he was doing an old friend a favor by rescuing me out of the funk I wallowed in New York. I had hit rock bottom, Carolyn. I had just been fired from a lousy job and had nothing…"

He sipped the beer.

"Sometimes, what appears to be the case often isn't? When David called me in Maine, I was irate that he was being persecuted for being gay. Now, I see his nefarious friends may have something going on beyond campus protest. But we aren't here to discuss Bernie or David. How is your delightful cottage on the ocean?"

"It's in a legal purgatory. Some title issue in Maine, so it's being resolved by lawyers, but it won't be mine anymore."

"I don't mean to be a Debbie Downer, but I almost hate to ask, because I understand your reticence to talk, but... about the *car* accident?"

She finished her second glass of wine and signaled for refills. His shrimp and her catfish had arrived.

"What can be said? The truck crushed their car and killed them instantly. I heard the truck driver was texting, but who knows. *He* survived. Kathy and Christopher were coming to visit me... to make up for all the lost years. What can you *do*?"

Carolyn leaned back.

"May I ask, *how* did you lose touch with your daughter?"

"After my wife was murdered in Chicago, I felt our little daughter would be best raised by my wife's sister, who was like her second mom. Elizabeth had other kids and a husband—a full family. Decisions made in an instant change lives forever. I thought that was best for her, while my daughter came to believe that I had abandoned her. There were long nights of regrets for what I *didn't* do. Kathy became a strong, intelligent, independent woman. She wanted me to meet my grandson, Christopher. Hey! I thought we were here to talk about tomorrow, and not yesterday..."

"I'm sorry. But you remain a life preserver for people in trouble... like for me in Maine."

"It was *more* than that, Carolyn."

"I know, Harry. I know... the feeling was mutual back then. But as you know, life can become quite complex."

"And I'm a simple man who wouldn't understand?"

"I didn't say that, Harry. You're deeper than you want others to think. It's just that David's friends *bother* me. You know—a gut feeling? David is naïve about some things and people."

The waiter brought another round of drinks.

"You departed Maine to save him... or to escape from me?"

"Why do men always think everything is about them? It's not about you, Harry. In Iraq I received a medal, but I wasn't any hero. I survived a brutal attack that... that left me... reluctant to sustain intimacy with anyone who wasn't family. You've seen my scar, but there was worse damage internally—not something you write on a postcard."

Her eyes glistened and he held her hand atop the table.

"So what happens now? I understand your brother's situation is near resolution, and Bernie can run his agency without my help. Where does that leave us?"

Carolyn caressed Harry's paw like a doe touching a bear.

"I don't know, Harry. I feel strongly both ways. Didn't *you* tell me about Yogi Berra and coming to the fork in the road?"

"Yeah, you *take* it," Harry laughed.

Their awkwardness melted like the ice in their untouched water glasses.

"Well, I have my Army pension and a job at Thalian Hall. What are *your* plans, Harry?"

"Survival, I guess. I don't have a clear view of tomorrow."

"You could still catch the bad guys, and Wilmington is a great place to live. You have the ocean and…"

Carolyn squeezed his hands and leaned across the small table to offer her lips. He kissed her. Memories flashed before Harry as he dove into her eyes. For that moment, he believed in redemption.

"You know, Harry, my apartment is nearby, if you're interested in… dessert?"

She raised a thin eyebrow and looked at him with an alluring smile, her cheeks reddened.

"Are you sure, Carolyn?"

As Carolyn looked down at her hands, her smile diminished.

"I think so."

She nodded with a slurred voice that told Harry she'd had too much wine. Encouraging words, but he saw a distant look and a heart closed. *Perhaps all those shared silences under the stars in Maine were due to her reluctance to share deeper truths with me?*

Despite lonely nights in New York, where he imagined such an opportunity, the situation didn't feel right. *If she wasn't offering a sober heartfelt "yes," will I be taking advantage of her?* She noted his hesitation.

The waiter cleared his throat at that inopportune time.

"We have the most scrumptious desserts, like Key Lime pie, or perhaps an after dinner drink?"

In the disdainful look Carolyn shot at the enthusiastic waiter, Harry recognized the Carolyn he'd met since he came south. He recalled a scene from Broadway's *Jekyll and Hyde,* where the lead actor altered his voice and appearance to instantly change characters and expose his façade. Before him, Carolyn became almost as two-faced as Jekyll.

"No, thank you. Just give me the check," she said curtly.

"I guess I'm not a spontaneous type of guy," Harry admitted.

Carolyn pulled out her purse and produced a credit card for the waiter. He watched as she suddenly seemed hurried to leave the restaurant, and him.

Harry reached for his wallet.

"I've got the dinner, Harry. After all, I'm the employer. Besides, Mannion Associates would just bill this meeting back to me anyway."

She prepared to leave.

"*Meeting?* I thought this was... personal?"

"I guess we were *both* wrong about tonight, Harry."

She signed the bill and rose from the table, with a slight weave in her departure.

"Good night, Harry."

"Maybe I should drive you home?" he suggested.

"Please, I'm quite sober. I don't need any pathetic patriarchal attempt to protect me like... I'm your daughter."

She walked with a flourish through the cacophony of diners up the wooden nautical stairs to the parking lot. He started to follow her, but he stopped and watched as she drove away. Immediately, he challenged his decision and wondered if this had been the worst choice of his life—*or the best?*

~~~~~~

JD Henzlein parked under the yellow awnings, which were the only thing new about Louie's. The diner sat in a strip mall with a Dollar Value and Chinese take-out. Where some modern places mimicked the retro 1950's look, Louie's was the real past, unfettered by improvements. As promised at their funeral interaction, Lloyd Curtin shared a meal with JD Henzlein.

"Thanks for the grub, bro," Lloyd gushed, jabbing a fried chicken thigh toward JD. A tattoo of a grizzled pirate with an eye patch and a knife in his salacious mouth stared up at JD from Lloyd's left bicep.

"Yeah, I thought we could catch up here," JD mumbled as he dabbled with his brown leafed salad.

Lloyd's crooked smile exposed several pointed yellow teeth.

"Is Ruth Chris closed?"

"I thought here was more private, since I have a business proposition for you. How much do you make moving people?" JD asked, offering Lloyd his business card.

"I supervise relocations, bro. I make fourteen bucks an hour—off the books, plus bonuses. I now get unemployment checks, too. But..."

"What kind of bonuses are you paid?"

Lloyd spoke through a mouthful of food.

"The five-fingered bonus, bro. Like when I find some shit for takin—it's a bonus, see..."

"You mean you *steal* stuff from the people you're moving?"

"No shit, yeah. Most people we relocate got so much crap they never miss one little thing or two. And if they *do* notice something missing, the insurance covers it. Everybody does it. Man, we're just redistributing the wealth."

"Well, what I'm considering is more serious than pilfering cuff links," JD offered.

"What? Like I don't read the papers? I see where the Cultural Archaeology people or somethin recovered a canon from Blackbeard's ship, man—right here in North Carolina. Our grandfather pirate still lurks! No tellin what that crazy cat buried under houses along the Cape Fear. We have rights to that booty, don't we, dude?"

"No, we don't. I don't know from where you're drawing this mythology of a pirate lineage. We had a few poor relatives in the Port City a century ago. They mostly picked peanuts, and I never heard anything about real pirates in the family tree."

"Maybe not on *your* side of dear old daddy's planted sperm seeds, but my momma's momma fucked sailormen that parked their boats in the Cape Fear Harbor, and surely buried doubloons in the cellars just like they plunged their dicks into the local pussy."

JD examined the disheveled man whose eyes seemed to be dancing.

"*Parked* their boats? Are you tweaking again?"

"No, man, I'm clean."

JD shook his head in disbelief.

"Anyway, I thought I may need your help in fixing a problem is all," JD said, beginning to regret approaching Lloyd.

"That must mean something illegal—else wise you'd do the shit yourself, right?"

Lloyd wiped his face and grabbed another piece of his greasy feast.

"You know we lost touch when you were incarcerated and…"

"I was in prison."

"Regardless. How far would you go to make a buck, Lloyd?"

"Depends on the buck. Money talks, bullshit walks. All the way, I guess. You got somebody bothering you?"

Lloyd's yellow teeth tore meat off the bone.

"This is a contingency plan, where I may want to eliminate some minions."

JD pictured the trio he called the stooges. After July fourth, they wouldn't be anything but witnesses. *What did one of my law professors say? 'If your car hits someone, better to reverse and drive back over the victim than to leave a witness.'*

"Eliminate? If you're fuckin wheedling about asking me if I would off somebody for cash, the answer is yeah!"

Lloyd continued shoving greasy chicken into his mouth.

"How much cash we talkin?"

"Keep your voice down, Lloyd. Maybe a thousand. That okay with you?"

He wondered how Lloyd remained thin eating so much, surmising drug abuse.

"Two sounds a lot better!"

"Two thousand each? There's no way!" JD scoffed.

"Each? You gotta big fuckin deal goin down, bro? How many?"

JD raised three fingers.

"You figured you got this pirate in town. He's been a jailbird, but now your bro can serve a purpose doing shit for you? You may dress all fancy, but deep down, you know we ain't no different."

JD placed his fork on the table, leaning toward Lloyd.

"We are *half*-brothers!"

"And our old grandpa pirate married your mama but not mine. You got the fancy education, while I wound up with shit in land-locked Indiana."

"What do you want, Lloyd?"

"Gimme five for stiffing the three… and a grand cash up front. Then we gotta deal."

JD smiled. He came prepared to pay ten thousand for the three hits and got away with half that!

"Deal, my friend," JD nodded as he shook the proffered greasy hand of Lloyd Curtin.

Under the table, JD squeezed a small plastic bottle of alcohol cleanser into his palms to sterilize his trembling hands. *Had he just made a deal with the devil?*

CHAPTER TWENTY-THREE

"You got the whitest face here, boy, but don't fuck up," the bearded man warned Lloyd.

The truck driver examined his arms.

"No drugs when you're working, and you lift what I give you, got it?"

The men stood at the depot, where moving van drivers selected crew to relocate people for the national moving companies.

"I do a day's work for a day's pay. I can lift as much as any fat slob here," Lloyd assured him. *I been down this road before.*

The tee shirt Lloyd wore prompted the question.

"You ever work for Weston?"

"Yeah, lots of times!"

He wasn't about to tell him that he found the tee shirt in a garage.

"Okay, sure. Well, we're loading the Mayfield truck tomorrow at Masonboro Loop, and we're headed up to Williamsburg, Virginia."

"Can I hitch a ride in the truck?"

"No room. You've got to provide your own ride there and back. I give you a hundred a day, and you pay your own way, got it?"

"I dunno. I need a place to sleep, and motels cost like fifty a night up there."

Lloyd avoided eye contact. He figured he could weasel a few more bucks, even though he could sleep in his van.

"Look, shithead—it's a day loading here and travels and unloads up there. Actually—two days total time, and I give you two hundred cash. Sleep wherever you want. You want it or not? I can get somebody else right here, right now!"

"Okay, I'm good," Lloyd mumbled.

The urge throbbed again for another woman, and maybe a road trip was just what he needed. Wilmington had started to feel crowded.

"Okay. Be at Masonboro Loop at eight sharp tomorrow morning, and if I smell any shit on you… your ass is gone, got it?"

The next morning, Lloyd carried the heaviest loads to show off his strength. The other loader wore ear plugs and talked to no one. The driver boxed and arranged. Before noon, they departed.

Lloyd followed the moving truck in his pirate ship on the road north to Williamsburg, Virginia. He fantasized about what the pirate would find in the Colonial Capital. Before unloading the truck, Lloyd parked his van around the corner from the house. He could smell the hops odor from the Budweiser manufacturing plant nearby in the area called Kingsmill.

The client walked around in a starched shirt, with sleeves rolled up like he was working. This guy was a professor, who was joining the staff at William and Mary College, and who made over six figures. Lots of heavy-ass boxes with books. Not a lot of loose stuff to give Lloyd an opportunity to pilfer.

The wife didn't seem the type for much jewelry. Lloyd figured her for someone who sat a lot. *Not only too old and ugly, but Mrs. Professor has a husband lurking about.* Lloyd finally grabbed a shiny silver Cross pen that looked like it was worth a six pack.

They completed the job and Lloyd stuffed two hundred bucks into his Wranglers. His urge for a target grew intense. Opportunity abounded in Williamsburg, as tourists filled the streets. Pieces of black electrical tape applied to his license plate converted the number ones to fours and threes to eights. As he pulled the Pirates baseball cap over his forehead, he laughed that he had never been to Pittsburgh.

As he drove around the campus of William and Mary College, he felt history talking to him. *This is where the governing elitists lived.* Williamsburg was almost the opposite of the rebellious pirate history—like in waterfront Wilmington. Summer traffic slowed progress among the old brick buildings. Where once great patriots mingled among these edifices, Lloyd, the pirate, roamed the streets. Inside the buildings that Lloyd would never enter, college teachers filled the heads of wealthy students with their own biases. And none of those educated snobs could change the oil in an engine like Lloyd.

Locating the sign for a pet store, he parked and made his purchase. Carrying the baby ferret back to the van, Lloyd recalled his mother screaming after he had a urine accident during the night. The image stained red as he gripped the steering wheel tighter.

He cringed, recalling that morning when her sausage-like fingers fed a writhing Skippy2 into the sink compactor. She glared at little Lloyd when she flicked the grinding switch. Blood and guts splattered onto the sink—Skippy2—gone forever. Lloyd stood in the doorway and howled a soundless scream, while she scolded him.

"Stop pissing on the sheets!"

Lloyd drove aimlessly. There were more families visiting Williamsburg at that time of year and less attention paid to him. His great grandfather had been a pirate, and even though JD denied any linkage, Lloyd knew that genes were always passed down.

Maybe it was reincarnation that allowed Lloyd to recall these streets. He imagined an ancestor being hanged in Williamsburg after being convicted for crimes along the coast. He figured that, centuries earlier, the Curtin men who preceded him scoped streets like these for targets. *They probably had the same urges as me.* Behaviors never changed, it was in the genes. Months on the ocean made for randy men in a town with willing women. The beginnings of the new country called America loomed all around him.

He eased down a side street with a bookstore and a restaurant on the corner. Workers were discharged and tourist shoppers were tired. He waited and watched, but he soon became impatient.

He walked around the cobblestone streets. At the stockade blocks, he paused to examine where incarcerated prisoners were punished for the entire village to witness. He felt like he had been there before. *Maybe an ancient uncle ended up here, caught doing nasty things in the capital.* Lloyd felt a part of this American history, carrying on a tradition, the legacy of crime.

As the sun settled, he returned to his parked van. The ferret slept. Down side streets, he resumed driving in search of a woman. History buffs wandered back to hotels as a peaceful summer day came to a close. Parking lots began to empty. Children were returned to hotel rooms. Plenty of trees offered cover. He sought only one woman.

Then he saw her, walking alone on the sidewalk. Maybe she was past thirty, but she had short, blonde hair as she sashayed toward a line of parked cars. Her ass raised high, like a younger woman, though her neck betrayed some mileage. Atop khaki shorts, she wore a pink top. A *Barnes & Noble* plastic bag with a Poe caricature on the side hung from one hand. She spoke into a bright pink cell phone as she approached several parked cars.

Lloyd drove next to her. He slowed and leaned across the front seat out the open window.

"Excuse me, Miss. I'm kind of lost. I'm supposed to deliver some books to the college bookstore. Am I near there?"

She looked at him and kept talking on the phone. Her lightly-tanned face highlighted pink lipstick beneath a large nose. To Lloyd's consternation, she didn't approach the van and ignored him. She accelerated her pace down the street. She pointed her hand at a silver car, and its taillights blinked as she approached the roadside door.

Lloyd pulled down hard on the brim of his cap. He slipped on the surgeon's gloves and encouraged his oncoming erection. He shifted the van into reverse and skidded backward toward the silver car. Leaping from the driver's seat, he slid open the side door of the van. His right hand grabbed the woman, while his left hand tasered her. She dropped her phone and keys. Lighter than he expected, he tossed her into the van. Slamming the door shut, he got in and drove off.

He grinned as he looked in the rearview mirrors. Preoccupied visitors and bored workers—*no one saw anything*. Driving through the crowded intersections, he entered the quiet residential streets.

"Gotcha, Pinky!" he said to the unconscious woman.

From the shattered pink cell phone lying in the street came a tinny voice shouting, "Evelyn, Evelyn… what's going on?"" The phone was crushed by passing cars.

Meanwhile, Lloyd drove to a darkened, tree-covered street near the closed, restored colonial houses.

The next twenty-four hours were the worst of Evelyn Nesbitt's life. Squirming against the duct tape, she pleaded for mercy, which only enhanced Lloyd's excitement. He liked how she smelled of sweet strawberries, until she wet herself in fear.

She would be tortured, raped and sodomized, cut repeatedly and beaten. The last words Evelyn Nesbitt heard were whispered into her half-bitten ear.

"Ignore *me*? Do you *know* who I am? I'm worth a hundred of you! I'm the Pirate King and I *own* you!"

After he inserted the baby ferret into her, she eventually passed out in pain. Atop her, Lloyd squeezed her wrinkled neck until she ceased to whimper. His thumbs pressed down on the bones until her life spirit passed from her into his hands.

When her breathing stopped, his sexual release was encouraged. He lay next to her with her ass pressed into his crotch. Eventually another urge demanded his insertion into her. During the night, the van rocked unnoticed near a closed Revolutionary War Tavern just past the stockades.

All the history buffs had vacated the darkened streets and the colonial homes were mostly unoccupied. Lloyd believed ghosts of his criminal ancestors had watched his attack and encouraged him. His activity on the dark colonial street continued the timeless pursuit of rape and pillaging by a misplaced pirate, who eventually fell asleep.

In the dark early morning hours, Lloyd awakened in the van. He smelled urine and death. After tying the used condoms for later disposal, he wanted to be rid of Pinky, but he tempered his immediate desire with a plan. He slid Pinky into the wheel well under the plastic covered mattress.

He drove at the city speed limit south towards Wilmington. Between there and Williamsburg, he considered disposing of Pinky in the miles of woodlands. He liked the idea that coyotes would destroy identification and Pinky would return to nature. While he knew the water in Wilmington had been good to blur forensics from the cops, he missed his life-size trophies. He now had a place.

He stopped at a Marathon Gas station to buy another cold six-pack, glancing at the headlines of a newspaper in a machine: *Goat-Man Serial Killer in Wilmington.*

The water burials aren't working. No matter, he had a place now. At the unfinished house, he could begin another collection.

He passed Jacksonville and Topsail Beach, and soon drove through Hampstead. As he neared the northern tip of the Wilmington city limits, he made a sharp left turn off Highway 17. The tattered and abandoned *Willow Estates* sign welcomed him. The gravel road led into an incomplete building development that had been abandoned. A partially-built model home sat behind the weed-infested trailer office. He had camped here with Auntie's treasure chest. Now it would become his domicile.

As indicated by the relatively small Henzlein Realty sign, Lloyd figured his half-ass half-brother wanted to ignore that failed investment. Lloyd would eventually coerce Jeff into letting him officially crash in the unfinished model. Summer weather meant no need for electricity, which worked out well, since none was connected, but Lloyd had added a sleeping cot and the ice chest for beer.

He pulled the van to the back of the house and dumped the beer and ice into the cooler. A couple of small rats or large mice scurried along the foundation. Blocked visibility from the road simply reconfirmed his choice. Like his ancestors, squatter's rights made him a homeowner.

Sandy soil allowed easy digging among the weeds. He retrieved his booty from the van and scraped a shallow grave and dumped Pinky in. This way, he could always have her nearby in case he wanted her again. Before he covered her with dirt, he snipped hair to add to his collection. After covering the grave with coastal Carolina dirt, he sat down on a step and popped open a can of icy cold beer and drank in peaceful satisfaction. The pirate had initiated a new farm for cultivation. Lloyd beamed at the vast space that invited him to contribute more trophies.

~~ ~~~~

JD Henzlein ranted on the phone.

"This little Goth bitch thinks she's going to extract money from me?"

"She didn't seem like the extortion type. She doesn't know shit about all we have planned. Give her a few bucks, you got plenty," Dave said into the Bluetooth ear device as he drove south to meet Carolyn.

"Yeah, *smart* guy—maybe I should give her *your* share!"

He knew telling Dave the truth wouldn't help—telling him that KiKi had attempted to protect her boss, Bernie, from getting into some illicit deals. What gall she displayed, threatening him with exposure if he didn't bail out Bernie from the real estate scam. *Who the hell is she? Not a lawyer, for sure.*

"Hey JD, she's nobody—just a secretary. What could she know about explosives and smoke bombs? You want me and Rock to scare her, maybe slap her around a little? I got no love for her anyway."

JD owned the real estate investment scam. Rock and Dave knew about a fireworks demonstration and damage to the USSNC, an unoccupied symbol. Annabelle invested money, but she didn't want to know too many specifics for plausible deniability. Her boy, Karim, knew all the details about the symbolic as well as actual target for MLF—to destroy the munitions plant MOTSU. That wasn't JD's goal. He was the juggler and these fools were his tools. He knew what separated class levels in America- cash.

Bernie must have leaked the real estate scam deal to his girl. Somehow she found incriminating links—like maybe the news report on missing explosives? Who knows what's on the net today? Some people were too clever for their own welfare. JD wasn't going through so much without the monetary incentive—like he'd never kill somebody without taking their jewelry and cash.

"Slap her around would do exactly what? She's smarter than I thought and has a big mouth. And with her connections to two ex-cops, she spells trouble. If they see bruises, they'll ask questions. We don't need interference—especially right now. *You* may be gone on July fifth, but I *live* here, my friend!"

"We can select body parts no one will see. When they're paid off, extortionists don't usually squeal. What does she know about?" Dave asked.

"Apparently, she knows enough to expose too much—if she isn't paid. So she needs to be shut up." JD demanded.

Portraying the girl as greedy would help motivate the hulk.

"If you *aren't* going to pay her, what do you want, JD?"

"It's what *you* want, Davey, my friend. You want to go to prison? All this ties together, and the Marines would love to be fed information that implicates you with fraud and a terrorism rap. You will never see the light of day again, pretty boy!"

"Terrorism? You mean some smoky explosions in a peaceful demonstration? No way is it terrorism, man. What are we going to do to shut her up?"

JD thought aloud.

"You pay once and you keep paying. What do you *think*, Dave? Despite the shrinkage from steroids, maybe between you and Rock, there's one set of balls?"

"Wait a minute! We can't—" Dave protested.

"Well, if *you* can't take care of things, then maybe someone *else* in your family can."

Dave punched off on the device in his ear and continued driving while opening another beer. Jacksonville to Wilmington was a six-pack drive. He considered JD's threat and knew he wasn't going to return to the grasp of Marine justice. Incarceration would definitely inhibit his Costa Rican surf shop with Rock.

He pulled off the highway and parked at Carolyn's condo. She was cooking dinner for him that night. He had brought a chilled bottle of German Riesling. That night would be an improvement on the old days, without an audience—days when their mother encouraged her children's closeness for her own viewing pleasure.

The humid evening drew sweat as he climbed the stairs. Before he could knock, Carolyn opened the door, dressed in a black silk robe. Her toenails were painted a bright red.

"Come in, dear David. I've been waiting for you."

Dave grinned as he entered. Carolyn sat on the couch with her legs crossed, motioning for him to join her on the couch.

"Damn, I left the wine down in the car!"

"Here's a Blue Moon for you. I already have a Pinot Grigio. Sit down here and relax."

"While driving here, I thought of how Momma made us share that tiny bed together—how she explained that there wasn't space for two beds, and then she sat there smoking and sipping a Bacardi and Coke while encouraging us to—*cuddle*. Remember?"

Carolyn smiled softly, rubbing his thigh as she spoke.

"Of *course* I remember!"

The opening in the black robe exposed her pale leg, through the slit.

"You and I stuck together then. You told me that you would always protect me," he mumbled.

"David, you know that I love you more than anyone *else* could, right? I will always protect you, you're my *only* family."

"Well, I need your help now. Someone wants to *hurt* me."

He shared the threat to his freedom posed by KiKi Sanchez, and then he lay back on the couch and stretched out his long legs.

"I won't *let* anyone hurt you, David."

Carolyn slid her left arm behind his head and stretched her right leg over him, like a praying mantis. Holding his head in both hands, she kissed him and forced his teeth apart with her tongue.

Sheryl Crow sang from the speakers as Carolyn straddled the man beneath her. If it felt so good, it had to be right.

No one will ever harm my brother. To defend your family and their freedom isn't wrong.

CHAPTER TWENTY-FOUR

Harry chewed chilled grapes and watched waves crash from his wobbly beach chair. He never saw television procedural cop shows portray a detective just thinking about the case. A *Wilmington Star-Gazette* sat in his lap, but his mind worked to fill a large blank slate, registering notes. In reality, detection meant more thinking than car chases and shoot outs.

It had been only a matter of time before someone leaked the connection between the murders in Indiana and the women found in Wilmington. The media ate it up as a chance to sell more copies with the titillating content. The Internet flooded with reports and myriad blogs about the relocated serial killer. Yahoo News even carried a reporter's fantasy, implying the killer may actually be part goat, based on reports of the nearby goat farm. Another inferred a link to the colossal bronze statue in Detroit of Baphomet, the goat headed demon.

Headlines decried the *Goat Man Strikes Again.* The FBI came to Wilmington and took over the investigation. The G men were embarrassed by their failure thus far to identify a person of interest in the killings in Indiana and Highway 70 rest stops. They had searched national databases like VICAP, and a massive manhunt was underway. Law enforcement reputations were on the line, and the way in which the media framed the progress would enhance or diminish careers.

Harry considered the deaths of two women—a young woman he never met, filled with hope, had her life ended too early—and the dead woman found near the library, who didn't fit the target profile. *Is the killer decelerating to the scary point where he'll now take whoever is convenient? Bodies can pile up in Wilmington, if that's the case.*

The victims were both dumped in water, which screwed up the forensics and delayed perpetrator identification. It was a tactic so unlike the ground burials in Indiana, which raised the question whether this was the same killer. Almost a decade had passed between the Indiana farm and these local murders. *Are there multiple murderers or are all these dead women victims of the media named Goat Man?*

Like most newspapers, *The Wilmington Star-Gazette* lead story reported victims as beautiful, popular and talented to increase reader empathy. They were purportedly loved by everyone, despite someone having just killed them. For once, Harry would have liked to have read a version that described the victim as ugly, untalented and disliked—which was at least sometimes the truth. Soon, such reports would make every local woman afraid for her life.

A composite artist rendering appeared on page one. Other versions would soon pop up on the Internet, despite no witnesses or confirmed photos of the killer. The blurry library video caught a van driver who was a skinny white guy in a dark baseball hat, which fit the usual profile of almost every serial killer.

Inferences were being made that other victims existed, but had not yet been discovered. There was a brief reference to a recent missing woman in Williamsburg, Virginia. *Maybe her disappearance links to the Goat Man and maybe it doesn't?*

If it did, Harry considered again what job would allow the killer to appear one day in Wilmington and the next in Williamsburg. Once again, Harry locked onto movers. The owner at the Strip Club referenced a guy in a Weston tee shirt as a skinny guy like in the library photos. While Harry had informed the police and FBI contacts of his ideas, he knew they rarely listened to outsiders.

As he turned the page, he noticed a full-page color advertisement for an Independence Day gala on the Cape Fear River. The ad filled with fireworks in the nighttime sky, above the waterfront. An insert invited parents with special needs children to contact a Special Activities group about a holiday tour of the former battleship the USSNC.

Harry recognized this as the same advertisement he had found in the dead PI Janakowsky's pocket in New York. *What's the link between Manhattan and Wilmington?* Harry began to feel he had the pieces of a jigsaw puzzle scattered before him, but he was unclear about what picture the linked pieces, when connected, would show.

In the paper, a small blurb described protests against celebrating the War of the American Revolution—with Chinese fireworks that polluted the Cape Fear River.

Before folding the paper on his lap, Harry checked baseball scores and saw that the Cubs had lost again. Sadly, some events in life were predictable. To block the bright sun's glare, he adjusted his faded Cubs cap. As his mind wandered from the headlines, images of the dead women dissolved into visualizations of other women in his life.

With Holly, he seemed to have an instant connection. *Was it possible to make one more comeback in life?* Life offered more than catching killers and, like the manhunt, the time remaining in his life kept shortening. Carolyn was the second woman he considered. *Why did I evade her offer of intimacy? A stupid sixth sense told me to beware.* That morning, on the sun drenched beach, he didn't regret his deferral as much as he had that night alone in bed.

Harry never dwelled long on the beauty of life, and soon the gray bloated face of Natasha Radinsky replaced the image of Carolyn. Since the FBI got the case, they had received a murder book and crime scene reports in addition their own national computer data bases. *What value could Bernie and I provide? Two ex- cops, intruding on a federal man-hunt, hardly seems practical.* Bernie had financial reasons, and Harry liked to finish what he started.

The beach became crowded with women lounging in bikinis as young men, displaying six-pack abs, strolled past. Harry watched the genders participate in the immortal social dance. On the beach, the games were transparent with few disguises—unlike the fancy hotel lobbies, where perfumed women in short cocktail dresses comingled with strutting men in fitted suits.

On the beach, physical attributes were visible. There, a guy shaped like a pear couldn't hide his flabbiness with padded shoulders in a tailored Armani suit. There were no façades at the beach—it was why Harry preferred it to any other location.

Harry watched people who had no idea *what* they were getting into when attracted by an appealing body. They could abscond to a beach condo and screw their brains out and connect with someone different each day. Life could be simple to the naïve, and yet his experience in dealing with criminals warned him that a tryst with a pleasant stranger allowed access by a potentially-sinister person.

The six-pack guy could morph into a date rapist. The perky blonde could prefer a stiletto goodbye. All the strangers who got together had no inkling that the person they hook-up with could be a saint or a killer. It was just the way Harry thought. Uncovering the *motivation* became critical to identifying a killer.

Harry recounted the dead bodies. He almost forgot the first one—the dead PI in the Albertson Hotel room. The notations on Janakowsky's business card *MLF DD Cmp LJ* became clear. He was looking into David Dodd at Camp Lejeune and a protest group that was anti-military, with a possible New York link.

Then there was the sudden death of a Colonel Bogart at Camp Lejeune, who was deciding the case of Dave Dodd. *Perhaps Holly's father-in-law, General Sabbatino, could shed some light on events at Camp Lejeune? And what happened to Dave's former lover, Jasmyne?* She was a leader in the campus protest group MLF. Both she and the Colonel were dead but apparently of an accident or natural cause.

The convenience of these deaths wasn't lost on Harry. Natasha and Ivanka, the library woman, were clearly murdered, most likely by the Goat Man from Indiana, along with a possible victim in Virginia. *Is there a link between these deaths and the killer at large, the Goat Man? Or is it two killers?*

Although intrigued, Harry sensed a connection without any proof, but he had to focus on the Radinsky murder. *What're the odds two active killers could be loosed at the same time in this small city?* To his knowledge, such a collision had rarely happened before, despite the FBI report that over 300 serial killers existed in any given year in the United States. A serial killer usually wasn't caught until he made a mistake—like Dahmer failing to devour his final target.

The beach became too crowded for Harry, but the sun soothed his knee and the waves inspired thought. As he walked toward the parking lot, his cell phone indicated an incoming text message.

It was from Spano, Police Chief of Wilmington.

"Meet me at the Holiday Inn Wrightsville Beach ASAP. Another victim—someone you *know*."

~~~~~~

Bernie Mannion watched the boaters gliding with white sails along the waterway toward the expansive ocean. *I should be working with Harry,* he thought, but he sat alone and finished a flounder sandwich at the Bridge Tender Restaurant. The table edge pressed into his stomach.

All he wanted was to supplement his police pension to live the good life, chase a few philandering husbands and collect fees. But now he felt involved in a subterfuge. He hated the handful of cops who took graft. The worst he ever did was scam a few free lunches. Now he was involved in a real estate deal with slime buckets, and maybe worse.

But this deal would make a serious down payment on a boat. A Shakespeare 830 glided past. Bernie *loved* that boat. He envisioned himself as the captain at the helm with a bevy of bikini-clad fawning admirers, while he glided into a peaceful sunset.

His phone alerted him to a text. The curt message from his local cop connection told him the body of someone he *knew* had been found next to the Holiday Inn in Wrightsville Beach. He paid his bill with a twenty and did not wait for change. His cane remained on the restaurant chair, as he climbed into Moby Dick, his hands gripping the steering wheel so hard they tingled.

Who the hell do I know that could be a victim? Near the oceanfront hotel, the police and ambulance activity made him slow down. Yellow crime scene tape stretched out around red and blue flashing lights. Scanning the crowd for familiar faces, he saw the Sheriff of Wrightsville Beach, talking with a bunch of troopers and dark suits.

Several thirty-year-olds in suits with short hair and ear pieces walked about, probably the Feebs. Now those headlines brought broader attention about a possible serial killer, the FBI assumed every aspect of the investigation. *Someone I knew.* A chill filled him and came with the question—*why call me?*

The beach public access parking lot spread next to the hotel. The middle of the lot served as the delivery area for the hotel, which also discarded its garbage into green dumpsters. He saw a body bag and a stretcher next to one of the opened dumpsters on the hot gray asphalt. IV bags were attached. Paramedics hovered. Bernie knew the drill and cringed at another victim. *Someone I know.*

He noticed Harry was already there, talking to Chief Spano, who was beyond his jurisdiction. The Wrightsville Beach Sheriff was walking around in her turf, talking to Feds.

Bernie walked away from Moby Dick as Harry approached him.

"Hey Bernie, this is bad. You don't need to look."

"What the hell are you talking about, Harry?"

Bernie brushed past Harry to see what the officials had found. The big man walked quickly toward the stretcher. A small white foot extruded from the corner. He saw the green turtle tattoo on her ankle. A petite technician blocked Bernie from touching anything. They were all in a rush of activity to move the stretcher into the ambulance.

Chief Spano stood next to him.

"Hello, Mannion. We got a call and the locals thought they had another murder victim, but one of the medics told us she's still barely breathing. Beaten up really bad with multiple wounds—she's headed to the ER right now. I understand she was—*is* your assistant?"

Bernie stood frozen in the hot humid air. His wide body weaved in the oceanfront breeze. The tattoo was hers, but from her swollen, battered face, he couldn't tell it was KiKi.

"Is this the damn Goat Man? I've got... I just want to see closer to be sure!"

The Chief nodded to the busy young tech who responded.

Bernie bent down with hands on his knees and looked at the round face of KiKi Sanchez. Black eye make-up spilled over her puffy purple cheeks. Blood coagulated near her nose and swollen lips.

His lip quivered and tears filled his eyes. He straightened up. Who would do this to her?

The medics rushed her into the flashing ambulance and took off with sirens blasting through the peaceful beachfront.

"That poor kid. Why *her*? We've got to get this scumbag," Bernie said to no one in particular.

Everyone nodded in somber agreement.

One of the uniforms standing nearby spoke to another cop.

"She was a piece of work. Did you check out that short skirt, and her hair was green striped. She was *looking* for trouble!"

Bernie turned to the cop.

"Shut the hell up, you fuckin asshole. You know nothin about her. She's good people!"

Harry stepped between his irate friend and the uniformed kid.

"Easy, Bernie. He's just a kid—mouthing off."

"Yeah, I know," said Bernie. "Son of a bitch!"

Chief Spano walked over to see what was happening.

"Does she have any family we can notify?"

His impression from the medics was that she wouldn't make it.

"The guys who reported the body thought she was dead. When we arrived, we thought she was gone. Damn close, but a sharp medical tech found a slight pulse. Whoever dumped her thought they'd killed her."

"I think she had an aunt up in Raleigh," Bernie interrupted. "I'll check the files at the office."

Harry placed his hand on Bernie's shoulder. Neither man moved for a few minutes.

"I'm sorry, Bernie. She's young and tough, so she can make it. We'll get this guy!"

A broad man in a dark suit approached.

"Are you Harry Powell? I'm Special Agent Niese,"

They shook hands.

"Do I *know* you?" Harry asked.

"Years ago, I was a criminology student in Chicago when you were on the force there. You showed our class around the police station. You seemed like a guy we could trust—spoke the real deal, as I recall. I'm Zack Niese. Now I'm with the FBI. What are you doing now?"

He held open his massive hands to emphasize the question.

"Well, I'm now doing private investigation. This is my boss, Bernie Mannion. The victim here was our office assistant. Was this the Goat Man?"

Harry handed Niese one of his business cards, while Bernie stood like a salt statue.

"Okay. I've just been over the murders in Indiana. The Bureau has now taken over control of the investigation here. You know 'the goat' at West Point was the cadet with the lowest ranking? Anyway we don't encourage the media to create a branded image like this. We'll refer to him as 'the Unsub'—unknown subject of the investigation. You and Mannion *both* worked in Indiana?"

"Yeah, sure. Bernie was a decorated cop there, a member of the IPD—the Indianapolis Police Department. We were looking for a missing person who turned out to be victim number one. Are you sure this is the same perp?"

"For now, we're working the assumption that she was attacked by the same guy. Our VICAP database records all similar violent acts and we're processing any links. More tests will confirm that. I'll call you."

Niese nodded and walked back to the group of dark suits.

Chief Spano approached.

"*Another* old friend?"

"Someone I must have met when I was giving talks to local kids back in Chicago about 'the police are your friends.' I honestly don't remember him, but he's now Special Agent Niese."

"Looks more like a linebacker for the Chicago Bears to me. A *mean* linebacker," Spano said under his breath.

Special Agent Niese heard the comment and responded by walking toward the men.

"Actually, I never played sports—I know that goes against the stereotype for my physical presentation, but I was busy graduating *cum laude* from Georgetown. We have the Evidence Collection Unit (ECU) on top of this. As I told your Wrightsville Beach counterpart, these attacks are the FBI's case, Chief. Are we clear?"

"I hear you," Chief Spano replied, looking up at the federal agent.

Not long after, Niese and his agents departed in black Envoys.

"KiKi's *got* to make it," Bernie pleaded, his lip quivering.

"Are you thinking KiKi's attacker is the Goat Man that killed Radinsky and Ivanka Fields?" Harry asked Spano.

"Don't know yet, Harry. Those women were both dumped in water, while KiKi is found in a *dumpster* near water. Who knows? I understand that eighty percent of attacks on women include a sexual component, and initially this doesn't. But Wilmington was a peaceful place, and now all of a sudden, we got three women attacked in a few weeks.

"The Feebs may be leading this case, but there are still too many dead Wilmington women for *me* to ignore. He can be in charge, but I investigate what I want. Besides, I'm not sure Mr. Niese has smelled the blood—you know what I mean?"

"Yeah, it's about the value of *experience*, Chief. Thanks for the call. This is *personal* now."

Within several hours, the parking lot emptied of most law enforcement. Sporadic visitors were directed to walk around the crime scene tape to the beach. Life continued as if nothing had happened.

Harry drove off the island. Also personal was a police call Harry received when he lived in Maine. No loss could exceed the impact from that one horrific phone call: that morning, he had shopped for Fruit Loops and Gummy Bears for his grandson's afternoon visit.

When he returned to the cottage, his antiquated answering machine glared with a red flashing light that a message awaited. The Portland police voice said they stopped by when no one was home, so they had to leave this phone message.

The voice informed him that there had been a serious car accident and he should come to the Portland General Hospital as soon as possible. Since Kathy and Christopher were due to his cottage within the hour, he wondered if he should leave. It was Maine, so he left the front door unlocked in the event they arrived in his absence. He even left a note on the table that read, *I'll be back soon, make yourselves at home.*

Harry drove to the hospital that was fifteen minutes away, assuming one of his elderly neighbors had been hurt. The disinfectant stench of the hospital hit him initially. His eyes squinted in the fluorescent-lit linoleum hallway. A brown uniform with black shoes met him.

After confirming who he was and that he had family by the names detailed, the cop delivered the news.

"I'm very sorry."

Both had been DOA—dead on arrival—at the hospital from a car accident. Kathy and Christopher were gone.

"Can I call someone for you?" the officer asked.

That's when Harry understood they were dead. There was no one to call. No tears came as he sat in numb disbelief. His little guy, Christopher, never had a chance to live. Harry's blood seemed to stop flowing in his body.

The cop told him that they had been killed instantly from a head-on collision as they neared Portland. The truck driver wasn't drunk, but he was apparently texting a picture of himself to his girlfriend while driving. Harry blamed himself for all the wasted time disconnected from his own family—*too many years that could never be retrieved.*

He felt alone on a desolate island, where water kept rising around him. He knew it was only a matter of time before he drowned.

His mind returned to the present.

The next day, Harry sat at his desk and muddled through worthless mail. Any office vibrancy disappeared without the ebullient

KiKi Sanchez. The hospital reported she was in a coma. Harry was reading Yahoo News when a headline caught his attention *Hindu Human Sacrifices by Goat Man.*

Some reporter had gone national with a tale that these murders had a cult motive. The self-entitled journalist postulated that a modern-day worshipper was sacrificing humans to the goddess Kali. This was the Hindu god of destruction, who once inspired human sacrifices. Recently, humans had been replaced by goats! In his muddled logic, the columnist linked the recent murders in Indiana and North Carolina to the cult.

The phone vibrated.

"Hello, Harry Powell. This is Special Agent Niese. I just wanted to let you know that the FBI will *not* pursue the case of Ms. Sanchez."

"Territorial battles deferred?" Harry asked.

"No. We do not believe this to be the same attacker that we saw in the other cases. The docs can't explain why she isn't dead. There are other confidential inconsistencies."

"Like the creature insertion?"

Niese hesitated.

"I can't discuss the ongoing investigation in Indiana. We have alerted the National Center for the Analysis of Violent Crimes (NCAVC) at Quantico for help. We expect the media to run with a continuation of their Goat Man saga, with Ms. Sanchez as his latest victim. We'll focus on Ms. Radinsky and Ms. Fields. However, I do want to meet with you to learn what your Radinsky investigation uncovered."

Harry felt that KiKi's attack was being abandoned.

"That's fine for you, but. KiKi is in a coma. Her attacker must be found! On the other two women, any progress *you* can share?" Harry asked.

"Well, there were twenty-three individuals who lived in Indiana during that spree who now reside in the Wilmington area, including you and your partner Bernard Mannion. We've cleared most of those other individuals. There are always outliers, but our databases are coming up blank for any cohabitant."

"Maybe he's a transient who doesn't pay taxes—like someone paid in cash working for a *moving company*?" Harry offered.

Harry had agreed to meet with Niese before his phone notified him of a second caller.

"Hi, Chief. What's up?"

"Hey, Harry. I tried to reach your partner, but he doesn't pick up. I wanted you guys to know that the son of a bitch who attacked Ms. Sanchez will be investigated by my team, locally, so we'll need to talk more. You know, she's alive, but in a coma and can't talk? Quite frankly, the docs aren't optimistic. It's efficient, if I can get you guys together? Perhaps at your office, where we'll check out her desk and computer?"

"Can we meet at our office later *today*?" Harry asked.

"I'll be there at four. Make sure Mannion's there, Harry."

"How was the MO with KiKi different from the others, Chief?"

Harry glanced at the newspaper headline, extolling the continuation of Goat Man attacks. What looked like a high school yearbook photo of KiKi Sanchez made the front page of the morning paper—as the serial killer's latest victim.

"We're keeping this quiet, Harry, but with Ms. Sanchez, there were no cuts and no sexual assault or animal insertion. In addition to other aspects, the other women were choked with pressure on the hyoid bone, while Ms. Sanchez had her neck snapped. Her attack was more like a brutal beating than the sadistic tortures found in the previous two dead women. The newspapers have it wrong, but that may help us if the attacker thinks he's home free. Maybe somebody figured they could hide a local crime inside the Goat Man story? Can you think of anyone who might have been this angry at Ms. Sanchez?"

"Not that I can think of, but obviously there's at least *one* person who wanted her dead," Harry answered as he considered the angle of no sexual assault. Ginger told him that eighty percent of all attacks on women were sexually-related. *Does that mean her attacker was a male who was not interested in sex with a woman? Or was he interrupted? Or was her attacker a woman?*

Harry's cell vibrated to reveal a call from Bernie.

"We'll see you at four o'clock, Chief."

Bernie was shouting.

"Harry, the shit's hittin the fan! We gotta talk, *now!*"

~~~~~~

In the parking lot, Lloyd sat in the van, turning the pages of the *Wilmington Star-Gazette*. Between bites of a Gyro, he searched for the continuation of the front page story, *Goat Man Strikes Again*. The headline enticed anyone to read the gory lead story. Lloyd gloated at being an officially recognized killer.

While he liked having a moniker, *Goat Man* pissed him off. *What do I have to do with goats? I'm a fucking pirate!* They located the Indiana bodies and linked them to his Wilmington conquests. Yet, they made no mention of little Lloyd—*so how did they connect the murders here to Indiana? Did I leave some hint in Indiana? Why the goat farm? I'm sure as shit no goat man—I've never even touched a damn goat. These know-it-all reporters will need to change their story. I'm a pillaging pirate!*

The end of the report mentioned a third victim of the Midwest serial killer had been found in a Wilmington dumpster. They showed a photo of some wild-looking kid named KiKi. He never left anyone in a dumpster. *That is disgusting!* And she was barely alive but in a coma. *How stupid do they think I am? Leave a witness?*

Lloyd knew better, but maybe it was just as well to gain credit and build his legend. Someday, they would find other bodies behind the truck stops along Route 70. If only he hadn't wasted those years in prison, the count would be higher. Someday, a black and red covered *true story* book would be written about his life. On the cover would be Lloyd, in a red bandana with a black eye patch and pirate's knife—*not some fuckin goat farmer!*

The newspaper also referred to an Evelyn Nesbitt—Pinky—in Williamsburg, who had recently gone missing. The FBI considered her another potential victim. Lloyd was impressed. The reporter surmised her location may indicate the killer had headed north.

Lloyd regarded such supposition as ludicrous, since he wanted no part of the Yankees. He laughed that they would never find Pinky in the woods behind the model home—unless the housing market boomed, and by then he'd be long gone and coyotes would have devoured any remains.

He laughed at the artist's rendering in the paper. The ball cap and shades made him look like anyone. The supposed killer was being drawn to look something like a goat. *Yeah, that's me—a human goat.* The picture didn't look anything like him. *Maybe I should regularly wear the eye patch to enhance my image as a pirate?*

He read somewhere about a charlatan in Chicago who sold goat testicles as the key to immortality. That was him, Lloyd Curtin—con man, pirate and now immortal goat man. *Maybe I should write a letter to the newspaper or go on line and tell everyone that I'm not a goat man, but a pirate? A lust-hungry, pillaging pirate!* He would also educate them that he was no rampaging intruder, like General Sherman, but a favorite son, returning with a vengeance.

The front page article quoted some FBI big shot named Zachary Niese. The Feds would profile the killer and get some of it right— like it took a genius to describe a serial killer as a white male in his thirties. Lloyd watched television too. *Big deal, who else could accomplish so much? Some punk kid or old coot isn't realistic.* Yeah, he didn't grow up in a balanced family, with two loving parents and supportive siblings. *Wow!* That really narrowed it down to most of America.

If he didn't get stupid and make mistakes, they would never catch him. He would act when the urge made him. He became a vessel to perform pre-ordained deeds. It was just the way he was. *What can a person do, but play the gene cards they're dealt? Continue to fulfill their destiny until stopped. What other choice do I have?*

What Lloyd read in the newspaper convinced him that the cops and FBI had no clue about his identity. *No eyewitnesses. No links to the victims. No forensics evidence.* Pinky's body hadn't been found and never would be. They were trying to connect the prey by some common social interaction. That was why he had been so productive for so long.

There *wasn't* any link to connect him to any victim. No female in Wilmington was safe from him, unless they were little kids or old. *After all, I'm not perverted. Maybe on my next target, I'll leave a calling card, correcting the Goat Man error? Maybe I'll leave a skull and crossbones patch? I'm the Pirate King, who owns women—and not some damned Goat Man!*

He crumpled the Gyro wrapper and closed the newspaper, recalling one woman from his church list in particular—Army Girl. The urge grew as he imagined her, tied down in the back of his pirate ship!

CHAPTER TWENTY-FIVE

JD Henzlein hated subterranean meetings in the dank basement. It reeked of urine and stale beer, which seeped from the upstairs bar on Front Street. He traded ambience for privacy to avoid being publicly linked to the three stooges.

Over a hundred years ago, the space had been the cellar of a whore house, where pirates stored their booty before getting laid upstairs. JD always figured if he dug under the wood floor, he would unearth treasures. But after a brief attempt one year, he gave up.

If he told his idiot half-brother Lloyd about the location, the tweaked fool would be down there, digging with a spoon. The moldy brick walls even held pirate memorabilia from upstairs before *The Corsair Coast* morphed into *Balls*. People today preferred current games to history.

JD liked fellow southerner, Tennessee Williams, and recalled the playwright's definition of talent: *Being able to get away with something*. JD had accepted that as his major talent.

Sitting next to Rock, Dave Dodd slugged a bottle of Blue Moon. Rock slouched in disinterest, guzzling a Corona. The third guy, did not match up in size to the other two men, but Karim Nissim possessed a powerful, energized look. He was a believer and was brought into the plan after Annabelle vetted him and his sister from her campus group.

The political radicals had an additional agenda that JD tolerated, as long as they served his purpose. Besides, Annabelle provided the money and thought she was calling the shots. While Dave and Rock could use their military employment to help obtain weapons, Karim knew what to do with the toxic tools.

"Okay, gentlemen, if I can interrupt the early drinking..."

"Hey! It's damn noon *somewhere*!" Rock complained.

JD consciously anointed Rock as the first elimination target for Lloyd.

"Whatever. We're nearing our event across the Cape Fear River. Do you guys have all your materials? Are you clear on the plan and timing for Independence Day?"

Holding a tan file folder in his hands, JD placed it on the dark pine table. Trying to write atop the wood remained a challenge, due to the proliferation of customer engravings from the past. None of the others had any notes or paperwork.

Rock held out his android phone and wagged it at JD.

"It's all here, man. Maps, schedules, materials list—we're good to go!"

He smiled at Dave as they toasted their longneck brews.

"Where are the diagrams I gave you?" JD asked.

"Scanned into the phone and burned the hard copy," Rock replied.

"You know, JD—you're real old school and should destroy that archaic paper bullshit," Dave sneered, referring to JD's folder.

JD pounded his fist on the tan cardboard that held more than the three stooges needed to know.

"*Results* matter—not style!"

"I have my press release right up here," Karim announced, tapping the side of his hairy head with a nail bitten hand. "You Kufars should throw away cell phones, like I have. Otherwise, authorities can track your asses with the GPS on your androids."

"Okay, paranoia Pete," Rock chided.

He and Davey would be in extradition-free in Costa Rica by the time anyone looked for them.

"Remember, the battleship is a symbol we need to set afire to lure first responders. Smoke bombs in the warehouses bring other distractions. Karim will... worry about the message sent to the munitions plant in Southport, called MOTSU."

"That's right. They protect New York and San Francisco, but Wilmington? Too many troops sent from Cape Fear to kill my brothers and sisters. The fuckers murdered *Jasmyne!*" Karim growled.

"Hey JD—I thought this was a *harmless* message demonstration?" Dave asked.

"Yes, yes—with just a little louder fireworks for the active military," JD answered. "No cause for alarm."

"We ain't blowing up the munitions plant, JD. I didn't sign up for that shit!" Rock complained.

"Not to worry, my friends. Nothing so extreme... demonstrations, and warnings..."

He stared into Karim's eyes to convey a need for privacy.

"Don't get fuckin crazy, Karim!" Dave warned.

"Nobody gets hurt here," Rock added.

"Fuck you! Just do *your* job!" Karim countered.

JD examined the three faces before him and worried. *Can this trio really pull off the forthcoming events?* To assuage his fears, he spent the next hour going through the details planned for July fourth. Like a lawyer preparing a trial witness, he drilled them to repeat their individual roles. There could be no mistakes, and the timing had to be precise.

He felt like a coach, wanting to win more than his players wanted to practice to win. Only Karim seemed impassioned. On a flip chart, he listed each step and they discussed:

✓ Materials obtained. Weapons "transferred" from MOTSU to combine with black market purchases

✓ Jacksonville storage emptied

✓ Confirm the exact nautical locations for Karim

✓ Rubber suits obtained

✓ Weaponry to fire mortar acquired

✓ RHIB (rigid hull incrusted boat) to join the flotilla on July fourth

✓ Amphibious landing at 0300 (3AM)

✓ Eagle Island fireworks enhanced (across from the public dock)

✓ Smoke bombs set up PM July 3rd in identified warehouses for distraction

✓ Plastic explosives (G3) to be installed on the USSNC during the early July fourth day tour of the battleship

✓ Wireless remote detonation devices to be used along the waterfront to be synchronized

✓ Press release to the local newspaper for the July 5th headline

✓ Target time for the show: 2100 (9 pm) on the Fourth. Coordination with the music and the fireworks

✓ Plan for personnel extraction (escape).

JD checked off each item with a red highlighter.

"Are we clear, my friends?" he kept repeating.

"Crystal," the trio began to chant in sarcastic unison.

Karim looked at the men with his dark eyes and kept the secret shared only with his cell leader. The coordinates set for the most destructive mortar would not just warn the MOTSU facility, but destroy it. *These Americans are tools to help me damage the military—like it is Pearl Harbor all over again.*

JD handed each man a single sheet of yellow paper.

"I'm giving you the escape plan. You go over the bridge to Leland and then south to Myrtle Beach. No one will find you in those crowds."

He spoke like he cared, fully aware that Lloyd would eliminate all three on a dark road in Leland.

"Color coordinated directions—like we're kindergarteners? Were you in the military service, JD?" Dave asked.

"No, I had flat feet and was 4F."

"Still seems like fuckin overkill on some of the explosives for a warning," Dave complained, perplexed. "You know there's an old military adage that says 'no battle plan survives the first contact with the enemy.'"

Rock and Dave smirked at JD and his plans.

JD's folder included other critical documents. There was a notarized contract to purchase downtown properties after the smoke explosions lowered their values—all pre-dated and pre-signed. Protests served a purpose, but JD believed that the reason to get up in the morning was to make money. Otherwise, a man should stay in bed and fuck all day.

"We'll reconvene on the second of July when all acquisitions must be fully completed. Are there any issues?"

JD looked at his trio of erstwhile warriors. Two thought they were making a noisy protest, while one wanted more. JD just wanted to make a buck. JD knew passionate players are more reliable than the mercenary.

"No questions? Then we're adjourned."

As the men climbed the creaky stairs, Rock mumbled to Dave.

"Is this *black flag* warfare?"

The term meant that people would die, and thus the two soon-to-be ex-Marines began to question their involvement.

The four men exited into the bright light of day. Dave and Rock walked south toward the river in animated discussion. Karim went alone up the hill, lost in thought. JD locked the bar door behind him and walked to his car.

He held the tan folder with an unshared schematic of where each man would be located on July fourth at 9:00p.m.—so that he could verify everything from his eagles nest location.

When the band played *and the rockets' red glare*... on Independence Day, the detonations would commence.

CHAPTER TWENTY-SIX

Harry watched as Bernie pushed open the agency's front door and approached.

"She wants you fired, Harry."

The men moved to the cluttered back room. The hospitalized comatose condition of KiKi Sanchez was unspoken, though ever-present.

Harry observed the exaggerated lines on Bernie's face in the fluorescent light. His friend's disheveled shirt popped out of his wrinkled tan suit slacks, and his socks hung down to his ankles. Bernie smelled stale.

"*Professor* Annabelle? She isn't happy?" Harry asked.

"Progress and communication! She doesn't *hear* from you."

"I'm not here to flirt with her, Bernie. I've looked into Natasha's disappearance—who now appears to be a victim of the Goat Man. I gave what I learned to Niese, and the FBI will be all over this guy. They have the databases, like VICAP, and connections."

"Harry, Harry—we don't make *money* telling clients the Feds will take care of their concerns. *We* take care of their concerns and get paid by the hour, plus expenses!"

Bernie wiped his sweaty brow.

"It's all about cash flow in the private sector, Harry. Unlike the government, *we* have to make a profit!"

"So I hold her hand and make *up* progress reports? That bullshit isn't for me, Bernie. You *know* that. Besides, didn't you say *you* would be the link to her? I want to find who tried to kill KiKi."

Bernie shook his head in defeat, but Harry continued.

"We know the MO linked to the murders in Indiana. Unless some local whack job came up with the same weird MO, it's the same guy here. The Feebs have searched VICAP and other databases for any similar MO from other states. They found other victims along Highway 70—women at truck stops they called *lot lizards*. I can offer input, but it's really not our case anymore, Bernie. Besides, KiKi…"

"That *same* son of a bitch wacko slashed KiKi!" Bernie piped.

"That's probably *not* a link, Bernie. And with a serial killer loose here, there may not be much official attention to a beating."

"Not a link? Like there are two different creeps in this town, trying to kill young women at the same time? He's choking them to death. I don't care what FBI profilers say. It's the *same* psycho. *I* don't think there are two."

"Actually, I found out that, in the seventies, there were two serial killers at the same time in California. I'm just telling you what official experts believe, Bernie. But I think we should focus on KiKi's attack."

"The docs aren't optimistic that KiKi will survive," Bernie responded, his chin trembling, his bloodshot eyes glazed.

"She's young and strong, and medical experts can be wrong. Besides, solving the attack on KiKi is personal," Harry confessed.

"I *hear* you!"

"Bernie, was KiKi involved with anything at Camp Lejeune?"

"No, she never even met those folks."

"What about any involvement with the campus protest through MLF?"

"No way! KiKi had another life completely."

"Anything to do with your real estate deals with JD?"

"What deals? No. Well, just filing some papers—which was her *job*. What do you know about that shit?"

Bernie took a deep breath, calming himself.

"All right, I hear you. We need to find who tried to kill her, but we still *need* to keep earning a paycheck. I can't afford to lose this business!"

Harry recalled a scene from *Requiem for a Heavyweight*, where the aged boxer McClintock's career ended and he donned the garish fake headdress of a Native American to perform as a money-making fake wrestler. He attempted to retain his pride, but management ignored his pleas to cease.

He ended up in a struggle between lost dignity and the need to earn a paycheck to survive. Harry expected more from his friend, Bernard Mannion. Harry had come to believe that if money became the only goal, life bordered on a meaningless waste of time.

"I can keep checking for local clues, but..."

"Keep doing that, Harry, until I tell you to stop. I'll deal with the professor's billings. The meter is running. Don't give me that freakin look, Harry!"

"*What* look? You pay the bills."

Harry knew he would be looking into KiKi's attack regardless.

"I *know* that disparaging look, Harry. I make no pretensions. I'm in the twilight of a mediocre career."

Bernie took a long sip from the giant plastic Sweet Tea cup from Mickey D's. Harry smelled the scotch.

"*Somebody's* gotta pay the rent, Harry."

"I understand, Bernie. But just so we're clear. My condo lease expires soon. Your leg is healed. I'll help you over the next few weeks in any way I can, but then I think it would be best that we part ways and stay friends. But foremost now—I want to find the bastards who did this to KiKi and make sure they pay for it."

"I get it, Harry. But think about it. I have a really big deal cooking that could bring in some cash and help the agency expand. I can make you a fifty-fifty partner soon," Bernie urged.

"Thanks, Bernie. No pun intended, but that boat has left the dock."

Harry felt another chapter in his life closing. He figured Bernie had some questionable business deal with that weasel, JD. Through investigation, he learned the MLF were vocal opponents of various military actions, but non-violent. The professor hated the local military. All these peripheral angles could be linked, but for the time being, he needed to find who attacked KiKi Sanchez. Someone once advised him not to take things personally, but Harry realized that his passionate energies always failed to enflame until it *did* become personal.

"What do you know about KiKi's *personal* life?" Harry asked.

"She was like a daughter to me, Harry. She didn't have an angry bone in her body. I can't imagine why anyone would hurt her. I still think maybe the Goat Man got interrupted. She had no ex-boyfriends. No close girlfriends. She worked here and went to school and..."

He watched tears form in Bernie's eyes.

"I need names of who she interacted with beyond this office," he insisted.

"She took courses at Cape Fear Community College and wanted to be a forensics investigator—like on that CSI TV show. She was receiving a certificate in that, and she was looking to enhance her income. Ironic, isn't it? She wanted to investigate crimes and ended up being the victim of one. I think she also did some club singing."

"You said she lived *alone?* Give me the address. I'll check out her apartment. You have a key?"

Bernie looked at Harry in a stunned manner. His face reddened, and he answered in a loud voice.

"Why would I have a key, Harry? What the hell are you askin? I told you she was like a…"

"A *daughter*—I believe you. I just asked for access to see if there's anything in her apartment that might help us—that's all!"

"I don't have a key, Harry. Maybe there's one in her desk. I gotta go see some people."

Bernie grunted a few words to himself as he rose and stormed toward the exit.

"Bernie! Don't forget—Chief Spano expects you and me here at 4:00 p.m. today."

Only the doorbells answered when the front door closed.

Harry stood at KiKi's tidy desk. The middle drawer contained the usual clutter of innocuous stuff. Under a flowered notepad, he found a key, which he hoped was to her apartment. He winced, due to his stiff knee, when he stood. As he departed the office, he reached up and tore off the bells above the door. They would ring no more. It was his silent tribute to his wounded colleague.

"I'll bring *down* whoever did this, KiKi."

Flipping the sign in the front door to read "*Closed,*" he locked the door.

Within minutes, Harry parked in front of a gray building containing four apartments. One belonged to KiKi Sanchez. Cracks in the concrete parking lot were filled with weeds. There was peeling paint trim and a hanging drain pipe on the building. He smelled the fried food of a Church's Chicken on the corner, while he noted KiKi's lime green Volkswagen beetle, sitting in the corner of the lot. He found the car locked and saw nothing strange inside.

Luckily, the key from her desk fit the dented metal door of apartment two. Happy to escape the hallway's stench, he entered. Sweet smelling lavender greeted him, followed by stale food odor from crumpled Church's wrappers, scattered around the room. He saw the contrast between the *work KiKi* and the *personal time KiKi*. While her work desk in the PI office remained orderly, her apartment presented a cluttered mess—the usual conflict of people who defied stereotyping.

A cushioned couch faced a small television. In a corner was a bookcase, packed with well-creased paperbacks. The titles emphasized crime-solving stories and displayed red and black spines. A kitchenette with upturned clean plates and glasses occupied the other corner. A door on the opposite wall entered the bedroom. A black bra hung on the doorknob.

Harry maneuvered across the cramped quarters into the bedroom. Pink sheets showed under a floral comforter at the bottom of the bed. The closet was nearly filled with casual shoes and clothes, folded on shelves. A small bag of what Harry thought *looked* like oregano but knew was pot sat in her nightstand drawer, along with several cheap lighters and wrapping papers.

Harry thought of the clutter in Natasha's apartment and thought it was much more interesting, if that meant anything.

Returning to the living room, Harry searched for any indication of what might cause someone to hurt the young woman. A surfboard rested against a wall. One of the walls contained prints of waves and surfers, and another displayed a poster with scientific Petri dishes from the television show *CSI*.

The small coffee table in front of the couch held a couple of text books, with covers that indicated a connection to forensic evidence. Cape Fear Community College was stamped on their sides, and each spine held a bright yellow "*Used*" sticker.

He glanced at the messy pile of papers, but noticed nothing unusual. Some were music sheets for songs he didn't know. The apartment didn't look like a place where trysts might occur. Harry noted to follow up on local music gigs and surfers. Sometimes, what *wasn't* present provided more clues than what was—such as the scarcity of any family photos in the apartment?

Sun lighted a table, drawing Harry's attention. A clear glass bowl sat near the window. It had gravel and grass in the bottom. Harry saw movement from the tiny turtle resident as it crawled into a corner.

"Hey buddy," he whispered as he sprinkled food from a container into the bowl. The turtle swam to the surface and began devouring the food.

He couldn't imagine a second adult person entering the hovel. He saw a woman, with minimal income, living her life alone, with active interests in learning and surfing and music. KiKi aspired to better herself through work and education. Her car appeared untouched and her apartment was locked.

He found no wallet or pocketbook, which might indicate she was out in public view when she was attacked. Her surfboard and wet suit were there, so she wasn't surfing. It seemed her school books were there, indicating she wasn't at school. *Who would want to kill you, KiKi?*

Harry looked for a computer, but found none. He scanned around for any stray flash drives, but he saw none. The absence of such a tool seemed odd to Harry. Perhaps its absence indicated a motive.

No money, no jewelry, few drugs. The pile of unopened mail contained mostly bills and advertisements. Like most young people, she likely lived on her portable electronic devices—all of which were not there.

He would need to check with Spano to see if they were found with her body. He felt guilty that he hadn't paid more attention to KiKi, but he would find her attacker and see that person punished.

If her personal life elicited no murderous connection, then could something at the office have linked her to a killer? Was Bernie into some nefarious activity that involved KiKi?

As he was about to depart, Harry thought about his childhood and where he would hide things. Returning to KiKi's bedroom, he lifted the mattress. Underneath, he found a small, floral diary. Distracted by noise outside, he shoved the diary into his pants pocket and grabbed the turtle bowl. He walked out the apartment door with bowl in hand as he locked the door.

A familiar voice greeted him in the parking lot.

"You aren't investigating a *crime*, are you, Harry? Tampering with evidence?" the chief asked.

Spano stood next to an official blue sedan, wearing a rumpled gray business suit. He removed the unlit cigar stub in his mouth.

"Hi Chief. I was just checking up for an injured employee. I figured *this* little guy wasn't *evidence*, and he'd need to be fed."

"I see. By the way—we received an update on Ms. Sanchez from the hospital. They confirmed none of the cutting and torture—like the others, and no perverted insertion. Her torso was beaten badly. Also, someone tried to snap her neck, military-style. Nothing sexual.

I hate to tell you this, but the docs say her chances are less than 50-50. Sorry, Harry."

"So she wasn't likely attacked by the Goat Man, right?"

"That's true, Harry. Is your partner with you?"

"Bernie? No. He's got other cases…"

"He isn't here *now*, you mean. But he gave you *his* key to the chippies' apartment?"

"I got the backup key from her desk in the office. No way was she his chippie. KiKi and Bernie? His relationship was paternal."

"All middle-aged Don Juan's claim that about young assistants."

"Don Juan? Bernie? Come on, Chief. And *definitely* not with KiKi!"

"We'll see. What do you *really* know about your partner's relationship with Ms. Sanchez?"

"Bernie thinks of her as his daughter—very protective for someone he met since he came here. She was even studying for a certificate in Forensic Science. They seemed close, but not in the way you are inferring. Men and women can be friends without some subterfuge and sex."

"Hey, I just asked. I'm a detective. I detect. Is your boy, Bernie, married?"

"No, his wife died."

"Bernie *killed* his wife. You *know* that, Harry?"

Harry suddenly noticed the humidity.

"It was a horrible accident. It happened just as he was retiring from the Indiana Police Department. If you know all this, why are you asking me? Are we playing some kind of game about, Bernie? He's a good man."

"Just asking questions, is all. You want to give *me* the key?"

Harry gave Spano the key, and the chief directed his men to examine the apartment.

"Did you see anything of use in the apartment?"

"No, it was just a sloppy one-bedroom that one person lived in. Low rent, but high expectations in the resident. No laptop or any paper trail. It's odd that there are no personal photos. No family. No friends. Just this little guy."

Harry indicated toward the turtle.

"Her car is still here, right? You have a key to that, too?"

"No. I didn't see any car keys. That green VW is hers."

"I figured *that* much," Spano nodded. "You know, your widowed partner is linked to *two* young women—one dead, and one *left* for dead. And he was around Indiana when twelve murders occurred there. He *will* be with you at your office at 4 p.m. today, like we agreed, right?"

"Absolutely," Harry answered.

"Also, the FBI offered us some surveillance cameras of Ms. Sanchez, waiting to go south at the bus stop over on Market Street."

"She was attending Cape Fear Community College. Maybe she took that city bus to the downtown campus?" Harry suggested.

"Good thought, Harry. By the way, the Radinsky car turned up in the county car lot. It had been towed from an expired meter in Wrightsville Beach. You were right. The keys in her apartment turned out to be an extra set to her mother's Mercedes—not her Eclipse. Maybe we should be listening more to you!"

"Were KiKi's electronic devices or wallet found on her body?" Harry asked.

"Nothing there. She was stripped clean."

"As I think about it, maybe KiKi *wasn't* taking the bus to school, because her textbooks are still inside. Without her books, maybe she was headed somewhere else downtown where it's tough to park a car."

"The surveillance tape doesn't show her arriving at her destination."

"This investigation is personal for me, Chief. I intend to keep looking."

"You find something, Harry, you *tell* me. With budget cuts, I don't have much manpower. We'll focus on Ms. Sanchez for forty-eight hours. If we come up empty, we have *other* cases."

"Thanks, Chief. Did the hotel surveillance cameras near the dumpster show anything?"

"The camera shows her being dumped. Other than it was a big guy in jeans and black hoodie—we got nothing useable. They all wear those damn Belichick-inspired hoodies, so you can't make out much of their faces. It's like a uniform of the criminal crowd. We think it was a white guy from his wrists that were exposed above the gloves he wore. He wore a big-ass watch. But dumb luck—he parked outside the camera angle.

"It was almost exactly three in the morning—like that was the scheduled plan. She was beaten elsewhere and just dumped there. Maybe the attacker figured the trucks would collect the garbage and no one would notice a body. They use electronic pickup devices to empty the dumpster into the refuse truck. Ms. Sanchez was very lucky she wasn't shredded."

Harry recalled a diver's watch on the thick wrist of David Dodd.

"So how did *you* learn about KiKi's body?"

"Man, who can figure. A couple of the kitchen workers throw out bags of discarded food from the hotel restaurant. Only a couple of staff sharpies enhance the discarded lot, with prime steaks and stuff. Then they come back and retrieve the clean bag. They got a surprise when they were greeted by the body that covered their loot. One of them called the cops, anonymously. But the idiot used his traceable cell phone, and we picked him up right away. Ms. Sanchez was lucky the medic caught her barely breathing."

"For sure. These crooks weren't worried about the *cameras*?"

"They wore black outfits and must have known the cameras loop is for twenty four hours. They've been pilfering for a year. The restaurant manager couldn't figure why profits were down," Spano said. "I need to join my troops inside. I'll see you and Mannion later."

Harry placed the turtle bowl on his front seat and drove off. Strangely, a dread came over him—like he wasn't *alone* in the car. As he proceeded through several green lights, he thought he heard a hiss in the back seat. At a red light, he looked into the backseat, where a copper colored snake lay coiled, staring back, flicking its tongue. He raced into a strip mall lot and opened the back door, encouraging the snake to exit the car. He watched it slither onto the pavement and into the tall grass of a nearby field.

Sweat dripped down his back. *That creature didn't get in my car by choice.* His windows and doors had been closed, but not locked. Later, Harry learned the snake wasn't one of the many innocuous snakes in North Carolina. Its size and coloration identified it as a pit viper of the poisonous Copperhead species. Harry surmised someone who was annoyed at his investigations upped the ante—just when he began looking into the attack on KiKi. The investigation then became even more personal.

As he drove back to the office, the diary dug into his ass to remind him of what he had found. When Spano spouted suspicions about Bernie, Harry made a decision to read the diary before turning it over. After he parked the car near the office, he pulled out the diary with diminished expectations of finding anything related to KiKI's disappearance.

He discovered ramblings about movies and general thoughts about life. There were doodles of flowers and seagulls and a hundred faces. She dotted all letter i's with a circle. One page contained scribbled lyrics about loneliness.

Another page contained initials, with comments next to each. The top of the page had *BM* with a filled-in heart next to the initials of Bernie. Next to the initials *DD* she added, *Ass Hole*. Another was *JDH* and *slick Willie*. Harry noted the *HP* had a question mark next to it. She still wasn't sure about Harry.

There were music gigs and some medical appointments listed. The last entry gave Harry hope for progress: *Slick Willie wants to meet face to face. Balls!* Returning the diary to his pocket, he entered the office.

Since KiKi was attacked by someone *other* than the Goat Man, Harry believed the motivation was specific as opposed to random. Besides the diary, there were no clues in her apartment, though he thought her desk might still contain hints. He sat in the swivel chair and used the password supplied from Bernie to review her electronic folders and files. He was fortunate that her laptop was locked in the docking station and required no password.

There was one that caught his attention: *Willie,* like in *Slick Willie* her reference to JD Henzlein in her diary. He opened the file and found scanned papers. Recent documents looked like some building purchases for a corporation, with various signatures. They had all been signed by Jefferson Davis Henzlein and Bernard Mannion, along with several other names that sounded familiar. Harry took notice of the *day* the papers were signed—July fifth, which was odd, since it hadn't happened yet.

Harry hit the print icon and waited for the copies. Flipping through hanging folders with hard copies he opened a folder labeled, *Land Deal,* but it was empty. Perhaps it had contained the original hard copies that KiKi scanned into her computer. A thief might have taken them and ignored the scanned versions.

Maybe there was another less obvious break-in? For almost two hours, he looked but found nothing further of interest. He linked the investment deal with the entry in her diary, referring to Mr. JD Henzlein, or *Slick Willie*. He had no idea about the *Balls* reference.

He folded the printed contract pages and put them into his pocket. Spano would arrive within the hour. Once he had determined there was nothing bad about Bernie in the diary, he planted it in one of KiKi's desk drawers for the cops to discover. It was the right thing to do with evidence.

The vibration in his pocket diverted his attention to indicate a call from Bernie.

"Harry! They *just* beat the shit outta me! I need you…"

"What the hell? Where *are* you, Bernie?"

"I'm near the river—downtown in the men's room by the tourist boats. I'm hurt! I'm hurt *real* bad!"

He heard a thud on the other end of the line—like the blunt sound of a body hitting the ground.

CHAPTER TWENTY-SEVEN

Carolyn ran on the beach. The military helicopters roared above the ocean along Wrightsville Beach. She was familiar with the gyrating rotors, which she usually heard at night, flying near her condo. Noise blocked by her earphones, she saw their dark visage above the bright beach, which differed from the resultant rattle of glasswarein her apartment during their nocturnal practices.

But to a war veteran like Carolyn, the thumping sounds sometimes elicited nightmares of past interactions. On the sunny beach, the ominous war machines triggered memories of when she fought in the sandy desert beneath helicopter cover. Those days, she carried lethal weapons. Now in jogging attire, her only weapon was her personal strength and skills.

Carolyn neared completion of her morning run on that July day. Sweat dripped down her chest. After slowing her pace to cool down, she ran off the beach through a public access area. Few people appeared at such an early hour. At home, following a shower, she wrapped herself in a towel. When she exited the bathroom, her brother David stood in the living room, with his friend Rock.

"Hi Sis, glad we caught you dressed! I just stopped by to let you know we're going AWOL for a few days and not to worry."

Dave opened her refrigerator and handed a beer to his friend, taking another for himself. His offering to Carolyn went ignored, as she left the room to replace the wet towel with a top and shorts.

"I forgot the other night to present you with this special bottle of German Riesling. I know you'll love it, and at this price, you *should*!" he laughed.

"Does this AWOL have to do with your big secret project?" she asked as she flipped back her wet blonde hair.

"Yeah, right—a *big* project. You know me!"

Carolyn looked at the men—one, she barely knew, and the other had been her closest confidante for all her life. They beamed with confidence. While she felt happy that David would avoid military punishment, she regretted his imminent departure.

"And this deal you're into is nothing *illegal*, right?"

Rock stood and went into the bathroom.

"Look, I *know* you've supported me through all this Marine bullshit—*and* that blackmail attempt is almost resolved, but *this* time it's a legitimate business deal. Me and Rock are helping a friend and making some start-up cash for our Surfer's Shop in Puerto Limon. This is a short term farewell until you join me in Costa Rica!"

He finished the Blue Moon in one gulp.

"Be *careful*, Brother," she warned.

She had become re-accustomed to telling her brother what to do. At that point, he seemed engaged in too many activities with too many strangers.

"Hey Sis—you know me. I'm big and strong, but that doesn't mean I'm *stupid*. This deal is a winner. I'm *Ares* and Rock is *Adonis*."

Rock returned to the living room and sat next to Dave, who winked at Rock while simultaneously caressing Carolyn's shoulder.

"What's the latest timing for your official days in the Marines?" she asked, feeling a jealous glare from Rock.

"Well, the deal is signed with an official discharge, effective July 15th. But the power boys just want me out of sight and mind, so I'm officially on a medical leave until then. JD got them to agree to *stress related illness. I* call it a paid vacation!"

He exaggerated a broad smile that Carolyn recalled from their youth.

Rock glanced at his multi-dialed watch, exposing bruises on his knuckles, causing Carolyn to feel a tinge of regret.

"Where are you guys *headed?*"

"For now—Charleston to do a little project we're helping with at The Citadel, and then a little R and R—thanks to *your* help for closure on all this, Sis. You're the best!"

The men made Carolyn feel wary. Dave and Rock rose from the couch in unison, like they were being pulled by a puppeteer. They towered over Carolyn by almost a foot. She hugged David tight, as if in farewell. She nodded at Rock.

"Take *care* of yourself, Brother."

After the men departed, Carolyn returned to her bathroom and dried her wet hair with the blower at the hottest level, though the hot air couldn't untangle her concerns. She had done so much to protect David, and now he was off with Rock. Having known David all her life, she knew he was lying.

And how long can I protect him? I've been helping David all my life. Maybe following the final act, it will be time to cut off that sibling support?

Carolyn pressed her pelvis against the pointed edge of the sink. She lowered the aim of the hot dryer and closed her eyes. Her body warmed to the vision of her and David, together on the sand in Costa Rica. Her hips moved in sensual pleasure at the vision. The hairdryer heat soon intensified and returned her attention to the present. She snapped the off button of the dryer. *Too bad I couldn't do that with my life, snap switches on and off to avoid being burned.*

Her protective role nearly finished, she decided to go shopping. She walked down the stairs and entered the Corolla. The azure sky filled with gray clouds, rumbling like albino buffalo across the horizon. She never noticed the white van on the corner.

When she drove out the parking lot, the van started up and followed her. The driver squeezed the steering wheel and leered in anticipation. Lloyd Curtin was ready.

After Dave Dodd drove away from Carolyn's condo, he turned to Rock.

"You got everything we *need*, right?"

"Of course! *You* made the travel arrangements?"

"I have our plane tickets right here!"

The men pounded fists.

"I can't believe Carolyn thinks you'll be out of town on July fourth. And *she'll* clear up the loose ends? Man, she's like your personal pit bull protector," Rock said in amazement.

"Carolyn loves me and what do they say?—sometimes, love is blind. Besides, I'll share all this with her later. She has one final act to finish things up."

"And we get the *money* tomorrow?" Rock asked.

"Fifty percent up front and another fifty percent after the *deed* is done," Dave laughed. "Like *we* would be so stupid to wait around for the *other* fifty percent! Do they think we're saps? Once the crowd sings, *the rocket's red glare*, we are *gone*! "

Rock reached out his muscular hand to caress Dave's knee.

"Two tickets to paradise!" Dave proclaimed.

~~~~~~

Exceeding eighty miles per hour, Harry exited near the USSNC battleship tourist sign. The Taurus rattled over the bridge into downtown Wilmington. He pulled into a parking garage and jogged down Market to Front Street toward the River. Across the cobblestone avenue, he shouldered his way through stagnant tourists. The public restrooms were on the Cape Fear River Walk. Harry took a deep breath and pushed open the door to the Men's Room. To his surprise, it appeared empty.

"Bernie!" Harry shouted while looking under the stalls for feet. He saw nothing, and decided to open each stall door just in case. *Isn't this where Bernie said he would be?* The first two stalls were empty. The third one wasn't.

Cramped in a fetal position atop the bowl, Harry found a barely recognizable Bernie Mannion. Blood seeped from his bruised and swollen face. His arms were scrunched across his chest, while his knees pressed into his bent torso. At best, he appeared unconscious.

Harry reached out two fingers to feel for a pulse in his old friend's neck, willing a heartbeat.

"Bernie! Bernie! Talk to me!"

Bernie's eyelids fluttered and one eye opened, responding to human touch. He tried to smile through puffy purple lips and the dried blood on his chin.

"They fucked me up pretty bad, Harry. Help me outta this shit hole, will ya?"

"Maybe first I call an ambulance… and the *cops*."

"*No!*" Bernie shouted.

He grunted as he strained to move himself into a near vertical position.

"I don't need our brothers in blue. Let's talk and you'll see why. Let's find a gin mill somewhere."

Harry helped the broad man crawl out of the cubicle. At the sink, Harry wetted a paper towel and wiped blood off Bernie's face, all the while assessing his friend's state. Bernie seemed alert, but discouraged and in pain—wincing at every dab of towel.

They struggled up a cobblestone alley and proceeded into The Happy Times bar, where Harry commandeered a booth. Patrons ignored the pair, sensing that Harry was helping a drunken friend.

Bernie flopped into the booth, even ignoring the pretty waitress. His eyes were like oysters with splotches of hot sauce. After guzzling a pint of Guinness, Bernie sought another. His hand trembled as he held the glass. He wiped his hand gently across swollen lips and then shared his story with Harry.

"I got into this deal with JD to buy some property downtown as an investment. I just wanted to get that boat, man. What a jerk I am, Harry—just a silly old *fool!* Then somehow, the profit on the deal depended on activity by these college anarchist types, involved with the fuckin MLF!"

"I can't let the police know about that deal. I found out too late that there might be some squirrely connections. I guess the real estate profits are tied into some chaos caused on July fourth that I have nothing to do with. These college fuckers wanted to warn the military complex about sending warriors to other countries. Like without us, these places are *peaceful.*"

"You're confusing me, Bernie. Why are they kicking you around?"

"I think they believe I know more than I *do* about their shit activity planned here for the fourth. They claimed it was a peaceful demonstration, but if it was so fuckin peaceful, why *beat* me up? They said they couldn't trust me to keep secrets, and the beating was a warning not to tell anyone about what I know. Hey, they knocked out my *tooth*, Harry!"

He opened his mouth to show Harry the bloody gap with the missing tooth.

"Thirty *years* a cop and I *never* had this done to me, Harry! Nobody *ever* took me down this way! Bastards!"

"Who is *they*, Bernie, and what about this MLF group?"

"I swear to God—I don't know the specifics. The Military Liberation Front is some puissant little group that protests military activities and presence."

"Is *that* why you were in New York City?"

"Yeah, and the shitheads didn't even have an *office*—more like a mailbox! All I heard was some kind of big demonstration downtown on the Cape Fear River during July fourth celebrations. Exactly what—I don't know, and I *told* them that. The guy I met was this little guy, Karim. He was radicalized at some mosque in Tennessee. Now he's a student at WC. I'm guessing the other two big guys with him were college guys *too*."

"How did you *meet* him?"

"I think he may be a client of JD. I met him at some barbecue party JD had."

The detective mind of Harry raced through information from various sources. *What did any of this have to do with the attempted murder of KiKi?* Bits of facts flooded his mind—from the newspaper report about military arms thefts from the Southport Depot nearby, the symbolic presence of the USSNC, the newspaper advertisement about a night of fireworks, the downtown investment, meetings with JD, a dead Colonel in Camp Lejeune, a dead radical named Jasmyne, a dead detective in Manhattan and ties to the MLF. *People don't usually get murdered over legal court cases, but they do over subversive plots!*

In the Wilmington bar with a battered Bernie, Harry revisited the question.

"Are you going to tell me the *truth* about that Janakowsky guy in New York?"

Bernie dabbed his bloody lips and shook his head in disgust.

"I didn't want you involved in this, Harry. Janakowsky guided me into this private investigation business here in Wilmington, and then he sort of retired, handing some of his clientele off to me. Retirement bored him so, I paid him to help out on some cases—you know, check stuff out.

"I had him look into the MLF, who are *supposedly* headquartered in Manhattan. I didn't think he connected with anyone. Then all of a sudden, he's found dead. How *did* Janakowsky die?" Bernie asked.

"Cause of death undetermined, but maybe not so natural."

Harry looked at the bloody tooth in Bernie's hand.

"It's your canine tooth, Bernie. No more meat for you!"

Harry tried to offer a smile, but it felt weak at best.

After two additional mugs of Guinness, Bernie seemed to move around better. Maybe after so many years, Harry had under-appreciated the restorative powers of beer. The ice applied in a napkin helped the facial swelling, and the winces from the ribs seemed less severe. Harry felt more comfortable about not rushing Bernie to Brunswick Hospital. Getting beat up by college kids was humiliation enough!

"I'm bad news, Harry. People I touch get killed. My poor Ethel under that car and… I *sent* Janakowsky to New York. And now *KiKi* is nearly dead? I'm sorry I *lied* to you. But *you* better be extra careful yourself, Harry."

"How did KiKi fit into *all* this, Bernie?"

"KiKi? Nothing, Harry. No way. Are you shittin me? I would never involve her in anything dangerous. You got any pain killers?"

Harry slipped him Advil from the cache he carried around for his knee. Bernie washed the pills down with the dark Guinness.

"She's a good kid. I loved her like she was my daughter, Harry. You know that."

Bernie grimaced, touching his swelling lip.

"I just had her copy and file stuff. Why?"

"Well, someone put a poisonous snake in my car, so I figured no one was threatened when I looked into the Radinsky disappearance. But now someone may want me to stop looking into KiKi's attack. Maybe there's a connection?"

They continued their discussion over more beer.

~~~~~~

Standing outside The Happy Times bar and leaning on a parking meter, the short, burly young man spoke into a Bluetooth ear piece.

"I *told* you we couldn't trust that old fart. Now he's crying his heart out to that Harry guy about what's going on. *Somehow*, they're going to screw everything up!"

The man awaited the arrival of his cohorts from campus. For the moment, he spoke to the person who controlled the local MLF cell. The voice came across clearly to the man in front of the bar.

"The campus lessons were all talk. Historical examples prove that only action influences change. Those bastards shipped boatloads of troops from the Cape Fear River to kill your family in Iraq. Now it's time to convince them to stay home and stop trying to police the world and convert everyone to democracy."

"What is your plan of what to do with these two old guys? Seems like they aren't scaring off like we hoped," the man said.

"We must react swiftly against anyone who represents a threat. They can't diminish our Independence Day. We will need to get rid of them *both*!" the woman ordered.

"*Got* it!" the man snapped, standing straight up, glancing along the tourist filled busy sidewalks.

Before he tapped the ear bud to disconnect, he heard Professor Annabelle Radinsky-Wade repeat the order.

"Get *rid* of them... permanently!"

CHAPTER TWENTY-EIGHT

In the bar, Harry felt his phone vibrating, displaying a text that Chief Spano was at the office, waiting for them. Another text message came from the FBI's Niese, who demanded to meet immediately. Harry's priority was to take Bernie somewhere safe, while explaining events to the chief and then connect with the FBI.

Along with a serial killer, a *terrorist plot* seemed active in Wilmington. *Are any of these deaths linked? What will tell me who tried to kill KiKi?* How many more lives are at risk? He needed a plan that would require the help of others to prevent further deaths.

He ordered a final Guinness for Bernie and a Red Bull for himself. While Bernie drank and moaned, Harry wrote notes on a bar napkin. He created a *to do* list of people he needed to talk to immediately. The Fourth of July was just thirty-six hours away.

Looking every bit like the war veterans they were, Harry helped Bernie limp to the garage. A few grunts later, he squeezed Bernie into his car. Driving north past Ogden signs, he followed mumbled directions from Bernie, who seemed ready to sleep. They travelled Middle Sound Loop, past a Burger King.

"Want a Whopper, Bernie?"

"You're not *funny*, Harry."

"Last *offer*, Bernie—let me take you to a hospital… at least a Medac clinic?"

He looked quickly at his wounded friend, who dabbed wet paper towels across his swollen lip.

"Take me home. I'll be okay. They knocked out my *tooth*, Harry!"

They pulled up in front of a modest house, with a live oak that spread a century of branches and blocked street views of the front windows. After settling Bernie in an oversized recliner in the living room, Harry seized a bottle of Johnny Walker Red and a glass of ice. He found some Advil in the bathroom and served the combination to Bernie.

"Thanks, man. Giving me more pills and booze?—*just* what the doctor ordered. I'll be fine."

Bernie gulped the pills and swallowed two fingers of scotch. He laid his head back and stretched out his legs.

"All right, I'm leaving," Harry said quietly. "*You* rest. If you need anything, call my cell phone—hear me?"

Bernie nodded and closed his eyes in exhaustion. Harry walked toward the front door, accepting that life is the only killer we can't stop as time drives to an inevitable conclusion.

"I didn't *do* you right. I *owe* you, man," Bernie mumbled.

Harry exited the front door, double-locking it behind him. He realized his dinner date was not going to happen tonight, so he called Holly.

"Let me *guess*—you can't *make* it," she said, even before he could say a word.

He had to get used to this caller ID exposure!

"Bernie got beat up and I need to follow up on some serious stuff. Sorry."

"How is he? Did you take him to the *hospital*?" she asked.

"He's getting better, but he wouldn't go!"

"You *do* know I'm a nurse. Can I help?"

Harry got in his car as they talked, watching the traffic congestion before him.

She sounded concerned.

"*I* could help him, Harry."

"What about the *kids*, Holly?"

"Oh Harry Powell—please join us in the twenty-first century. We are superwomen—combining motherhood and careers. You might have *heard* about us?"

Harry could almost see her warm smile. He considered his two worlds colliding—with the retired on-the-beach Harry friends meeting the criminal-chasing Harry contacts. Holly would become a rare cross-over to both lives, which made him hesitate before replying. *Is there any danger in her getting involved?*

"Okay, but please be careful. There are people out there who want to *hurt* us. If you could come and check on him, that would be great. The small garage side door is unlocked. Thanks!"

"Do you know who *did* this to Bernie?"

"*Another* long story, and thanks again for setting me up with your father-in-law, General Sabbatino. We had a long talk yesterday about activity around Camp Lejeune. He's a *good* man!"

He gave her Bernie's address and ended the call before driving past red, white and blue banners on a fireworks stand with *bargains galore*, on a seasonal lot. After accepting Harry's excuses, Chief Spano said he would go visit Bernie personally. Not long after, Harry found himself in a nondescript business center office, seated across from FBI Agent Zachary Niese.

"Technically, it's *Special* Agent," he said to Harry.

Harry read the office walls to learn more about the man facing him. Unfortunately, the temporary office in Landfall displayed generic pictures. Next week, the space might be occupied by someone trying to sell seniors overpriced annuities they didn't need.

"So, I have your report on what you learned about Natasha Radinsky here. Thanks for your observations and thoughts, Powell. It will save us time, *quid pro quo* communications. We try to keep the specifics to a minimum with the media and use *homicide violence*."

"*You* didn't demand my presence here for *appreciation*, did you?" Harry asked.

Maybe it was the Red Bull, but he felt anxious about merely talking, and not *acting*.

"And *you* didn't come here just because I *asked*, did you?" Niese countered.

He examined Harry's appearance.

"That *blood* on your shirt?"

"Just helping a *friend*, after he was... hurt."

"I called this meeting regarding the serial killer. We think the killer suffers from *picquerism*—he derives pleasure causing pain—through *puncturing* his victims. The displayed rage on the two bodies and the knife slashing are typical of such a killer. The old time profilers called them "anger excitation" types. We have new terminology today, but the basics are the same."

"He gets off on the torture and control of the victim, with the murder only a final statement. This unsub strangles them so he can *feel* them dying. He has to contain them so he can *possess* them. There are indications that he performs these heinous actions in a remote domicile, or a moving venue."

"Like the white *van* seen at the library and by the cop on the bridge?" Harry concluded.

"Yeah, and there are a few of *those* around, Powell. We haven't *got* much at this stage—only a skinny white guy in his thirties, who drives a white van and wears a baseball hat. That doesn't narrow things too much."

Harry leaned forward as Niese continued.

"We'll let the media assume Sanchez's attack is *related*, so maybe it will help flush this guy out. The results of a CODEX search for the *modus operandi* of the killer showed animal insertion pre-mortem, which matched events in various locations from Lebanon, Indiana to Wilmington, North Carolina, with several bodies found along State Highways in Tennessee and West Virginia. The timeline indicates an almost *eight* year gap from the Indiana murders."

"So it's the *same* guy?" Harry asserted.

"Most likely. This guy seems to have been hard at work killing in Indiana—most likely as a resident. Then he seems to have almost disappeared for almost eight years, but we don't know that for certain. Just because we haven't found *bodies* doesn't mean he's been dormant. The roads from Indiana to North Carolina are long and mountainous. There could be bodies in remote areas, beyond the larger truck stops."

"That eight year gap—I'm assuming you've checked jails for any incarceration along the journey east?" Harry asked.

"We're working on that. It may have all began when your partner, Bernard Mannion, worked as a cop in Indiana. And where were *you* during that time, Powell?"

Niese looked at the assorted pages in front of him, as if he had the answers and was waiting to see if Harry would confirm or deny. Harry was familiar with the technique.

"Bernie being in Indianapolis when those bodies were buried in Lebanon means *what*? They're *different* jurisdictions. And to answer your question—I was working in *Chicago* during the first few years those goat farm murders occurred.

"You were a *cop* in Chicago."

"Yeah, remember—you mentioned how we *met* in Chicago back in the day? I'll bet *that's* my whole history from the Chicago PD there, right in front of you! So *why* the games?"

Niese looked up from the papers with a steely glare. If he meant to intimidate Harry, he had failed.

"No *games*, Powell—I'm just stating a fact. We're trying to link our unsub from Indiana to Wilmington. Your *record* intrigues me. How does a guy go from Chicago *gold badge detective*, to security work at an Indiana drug company, to the night shift at a third-rate New

York hotel, to unemployed in the exact *same* timeframe I'm trying to identify a killer?

"And *then* he shows up in *Wilmington* with a business partner—who was in *Indiana* at the *same* time as the *murders* there? Seems *unlikely* there's no connection, *doesn't* it?"

Harry noticed Niese had a manicure.

"*Coincidence*, Special Agent. You have the record of my life in the papers in front of you. I don't feel a need to *defend* myself—or Bernie, for that matter."

Niese smirked at the response and proceeded to read through the papers.

"You're a piece of *work*, Powell. You *hit* a superior officer while in the army? In Chicago, you *killed* the men who supposedly murdered your wife. I guess it doesn't pay for a woman to marry you or Mannion—they all end up dead. And then you lost your *house* in Maine to foreclosure? Tough times, and your friend, Mannion, helped you out? You *owe* him. I can appreciate that!"

Harry shifted in the uncomfortable chair, hoping the discussion wouldn't get any more personal. *He needed to find who attacked Bernie.*

"That's all *mostly* correct—except that '*supposedly*'—no, you're wrong there. Those punks *did* kill my wife. And I didn't *murder* them. They were committing a felony when I shot them to save another victim. But what's your *point*? I shared all I know. Why am I here now?"

"Lebanon, Indiana. One of the cops at the location of the twelve murdered women just happens to be your partner's cousin, another Irishman by the name of Robert Mannion."

"Like I said—*coincidence*!"

Helping to catch a serial killer interested him, but dealing with the special agent's absurd innuendoes did not. He had to find who attacked KiKi and thwart a terrorist attack that threatened Bernie and others. He debated sharing what Bernie had told him with Niese, but asking for help didn't come easy.

"And now Ms. KiKi Sanchez is attacked—right here in Wilmington, and she's an *employee* of the Mannion Private Eye Company *and* a close personal friend of your partner."

"Well, let's get *this* straight, Niese. KiKi and I *both* worked for Bernie, who is a retired and *decorated* cop. He's a licensed private investigator, paid to help clients. I don't get your focus. You have a rampant serial killer and potential terrorism and… and you're dicking around with *us*?"

Niese jerked his head up and shot Harry a glare.

"My focus is *my* concern. I'm the FBI profiler and Special Agent, Powell. You're nothing but a disgraced former cop from another century with a history of violence—who last worked a graveyard shift security job in a fleabag hotel. And what are you referring to as *terrorism*?"

Harry felt the words slap him across the face, like gloves challenging him to a dual, but he focused on the question.

"You should *know*. Apparently, there's a campus cell of the MLF here in Wilmington that's planning some sort of protest on July fourth. That's all I know!"

"MLF on July fourth? We'll look *into* that. By the way, do you *know* a Fred Janakowsky?" Niese asked, again reading the pages in front of him.

The name hit Harry like a left hook from Smokin Joe Frazier and pounded his gut—when he expected a soft jab. He said nothing.

"You *know* him, Powell? He was *also* a private investigator from North Carolina, who was a partner of your buddy, Mannion. Only *this* guy was found dead in a hotel in Manhattan, the *Albertson*. Does that sound familiar, Powell—since it is where *you* just happened to *work* at the time? And it was *you* who called the NYPD? Any flashbacks on all this stuff—or is it just all a *coincidence*? There's a lot you *aren't* telling me."

An ominous reflection of the dead Janakowsky at the hotel became a harbinger of Harry's lonely demise. *Can a man subsist alone? Maybe not thrive, but a man could survive.* Harry was living proof of that minimalist expectation. He believed a man with a will to survive could outlive any tragedy. But there would come a time when the propellants of death would eventually pummel him. Alone, he grew closer to such a final scene. *Will I curl up in the sand to await the drowning waves of time?*

"Hey, I told you about the MLF protest. Janakowsky was in New York looking into that group, but he found nothing. They'd done a campus protest at WC, and one of Bernie's clients got involved. You're the FBI. Surely, you know about them. Are you guys looking *into* that?"

Niese avoided eye contact and Harry continued.

"I *told* you about the Goat Man possibly working as a mover, and you *ignored* me. And have you even *checked* prison records on the killer's route for those eight years? And yeah—*I* called in Janakowsky's death. So *what?* I didn't know him or what he was up to when I was in New York. He could have been a John Doe, for all I knew at the time."

Harry's words were tinged with a passion he hadn't felt in years. It felt *good* to be angry!

"I don't ignore anything, Powell. I have a serial killer to catch, and I can't worry about some puissant MLF protest. As far as I know, they're insignificant. Besides, Homeland Security now oversees terrorism groups. And college radicals don't serially kill."

"I get it, but a terrorist can kill more in minutes than a serial killer in a year."

Harry sat unmoving. He struggled to continue a dialogue, being clearly outmatched in facts.

"I want to know everything *you* know about what's going on here, Powell. There *are* connections. I want to know everything you know and I want to know it *now!*"

"You mean about the *Goat Man?* I gave you my report."

He deliberately added the media tag, hoping it would annoy Niese and throw him off his dominant game.

"I want what's *between* the lines. You need to *talk.*"

Harry leaned forward.

"Seriously? You want *my* help? *You* accuse Bernie and me of being some link to the crimes and…"

"Look, I *understand* you resent the Fed—I see all your authority conflicts from the records. But you could help catch a killer by sharing all you know."

"It seems that you know more about *me* than you do about the Goat Man, Niese. Besides, I have to *find* who attacked KiKi."

Niese looked up from the papers.

"Maybe there's some local familial connection here for the unsub? Maybe he's a member of the Mannion clan? After all, he did come here from Indiana."

Harry sat on the edge of the chair. He could walk out and let the Feds wait until Goat Man killed again. *But how many innocent women might die if my recalcitrance delays possible resolution? Is Holly a target? Is Carolyn a target?*

Harry recalled the stale room where Janakowsky died alone as well as Bernie's trembling arms after the attack. Most of all, he remembered KiKi's face as she lay in a coma at the hospital. He hesitated before deciding to take the approach he usually did—which was to tell the truth. "I'll share all I have on these events, so you can nail the Goat Man and be a media hero. You'll maybe even get yourself promoted, Niese. Maybe that MLF is nothing, but they do need to be scrutinized. Remember the Boston Marathon? But in exchange for my complete cooperation, I want some help to find who tried to kill KiKi Sanchez. Is that a deal?"

With glaring red eyes, Niese nodded consent.

Harry shared his knowledge with the FBI profiler, skipping the investment role of Bernie. He referenced his gut feeling that the deaths in Camp Lejeune and the July fourth protests were somehow linked. From Ginger, his Indiana source, he shared a recent tidbit with Niese.

"I'm *sure* your people checked the scene in Indiana. With all the crap, there was an eye patch found—like what a pirate might wear— like the Pittsburgh baseball cap I heard about at the strip club. Your serial killer may be someone with a local link to the history of *pirates* in Wilmington."

Niese nodded as he took notes.

Harry shifted his focus to KiKi. Over the decades, he accepted ownership of the ultimate justice done to those who assassinated his wife, and he planned the same results for those who tried to kill KiKi. Some attacks a man cannot avenge, but at times when he can, he owes it to the victim.

"Okay Powell, we're making *progress.*"

In the hunt to stop potential deaths, Harry felt rejuvenated. Being part of the team driving to stop a serial killer also drew him closer to providing his own justice. The Goat Man didn't beat up Bernie or leave a snake in his car. And the Goat Man didn't try to kill KiKi, but Harry was beginning to understand the link between those who might be involved.

"Now, *beyond* the Goat Man and to some *oth*er matters," Harry insisted.

CHAPTER TWENTY-NINE

After the interchange with Niese, Harry completed several phone calls. The hospital said only family could learn status on the phone, so he claimed he was KiKi's uncle. They told him she remained in a coma, but her life signs seemed to be stabilizing. Confirming that Bernie remained sore but was doing okay, Holly became a peaceful addition to the chaos in Harry's life. *Time for his one more comeback!*

The dusk sky became a mauve canvas. What did his grandmother say—*red sky at night, sailor's delight?* He parked the dirty Taurus and climbed the stairs. Less than two days remained before the fourth, and Harry would need to vacate this condo. Fortunately, he travelled light and hadn't yet removed items from his rental car— like the gun locked in the glove compartment.

To empty the refrigerator, he grabbed two cold Amstels and lay down on the couch. The first beer tasted great. He placed the second bottle under his right knee for cool comfort. He perused the scattered notes that covered the tabletop and retrieved his old black notepad. It was like his life—battered and used, but with a few more pages open to complete.

He created a page for each person. The cheap pen he used made him laugh, as it read Albertson Hotel, NYC.

KiKi—*Different MO probably means different attacker. If not psycho, motive? Nothing personal, but business files about downtown deal & diary about meeting with JD = linked? If deal is illegal it jeopardizes JD and others listed. Choking method by a pro (military?) is not done by a sexual sadist. WTF is Balls?*

Bernie—*good man with questionable connections, just wants cash for a boat. How is real estate deal w/JD linked to events on July fourth linked to MLF group? Bernie's attackers= College = MLF? Names? Does Annabelle know them? Natasha link?*

Janakowsky—*Dead PI in NYC linked to Bernie. NYC linked to Wilmington – MLF w Bernie. Link that drew in Harry. Get help to learn more —contact Homeland Security?*

General Sabbatino—*Camp Lejeune deaths. Were they both murders? Motive? Terrorism/ homophobe? F/U more info –need facts not rumors.*

Natasha—*Goat Man victim – FBI on serial killer. Did Goat Man see her dance? Jog? He attends strip joints? Were any of the dead Indiana women joggers? Press activity near beach and jogging=car found. Guy at strip club with Weston shirt and Pirates hat – is he the guy? Info shared.*

Prof. Annabelle—*Money + political clout. Views in class link to MLF? Check WC websites and publications. Annabelle and JD close? Business and/or personal? Both capable of illegality, but her daughter murdered? College radicals link to $$? Link to her?*

JD Henzlein—*Real estate deal makes a buck. Any link to terrorism? Is murder out of his league? Politics not his gig--unless it can help $$. Link to Bernie on real estate deal downtown. KiKi copied contracts. KiKi diary meeting with JD: What did he or she want? July fourth link? Balls? JD clients are Dave+Carolyn+Bernie (ties to military/murders?)+ Prof= He links to all!! Any link of Marines to radicals? Dave Dodd and his dead girlfriend?*

Agent Niese—*MLF is not on FBI watch list? Homeland Security? Utilize Federal databases on terrorists and serial killer MO research. Reinforce suspicion of Bernie misdirected. Is KiKi attack linked to any of the local deaths? Link to JD and diary – Balls?*

Dave Dodd—*Trained in weapons + wristwatch indicates he is an underwater diver? Video of KiKi body dump sees such a watch. Kiki a surfer - any link? Sharp eyes = appearance deceives as more brains than muscle? Any links to JD beyond court martial case? Is he an active member of MLF group? dead girlfriend was a link? Her death an accident or murder? DD resents Marines but terrorism from within? Why not - Fort Hood? He may not be radical, but his associates are? Any link to KiKi? Military choke? Real estate deal? What does he want?*

Colonel Bogart—*dead on WB. Another coincidence? He pushed prosecution of Dodd- Was he anti-gay or anti-terrorist or both/neither? Re-Check cause of death and link to MLF.- Jasmyne and Karim! Why was he in WB? Does General Sabbatino know?*

Goat Man—*usual FBI profile as 30-35 yr old white male. With ties to IN and now to NC + VA? Transient job. Where does he buy gerbils? Why bodies in water versus another "farm?" Possible jobs for transient in construction/movers/landscape? Cash based =untraceable. After recent murders, why change MO on KiKi? He wouldn't. Weston mover and pirate – link to locals-who? 8 years MIA- f/u FBI check jail records TN, KY, etc. Pirates cap-Pittsburgh or a pirate? Links in WNC to pirates? The eye patch in the killing field in Indiana. Seen here? Long history in area – JD Henzlein!!*

Harry saved the last blank page for the person he least understood:

Carolyn—*truth on relocation to NC? Relationships -with brother? with JD? Bernie? No link to JD, Annabelle, or KiKi - Dave Dodd is key. Her changes in demeanor means what? Cold eyes. Her history as a trained killer pertinent: military choke on KiKi but no link. Is she a target of the serial killer, or a killer herself? Future link with Harry?*

All the names were duplicated on two pages, except for Holly. She apparently had no connection, except a dead husband once stationed at Camp Lejeune and a father-in-law General. Harry finished the bottle of Amstel and removed the other from beneath his knee to drink it. With more questions than answers, he felt there was a connection. Again, the pieces in the jigsaw bounced around, looking for a link. Some pieces were coming together, but the picture still escaped him.

A new word repeated in his notes—*balls*. He searched Google for "Wilmington" and "*balls.*" And there it *was!*—a sports bar in downtown Wilmington—with no website and no phone number. Business hours began at 5:00 pm. *Why would KiKi be meeting Henzlein at a sports bar closed in the daytime?*

Turning the pages, he reviewed his scribbles, looking for a link. *Maybe nothing connected, and maybe everything?* The FBI would chase the serial killer using VICAP and make progress on the two local murders. Niese could link to Homeland Security to track down the MLF group and local members. Radical thought was the norm on some campuses, but had the professor expanded beyond being a theorist bloviating to novices? Spano was at least looking into the beating of KiKi, and Bernie.

There seemed to be more from the Camp Lejeune perspective. *Holly's father-in-law can help some more. A dead colonel who pushes to court martial David Dodd, whose sister came here to help him? Plus, Dodd has a radical girlfriend whose death didn't appear to devastate him.* Harry learned they had originally met on the WC campus at some Mujahidin Youth Movement rally.

Does Annabelle know either of them? So many murders in the shadow of military protection could *not* be attributed to a random serial killer. Harry didn't believe all these attacks were random. His gut told him that, while there were coincidences, there were also links to some plan of murder and possible retribution. It was as if two killers were operating in peaceful Wilmington at the same time.

And despite the horrific, singular deaths from a serial killer psycho, those killings would pale to a potential massive slaughter by terrorists. The image of people falling from the World Trade Center before the building collapse remained indelible in Harry's mind.

Harry compartmentalized the links to a serial killer and focused on the beating of KiKi. *Was her attack connected to the upcoming demonstrations of July fourth? Did the JD real estate deal have anything to do with her attack? July fourth seems to link MLF demonstrations and the warehouse purchase deal—and that was less than two days from now. Is it all just a coincidence?* From what Bernie told him, the beating indicated a state of panic as Independence Day loomed.

Bernie had more answers, and perhaps Spano could extract more from him. If there were a campus terrorism link, Niese could probably draw more from the professor. The biggest unanswered question in the pages before him was the notation in KiKi's diary of a meeting with JD. *Tomorrow morning, I'll visit Slick Willie.*

He tossed the two empty beer bottles into the garbage and grabbed a third from the near empty refrigerator. The next day was July third, and Harry needed a good night's sleep. Opening the glass doors, he stood on his balcony and looked past palm trees at the distant charcoal sky. Bright, peaceful moonlight penetrated the darkness.

Without notice, the glass on the sliding doors shattered, causing Harry to drop instinctively to the stone patio. The beer bottle also dropped from his grip and shattered on the cement floor. He recognized the filtered sounds of a silenced gun. The shots continued hitting the area above him. Glass shattered everywhere. The shots sounded like they came from below. *Someone is definitely shooting at me!*

Harry stayed down and lied still. His heart rate accelerated to palpable levels—like he was back in Vietnam—when unseen Cong snipers targeted his battalion. He peered through the balcony railing, but he saw no one. The quiet returned when the shooting stopped. Beyond the shrubs came the sound of squealing tires, which broke the sounds of silence.

Harry grunted and rolled off his back to crawl over to examine the shattered apartment doors. He moved like a cat to avoid glass shards on the balcony. Holes on the walls were visible, but he had heard more shots. After rising to a crouch, he duck-walked back inside the condo, cautiously standing against a solid wall, pain shooting through his throbbing knee. Looking down at his chest, he saw no blood—just pieces of glass.

Yanking his phone from his pocket, he punched in the number.

"Hi—it's Harry. Someone just *shot* at me! I'm home at the condo. Yeah, I'll be here. Thanks, Chief."

He limped downstairs to his car and opened the glove compartment to retrieve his own gun.

CHAPTER THIRTY

Carolyn awoke as the bright morning sun spread warmth across the bedroom where she crawled out of bed. Hurried, she dressed for running with the goal to reach the beach before too many tourists arrived. It was July third, after all, and Wilmington was filled with visitors. After eating a Greek yogurt, she jogged out the door in search of the cooling ocean breeze that cleansed her skin and her mind.

~~~~~~

Lloyd Curtin devoured a jelly donut and wished the van's air conditioner worked better. Glancing in his rearview mirror, he admired his shiny earring. *Today is the day I'll take Army Girl!* Knowing her routine helped him wait in confidence. After following Army Girl several times, he knew she lived alone and went jogging on Wrightsville Beach at six thirty every morning.

Her route included two blocks next to the Blockade Runner Hotel. Lloyd appreciated the hotel's name. Besides running blockades, his pirate ancestors aboard corsairs plundered merchant ships sailing too close to the Confederate Carolinas. He read about the shipwreck of the "Modern Greece," found off Fort Fisher, which failed to evade Union vessels to deliver supplies to Wilmington during Lincoln's War. That was Lloyd—a blockade-running pirate about to attack booty running too close to shore—Army Girl. *A man is what a man is!*

He rolled the van into a side street parking spot near the beach access sign. He kept the engine running to keep the air conditioner working. Hung-over tourists slept in rented rooms in the low country beach homes. No cops would hassle him at this hour.

In his rearview mirror, he watched like a lookout on a pirate ship. Then he saw her stretch her taut white legs in tight red shorts. Her inviting high ass made the urge enlarge in his jeans. She walked, while stretching with purpose along the street. Soon, she disappeared through the sandy beach entry among the high grasses. Lloyd looked at the dashboard clock. For thirty minutes she would run and then return at the same spot where she had just departed. Lloyd tingled with anticipation. *In thirty minutes, Army Girl will be mine!*

"All ready, little Lloyd?" he asked the encaged starving ferret.

~~~~ ~~

Carolyn enjoyed the strain of stretching muscles as she walked. Wrightsville was such a peaceful part of what was once the busiest Confederate port. After crossing the walkway, she smiled at the welcoming horizon, filled with sparkling ocean. Cloudless blue sky met green water, a peaceful place filled with optimism.

Jogging slowly in place at first, she accelerated to a full run. There were no helicopters yet that morning. Her legs kicked high as her blonde hair bounced behind her, like a frisky pony, running with joy and abandon. Waves sparkling like diamonds, she never felt more alive.

~~ ~~~~

Lloyd climbed into the back of the van to straighten out the hanging picture of a pirate he had torn from the newspaper. Carefully, he rechecked his kit. The taser contained a full charge. Duct tape, knife, binding ties and cheese were accounted for. A box of Trojans awaited his use. *All is ready; Army Girl will soon be mine.*

He restrained the growing erection in his Wranglers. While he had the urges since childhood, he now believed they came from his pirate genes. Beyond the air conditioner, he only heard the feint squeak of the baby ferret, rattling its cage. Lloyd smiled and resisted rubbing himself so he could wait the remaining twenty minutes until Army Girl's run concluded—and then, he would *own* her. His palm itched in anticipation to yanking the blonde ponytail and tearing off her silky red shorts. Fifteen minutes remained, but it seemed like days!

~~~~~~

JD arched his back, exploding inside Amber. The summer intern smiled and pushed the crisp new hundred dollar bill into the lace covering her budding breasts. She bounced off him like an Olympic gymnast, and off she went with a farewell shake of her ass.

He smiled and pressed his lips with two fingers in an air kiss. They were the first to arrive at the office that day. The staff called Amber "Sis," which he originally thought was a term of endearment. He learned later that the office staff used the title as an acronym for *Summer Intern Slut*, or SIS.

He looked out the window as gray clouds began to roll across the clear skies. Inclement weather usually passed the waterfront area before any rain fell, but to JD, *these* clouds appeared darker than usual.

Mortgage documents spread across his desk—loan applications for Fannie Mae that he had created for applicants—all deceased. There was even a form for old Aunt P. *That* was why he had Amber do the copying. Even though they were airheads, his regulars might have eventually caught on to his phony machinations. Amber, however, would return to school in a few weeks, clueless, but with a cash bonus and fond memories. Trailer parks were filled with grateful girls like her who *understood* what to ignore.

As he placed the applications in the envelopes, JD laughed at how stupid bureaucratic government-controlled agencies were—they were like rubes, begging to be taken advantage of by anyone with brains and balls. It was as easy as checking a box to declare your eligibility for a federal hand out.

JD saw most people as content to grovel for pennies and celebrate with six-packs for the weekend. When agencies were billions in debt, what pencil-pusher punching a clock for a pension would question mere millions in mortgage requests by the destitute in little North Carolina?

Hell, I didn't blame the recipients. If someone wants to hand you a free house, you take it. JD was getting his piece of the pie. Few residents were actually evicted, which meant the chance his dead applicants would ever elicit scrutiny became a low risk. And if they *did* receive notice, it would just serve as a directive to depart the premises and never be heard from again.

The mortgages were not as lucrative as what he had planned downtown. Claiming damage on those warehouses would also lure government payouts. This scam would fill his Cayman Islands bank account and afford him a sabbatical there at the Ritz Carlton Resort.

Maybe even take a summer intern along for amusement? JD loved the deal and the chance to prove his brilliance. Either way, he would buy low and gather high returns with the refurbishment of downtown Wilmington—*thanks to government support.*

His idyllic daydreams were interrupted.

"JD, there's a man her to see you—a Mr. *Powell,*" Amber announced.

Harry barged right behind her.

"What the fuck! Okay, send him in."

JD moved his mortgage papers into a pile and covered them with a copy of *Wrightsville Beach* magazine. It was an old issue with a cover that featured grinning Businessman of the Year, Jefferson Davis Henzlein.

JD stood, extending his hand.

"Harry Powell—my *friend!* Have a *seat.* Do you want some sweet tea? How's the condo? I have…"

Harry sat down, in an aggressive crouch.

"Forget the condo and the bullet holes and shattered glass!"

"*Bullet* holes? What are you…?"

"Someone *shot* at me last night," Harry erupted.

"Sounds like a mistake, Harry. Maybe it was some early Independence Day revelers?"

"It was no *mistake,* but *that's* not why I'm here!"

"You're panicking about the *lease* expiration? I take care of any pal of Bernie's—I'll get you a *better* place!"

"I'm not here to talk about *my* apartment, JD. I'm here to ask about a future real estate deal *you're* working on in *downtown Wilmington!*"

A cold hardness overcame the disingenuous smile on JD's face. He looked at Harry like he was aiming a loaded weapon.

"Deal? I'm always doing *some* real estate deal. You may have noticed the sign out front on your way barging in here. This is a *real estate* business, and I'm an attorney. Deals are what I *do.*"

"*This* deal involves contracts for city-owned foreclosed properties—at a steal of a price—and all signed and pre-dated *before* the transfer date of July fifth—like you already *know* about some disaster that will further diminish their value.

"It's sort of like a company insider buying puts, while knowing about future events that drive the business down. You have assorted influential partners, as well, including my friend—Bernie Mannion."

The folded copies remained hidden in his pocket.

JD paused. *How the hell does Powell know about that deal? Blabbermouth Bernie must have told him!*

"Bernie Mannion is a *small* investor in a real estate investment, oh yes. It's nothing out of the ordinary. Buy low and sell high. It's all perfectly legal, and it will help my friends earn a few bucks. I always look out for my friends, Harry."

"Well, Bernie is like a *brother* to me, and he's your *friend*. Bernie was badly beaten up yesterday, by the way."

"What? When did *this* happen? Who would *do* such a terrible thing? I'll call Bernie right away."

JD pulled out his iPhone with a theatrical display of effort to emphasize his concern.

"He's resting right now. Better to leave him alone."

"What *hospital* is he in?"

"Don't worry. He's in a *safe* place… with guards," Harry sneered.

JD hesitated.

"I guess *he* told you about this… investment deal?"

"No. He actually didn't say anything… not until I *asked* him about it. I learned about it first from *another* source."

JD stared at Harry, evincing a warning that such "openness" endangered his health.

"Like I *said*, it's pretty straight forward—nothing out of the ordinary."

"Were *zoning* laws changed to help your odds at profit? The papers are dated July *fifth*. What's happening July fourth?" Harry pressed.

"I can't get into all the nuances of this *private* contract. It's just one of the many pies I have my fingers in. Maybe I can cut *you* into a future venture? A man has to pay the rent, doesn't he? But I assure you— there's nothing in this business transaction that would involve Bernie getting hurt. He's in *Cape Fear* Hospital, you said?"

"I didn't say *where* he was!"

Harry stared at JD, his fists clenched.

"And you wonder why people *shoot* at you, Harry? You must be putting your detective nose where it doesn't belong. I thought you were working on the *Radinsky* case—or has *real* law enforcement taken that away from you?"

JD touched the magazine on his desk.

"I thought my getting shot at was an *accident?*" Harry countered.

"What do you *want*, Powell? I'm a busy man."

"The FBI is working on the Goat Man murders. *Let's* just say that this is just my own curiosity about the attack on people I like very much—first KiKi Sanchez, and now my friend, Bernie. And I get *shot* at? That makes it really *personal*. You know—an amateur sleuth with *time* on his hands."

"Well, I'd let the federal *experts* run the show, Harry. I thought your little clerk was a victim of the Goat Man—who's from *Indiana*, isn't he?—where you *and* Bernie used to live, I believe?"

"Did your downtown deal include meeting with KiKi?"

JD looked at his garish Rolex.

"KiKi? Oh, the Sanchez from your office—the Goth, hippie girl with tattoos with whom our friend Bernie became so enamored? Not such a hot Latina, if you ask me—no offense intended. As to meeting with her, I hardly knew her name. She wasn't what I would call *investor* potential."

"You mean you couldn't soak any money from her? She's a good person."

JD looked around the room to avert Harry's penetrating glare, which he feared saw through his own criminal façade.

"Well, I'm certain the FBI will find who attacked her like the other women. Now, if you will excuse me…"

JD stood.

"So you *never* had a meeting with KiKi Sanchez?" Harry repeated.

"No meeting—no way. I hardly knew her. *Not* my type!"

"Ever hear of an MLF group?"

"Are they a rock band? I'm not very political, my friend. I'm just a businessman, trying to pay the rent. Now if you would be so kind…"

JD shuffled some papers, indicating it was time for Powell to leave.

Harry, however, didn't move, his silence taking effect.

"Who the *fuck* do you think you are, Powell? An over-the-hill private eye wannabe? You're nothing but a carpetbagger Yankee, interfering with southern *business* initiatives. Go back where you *came* from! You're not needed or *wanted* here!"

Henzlein stood.

"What about *Balls*—it's a bar downtown. Do you know anything *about* it?"

Harry watched carefully for any signs from Henzlein.

"I'm not *into* sports bars. Now, Mr. Powell, please *leave*."

"You're a lying asshole, Henzlein."

"Good-*bye*, Powell."

JD walked Harry to the front door. He slammed it shut after the detective left and peaked through the window to watch Powell enter his car and accelerate out of the parking space. JD tapped his phone and strummed his fingers on the desk. The call rolled into message answering. In a diminished tone, he spoke.

"We've got *troubles*, Annabelle. Call me."

Professor Annabelle Radinsky-Wade walked between Kenan Hall and the Campus Center on the idyllic campus of WC. Crepe myrtles bloomed like the young, febrile summer students, passing the professor. She regretted Natasha would no longer experience this cocoon life. Annabelle's existence revolved around her power among these students.

As a tenured professor in a state school, her position remained untouchable. As long as she showed up for a few hours of classes, she could teach or not teach, say anything she wanted, and the administration could do little to her. One passing student nodded, and though she couldn't recall his name, she knew he looked good in tight jeans. Annabelle needed to grab a salad before her next lecture, so she turned toward the cafeteria.

The MLF cell had been a welcome addition to her influence on campus. She mourned Natasha, but seemed to miss Jasmyne more. She was a strong, dedicated leader and the loss was palpable. While Jasmyne's brother, Karim, fulfilled the upcoming technical needs, he lacked the vision for long term influence.

Her iPhone signaled a missed call during the previous lecture. Without breaking stride, she listened to JD's message. She returned his call, but he didn't answer. She loved being on campus, because most of the people there agreed with her. Her views were consistent with all campus speakers, as they blocked any opposing ideas.

A college campus was not a stage of life to consider options, but a time to be told what to *think*. When outside recruiters who held her same beliefs visited the campus, she greeted them openly. Her beliefs coincided with global MLF, which started with constructive intentions, as did most extremists, but then they became filled with dystopian views of America and opportunistic power.

But her beliefs served her greater purpose in the progression from *talk* to *action*. Like Saul Alinsky said, *first you negotiate for a small piece, until eventually, you take the whole pie*—Like cherry pie, on the fourth of July.

Her goal was simple enough—to direct the thoughts of young people. *Isn't that what a teacher is supposed to do?* She ignored standardized textbooks that had to pass through a committee. *Fuck any core curriculum.* Her acolytes needed to hear the truth, as she saw it, not some homogenized academic bullshit.

She was the person who formed the student's belief systems— not some dusty textbook, written by old white men. MLF members shared professional reports and hand-outs that she gave to students.

Students weren't complete fools—they accepted that to receive an A meant compliance to her views. A university thrived because of a single consistent viewpoint and a hot house for the growth of a consistent progressive belief system. The only protests on campus were against outsiders, who didn't share their views, or a society not yet conformed.

Students were malleable pawns in her view. Visiting speakers and new professors who tried to preach an opposing view found out there was no tolerance or debate. Try to locate one of those disagreeable dinosaurs on a modern campus. She laughed at the takeover of the thought process in a controlled campus environment—now the most authoritarian locale in America.

The consistent campus thought process now had to be applied to battering the beliefs of the general public. *No military on campus and no military in Wilmington!* Fortunately, the media scorned anyone who disagreed with her views, and public thought would soon comply with the campus. That inevitable evolution needed to be accelerated through actions—sometimes violent.

She walked past the poster-plastered walls of upcoming events. Colorful signs extolled visits to Chapel Hill by former radicals from the sixties. The North Carolina public universities were aligning nicely. There was a one-hour seminar for the USMC and Navy, but attendees were ridiculed.

She strode into the dining area. Ignoring the bountiful salad bar, she settled for coffee and a piece of organic cherry pie. Among the scattered scruffy students, she observed—despite all having the same beliefs— that they *still* perceived themselves as rebels. Annabelle laughed!

While eating the pie, she read a text from the panicking JD about exposure. *Harry Powell has suddenly become Superman in the scared eyes of JD Henzlein. The man has no balls.* She lowered her chin and calmly entered a reply to JD, *Don't worry everything under control. Proceed as planned. Don't panic about one old man. Come by the house tonight to relax.*

Returning the iPhone to her Prada bag, she walked back toward the lecture hall, where the next choir to whom she would preach sat waiting. She smiled at the invigoration of power.

A few miles south of Pleasure Island and the historically preserved dunes near Fort Fisher, senior citizens Tony and Tara Smith were getting ready for bed. As usual, Tara made sure the lights were turned off. Tony checked the doors, to see they were locked— habits they brought from Boston. Tara checked on the food for their cats in the laundry room at the rear of their home.

Had she looked out that *particular* window, she may have noticed several backyard visitors. But she hadn't and she joined Tony in their front bedroom. Within minutes, they were peacefully asleep in the safety of their oceanfront home.

In the Smith's backyard, among the wild grass and sandy beach, three men in black wet suits were busy setting up base plates and bipods to fire mortar. Two of the men were soon-to-be ex-Marines, and the third was a young man they'd met on campus, who was a technical expert, connected to the MLF group. The men worked like feverish giant frogs on the sandy knoll, hidden behind oleanders.

Dave Dodd whispered urgent orders, while Karim provided expertise at enabling the weaponry. Rock moved the devices for balance. Karim aimed five units at the MOTSU Southport munitions distribution facility. He knew the Army shipped weapons from there around the world.

Karim also aimed "one, for good measure," at the warship, the *United States North Carolina*, which sat peacefully retired in the harbor. Although the trio would also have C4 explosives planted on board the ship, Karim liked the idea of overkill. Further explosives would also be sneaked onto Eagle Island, next to the battleship.

The plan was simple—celebratory fireworks would be succeeded by explosions aboard the symbol of the military for first responders and the crowd of spectators. Then smoke would be unleashed from warehouses along the river. Finally there would be destruction at the massive munitions plant in Southport.

Karim called this "show and go." He focused on the 'go' that disabled the military and let the two Marines focus on the protest "show" that sent messages. Karim visualized news reports similar to 9-11. It was time.

"No more messages. Now we make *headlines!*" Karim whispered to himself as he worked the launch equipment they carried on the amphibious boat. In the moonlight, Dave looked at Rock and shared a silent tolerance of Karim. Each man worked the set-up and then deferred to Karim to finish the precision calibration work.

Once the mortars were set, the three men disappeared into the black ocean. They swam a short distance to the amphibious boat that brought them there. The timing of their endeavor fit perfectly between the patrolling helicopters. They quietly motored south to the rocky shores of federally-protected Fort Fisher Park.

From there, they took the Jeep and drove downtown to align explosives in the swampy land called Eagle Island, next to the battleship. Rock wore tall rubber boots and planted devices in the wetlands, while Karim maneuvered around the stacked Chinese fireworks that had been dropped off for the Fourth of July celebration. He added a few special surprises of his own to create fear from chaos.

"That takes care of distraction from the boat," Karim concluded.

"For the *last* time, it's a *ship*," Dave complained. "You know the difference? A ship has a *captain*—a boat has a frustrated *husband!*"

The men shared a laugh that slightly lessened the tension.

The next morning was July fourth. Dave and Rock would dress for the final time in their full Marine attire and join a morning ship tour of the USSNC. They would sporadically stop to share an intimate embrace. Such affectionate displays would cause others to look away.

Without scrutiny, the men would place plastic G and C4 explosives in various strategic locations on the ship. They particularly liked the former medical surgical center at the middle of the ship. By noon on Independence Day, the explosives would be in place and linked to wireless remotes that each man held at different locations. Dave and Rock would be situated along the railing on the Cape Fear River Walk.

"They sent troops from here to kill my *family*," Karim complained.

"They wanted to toss me in the *brig* for love," Dave grumbled.

"We *need* money for the surf shop in Costa Rica!" Rock exclaimed.

Karim looked at the two giants, wanting to kick them.

"We assume our positions at zero eighteen hundred," Dave reaffirmed. "*After* the explosions, we reconnoiter in Leland for escape, as shown on JD's map. Are we clear?"

"Sure—by then the warehouses will be smoking and the battleship will be ablaze, and people will be scrambling from the additional fireworks explosions," Rock added.

"Payback is a *bitch*!" Karim declared.

The three men parted with nods of anticipation for Independence Day.

CHAPTER THIRTY-ONE

As if on schedule, Carolyn came off the beach. She slowed at the sight of the unmarked white van parked at the curb. Exhaust indicated the engine as running, which she found odd. The van wasn't there earlier, but *hadn't* she seen a van like this near St. Matthew's Church?

An inner alarm signaled her to imminent danger. Before her eyes, a desert scene flashed of the moments just before she was attacked in Iraq. She had felt alarmed then too, but the Iraqis had moved so quickly that she couldn't react fast enough.

Deceived by the sight of women and children—who were with apparently unarmed men—she thought it was a family outing. But she realized too late that the kids were just props for the combatants. Now, she felt uneasy by the situation before her—despite it being just an innocuous white van on a quiet peaceful street.

Increasingly concerned about the situation, she stopped jogging. The hair on her neck perked up. Ready this time, she ran in place, with her blonde ponytail swaying, her legs churning up and down. *Think!* She commanded herself. *What reason would a van have to appear upon the conclusion of my daily run?* Such a nondescript vehicle could harbor anything.

It definitely seemed out of place and was illegally parked. Beachfront breezes blew smoke exhaust from the tailpipe. Through tinted glass, she couldn't see a driver in the front seat. Her mind raced to action mode as she surveyed the scene about her. Running faster in another direction became an option she immediately negated. *I'm not running anymore.* The side doors would be a logical point of attack from the van. Carolyn crouched.

Inside the idling van, Lloyd leaned low across the front seat and watched Army Girl slow down. *Is she just cooling off or is she suspicious? Maybe I should abort the attack. There are plenty of other targets at the church every week, so why take a risk?* The urges forcing blood to surge to his extremities became stronger than ever. His body electrified. Army Girl probably smelled like she looked—sweet vanilla. He felt blood engorging his manhood and his arms pulsed. Even his teeth tingled in anticipation.

His head filled with rapid fire snapshots of previous victims as he recalled how they begged him to stop. *I'm better and smarter than all of them, so why hesitate?* He reconfirmed the presence of the serrated hunter's knife. With the gear shifted to park, he crawled into the rear of the van, the taser in his right hand fully-charged. To keep one hand free, he held the knife in his teeth. He reversed the direction of his cap.

Gripping the handle on the sliding door, which was already warm from the morning sun, he was ready to pounce and pillage—like a pirate, leaping from an attacking corsair upon a ship, filled with booty!

It was as if time had switched to slow-motion.

The would-be pirate driven van idled at the curb. The van driver leaned on the side door. Taser gripped in his hand, knife held in his teeth. His other hand gripped the door handle.

The army veteran froze in position. The woman crouched and rose on the balls of her feet. She possessed no weapons except her alertness and strength.

No one else walked nearby at this hour. Large oleanders and mature Pindo palms blocked the view from the access walkway. Nature stood silent, watching human activity unfold.

In a flurry the side door of the van slid open and the pirate leapt from the vehicle. He growled and reached out a grimy hand for the pony-tailed blonde. Taser sparks filled the air. Saliva spilled down his chin as his teeth gripped the knife.

Carolyn shook her head, as if to clear past images. Her brain directed all her limbs to focus on the present situation. Instinctively, she bent her knees lower in the crouch, ready to spring forward. Her hands rose to her face, with elbows extended in a defensive posture. The sound of movement caught her attention.

She squinted at the side door of the van, as it suddenly slammed open. Her feet shifted to point at the activity. She heard the growl of her attacker before actually seeing him. Like all her training dictated, she responsively pushed down on her feet to thrust forward at her enemy. One man. One attacker.

When the skinny guy in a tee shirt leaped from the van, he had a knife in his mouth and raised his right hand to strike her with what looked like a gun. He missed her. She sprung out of her crouch and slid to her right.

Carolyn struck Lloyd Curtin in his face with her upturned palm, which pushed nose cartilage into his skull. The shattered nose sprayed blood in a Pollock pattern on the side of the white van. The soaked Weston Van Lines tee shirt became unreadable. Lloyd's jaw fell open and the knife clanged onto the pavement. In reflex, his hands flew to defend his shattered face, releasing the taser, which also dropped to the street.

In a panic, he turned back to the van in an attempted retreat. He scrambled into the open side door and crawled toward the front seat. Carolyn retrieved the knife on the sidewalk and pursued Lloyd into the vehicle. She could see the back of his jeans as he crawled toward the front seat, and she grabbed his belt to prevent his escape, dragging him back onto the floor of the van.

She jumped on top of the squirming attempted attacker. He cried for release. Like riding a horse, she spread her legs around him. Corralled, the wiry man had been stopped and could not reach the driver's seat. Despite squirming and twisting, he went nowhere.

He squealed like a pig when the knife penetrated him. Carolyn *knew* this man wanted to kill her. Like those hyenas in the desert, he was going to rape and torture her. *But not this time!* This time, it was her turn on top.

Silently and efficiently, she held the serrated knife and shoved the blade into the back of his neck—like pithing a frog in high school biology class. The man's long taut body released several spasms and his hands ceased reaching for the steering wheel. The inserted knife blade caused his neck to weaken so that his head hit the van floor. He was floating in a pool of darkness—trying to swim, but failing. Lloyd Curtin heard the chattering of nearby little Lloyd.

Carolyn slammed the side door shut and tightened her grip on the knife, continuing to attack the Goat Man.

~~ ~~ ~~

The apartment crew replaced the glass in the sliding doors and removed the shards. Harry tipped each guy a twenty for their fast work. The cops found no evidence in the parking lot. Maybe some July Fourth revelers were fooling around they said. Harry knew better. This was targeted and, if it was a pro, it was only a warning.

He opened the refrigerator to grab a leftover slice of Brooklyn Pizza. Near the window, he looked at the glass bowl he had appropriated from KiKi's apartment. He sprinkled food into a corner for the tiny turtle.

"There you go, buddy. Are you okay? You guarded my apartment today, right?"

It felt good to talk to somebody. It was not exactly Olivia or Elaine, but it was a step toward connectivity.

On television, the beautiful WILM Fox News hosts introduced a breaking story, and the imposing presence of Agent Niese appeared. He seemed comfortable behind the forest of microphones. Below him on the screen ran the caption *Goat Man Killer Update*.

"I am pleased to announce that the citizenry of Wilmington no longer need to worry about a serial killer. Working with local Police, FBI agents have located the man responsible for recent murders in Wilmington. These cases are being marked solved by the FBI."

Lights flashed all around Niese. Harry noted the crowd standing around Niese and identified Spano in a wrinkled, tan suit.

A reporter shouted a question into the bevy of microphones.

"So the Goat Man is in custody, Agent Niese?"

"It's *Special* Agent Niese, and the person we believe responsible for the local murders *is* in custody."

The local journalist was insistent.

"We understand it was the Wrightsville Beach Police who located the killer. Is the chief available to answer questions?"

Niese pressed the whitened knuckles of his massive hands on the microphones.

"This Interstate criminal has been under FBI investigation since Indiana. The killer is now in our custody. We have no further information at this time."

Harry watched as the two local chiefs, Spano and Belvich, stood at attention behind Niese. He hadn't received a call from Spano since the WB police had located Goat Man. *Was he arrested or dead?*

"Can you tell us the Goat Man's *name*, Special Agent?"

"Not at this time. Our purpose is to let the citizens of Wilmington know they are now safe from this monstrous killer."

"Are you *sure* he's the 'Goat Man,' Agent Niese?"

Niese shot a look of annoyance, but he remained calm under the scrutiny of the voracious media. He then spoke, in a slower and more deliberate voice.

"We are *certain*."

"Where is the Goat Man right *now*?" a gray-haired, paunchy former news anchor asked.

The cabal of hyenas swarmed around him for another tasty tidbit to feed their audiences. Bright lights flashed and everyone stared at the Special Agent.

"Let us just say, at this point in time—our perpetrator isn't going anywhere. We have him secure in custody."

The press conference ended and the TV reporters returned to general news.

Niese returned to the Medical Examiners, who were on break. Despite the media questions, the special agent preferred the strobe light press conferences to looking at corpses on stainless steel tables. He had seen comrades with torn limbs and bodies blown apart when he fought in Afghanistan, but the repulsive, disgusting visual before him was worse.

The police had received two citizen alerts. A resident walking his dog saw the taser in the street and the blood splatter on the van door. A hotel employee, taking an outside cigarette break, thought he heard screams and called 911. The police concluded that the source of the screams was the corpse they found in the white van, parked near the beach.

The interior décor and tools indicated that the vehicle served as the roving home of the unsub who the media called the *Goat Man*. From the way he decorated the van, he could have rightly been called a pirate. Initially, they considered that the corpse might have been another victim, but as the investigation proceeded, he realized that apparently, when the killer attacked his final victim, he bit off more than he could chew.

Niese examined the knife punctures that dotted the dead man's chest and stomach. Unlike their initial impression, they weren't the cuts, related to torture, as seen on previous victims, which were methodical and precisely planned. In this case, the knife penetrated deep, with fatal intent.

The examiners counted forty-eight separate stab wounds—clearly indicating a rage attack. His throat was sliced in a bizarre, horrific smile that almost caused decapitation. The dead man had been castrated, and his package was stuffed into his mouth.

The ME whispered to Niese that a ferret had been found inside the dead man's rectum. Several agents inquired whether it was another victim or the unsub. Niese always believed the van contents would confirm the decedent was the guy who was killing the women. After arriving at the scene to take charge, he let the forensic and evidence tech folks take over.

This guy wasn't killed—he was slaughtered. Whoever did this is capable of savagery—maybe a relative of a previous victim seeking revenge, or one seriously messed-up person themselves?

And since the unsub only targeted women, Niese came to the conclusion that the perpetrator of the slaughter was a *woman*, a chill went through his extremities. He considered a wild option that the dead guy was actually another *victim*.

Maybe this guy somehow interfered with an attack? In that case, the unsub may still be at large. No, I just told the media we had the killer.

The FBI needed to confirm that slaughtered man in the van was indeed the Goat Man. Either way, Niese accepted that two crazed killers had *collided* in Wilmington. He exited the morgue to join some colleagues and answer additional inquiries. It was his opportunity to end the fear and speculation and confirm that they had captured the unsub, the Goat Man.

"Hey boss, it's the *guy*, alright," Agent Zoey insisted.

"You find something new?"

"Well," Agent Kent interrupted, "The van was loaded with *pirate* stuff and a kill bag for abducting. It must have been this guy's van, or why leave it? His killer could have driven it off, as the engine was still running. Our guy probably killed previously in that rolling death trap, and he kept relocating."

"Was there a name on the van *registration*?" Niese asked.

"Documents in the vehicle are all phonies, the plates were stolen, and there was nothing in the van to identify the dead guy," Kent answered.

"But we have a BCOE compatible print just in," Zoey added.

"Okay, stop the suspense and tell me! Who the fuck *is* he?" Niese demanded.

"His name is Lloyd Curtin, a meth dealer who did time in Tennessee and had an old domestic battery beef in Indiana."

Niese had the damned Goat Man! *Curtin, it's over.* Soon, the National Center for Analysis of Violent Crime in Quantico would feed them more of the data than they needed. Most agents would focus on celebrating the crime resolution, but Special Agent Niese had another opportunity.

He would direct the closure on Curtin, as most people in his position would do. But what made Niese special was this chance to multi-task and show his superiors that Homeland Security wasn't needed.

I'll take down a domestic terrorism attack and save a city!

His focus had expanded to a purported terrorist attack.

~~ ~~ ~~

Harry watched the press conference end. He felt Niese didn't appear as confident *after* catching the Goat Man as he had during the hunt. *Was everything they knew being shared? Why hadn't the police chiefs spoken? Is it truly over?* For Harry, the announcement brought closure to the murder of Natasha Radinsky and others, but did nothing about finding the attackers of KiKi.

The TV screen filled with scenes of anti-American riots around the world. When a jewelry store commercial replaced global unrest, Harry became uninterested and examined the condo doorway. The next tenants would never believe a recent gunshot attack had occurred. If intended, the bullets should have killed him.

It was a warning—like the snake in his car and Bernie being beaten. No one had seemed bothered by his inquiries into Natasha's absence but, after only a few days checking out KiKi's attack, he was visited by a Copperhead and was the subject of target practice? There was more going on than the claimed capture of a serial killer. He had phone calls to make and plans to initiate.

The engine roared overhead and Harry watched the Osprey military plane fly past, the government preventing penetration into U.S. airspace. Protection was what they did better than anyone in the world. Enemies always existed, but their names changed. *Too often the only time we noticed the military protection was when something went wrong, but what about the daily heroes that let us live peacefully?*

He had read about the Japanese attack on naval bases in Hawaii and German submarines off the coast of North Carolina. Vigilant protection was essential. *Never again should we be fooled by enemies with a goal to convert or kill us by using civilian planes like the Muslim terrorists on 9-11.* He had watched the planes hit the WTC.

Thirteen years had passed without enemy success on U.S. soil. *Will the next attackers be homegrown terrorists, like the students at the Boston Marathon?* Harry could still hear Miguel, at the Albertson Hotel, warnings to him.

Radicals knew the U.S. had become a society grown fat and lazy that had lost the edge. Internal moral decline, combined with envious enemies fueled a potential American collapse. Local initiatives could begin a national trend. Harry Powell had to stop watching events unfold and take action.

The first casualties may not be the result of the witches and demons in TV's *Sleepy Hollow*, which they filmed in Wilmington. The perpetrators would be hate-filled so-called Americans!

He turned off the television and tossed his notepad on the table. He believed that individuals could most change society, for good or for evil. One person could lead the way, but that person had to coordinate with a broad group that helped implement ideas into results.

Despite being an unofficial outsider, Harry needed to assume the role of coordinating leadership. More concerned with what he had to stop than why it began, he strained to foresee a catastrophe created by a handful of zealots. And the timing was crucial.

After an hour of phone conversations, Harry felt satisfied that he was doing what he could to affect positive action. They were better off working together.

KiKi wasn't so much a warning as an assumed kill. As best, Harry concluded that she only connected to events because of the business deal filing she did for Bernie and the meeting with JD. He believed he would find her attacker by unraveling other events, possibly linked to the MLF. He needed more answers and knew where to find at least some of them.

When he called to the hospital to check on KiKi, a nurse explained that there was "no change in her comatose condition, which remains critical." He said a silent prayer to St. Jude.

Harry continued with notes. On a blank page, he detailed correlations on three key people he had called, and he summarized what they could provide.

Chief Spano—//JD & local business deals/KiKi attacker/Wilmington citizens and tourists endangered in Cape Fear July fourth riverfront celebration

Agent Niese—//MLF terrorist members?event? Links? Involve Homeland Security, //serial killer//national monument in harbor-USSNC checked+ evacuated/Federal links + databases/technology knowledge?

General Sabbatino—at LeJeume - Dave Dodd and friends court martial motivation// Colonel Bogart death update? Missing weapons MOTSU on alert? Local sea attack prevented.

The one name from Harry's notes that seemed elusive was supplied by Bernie— Karim Nissam. He wasn't military, and he was not registered at WC, UNCW, CFCC or any local school. There was no residential info to locate him. No phone. No taxes paid. No driver's license. *Who is this guy?*

Harry knew from personal military experience about the Marine Recon. They were the Corps elite special warfare unit, which in the U.S. Army was called Special Forces. The Navy had their SEALs. They were the worlds' best units. These true American heroes could prevent just about anything. Harry needed help. Cooperation could create protection against anyone, so he had to help make that happen. *One man can make a difference.*

"Ring the bell" signified the end of training and becoming a SEAL. When American citizens were about to be attacked, it was time to go to the professionals. Harry always got by with a little help from his friends, and they would help him implement a successful plan. Harry had rung the bell. Tomorrow was the Fourth of July.

CHAPTER THIRTY-TWO

Three black Envoys turned sharply into the parking lot of Henzlein Real Estate & Development. Niese directed his agents on their plan and led the entry. On the holiday weekend JD was almost alone. When he heard Amber screech in the outer office, he leapt from his desk. Scanning his desktop for incriminating mortgage documents, he turned on the shredder. He froze when he looked up at a man in black combat gear, with fire in his eyes, pointing a gun. JD struggled to swallow.

Niese wasted no time in establishing who was in control.

"Sir, are you Mr. Jefferson Henzlein?"

"Yes, I go by JD. What *is* this, my friend?"

"Show me your hands, sir. Get *away* from that shredder!"

JD stood still, heart pounding to escape his chest. *Has the Fed learned of the mortgage scam? Or has one of the three stooges blown the July fourth warehouse scam and demonstration?*

One of the agents told JD that one of his business cards was found in a van that was the scene of a violent crime. Hearing the words, JD breathed easier. The government team continued holding guns in an isosceles brace position.

"Okay. Take it *easy* with the hardware. I'm also an attorney. Are you *arresting* me?"

He felt his legs still shaking beneath his silk slacks.

"That depends on your *answers*," Special Agent Niese warned.

Two of the other agents searched JD, confirming that he was unarmed.

JD counted more than six agents, all dressed in black.

"Now, either tell me what this is all *about*, or leave my *office*... please," JD demanded.

"Do you know a Mr. Lloyd Curtin?"

"Yeah, I know him. He's my half-brother. What did that half-wit do to warrant all *this* firepower?"

"Did he *work* for you?" Niese asked.

JD laughed nervously.

"*Work* for me? No! He was a loser ex-con who came to Wilmington recently for my aunt's funeral, and he just looked me up for a handout is all. Where is he *now*?"

"He's *dead*, Mr. Henzlein. We believe he may have murdered several young women here."

"Lloyd was the *Goat Man*? Wow! I had no idea! I knew he'd been in *jail* for some drug stuff, but… the Goat Man, huh? He really stepped up a grade. You *shoot* him?"

Becoming more relaxed, JD realized the federal invasion had nothing to do with him. The officers lowered their weapons, and several walked out the room, waiting to obtain search warrants to examine files.

"When was the last time you *saw* your brother?"

"Half-brother, please. I probably saw him a couple of days ago. Quite frankly, we weren't close."

Niese spoke slowly, as if a lawyer were listening to his every response.

"Do you know where he was *living* in Wilmington?"

"Not with *me*, that's for sure! Well, I understand he was a squatter at an old property I own… in an unfinished development called The Willows. It's up in Hampstead."

A young woman agent tapped notes into a smart phone.

"What did your brother do for a *living*, Mr. Henzlein?"

"*Half*-brother. We are different. Shit, don't link me too much to this guy. I mean, I don't need that kind of publicity. I think he moved furniture and did odd jobs."

"Did Mr. Curtin ever live in Indiana?" Niese asked.

"Yeah. Yeah, he did—years ago. I never made the connection from the papers about some goat farmer. He…"

"Did he perform any odd *jobs* for you, Mr. Henzlein?"

JD hesitated and looked away from the agent.

"No, he didn't work for me or anything. Like I said, we *weren't* close."

Over the top of the dark suits belonging to the invading government agents, he saw Amber's scared face. A tall female agent seemed to be interrogating her, which made JD nervous.

"Okay, you're going to *show* us where he lived," Niese demanded.

Escorting JD from the office, the Envoys scattered dust as they exited in the direction of the abandoned home. Within minutes, agents combed the area around the model home in search of clues. They were looking for anything that would link Curtin to the Wilmington murders. They looked for the predictable trophies that serial killers kept from their victims. Mostly, they found empty beer bottles, fast food wrappers and a dilapidated chest, filled with moldy crap.

Before departing the office, Special Agent Niese had coached Agent Zoey.

"This employee is Amber, a summer intern. While we have no search warrant for all the files in the office, an employee can give us information. You can bluff Amber, telling her that she can leave if she voluntarily gives us the papers we need, and if she agrees to say nothing about it to her boss. Use your commonality as young females. Flash your badge if you need to intimidate her. Do it right, Zoey, and your career advances. Okay?"

Amber delivered documents and provided papers to Agent Zoey that, properly debriefed and analyzed, would direct actions to save a city.

Niese directed their search beyond the barren unfinished house into the shallow woods and shrubs. While in the field, he pointed out a raised area.

"There, see that mound? Be careful," he told an agent, who brushed away the topsoil and debris.

The outlined remains of a woman was visible to the team.

"A new *farm* for the Goat Man!" the agent mumbled.

Niese walked off to make some calls. He directed the Medical Examiner to the house, guessing they had found the missing woman from Williamsburg. No other graves seemed obvious. As he walked, Niese considered the savage killing of Lloyd Curtin. Anyone who could perpetrate the type of violence unleashed on the Goat Man was someone of particular interest. *Maybe the killer did us all a favor by stopping this mayhem, but maybe the vicious actions exposes more than intended? But what does any of this to do with a terrorist plot that Powell keeps harping about?*

"Agent, can I *leave* now?" JD interrupted.

"Sure, we'll be in touch," Niese nodded, enjoying the sight of the man's Adam's apple, which jumped in response.

He watched the lawyer depart. There was something *about* that JD Henzlein coxcomb. *He looked guiltier than many perps! Maybe he isn't connected to his brother's murders, but something isn't right.*

The agents continued to seek anything related to Curtin, but they found little more. Niese felt his phone vibrate and read the text from Agent Zoey.

Meet me at the office ASAP. We have documents and plans for an attack on July fourth!"

Niese's suspicions had proved correct, as the summer intern had talked non-stop to Agent Zoey. For Niese, the case began to feel like peeling an onion, with layers of crime being exposed at each strip. The new turn of events delighted Niese, who envisioned more press conferences and headlines, extolling his leadership and success.

~~ ~~ ~~

Chief Paul Spano walked with trepidation up the cracked steps to the house of Bernie Mannion. The massive live oak roots created weed-filled cracks along the walkway. *The past impacting the present.* Spano always disliked questioning former cops about links to crimes. It seemed like severing a long line of blue bloods. If they were guilty, he was okay with nailing the betrayers of trust. But if they were innocent, he felt it displayed his own lack of trust and thus his own betrayal.

A Wilmington Police squad car remained in the driveway, with a uniform at the wheel and the lights flashing. The chief spoke to a closed front door.

"Bernie Mannion? It's Chief Spano."

He put the unlit stub of his old cigar into the baggie in his pocket. Southern courtesy caused him to knock before he rang the buzzer. In the late afternoon, Spano heard the beginning of local fireworks, being exploded in the distance. He hated the Fourth of July because the distracting sounds of fireworks could hide weapons fire.

When the front door opened, Spano hardly recognized the man standing before him. Mannion's shirt hung outside his pants and the belt was open. His socks had a hole in one big toe. Purple and yellow welts swelled on his face so that he glared back through slits.

"Hey, Chief Spano, what are *you* doing here? Come on in. Is KiKi okay?"

Spano followed the wide man as he shuffled to a recliner. The room reeked of booze. Spano sat on the worn couch.

"Last I heard, your assistant was critical but stable. Are *you* doing okay, Mannion?"

"Yeah, a nurse friend of Harry's stopped by. I looked a lot worse before that. She helped. Holly something or other—real cute. I'm doing better. They knocked out a tooth."

"Sorry to hear that. You want to tell me who *did* this?"

The men sat in silence for a moment.

"I'm sure you've *heard* about the dead guy they found in a van near the beach. The FBI thinks he's the *Goat Man*. Well, I just heard the FBI found a body they think is the missing woman from Williamsburg. This means Goat Man was apparently killing *outside* of Wilmington on the day that your assistant, Ms. Sanchez, was left for dead. It seems to confirm that it wasn't the Goat Man who did it. Perhaps your beating and the attempt on Ms. Sanchez are connected? I have ordered 24/7 police protection here at your house for you just in case. Tell me all that you *know*."

Bernie grabbed a blood-stained towel and wiped his mouth. Glancing over at Spano with rheumy eyes, he lowered the towel and mumbled through his swollen lip. As he lowered his head, Bernie wept into his large hands.

"Chief, I've been thinking a lot and… *I* did it. *I* caused KiKi to be attacked. If she dies, I *killed* her!"

CHAPTER THIRTY-THREE

The July Fourth afternoon sky filled with lavender streaks as the sun hid behind gray clouds. Sporadic helicopters patrolled the beach, like giant black mosquitoes. Earlier, the Blue Angels squadron had flown over the Cape Fear River Independence Day celebration. Around town, bands played and people barbecued. The Tenace Family experts were readying the fireworks on the wetlands called Eagle Island.

Onboard the USSNC, volunteers in Uncle Sam outfits guided the tour for special needs children. The group of almost one hundred kids had boarded the ship museum to finish the tour in time to enjoy a hot dog and fresh corn dinner on the ship. They would witness the fireworks display from the deck of the USSNC.

Various ships floated along the river, representing divisions of the military. Thousands of visitors and residents filled cobblestone streets and loaded the pockets of the restaurateurs. A long line crossed the street for Kilwin ice cream cones. Almost everyone shared the festive mood on the warm day. Red, white and blue banners hung from streetlights and window ledges. The music from recorded bands played patriotic tunes above the crowd noise.

Free of his uniform from the ship tour, Dave Dodd's silk shirt of the Costa Rican flag hung loosely over Tommy Bahama tan cargo shorts. The spikes of his blonde hair bristled in the breeze. While he walked along the cobblestone streets past the Cotton Exchange shops, he talked on his cell phone to a compatriot.

"I wish you were here to see this display, Karim. Did you locate the *problem?* "

"The *biggest* problem is wasting my time. Somehow, I got the amphibious to the location without too much attention. There must be a connection glitch in the wireless. I'll detonate these manually and then take the amphibious down to the harbor to finish my tasks, up close and personal. You guys all set?"

Karim never divulged the extent of his arsenal to anyone but his cell leader.

"Rock and I have planted the C-4 plastic explosives with batteries on the ship and have the detonators in our pockets. The fireworks you added on Eagle Island also links to our command. By the way, Rock and I confirmed the connections before we left them."

"So did *I*, Davey boy. I checked all the links. They must have become dislodged. Maybe one of you guys didn't…"

"Fuck you, Karim," Dave interrupted. "Just be sure to finish *your* job!"

As Karim heard the phone click off, he knew the two hormonal hulks had no idea of the depth of the demonstration tonight. On the previous night, Karim had placed additional detonation devices, critical to his launches aimed at MOTSU.

No need to risk stealing. As with most things in America, money could buy a person anything required—including explosives. He had vested sources for the cash. By nightfall, fire and brimstone would rain upon the celebrating Americans.

Dave had tapped the Bluetooth to disconnect and walked slowly among the crowd. He thought of Jasmyne and the other college radicals, and he considered the message they wanted to send. They were so intent on making everyone believe *their* viewpoint. Dave had a simple credo *everyone lies, so why believe anything? Look out for number one.*

Dave exalted that the bigwig brass, beyond Colonel Bogart, would receive the message. They didn't want his *kind* in the Marines? How would they feel when the pain their hurtful views spawned was reversed on them? *Payback is a bitch!* He pushed through the crowd of happy oblivious patriots, in search of the man he considered his soul mate.

He couldn't miss Rock, leaning on the Cape Fear waterfront railing. The man wore a shocking pink shirt, hung over white shorts and a blue Ultimate Fighter cap. After a hug, Rock confirmed the wireless detonation devices were ready to go.

They would separate a hundred yards apart along the river front, as JD had outlined. If anything went wrong, no one could possibly grab them both and stop the detonators. The wireless remotes would detonate the C4 explosives inside the USSNC ship museum. All these explosions, around and inside the former battleship, sent a message. They anticipated the visiting flotilla would also burn from collateral damage debris.

"Our *boy* in place?" Rock asked about Karim.

"That little fuckhead is accounted for and everything's in working order. He'll release his loads exactly five minutes after we push the remotes. All hell will break loose, and during the ensuing chaos, we'll depart together. We're supposed to meet Karim in Leland, according to JD's plan but *that* isn't going to happen."

"Your sister closing things out tonight?" Rock asked.

"Yeah, hopefully she figured out my farewell hug. She'll understand, once events unfold."

Then Carolyn would join him in the extradition-free paradise of Costa Rica.

"Well, it's almost go time, Davey. You have the cash from JD?"

"Of course, and it sits locked with all our shit in the car trunk in the Thalian Hall parking lot—thanks to my sister's employee pass. We're ready to accelerate out of town as soon as the skies explode. This is going to be awesome. You also set up the smoke devices in the warehouses?" Dave asked.

"Yeah, there were three vacant brick buildings up the street that JD identified—warehouses like some useless historical shit. Smoke bombs are timed for 2105, so people will think they're being attacked from every direction. Shit still seems like *overkill* to me!"

Rock and Dave leaned on the railing and watched the party-like scene unfolding before them. So many happy people paraded around them that they almost felt part of the group. But they never connected to those around them, since they didn't believe in any cause beyond theirs.

A half-dozen protesters with placards, berating the celebration of war with pollution by foreign fireworks, marched about. They went mostly unnoticed by the crowd.

"Does Karim have an alternative escape plan, since he isn't *here?*" Rock asked.

"Who *gives* a shit? That's *his* problem. He's got the amphibious. He'll probably head north afterward."

Rock placed his hand on Dave's forearm.

"This almost seems too good to be true. We cut our losses with the Marines and get out of here with cash in hand and a new beginning for us. I can hardly wait for Costa Rica!"

"Yeah, the patriotic orchestra will begin soon," Dave nodded.

"I like our cue, *the bombs bursting in air…*"

They laughed at the impending destruction.

~~ ~~ ~~

High atop the crowd loomed the riverfront Hilton Hotel, which contained Ruth's Chris Restaurant. Seated at a table, Annabelle felt satisfied and relaxed that the preparations were done.

"Well, my little acolytes are all down there along the waterfront, marching with their protest signs."

She smiled as she glared down from the restaurant window. Like she was attending a Presidential Ball, she was dressed in red silk, while her companion slunk in a wrinkled suit with disheveled hair and a furrowed brow.

"How many students from WC are protesting?" JD asked.

"Well, we told the media several hundred, but between you and me, I think it's about a solid dozen. But they get prime time on the TV."

"What do the placards say?"

"*Don't celebrate war here! No more troops from Cape Fear!* Poetic, isn't it? They contain the usual banal comments that are sadly ignored. It's why acts of violence become a necessity."

The final text she received from Karim was clear—*All set to go.*

JD Henzlein and Annabelle Radinsky-Wade sat across at the white linen covered window table that she had reserved, allowing them a perfect view of the impending fireworks. She sipped her Cosmopolitan and waited for a rare filet mignon. JD, having no desire to eat, ordered a second Glenfiddich,

"Relax, lover. This is just foreplay for the orgasmic splendor about to display. Afterward, we have a suite upstairs, where I promise you the best sex of your life!"

Annabelle stared at him with a glow that appeared surreal to JD, like a goddess on high.

"Yeah, it should be a memorable night. The materials and the three stooges are in place. It's less than an hour to show time. I didn't expect the kids to still be on the boat this late. I expect they'll get off before…"

Between furtive glances at the window, he drank with his right hand and looked at the Rolex on his left wrist

"The USSNC is just *one* of the *ships* in the harbor. Others represent all branches of the *military*. Delightfully, *all* of them get to experience the message firsthand to cease military intrusion!"

"*Whatever* the hell the boat is called! The kids…" JD protested.

"Not to worry. Think big picture, JD. First, control land by conserving public lands. Then, manage money via the banks—infiltrate all youth education - from day care through college. Now healthcare, and then the military. You *never* see the bigger picture, JD!"

Annabelle wore full make-up and her clinging red dress displayed sufficient décolletage to attract the waiter's look.

"All that political shit is *your* thing. I never signed on for any children casualties," JD differed, taking a long drink.

"Well, the kiddies aren't *going* anywhere, since the tour *includes* a view of the fireworks *from* the battleship," Annabelle smiled.

"What? I thought…"

"Don't go soft on me, JD. It's way too early in the night."

Annabelle reached out hands with painted red nails, grasping his sweaty fingers.

"Besides, the explosions won't *destroy* the ship—they'll just cause a lot of *smoke*."

"Is that the *truth*, Annabelle?"

"*Trust* me, darling. Anymore word on your wacko brother, Floyd? That sick bastard killed my Natasha, and he's apparently now gotten what he deserved. I heard he was *castrated*."

"What? His name is *Lloyd*. He was my half-brother, damn it! *What* word? He's dead. I'm sorry about Natasha. There were a dozen more in Indiana. The FBI came to my office and snooped around. Then they made me take them to the abandoned model where he was crashing and waste a day.

"Lloyd was apparently cut to shreds by his latest intended victim. I guess he picked the wrong target. He was the Goat Man. Crazy dude is all I can say. But about the kids on the *boat*?"

"I *saw* the newspaper headline, Goat Man Caught, with his ugly mug on page one. You sure got the looks in the family, darling. *Tomorrow's* headlines will all be about tonight. Goat Man will be yesterday's news. The press release will wake America up to mind her own damn business. Is your little *deal* done?"

She sensed a need to distract the sweating fool.

He bit his lower lip, wondering why his office had been taped off as a crime scene investigation.

"What? Yeah, our deal has been the *easiest* part. The damages tonight will elicit hundreds of already prepared claims that will open the Fed checkbooks to the deprived warehouse resident owners. Checks will arrive in a few weeks. That deal is all covered."

He leaned back and continued swallowing the numbing Glenfiddich.

Blood oozed over the sizzling plate as Annabelle sliced into her steak. She overruled Karim and convinced JD that having Harry Powell neutralized was a wise strategy. Exposure of the deal meant losing money, which always motivated JD. He ordered another Glenfiddich.

Annabelle smiled, offering a toast.

"To a successful venture!—to making a difference and stopping the Fascists from invading other countries! *Fuck* the intruders!"

Several diners looked her way, but most ignored the outburst.

JD glared at her, reluctantly clinking his glass against hers. From his high school football playing days, he always avoided premature celebrations—as it was a jinx to victory.

~~ ~~ ~~

A single man in a wet suit worked feverishly in the shrubs along the beach. *If something can go wrong, it will,* groused Karim. He knew he had done nothing wrong, so it must have been one of those two steroid freaks. They had acquired some of the shit and probably got *old* crap! They took steak money and bought burgers.

As he worked on the delicate wiring, Karim thought about his deceased sister, Jasmyne. The letter *J* he carved on each device was testament to her. He had no doubt that bastard colonel had killed her. *Too bad she won't see her vision fulfilled in the destruction we'll cause in less than an hour.*

He crouched on the beach, confirming launch coordinates with several targets, including the Cape Fear River flotilla, the USSNC and the Southport Depot MOTSU. Messages were for Western Union and the steroid twins,—destruction was his goal.

Despite long summer days, Karim hated working with faded daylight, worrying if someone in a beachside house would see him. A military helicopter might fly past and see the mortar units. With such antiquated technology, he would do the best he could. Once the mortars were launched, he would escape the area.

He had no intention of meeting up with the steroid twins. Cell activities would continue in the Navy center of Virginia Beach. One man could impact the viewpoint of thousands and the lives of millions. This was just the *beginning* of the destruction of the U.S. from within!

~~~~ ~~

While the perpetrators of destruction fulfilled their machinations, Spano, Niese and Sabbatino were busy, directing their teams into a cooperative defensive action, formulated with the help of Harry Powell. Their focus on that night involved defusing the explosive attacks on Independence Day. Uncertain of the magnitude they faced or the reasons why, they focused on the task. They were able to track the movements of two of the three unsubs through the GPS in their cell phones.

Niese deployed wireless blockers, courtesy of the Defense Advanced Research Projects Agency (DARPA). The devices were in the hands of FBI agents on the Cape Fear riverfront. Niese navigated through the celebratory crowds, directing his agents through electronic communications. Federal high tech equipment afforded them the ability to track persons in the crowd. The USNCC would not go down on his watch.

With the guidance of Harry Powell, the agencies and military were in coordination and communication. There were stealth eyes in the sky via helicopters with night vision. Security cameras on buildings were coordinated in the impromptu black trailer headquarters in the Cotton Exchange parking lot. The Feds targeted the active players. The planners were the responsibility of local police.

Chief Spano applied all available overtime personnel. He directed officers to follow the leads provided by Harry Powell, and he utilized the information the FBI received from a frightened summer intern in JD Henzleins' office. Information shared by Bernie Mannion had also helped the local police.

The special needs children were evacuated from the ship as Spano walked along the riverfront. He had the two purported leaders as his team's responsibility. They had been under surveillance since earlier in the day, and now they appeared to be hands-off viewers. Perhaps they were creating good alibis?

General Sabbatino took responsibility for destroying any long range weapons use along the shoreline. His defensive focus centered on MOTSU. The storage was so vast that any penetrating strike could be catastrophic. A team of agents were all over the USSNC, with three Belgian Malinois, a scent-detecting German Shepherd breed searched out bombs. A Marine Recon team in a stealth helicopter departed Camp Lejeune. They knew terrorist actions would initiate within the hour.

~~~~~~

The helicopter could have been just another training exercise along the beach, but the drill had become real. While the team believed all the perpetrators were downtown, Powell thought they should double-check the shoreline for any secondary strike personnel. The pilot lowered the whirling bird near the beach, flying above the dark blue water into a gray sky. They searched the shoreline from Topsail down to Kure Beach, looking for possible terrorists and following the Generals' command.

The Recon team had a dual mission that involved incapacitating weapons and capturing terrorists. After recent media criticisms of the interrogation methods of their SEAL counterparts, the Marines had little intention of capturing anyone.

~~~~ ~~

As they crossed the Cotton Exchange parking lot, Chief Spano tossed his cigar stub into a waste bin. He walked up the inclined driveway and entered the Hilton Riverfront Hotel, followed by four uniformed armed deputies plus recent military additions to his team.

They marched through the glass doors of the Ruth's Chris Steakhouse entrance and talked to the greeter about their plans. Within seconds, they had established a perimeter around the window front table of JD Henzlein and Annabelle Radinsky-Wade. Staff escorted other diners to the bar area.

As the orchestra played a preamble to the National Anthem, and the crowd below began to press toward the waterfront, Spano and his team approached two diners. JD and Annabelle never noticed the approaching contingent with weapons pointed until they surrounded their table.

The police arrested JD and Annabelle and read them their Miranda rights. While uniformed officers handcuffed the pair, Spano personally confiscated their cell phones, which he handed to a young, plain clothes technician, who went right to work.

Spano looked at his watch: *it was 8:55 p.m.*

~~~~~~

Bernie sprawled unconscious atop his living room couch. The hospital said KiKi remained critical, but her condition had become stable—whatever the hell *that* meant. Harry's friend, Holly, had cleaned Bernie's wounds and bandaged several cuts. She even brought him a Whopper, making sure he was comfortable before she departed.

Bernie had divulged all he knew to Spano—even his guilt about having given business deal documents to KiKi that endangered her life. Bernie augmented his medical treatment with his own potion—an empty bottle of Johnnie Walker Red lay on the floor next to him. He heard the distant fireworks explode through his guilt-fueled dreams where they landed on his house, igniting him in flames.

~~~~~~

Strobe lights were aimed at the unoccupied microphones on the steps of the downtown Federal Building facing the Cape Fear River. A press conference with the FBI was scheduled for later. The media expected the purpose was to share more information about the Goat Man.

CHAPTER THIRTY-FOUR

Harry Powell looked at his cell phone as 9 p.m. approached. He rode the Hilton elevator to the top floor. Every event in the terrorist plan was to happen within the ensuing few minutes. He mentally checked off the list of shared responsibilities, like a conductor leading his musicians. Each military and law enforcement leader had their targets. He had one.

All the plotters and activists were covered by professionals. It wasn't like a movie, where a loner, like Rambo could cover all the plots. Through coordination and with the help from his friends, all the perpetrators were covered—except for *one* individual who most thought was a peripheral player. Harry believed otherwise.

Once upon a time, *Detective* Powell obeyed the police rule *to never enter a dangerous situation alone and unarmed*—yet *private citizen* Harry was doing just that. He did not want to believe he would need his gun with her. He exited when the elevator stopped at the top floor. He climbed a flight of cement stairs that led to the exit door to the roof, where she chose to meet him.

The beautiful blonde woman sat in one of the two chairs on the roof veranda. A single candle flickered atop a white clothed table setup for a special private dinner.

Her shimmering hair reflected the pulsing red glow from the airplane warning lights along the edge of the roof. The black sky surrounded them with sparkling stars. In the reflected lights, the man appeared younger than his years, but he clearly had a purpose. A Marine Osprey flew past. The crowd below cheered in appreciation of the warriors protecting them.

The woman leaned forward and spoke.

"Have a seat, Harry, and rest your weary knees. How *about* this?—two combat veterans, watching the fireworks on the Fourth! What could be more patriotic?"

She handed him a chilled beer from the small cooler between them.

"Thanks, Carolyn. But what made you bring us here tonight?"

Harry glanced around at the surroundings, awaiting her answer.

"I thought we could get together before I leave town, Harry. Old friends—getting together on a holiday—isn't that *enough*?"

When she tipped her sweating glass of white wine toward Harry, he tapped it with his bottle, thinking back to their days on Higgins Beach in Maine and all the hopes about connectivity that summer. Back then, he believed she could change his solitary existence.

Her translucent skin glowed. Her eyes were furtive under a shiny blonde mane. The loosened ponytail made her appear older and more serious. The crowd below grew louder in anticipation of the fireworks. The live orchestra was tuning up.

He examined each corner of the rooftop for movement, reminiscent of his state of readiness when he was in Vietnam. *We're alone.*

"Welcome, Mr. *Semper Fi!*" she said.

"Always faithful," he nodded, interpreting the Marine Corps motto.

Each imbibed while examining the other person.

"You know, Harry, you were my Marine oasis in Maine. You were the calm between many storms. But now, I guess that's all *changed*."

 From the streets below, strobe lighting flashed across the sky. Live classical music began to drift over the noisy crowd below as a preamble to the fireworks.

At eye-level on the streets, a sudden flurry of action caused a wave of excitement to ripple through the crowd. A hundred movements occurred in the span of minutes. FBI jacketed agents grabbed two large young men and escorted them away from the Cape Fear Riverfront, where agents tore inactivated devices from their grasps. Other agents cuffed them and led the duo to black vans.

The crowd celebrated the arrest with a cheer and returned their attention to the riverfront fireworks, awaiting the colorful explosive displays that would coincide with the singing of *The Star Spangled Banner.*

"I thought this would be a perfect location to watch the world below us tonight. Nothing fancy, but I figured you didn't like fancy anyway, Harry. Just a steak, some beer and fireworks!"

"You're right, Carolyn. I like things basic and honest."

The orders from General Sabbatino were clear—what to watch for and what to do. The stealth helicopter crew first observed the amphibious vehicle afloat on the eastern shore of Pleasure Island. Through night vision goggles, they observed a man in the wild weeds, surrounded by mortars and other weapons.

Karim heard the helicopter approach and mistakenly stood in defiance, but the wind from the copter blew him sideways. He tried to defend against the powerful thrusts by shouting at the crew. Then he refocused and turned to launch the mortar rounds.

Gunfire from the helicopter tore him apart, neutralizing his planned attack. Two Marine Recon team members jumped into the water and were instantly on top of the fallen terrorist. They disarmed the weapons and detonators within seconds and quickly communicated their success to teammates.

Inside the private residence, Tony and Tara Smith held each other, watching the scene unfold. Despite the billions of dollars spent on high tech surveillance tools, the crucial view of this couple made the difference. Their earlier phone call helped the Marines find *the needle in a haystack.*

"Surprised?" Harry asked Carolyn, after the live orchestra began playing the National Anthem and fireworks lit the nighttime sky.

As Carolyn sat, gazing down at the traditional culmination of the special American holiday, her iPhone sounded a reminder at exactly 9 p.m. She finished her wine and tossed the glass over the edge of the roof.

"That was dangerous, Carolyn. You could *hurt* someone!"

He placed his beer bottle on the floor of the rooftop and approached her. Seeing him, she opened her long muscular white arms toward him.

"Harry, I don't *understand* you! Under the stars alone with a beautiful woman and some liquor, and all you're worried about is some little civilian being hurt below? Besides, it only *looked* like glass. It was *plastic.*"

"Things aren't always what they seem. I'm beginning to understand that all too well, Carolyn. I know about the MLF plans tonight. They're not going to happen. Your compatriots are all under arrest. It's over."

She looked about the empty roof.

"I have no *compatriots!* I don't know what you're talking about."

Harry read his text message: *All steps successfully completed.*

"Do you hear the National Anthem? Do you see the fireworks exploding? No *extra* explosions. The children on the USSNC are safe and enjoying the celebration. The flotilla is untouched. MOTSU was not hit. It's *over*, Carolyn. The explosive display that you somehow helped has been thwarted."

"I don't know what you're talking about, Harry."

"In the end, who were *you* faithful to Carolyn?"

"*Faithful?* I'll tell *you* about faithful, Harry Powell. You think anyone was *faithful* to me after I was raped, or did the big shots just cover it all up to protect their *own* useless asses? Faithful? Get *over* it!"

She stood, glancing down from the rooftop edge.

"No one is *perfect*, Carolyn. There's good and bad in all organizations and countries. It's just that America is exceptional—we do more good than anyone else in the history of the world. These spectators and the kids on the ship had nothing to do with any target to protest."

"I protested *nothing*, Harry. You don't know what you're *talking* about. Where's David?" she asked with narrowing eyes.

"By now, your brother has been arrested with his co-conspirators. Also in custody are JD and the Professor. It's all *over*, Carolyn. The terrorist attack has been thwarted."

Her demeanor changed dramatically.

"You son of a bitch, Harry!" she sneered. "You damn Dudley-Do-Right. I didn't want to *hurt* you, but David is my only *family*, and he's *always* been faithful to me."

"He wasn't *hurt*. He's in FBI custody," Harry explained.

"David needs to be released. We're going to Costa Rica."

Her hands clenched.

"All these people you mention have *nothing* to do with me! I don't know any professor, and I barely know JD. Who made *you* the policeman for the world? You always want to play the hero, Harry. The world *kills* heroes, you fool!"

"How do people justify hurting *innocents* to protest anything? Does that make *any* sense, Carolyn? You and the MLF wanted to protest military presence by killing innocents? I thought you, of all people, would have more respect for the military."

"I don't *know* of any innocents. People *die* every day, Harry. I was innocent before I got sent to Iraq. I know!—shit happens! All I did was protect David. Blood trumps friendships and loyalties."

She shoved her chin forward like she had thrust a blade into Harry's heart. Her lips tightened.

"*You* don't know anything about protecting family, do you, Harry? You let your wives and your children die! And now you try to protect strangers? "

Harry stood in the face of attack, with focus and with restraint.

"You would do *anything* for your brother, wouldn't you? What happened to Colonel Bogart and Jasmyne? I *get* squashing a court martial, but the pregnant woman!"

Carolyn reached out to touch him.

"Oh, Harry. Sometimes—you believe too *much* in people."

"Maybe that part's my mother's legacy to expect people are good," he said. "But my *father* said *you can't trust anyone*. I understand protecting Dave, but what did *that* have to do with KiKi. Why hurt her? Was that JD?"

Carolyn looked away, shrugging her shoulders. Fireworks shot into the sky, reflected off the flotilla of military ships along the Cape Fear River. The Fourth of July fireworks display culminated in a repetitive burst of colors to the conclusion of *The Star Spangled Banner*. In the dark silence, the orchestra completed the evening with, *God Bless America*.

"You think JD could be a *killer*?" she scoffed. "He makes plans and talks a good game. He's a poltroon and couldn't kill anyone. That asshole only pursues women and money."

"So, *Dave* killed Jasmyne?"

"David? No! He's more a lover than a fighter. If you only *knew* the life we were brought into—nothing he or I did would surprise innocents like you. It isn't his *fault* the way we were raised. Experiences create the person. You aren't so smart *after* all, Harry."

"You're right. Thankfully, I have smart friends."

Harry saw a distant haunting in her eyes.

"You know, I talked to the waitress at the restaurant where Colonel Bogart had his last drinks—with a redhead, named Heather. The colonel was going to *hurt* David, wasn't he, Carolyn, or *Heather*?"

"I don't know what you're *talking* about."

"Oh, you *know*. And Jasmyne was endangering your brother with all her terrorist talk, so *she* had to go. I get all that. But *KiKi*? She hardly *knew* Dave. Why try to kill *her*?"

"You mean it wasn't the *Goat* Man?"

She laughed with a meanness he hadn't seen before. The look had returned—the same look from that night in the restaurant—the change to dark, soulless eyes of hate.

"The colonel wanted to expel David dishonorably for a biased bullshit reason. Yes, I took care of Bogart—as well as that little slut who tricked David into having his kid? She got what she *deserved*!"

"I get it. But KiKi had nothing to do with your brother!"

"Well, your buddy, Bernie—he gave her some papers and your little KiKi got greedy. She was threatening to tie David into some illegal activity, if she wasn't paid off. She wanted to ruin his honorable discharge and everything! The boys tried to convince her, and I just *closed* the deal. I must have screwed up, as I hear she's still *alive*?"

"Dave wasn't a part of that deal you mention, but *others* were, especially JD. Dave conned *you* into helping them by claiming he was in danger. You became their avenging protector. That *snap choke* to kill method was an army tactic—not the ploy of the sexual predator, Goat Man."

"People don't *screw* with me, Harry, not anymore!"

"So, it was *you* who slaughtered the Goat Man?"

"He tried to *fuck* me, Harry. He tried to kill me! I don't *get* attacked—I *attack*! Can you believe that wacko was a *relative* of JD's? He thought he was a damn pirate! What a joke. I did the only thing I'm *trained* to do, Harry. And it felt good!—self -defense against a perverted loser."

"When killers collide, bad things happen. Goat Man was insane, but what is your excuse for killing innocent people?" he asked.

Carolyn reached behind her back, nodding toward Harry.

"Like I said, there *are* no innocents. I don't regret *any* of them. I protected *David*. All those people were no good, Harry—not worthy of your concern. It was the right thing to do every time. No need to *confess* what feels good!"

Harry stood erect, speaking in a monotone.

"And you, Carolyn, are *you* worthy of my concern? Not that it matters now, but the attacks on me, was that *also* your doing?"

Carolyn stood like a pillar of salt.

"I don't do warnings, Harry. When I learned of your threat to David's freedom with your nosiness, I knew there was only *one* way to stop you—and this is *it!*

She produced a weapon that had been lodged in her slacks.

"Don't move."

With her confirmation, Harry felt like a giant anvil had fallen to squash him into near nothingness.

Below them, on the steps of the Federal Building, Special Agent Niese stood in front of the strobe lights of media cameras flashing around him. He handled questions with calm assurances. America and Wilmington were safe, since *he* and his FBI team had captured the perpetrators.

"First, the serial killer, Goat Man, was dead, and now, a violent protest had been averted." Niese had carefully followed orders and deleted the word "terrorism" from his prepared comments. Niese beamed in the spotlight, like a man who should be wearing a super hero cape. He felt like Superman as he shared his success story.

"What's that Glock for? What *now*, Carolyn? The events are stopped. David's going to *prison*. It's *over*."

"Now that you have figured all *that* out, you're going to have an accidental fall from the roof. I'll get David exonerated."

He repositioned himself, as he spoke.

"So, you're going to kill *me* too, Carolyn?"

"I made a commitment to shut you up. To observers, it will be a tragic 'lover's fall.' You gave this ring to me tonight, but I rejected your proposal and you leapt to your death. Sad and tragic— like a rejected lover, a sentimental old fool. Your life was no longer worth *living*."

"It won't *work*. I shared all I learned with others," he insisted.

"No, you *didn't*, Harry. You're a *loner*. No one ever *knows* the truth about people. They believe what they see. No one else will link *me* to any of this stuff. Only *you* figured that out, Harry. Events you described are over, and I wasn't *involved*. The police and military would all move on, but not you, Harry. It's not in your genes to move on. You'll never leave it alone."

Harry positioned himself in front of Carolyn, with his back to the new buildings across the street.

"Listen, Carolyn…"

She gestured with the gun.

"Get over to the edge *now!*"

Harry stepped closer to the roof's edge. He looked down to see the crowds, already dispersing.

"Your time is *over*, Harry Powell," she announced before raising the weapon and leveling it at his face.

"Even old men can be dangerous. If I don't jump, how do you explain the gunshot?"

"I don't need to explain *anything*. You live in the past."

She reached behind her and pulled out another weapon.

"There's no need for bullets. This taser will stun you enough to cause the fall. It will leave only pin pricks, with no obvious trace. You're just a sad lonely man who ended his own life—a man, down on his luck—who couldn't endure one more rejection from the woman he loved. We shared a last supper together. I'll scream in terror to alert the authorities. I'll be heartbroken. Now go ahead! Fall peacefully. Jump!" she shouted.

"Allow me a final silent prayer, Carolyn."

Harry made the sign of the cross. Then he raised his right hand to his brow and saluted.

She sneered at his final futile religious and militaristic gesture, but when Carolyn brushed a strand of blonde hair off her forehead, a red spot materialized.

Immediately, a black hole appeared in her head, below the blonde bangs. Her unblinking, lifeless eyes seemed to accuse Harry. With arms collapsed to her side, the weapons fell from her hands. Her body leaned and fell off the edge of the roof into the night. She glided into the darkness toward the black water, like a hawk floating to earth.

Harry saluted into the dark distance at Marine sniper, Kilty, who had done his job, as always. *Semper Fi.*

EPILOGUE

Lloyd Curtin, also known as the Goat Man, slaughtered over twenty women across state lines, the only respite came during his incarceration. Trophies were found in an unusual photo album. Each sleeve contained a photo of the victim with an attached snatch of hair. Other evidence was also located in the airport storage facility.

Bernie Mannion healed from his wounds. After declaring bankruptcy, he lost his home and boat and closed the investigation agency. He works for Block Department Stores, in security. Socially, he dates wealthy widows and enjoys watching boats sail from the marina.

Zachary Niese returned to Washington D.C. to continue his fast track government career. He became known as the man who singlehandedly hunted down the horrific Goat Man and thwarted a domestic violence plot. He would eventually host a reality television show on the ID Network about capturing criminals.

JD Henzlein served as his own attorney in court hearings. While in police custody for conspiracy and fraud charges, he was sodomized by another inmate and fatally stabbed. His bail hearing had been scheduled the next day.

Professor Annabelle Radinsky-Wade became temporarily mired in the legal system, fighting conspiracy charges. With the financial and legal support of the teachers union, she accepted a year of house arrest in her Landfall home, along with a three year suspension from teaching.

Chief Paul Spano continued his vigilance to protect the residents of Wilmington North Carolina, fighting daily against modern-day pirates. His favorite time remains Friday night dates with his wife.

David Dodd and **Rock McDaniel** were convicted of various felonies, including theft, terrorism and attempted murder. They now reside in different federal prisons. Their partner was removed from a backyard near Pleasure Island; **Karim Nissim** was DOA at the hospital.

Carolyn Heather Dodd Morderca murdered Jasmyne Nissim, Colonel Bogart and attempted to murder KiKi Sanchez before killing the Goat Man. Carolyn died from a sniper's bullet before she landed face first in the Cape Fear River. Her body washed ashore in the EPA protected wetland rice paddies across from downtown Wilmington.

Larry Janakowsky, the private investigator, found in New York City, was poisoned with thallium. His death remains an unsolved cold case. His last hotel visitor was an unidentified woman who carried a briefcase, embossed with gold initials: MLF, which some thought were hers.

KiKi Sanchez resides in Wilmington with her turtle, Tommy. She met JD to protect Bernie from the crooked deal. After a long convalescence, she survived the beating by Rock and strangulation attempt by Carolyn. She completed her assistant's degree in Forensic Science and got a job with the Wilmington Police department. She helps investigate violent crimes, under the mentorship of Chief Spano.

Harry Powell walks with a slight limp along the expanses of Topsail Beach. He occupies a cottage owned by Paul Spano. **Holly** gave Harry a gray kitten with blue eyes. They named it Scarlet. Harry and Holly are often seen together with her children on the beach, where they are said to look like a happy family. Acquaintances occasionally seek Harry to ask for his help.

ACKNOWLEDGEMENTS

Special appreciation to my wife, Mary Ann, for her patience, especially during years of solitary writing time. Our children and expanding family are the joys of my life. I have also been blessed by experiencing many friendships through several careers. My friends and family have always been a source of inspiration. I have truly been blessed.

In addition to Mary Ann, I would also like to share my appreciation to those who have helped with feedback on my various writing ventures by sharing their time and talent: Bob Elia, Kristine Lemke, Pat McDonnell, Cathy O'Connor, Kevin Sands, Lou Saulino and Bernie Tyrrell. I really appreciate your insightful comments and advice.

Tom Olsinski
Author Biography

Before turning to fiction, Tom Olsinski's previous writings paralleled his education and careers in healthcare and business. At Fordham University, he wrote and edited the college newsletter. As a pharmacist, he contributed a weekly newspaper column entitled *You and Your Health*. Then, as a marketing executive, he wrote the business column *Mind Your Business* for Hearst Publications.

In addition to writing numerous articles for a Fortune 100 company on subjects that included strategic planning and leadership, Tom has given lectures on ethics at business schools. Since focusing on fiction, he has written several crime novels. *When Killers Collide* is the most recent.

Married with three children, Mr. Olsinski resides in North Carolina with his wonderful wife and two cute cats. Visit www.tomolsinski.net.